THE DARK SIDE OF THE CROSS

A JAMES MACBRIDAN MYSTERY

JAMES S. PARKER

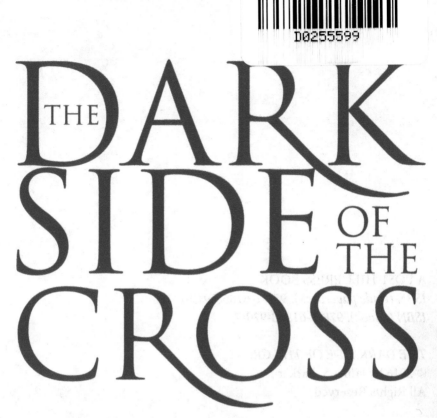

A POST HILL PRESS BOOK
ISBN (trade paperback): 978-1-61868-919-1
ISBN (eBook): 978-1-61868-920-7

THE DARK SIDE OF THE CROSS

Cover Design by Roy Migabon

Post Hill
PRESS

Post Hill Press
275 Madison Avenue, 14th Floor
New York, NY 10016
http://posthillpress.com

For my wife
Margaret

The Love, the Light,
and the Laughter
in my life!

CHAPTER 1

The dark, ominous morning skies that blanketed the New York City area were not all that unusual for the early fall. Temperatures had remained mild, and unless it rained, it was doubtful that many people would even pay that much attention to the solid wall of clouds steadily moving in. The wind continued to increase, but did so at a measured pace, masking the severity of the cold front that would soon engulf the city.

The front, and all its unexpected consequences, remarkably paralleled the events getting ready to unfold at a meeting being held at the Investigative Division of the Hawthorne Group—the quiet before a storm of unknown and unimaginable magnitude. James MacBridan, lead investigator, had arrived well ahead of schedule, all too familiar with the required punctuality of his boss.

"Here's what we know," said Dolinski, looking at the file on his desk. MacBridan sat across from him, having wedged himself into one of the overstuffed client's chairs, a tight fit at best. It wasn't that he was fat, actually quite the contrary. MacBridan's six foot one frame was nearly solid muscle, and he worked at staying in shape, which enabled him to handle many of the rougher demands of his job. He was particularly broad across the shoulders, his jacket size, depending on the cut, varied between size forty-six and forty-eight. His dark brown hair emphasized his blue, intense, penetrating eyes that tended to give MacBridan a hard look. As was his custom, MacBridan stretched his long legs out in front of him, marveling at the neatness of the Dolinski's desk. It just wasn't natural. "Over the past two months, seven Catholic churches have been burglarized in and around the Boston area, in addition to two others in Western Massachusetts. The relics that were taken are of extraordinary value, and not just to the church. It was important to understand that their value has been assessed not only on their religious significance, but also as to their value in the world of historical antiquities."

Peter Dolinski, the man MacBridan reported to at the Hawthorne Group, continued to stress their value repeatedly as the initial briefing went on. "Personally I don't agree with paying a ransom, never have, but I'm afraid the thief has made his point rather clear to our client. We either do things his way, or else. Archbishop Kerry has reminded me several times that each of these relics is quite old and must be handled with considerable care. That is primarily why he is insisting on paying the ransom. Understandably, they are rather fragile and won't fare well with too much exposure to the elements. The Catholic Church is willing to do what they have to in order to get them back."

"All right, I can understand that. Where is this pay off supposed to take place?" asked MacBridan.

"Hopefully, we'll know in the next couple of hours," answered Dolinski. He opened the right hand drawer of his desk, took out a cell phone and slid it across to MacBridan. "Two days ago, the priest at St. Margaret's received a call from a man claiming to have the artifacts. He gave enough detail to make his claim legitimate. Unfortunately, our thief didn't give them any room to negotiate. Either the church pays for the relics, or he will destroy them. This threat, of course, also holds true if the police become involved in any way."

"Of course. So, all things considered, the church is taking a bit of a chance even bringing us in," said MacBridan.

Dolinski leaned back ever so slightly in his high backed leather chair. It was about as relaxed as he ever got. "I've known Archbishop Kerry for several years, and he called me the minute he hung up with the priest. He actually wanted to handle the exchange himself and wanted my advice as to how to go about it. I convinced him that in the best interest of the church, he needed the Hawthorne Group to manage this for him. I gave him the number to this cell phone and told him to tell the priest to give the number to the thief the next time he contacted them."

"I take it he called back."

"Yes, he did, exactly at the time he said he would."

"Prompt. Good to hear. I like that in a thief. Could the priest tell if it was the same person?" asked MacBridan.

"The priest says that the guy has a very pronounced lisp and he didn't think he was faking it. He told him that the church has agreed to pay and that he is to call this number and ask for Father MacBridan."

A smile spread across MacBridan's face. "You're joking."

Dolinski just stared at him. "You know better. Keep that close to you. He said he'd be in touch in forty-eight hours, which would be some time this afternoon. Let me know as soon as you've talked to him."

***

MacBridan waited for the call with Cori Hopkins in her office. She had worked several cases with MacBridan before, and although quite experienced, she didn't look the part of a field operative. A tint of natural red ran through Cori's shoulder length, dark brown hair. She wore it loose, so that it framed her face, accentuating her pale green eyes. Her five foot seven figure was on the slender side and never failed to attract the attention of the men around her.

"If this guy has half a brain cell he won't call. He has to know it's a setup."

"You and I would know that, but that's only because we're bitter, old, and cynical," said MacBridan. Cori started to object to MacBridan's having included her in that characterization when the cell phone rang.

"Here goes," said MacBridan. "Hello, this is Father MacBridan."

"You should be expecting this call, so lissen up 'cause I'm only going to say things once, you got it?" The priest had been very accurate in his description of the thief's voice. The lisp was very distinct, and he sounded young.

Cori wrote down the number from the caller ID, turned to her computer, and went to work. "Yes, of course, I've been waiting for you. Please go ahead," said MacBridan.

The thief quickly told MacBridan the time and the place for the exchange. As they talked, Cori pinpointed the location from which he was calling, a pay phone outside a park in downtown Boston. She then radioed one of the teams Dolinski had on standby in Boston, and they immediately moved out, hoping to catch sight of the guy.

"Remember, you come alone. I see anyone else and tha's it. You underssand?"

"Yes, I understand. You've been very clear," said MacBridan, trying to give his field team as much time as possible. "But what if someone does come by, someone I don't know? I can't help that."

"No one but you, Father, no one. You juss better pray that things go the way I want them to." He slammed down the phone before MacBridan could say anything else.

"I couldn't keep him on any longer."

Cori's phone soon rang. Dolinski's people had made good time but not good enough. All they found was an idle payphone next to one of the main walkways leading into the park.

MacBridan immediately briefed Dolinski on his short call with the thief. Dolinski then called the archdiocese to let them know the exchange was on. With the wheels set in motion, Cori made arrangements for her and MacBridan to get up to Boston, as well as getting the backup they would need ready to move.

An hour later, an elderly priest, Father Vincent, arrived at the Hawthorne Group's building and gave MacBridan a clerical collar, a crucifix, and a prayer book. Father Vincent's hands trembled as he helped to put it on. MacBridan was surprised by the tight fit of the collar. He felt as choked and uncomfortable as he had when his mother forced him to perform as an altar boy a lifetime ago. Father Vincent, for some reason, was very nervous about being there but asked if he could pray with MacBridan.

"Father, I'm not sure how much good that will do. God and I are not on the best of terms and haven't been for many years," said MacBridan.

"God never forsakes us," Father Vincent snapped at MacBridan. "Even if we have turned our back on Him."

"That's good to hear, Father, but I doubt the work I'll be doing tonight will follow many of his teachings."

"Tonight you are doing God's work," said Father Vincent. "Go with God."

***

The car's engine throbbed under the hood, omitting a low, powerful growl, threatening MacBridan as it rounded the corner, creeping towards him. Although it did not appear to be in the best of shape, he could see that a significant amount of custom work had gone into the car. The windows were tinted, so much so that it effectively blocked any view of its occupants, giving the appearance of the soulless, dead eyes of a snake. The back end of the car was jacked up, further accentuating the car's image of a prowling, night hunter, poised to attack anything weaker than itself.

The large, dark-colored sedan continued its slow approach, a block from where MacBridan waited. Despite the late night hour, the car rolled forward without any lights. This would be its second pass in thirty minutes, presenting a complication MacBridan hadn't counted on. Multi-storied brick tenement houses, all in varying states of decay, lined both sides of the street. The tired, old buildings leaned against each other, crumbling monuments to the despair and violence that blighted this inner city neighborhood. Scant bits of light escaped from the few windows that weren't boarded up. The car, as battered as the neighborhood, crept forward.

MacBridan raised his hands to his mouth as if warming them with his breath. With his hands covering his face, he spoke into the wire connecting him to his backup. "Here they come again, and unless I'm mistaken, they're not with Welcome Wagon. There's a chance this could be our boy, but it doesn't feel like it."

His team, parked three blocks away, listened intently, ready to move. But MacBridan knew that he was on his own, no matter what went down. As close as they were, his backup was too far from him to provide any immediate support.

The cold temperatures, combined with the neighborhood's reputation, left this section of Front Street nearly deserted. Up until the car's appearance, there had been little sign of life in either direction. Well, that wasn't entirely true, MacBridan reflected. There had been a rat, the size of a small pony, which had disappeared into a pile of garbage not too far from the entrance to the alley. As far as he could determine, this run-down part of town had long been devoid of any improvements except, possibly, the addition of gang graffiti, defiantly streaked across various walls. In fairness to the few residents that still called Front Street their home, MacBridan tried to view the graffiti as urban art.

Tension laced across his shoulders as the car closed the gap between them, but he did his best to ignore it. He made eye contact with the driver, or at least with the part of the windshield where he thought the driver should be. MacBridan stretched to his full height, a little over six feet, not giving any ground to the slowly approaching car. He was naturally broad in the shoulders and the padding of the leather jacket he wore worked to his advantage, further accentuating their width. The expression on MacBridan's face was neutral; his eyes locked on the windshield, moving to the driver's window as it gradually rolled by. The car slowed down even more, nearly coming to a stop. MacBridan stood motionless, braced for whatever would happen next. Suddenly the rear tires squealed and the car shot off, racing down Front Street and disappearing around the corner at the next light.

MacBridan slowly let his breath out. He knew the car's occupants were taunting him, but the threat of their escalating things into something more remained all too real. Once again, he raised his hands to his mouth. "So much for the pre-show. Guess my obviously good-natured charm just didn't appeal to them. Our boy better show up before they come back, though, or I'm pretty certain we'll have a problem on our hands."

MacBridan checked his watch: ten till. If their man held true to the plan, the exchange would take place at 2:00 a.m. The waiting continued.

He zipped his jacket up as far as it would go and rubbed his hands together, trying to ward off the bone chilling cold of the night. It was only late September, but as far as MacBridan was concerned, it felt like the dead of winter.

As he waited, MacBridan considered how little he knew about the man meeting him to collect the ransom. The little he did know he didn't like. He glanced down at the canvas bag next to him, frowned, and shook his head. It held the one hundred thousand dollar pay off. A great deal of money, all to reward a thief.

The night air seemed to be getting colder by the minute. Not for the first time that evening MacBridan envied his backup, wishing he could think of a way to share the van's heater with the two surveillance men and Cori. This time MacBridan really was warming his hands. "All clear here," he said.

MacBridan's voice came across the speaker in the van with very little static. "Think he'll show?" asked Smithers, his massive frame crammed into the van's front seat.

"Yeah, he'll show," answered Harry. Harry was just as tall as Smithers, but had a tight trim build. The scar under his left eye gave evidence that he was no stranger to violence; still, he had usually come out the victor, a good man to have standing with you. "Question is, can MacBridan fool him into believing he's a priest?" he asked Cori.

Cori gave a small smile. Tonight she was operating the equipment that monitored both the wire MacBridan had on as well as the transmitter sewn into the handle of the bag containing the money. She answered, "I think we're safe, so long as our perp doesn't ask him any questions about the bible."

MacBridan had taken up position on the corner of Front and Twelfth, right where he had been instructed to stand, in plain sight. Once again, he looked around. Nothing moved. The payphone across the street started to ring. Carrying the bag, he crossed to the phone and answered. "Hello."

"You don't look like a priess." The lisp in the voice as strong as ever.

"Really? What did you expect?"

"You know man, a priess. An older guy, gray hair, the uniform," the thief sounded nervous, real nervous, like the amateur MacBridan figured him to be. This was not good. MacBridan knew that when amateurs got scared, people got hurt.

"Sorry to disappoint you. Not all of us are old. As to what I'm wearing, in case you haven't noticed, it's freezing out here."

"Open your coat. Turn all the way around. I want to see what's under there."

MacBridan lowered his collar and unzipped his coat. He let the phone hang by the cord and turned around. With the coat open, the clerical collar and the crucifix around his neck were clearly visible.

MacBridan zipped his coat up and picked up the phone. "Everything alright now?"

The thief did not respond. MacBridan worried that the extended silence might mean that he wasn't buying him as a priest. Was it because he was in reasonably good shape? There had to be priests who worked out.

Finally, the thief said, "You got the money?"

"Yes, but I don't give it up without the artifacts."

"Look man," the thief nearly shouted into the phone, "you don't make demands! We're doing this my way. You better be real nice to me. I'm doing you a favor. Weren't for me you'd never see any of this junk again."

"Sorry," MacBridan said. The guy sounded closer to the edge than MacBridan liked, so he didn't want to push too hard.

"You sure you're a priess? You don't sound like no priess."

"Guess I'm a little nervous," said MacBridan. "I've never done anything like this before."

There was no response.

"What do we do now?" asked MacBridan.

"You bring that cell phone with you like I said?"

"Yes, I have it. It's the same number you dialed earlier."

"Yeah, well, give it to me again."

MacBridan gave him the number.

"Okay. See the apartment building behind you? Number 1308?"

"Yes, I see it."

"Okay. Go to the top floor, apartment C9. I'll talk to you there." The line went dead. MacBridan smiled tightly. As was usually the case, greed had won out over apprehension.

MacBridan hung up the phone and looked around. There was still no sign of the thief. "Here goes," he said under his breath. Anxious to leave the night air behind, he moved to the stoop of 1308, walked up the steps, and went into the building. A single, low wattage bulb, halfway down the hall, failed in its attempt to light the hallway. MacBridan held the canvas moneybag in his right hand. With his left, he reached behind him and checked the gun he had secured inside the back of his coat.

Disappointingly, the temperature inside the apartment building wasn't much warmer than it was outside. The walls along the hall were cracked and chipped, and the building had a thick, putrid odor of its own. It took him a few moments, but MacBridan identified it as a mixture of old garbage, with a pinch of urine, spiced with the stench of decay. Nice. He wondered if the rat he'd seen earlier had an apartment here. There was no elevator, but MacBridan quickly found the stairs and started up. He didn't like the way this was going, or the position he was putting himself in. The fear in the thief's voice had come across all too clearly. By having chosen an apartment on the top floor, the thief had successfully cornered himself. MacBridan didn't care for the implications this presented.

MacBridan stopped and listened as he reached the third floor. Apartment C9 was down at the far end of the hall, facing the street, on the right. The only sounds were the sad notes of a saxophone straining out a blues tune that MacBridan didn't recognize, drifting up from an apartment on the floor below. Carefully, he moved down the hall to the side of the door labeled C9, The C having been replaced with a mismatched font.

MacBridan knocked. He waited, but no one answered. He tried the door and wasn't too surprised to find it unlocked. With his foot, he pushed the door open and waited. Nothing happened. He said, "It's Father MacBridan. Is anyone here?"

The silence mocked him. MacBridan looked back over the railing. His cell phone rang, making him jump.

He fumbled with the instrument and said, "Hello, this is Father MacBridan."

"You in the apartment?"

"No. There's no one home so I wasn't sure about going in."

"Come on Father, don't go ssupid on me. Go in and look in the box by the window."

MacBridan did as he was told. As his eyes adjusted to the darkness, he could see that the apartment had a one-room layout with a bare wooden floor, the kitchenette off to his right. There were no furnishings or anything else in the small, empty room. He knelt next to the box. Taking a small flashlight out of his jacket, he looked inside. Three of the smaller missing artifacts lay on the bottom of the box.

"You find it?" asked the thief.

"Yes, but it seems we have a problem. Where are the rest of the artifacts?"

"Those are just a free sample. Let you know I'm real. You may be a priess, but it don't mean I truss you. Open the window and look down."

MacBridan moved to the window. There, on the street below, stood the thief, calling from the same payphone MacBridan had used earlier. At his feet was another box, larger than the one in the apartment.

"Okay Father, here's how we do it. You drop me the money. I see if is's all there. You stay right where I can see you while I check. You move away from that window before I say is's okay and I'll grab everything and leave you with nothin. You underssand?"

"Yes." MacBridan muted his phone. As he leaned over to pick up the moneybag, he spoke into the wire, "Right after I drop the money, move in."

***

Cori looked at her two companions. "This is it. Get ready."

Smithers put the van into gear and waited for Cori's signal.

***

MacBridan yelled down to the thief, "You ready?"

"Come on man, drop it. We ain't got all night."

MacBridan dropped the bag. The thief caught it and immediately tore into it to get at the money.

"He's got it," MacBridan said.

The van edged out onto Front Street. Keeping a slow pace, it moved toward them, its lights off so as not to attract attention. Although still blocks away, the thief spotted the van almost immediately.

He looked up at MacBridan. "Friend of yours, Father?"

Without waiting for an answer, he picked up the box of artifacts and threw it into the street. The box came open, scattering the artifacts across the pavement. He grabbed the money and took off at a hard run down the street, away from the van.

"He's got the money and he's heading north," MacBridan yelled into the wire as he raced out of the apartment and down the stairs. "He's thrown the artifacts all over the street and there's some in the apartment. Get those first, then back me up."

MacBridan made it out of the building and into the street just as the van skidded to a halt, the left front tire barely missing one of the artifacts. He looked just in time to catch sight of the thief turning into an alley. As he ran down the street, he unzipped his jacket, reached behind him and pulled the gun free of the bindings that secured it in place.

MacBridan's luck held. As he entered the alley, he caught sight of the thief darting into a building two-thirds of the way down on the left. It didn't take him long to reach the same red brick structure. The thief had disappeared down a small flight of stairs, leading to what looked like the door to a basement.

"Cori, I'm going into a four-story brick building. There aren't any lights on that I can see. There's a green dumpster next to the door." With that, MacBridan descended the stairs and entered the dark basement doorway.

As soon as he entered, he flattened against a wall and listened. He didn't dare use his flashlight. There wasn't any sound, but at the end of the long hallway, he could see a faint light. He gave his eyes a little more time to adjust, then as quietly and cautiously as he could, he moved down the hall. The light came from a room, the door partially open.

MacBridan stood beside the door, gun ready. He didn't know what to expect on the other side, but felt sure the thief knew he was there, ready to take him out at the first chance. It had been too easy. He glanced around the doorframe and what he saw surprised him even more. The thief sat on the far side of the room at a small table. He was young, early twenties and bone thin. On the table were three candles, accounting for the light. The thief had the money spread out before him. He was counting it, as if he had all the time in the world.

MacBridan burst into the room, his gun leveled at the thief's chest. The thief stood up, knocking over the chair, but froze at the sight of the gun.

"You did some things right, but for the most part, you were pretty stupid," MacBridan said as he walked across the room. "Now, interlace your fingers behind your head and kneel down."

The thief stared at him. "Do what?"

Smaller words, MacBridan said to himself, use smaller words. "I said put your hands behind your head and kneel down. Now!"

The thief did as he was told. MacBridan stood behind the thief and quickly patted him down. In the right hand pocket of his jacket, MacBridan found a switchblade with a six-inch blade. Pocketing the knife, he moved to the table and began to put the money back in the bag. Trash covered the floor. A sleeping bag and a blanket lay next to the wall, in the corner. The thief had obviously been living here for a short time.

"Cozy," said MacBridan.

"You're not a priess. I knew you weren't no priess." The lisp was very pronounced.

"Maybe not," MacBridan answered, "but as is turns out, I do accept confessions. The way I see it, you're in a bad spot. Now, I'm positive you had help stealing this stuff. Tell me who they are, where they are, and I'll do all I can to help you."

"No way, man. You're crazy. I'm not saying nothin'. Those people are real spooky, man. They can do things you wouldn't believe."

"You're looking at serious jail time here. If I find them without your help, and I will, it's going to leave you with no one to turn to."

"Look man," the thief stammered, "I'm tellin' you, they got too much power. You don't underssand. Look, I'll give you some of the money—you can have half. I'll even give…"

The sudden change in the air hit MacBridan with a jolt. He blinked his eyes a few times, as the light in the room quickly faded. Glancing at the candles, he saw that even though they continued to burn, just as when he'd arrived, the light they put out had greatly diminished. MacBridan looked around, trying to find the reason that would explain what was happening. The thief, mortified, scooted back against the wall, his eyes wide, darting from side to side.

"They're here." The whisper of his voice so intense, so filled with terror,that it got to MacBridan. What little light there was continued to weaken and retreat back into the flames. "You gotta let me go!" The thief begged, tears streaming down his face. "We gotta get out of here now! I don't wanna die."

"Shut up," MacBridan nearly shouted. The thief's panic was contagious, and the unexplainable loss of light didn't help any. Then, just as suddenly, the temperature in the room plummeted. The cold, more penetrating than anything MacBridan had felt in a long time, cut through him with such force that it nearly brought him to his knees.

The thief's eyes locked on to something across the room. He pointed at the door and began to scream. MacBridan strained his eyes but couldn't see anything, at least not at first. But there was something there, something standing between them and the doorway, blocking their only way out. A darkness filled the space where the door had been. A darkness so complete, so intense, that light was absolutely useless against it.

Without any sound, it entered the room and began to glide toward them. A nearly paralyzing fear washed over MacBridan leaving his mouth dry, unable to swallow, and he felt the tingling needles of numbness rapidly spreading through his body. He tried to speak but couldn't form the words. He wanted to shoot at it, defend himself, but couldn't raise his arm. The lack of control over his body further fueled his mind with panic. He tried to grasp some understanding of what was happening, feeling as if he was drowning in a sea of darkness. It was his last thought as he felt himself falling, passing out on the floor.

***

"Mac, come on Mac, wake up. We're going to need an ambulance!" she shouted.

MacBridan could hear the voice, a woman's, but he didn't know who it was. "Maria?" he mumbled, his mind struggling to focus in on things. Finally, he managed to open his eyes. The room looked familiar, but why? Then he remembered. He was in the basement of the deserted building, still in the room where he'd found the thief. With a great deal of effort, he turned his head and saw that the candles were still burning. Their light, however, had returned and once again filled the room with a soft glow.

"Mac, are you all right?"

MacBridan sat up, struggling with every movement, every thought. He felt groggy, as if trying to wake up from a deep sleep, his mind trying to reorient itself. Cori knelt beside him on the floor, a gun in her hand.

"Did he get away?" asked MacBridan.

"What happened Mac? Who was here? Was there a woman involved?" asked Cori.

"A woman?"

"You said 'Maria.'"

"No, never mind that."

With Cori's help, MacBridan managed to get to his feet. The thief lay on the floor next to the table.

Smithers stood beside the still form. "Harry's gone for an ambulance, but it's not going to do this guy any good," he said.

MacBridan made his way over to Smithers and looked down at the thief. What he saw nearly turned his stomach, threatening the slim grasp he'd regained over his faculties. The man was dead, eyes wide open, his mouth gaping in a silent scream. The throat had been torn out so savagely that his head lay at an odd angle to the body.

"Mac, what happened here?" Cori asked again.

MacBridan stood staring at the body, unsure how to respond. "I don't know," he mumbled, his voice almost too low to hear. "I really don't know."

CHAPTER 2

Even though MacBridan and the rest of their team were now back at the van, the nightmare he'd just experienced lingered on. MacBridan's eyes never rested, continually moving up and down the street, expecting at any moment to see the dark form materialize out of the shadows and come at him again.

Cori's cell phone rang. "Yes, he's right here," she said. She handed MacBridan the phone and said, "Dolinski."

It was just past 3:00 a.m., and the thought of reporting back to Dolinski had completely slipped MacBridan's mind.

"How did it go, Jim?" asked Dolinski.

MacBridan hesitated, not sure how to answer the question, his mind still reeling from the shock, he found it hard to focus. "It went okay."

"Okay? What is okay? What happened, for heaven's sake? Did you recover the artifacts?"

Again, MacBridan hesitated. He wasn't prepared to talk about all that he had just witnessed, and he certainly didn't want to talk about how he'd been rendered helpless. "Yeah, we got them all. At least I think we did. Harry and Smithers are combing the area again." Try as he might to calm down, his voice sounded as if he was out of breath.

"What is it, Jim? What aren't you telling me?" asked Dolinski. "Someone go down? Did we lose someone?"

"No, it didn't get at us." MacBridan stopped again, hardly recognizing the monotone sound of his own voice. He had to snap out of it, he sounded ridiculous. "The thief is dead. He was killed after I'd taken him into custody."

"What? Just how did that happen? Did he attack you? What do you mean 'it didn't get at us'? Jim, you're not making any sense," Dolinski pressed.

MacBridan stood there mutely staring at the phone. He didn't know what to say or how to explain what had happened.

MacBridan felt Cori next to him and realized that she'd been closely watching the exchange. He handed the phone to her and walked away, listening to her as she continued to fill Dolinski in on the night's events. It had not been a good night for MacBridan, and it was far from being over.

***

The long night continued at the precinct house where the police questioned him over and over again. At some point MacBridan remembered a lawyer showing up, but the police had already decided not to file any charges against him, at least not yet. The Hawthorne Group had been working closely with them on this case, and Cori had backed up MacBridan's statement. The wire he had been wearing provided the best evidence that MacBridan had nearly become a victim himself.

After he left the police station, MacBridan called Dolinski back. Although he had a better grip on his nerves, he still could not shake the feeling of dread that seemed to drape across his shoulders like a shroud. Their conversation was short and to the point—get to the New York office as soon as possible.

***

The short flight back to New York was uneventful, and MacBridan took a cab to their Manhattan office. He waited as patiently as he could for the meeting with Dolinski. It was late morning and he was operating on very little sleep, his umpteenth cup of coffee nearly gone. As he sat his cup down, he noticed the slight tremor of his hand, the only visible sign of the nervousness that still lived within him. MacBridan wanted to blame it on caffeine, but that wouldn't explain the unrelenting tension between his shoulders.

He checked his watch. MacBridan was anxious to talk to Dolinski. He desperately wanted to know what the police had turned up.

As MacBridan waited in the private waiting room normally reserved for clients, his eyes rested on the modest, gold plated letters proudly mounted on the wall that spelled out "Hawthorne Group." MacBridan took a great deal of pride in his employment with the elite, private firm, knowing the high level of talent and skill that ran through every part of the organization. The Hawthorne Group's clients filled the ranks of the who's who in business, government, and the entertainment world, and they handled their client's needs with complete discretion.

The Hawthorne Group had started decades ago as a family owned law firm that, due to their considerable wealth, could cater to a select clientele of their own choosing. As the years progressed, the firm grew in strength and power and earned a reputation for protecting the special interests of its clients. Appropriately, as the demands of its clients grew in complexity, other divisions were added to support their needs.

There was a financial division, capable of working through the most delicate tax problems on up to the largest of corporate mergers. Dolinski was tasked with various security challenges, as well as private investigative services, and headed up the investigative division. Lastly, to divert the media's and public's attention, a public relations division was created, there in part, to quote Dolinski, to 'put perfume on the pig.'

Based on its reputation in all the right circles, the Hawthorne Group had been able to attract top talent and was well positioned to handle the most sensitive of issues. MacBridan had been one of the first that Dolinski had personally recruited into the firm. Based in New York, the Hawthorne

Group fielded offices in five countries, with six locations spread out across the United States.

MacBridan had worked for Dolinski for close to three years, and for the most part, he liked and respected the man. The two men shared a common background, both having served in the military, and then for different law enforcement agencies. But most important to MacBridan, was the fact that Dolinski let him run his own show without constant interference or direction.

On the other hand, the one thing that had, on more than one occasion, caused conflict between him and Dolinski was the man's complete ruthlessness. While this was not a prevalent tendency, it too often sprung up, seemingly out of nowhere. Dolinski's personality during those times closely resembled the dramatic swings that one would expect of Dr. Jekyll and Mr. Hyde. He would offer no middle ground and seemed to operate without a heart or conscience. The given objective would be met, period, and anyone who got in the way was simply a casualty. However, at the same time, and to his credit, it was important to note that Dolinski was very loyal to his people. He gave unwavering loyalty and expected no less in return.

The door to Dolinski's office opened and his executive secretary, Ester King, emerged. Ester never failed to amuse MacBridan. Her whole persona was based on being very prim and proper, almost to the point of severity. She was the perfect picture of the dour maiden aunt who had never married, with an air about her that told you she was not to be trifled with. During his tenure, MacBridan had never seen a full-fledged smile cross her face. The mouth would go through the motions, but the eyes never joined in.

"Mr. Dolinski is ready for you, Mr. MacBridan. Is there anything else I can get you?"

Nearly three years and it was still "Mr. MacBridan." However, being a master sleuth, he deduced that Ester, either couldn't remember his first name, or—more likely—she was desperately masking a strong sexual attraction to him. After all, she was only human. "No, thank you, I'll just go on in."

"Very good," said Ester as her face contorted into her twisted version of a smile, lightly pulling at the cheeks, still not reaching the eyes. At least, he guessed it was a smile.

MacBridan closed the door behind him, crossed the room and eased into his favorite of the two client chairs in front of Dolinski's desk. "Good morning, Jim," Dolinski said. He remained seated at his desk. "Sorry to have kept you waiting."

Dolinski looked the same as always. His hair was perfectly styled, and he wore a suit that had easily cost a grand or more. His tie and shirt perfectly matched the ensemble as if the style editor of *GQ* had personally picked it out for him. Much like Dick Clark, Dolinski never seemed to age. He appeared to be in his early fifties; gray dabbed at the hair around his temples and continued on from there, being lightly sprinkled throughout his mass of black hair. His deep voice matched the barrel chest, giving the distinct impression of a drill sergeant out of uniform. Although well under six feet tall, Dolinski could be a very intimidating individual when the spirit moved him.

"The Catholic Church is very pleased with your work up in Boston. Archbishop Kerry asked me to convey his deepest gratitude and to let you know that you are in his prayers."

"Not only well deserved, but good to hear," said MacBridan. "You have to admit, it is somewhat rare that one recovers the stolen items, as well as the ransom, all in the same night."

"Indeed. I have a report here on our thief. He has finally been identified." Dolinski opened one of three folders lying on his desk. The lack of clutter matched the immaculate neatness of his dress, something that never failed to impress MacBridan. MacBridan's desk was the polar opposite; always covered with various piles made up of reports, case files, unopened mail, and the occasional half-eaten sandwich that had been lost in the clutter. "His name was Gerald Vickers. Ring any bells?"

"None. Last night was my first and only meeting with Mr. Vickers."

"Not surprising. He barely rates as a small-time punk. He grew up in a small, rural community in western Massachusetts, New Westminster. At this point the police have no idea how he happened to come into possession of the artifacts."

"Have the local authorities in New Westminster been of any help?" asked MacBridan.

"Not much, and frankly there is not much to add. They were surprised to even get the call. From what I understand, they feel that the thefts were far and above Vickers' limited capabilities."

"I'd have to agree with that," said MacBridan. "He was just a kid, and not an exceptionally bright one at that."

"None the less," Dolinski continued, "our client is very pleased with your work. In addition to the bonus, the church is happily paying for services rendered, and they are now offering to double the amount if we can recover the one remaining artifact that is still missing."

MacBridan frowned, "I didn't realize there were any more. We covered the area pretty well. I'm sorry to hear we missed one."

"I don't think you did. I sent in another team first thing this morning to go over the same ground, just in case, and they came up empty. No, I don't believe that Vickers had this one with him."

"To offer that kind of money, this particular artifact must really be something," said MacBridan. "What makes it so special?"

"Archbishop Kerry went in to that in some detail. It is a cross, roughly fourteen inches long, made of oak and silver. It was brought over from Ireland in the early nineteen hundreds. It is of extraordinary value to the church, and—here is the really remarkable part—it is believed to have once been carried by St. Patrick."

"Now I understand," said MacBridan. "A relic with that pedigree would fetch a fortune on the black market. The Irish government alone would probably pay a great deal to get back a cross of that significance."

"Exactly," said Dolinski, "hence the generous financial incentive for us. He stressed the utmost importance of the assignment and our need to move quickly. With Vickers having already set the example of going independent for a quick score, the concern is that that kind of behavior could become contagious, spreading to the other people involved in the thefts."

"Perhaps," said MacBridan, "but his death certainly sets another kind of example of just how far that kind of behavior will be tolerated."

Dolinski reached for the second file folder. Before he opened it, he looked at MacBridan and asked, "Mac, how are you feeling? Things got a little rough there at the end."

MacBridan thought a moment before answering. "I feel fine. Truth is I really wasn't hurt, but I can't get it out my mind. For the life of me I can't figure out what happened."

"Have you been able to remember anything else? Anything at all since we last talked?"

MacBridan shook his head. "Wish I could. It was one of the strangest things I've ever experienced." MacBridan went over the scene in his mind once again. It took all he had to contain the fear he felt and the nausea that instantly filled his stomach. He clasped his hands together and rested them on his leg to keep Dolinski from seeing the fear that they betrayed. "Whatever it was, it seemed to affect the candles first. They continued to burn, but the light itself was actually sucked out of the air. This was quickly followed by an extreme cold. As you know, I've been to the Arctic Circle more than once, but I don't believe I've ever felt a cold such as that. It was more like some kind of force, so strong that it was capable of taking control of you, mind and body. I couldn't move."

"Cori found your gun beside you. Do you remember pulling it?"

"Yes. As soon as the light began to dim, Vickers reacted. As sure as I'm sitting here, I believe he knew what was happening and it terrified him. The last thing that I remember was looking at the door." MacBridan hesitated before continuing his narrative. "I don't know how to describe this any better than to say that a darkness, a shapeless, formless darkness filled the door. Then it came at us. I wanted to shoot it, but couldn't. The next thing I knew Cori was with me."

"The wire you were wearing recorded the entire incident, but it doesn't add anything to what you have already told us," said Dolinski. He opened the file folder. "I think you'll find the medical examiner's report is just as fascinating as your own story."

"Do the Boston police have any leads on who killed him?" asked MacBridan.

"Not only do they not have any idea as to who killed him, they have no idea as to *what* killed him. I have a complete copy of the report for you but want to touch on the highlights while you're here. Vickers's throat was mutilated almost to the point of decapitation. Marks on some of the neck vertebrate suggest the fangs of an animal, but—and this is interesting—not any animal that they can identify. Now, as interesting as that is, it's not the strangest part. Due to the nature of his injuries, the two of you should have been covered in blood."

"I don't think I have any on me," said MacBridan, once again going over it in his mind. How could he have missed that? What else had he missed that night? "Come to think of it, I don't remember there being much blood even around Vickers."

"Exactly! That is what bothers the ME the most," Dolinski continued. "The two of you should have been lying in a pool of blood, and yet there was remarkably little spilled."

"That doesn't make any sense," said MacBridan. "How do they explain it?"

"They don't. Even at the autopsy there was very little blood found in the body."

"But how is that possible? To clean up a mess like that would take several people, combined with a great deal of time and effort, and I don't think I was out that long."

"According to the report Cori filed, they were, at the most, ten to twelve minutes behind you. You didn't give them the best description of the building you were entering, but they found you none the less."

"I haven't had the chance to talk with Smithers or Harry. Did they see anything?"

"Nothing. When they arrived, both of you were on the floor." Dolinski stared at MacBridan. "Mac, are you sure there isn't anything else you can tell us?"

"No sir, I'm afraid that's it," answered MacBridan. There was, however, one other item worth mentioning, but MacBridan didn't think it would help, and he certainly wasn't all that anxious to discuss it. He, along with Vickers, had been flat out terrified. Whatever had killed Vickers had filled him with an overwhelming dread that promised to give him nightmares for some time to come, adding to the nightmares he already had.

"Very well then. Mac, I want you to go to New Westminster and see what you can find. With Vickers dead, New Westminster is the only point we have to begin our search for the missing cross. Almost all of the churches robbed were in the Boston area, but that may be where Vickers's accomplices are hiding." Dolinski handed him the third folder. "You'll find everything we have so far in there. There are also pictures of the cross you'll be looking for."

"Thank you," said MacBridan, as he rose to leave. "I'll see what I can find, but it sounds rather like a long shot."

"Perhaps, we'll see. However, while in New Westminster, there is one other thing I'd like for you to look into. Double duty, if you will, but this shouldn't get in your way too much."

"What would that be, sir?" MacBridan asked, taking his seat again.

Dolinski turned his chair and gazed out the window. He seemed uncertain how to proceed, and then said without turning around, "Mac, this is a bit personal, but I have family in New Westminster and she may be in trouble."

"She?"

"Yes. An aunt of mine—Ms. Katherine Chamberlin. Her real name was Katya Dolinski, but after she married, she changed it to Katherine. She must be in her mid-seventies."

"What kind of trouble is she having?"

"That's perhaps the most difficult part about this, Mac. It is hard to put into words. Perhaps the best way I can say this is that Aunt Katherine has seen some things that have her worried. She also thinks someone is watching her house."

MacBridan groaned to himself. Not only was he being sent on the improbable mission to find a gang of thieves who prey on churches—one of whom was now possibly a killer—in rural Massachusetts, but now he would also get to do some babysitting for an old woman. An old woman whose biggest problem was probably being a little afraid of the dark.

"Sir, with all due respect to your aunt, wouldn't she do better calling the local authorities? I'll be pretty focused on the search and may not be able to give her the time this deserves."

Dolinski turned and faced MacBridan. "Look, I know what you are thinking." The fact was he probably did. In the years MacBridan had worked for him, Dolinski had demonstrated an almost uncanny insight into people's thoughts. "This is not some frail, senile old woman afraid of her own shadow. You'll find that she is one tough old girl with a razor sharp mind. Besides, she has already called the local sheriff, and frankly they didn't take her all that seriously."

"I see. Well, what exactly has she seen and why would anyone be watching her?" asked MacBridan.

"Both excellent questions, but I'd rather she be the one to answer them. She can fill in the details so much better. I've already spoken to her, and she is expecting you tomorrow. Besides, you'll be staying with her while you are in New Westminster. She has a very nice guest cottage behind her house, and I'm sure you'll be quite comfortable."

"Do you think that is wise sir? If we are right, and I do find these people, I may end up putting your aunt in harm's way."

"Mac, I believe she may already be in some kind of danger. If I could get away from here I'd go myself, but there is simply no chance of that. I want you there and I want you there tomorrow," said Dolinski. His tone made it clear that there wasn't any more room for discussion. "Do your best to find that artifact."

"I will," said MacBridan. He got up and moved to the door.

"Mac," Dolinski said before he opened it. "I've known her most of my life. She and my parents were very close. There were quite a few summers when I'd go to visit them, staying for weeks at a time. I learned a great deal from her, about her beliefs, and I know that she doesn't spook easy. Something is going on there. If I didn't believe it was serious, I would not ask you to get involved."

MacBridan nodded and left.

CHAPTER 3

Holly's gaze drifted across the valley that ran down from their property, but her mind continued to reflect back on all of the changes that had taken place over the past year. It had been an incredible year with so many wonderful changes.

"You want some water?" Ian called from the kitchen.

"Yes, please," said Holly.

"Stay there, I'll bring it out."

They'd finished dinner an hour ago, and as was becoming the custom, Holly found herself resting on the front porch of their home, awaiting the sunset. The last twelve months were almost too overwhelming to think about. Just a year ago, she and Ian had been living in a small apartment in Boston. Now they were miles from there, settled in their own home.

So many changes had taken place, all happening so quickly, that she and Ian seemed to have been swept away in a current of change with little option but to hang on to each other and hope. Still, they were happy. She loved their home, and Ian appeared to be just as content as she was. Yet there was something wrong, something she couldn't identify.

Holly couldn't shake this feeling of uneasiness, a nervousness, which remarkably hadn't started until they'd actually moved in to their new home. Considering all that they had been through, the nervousness should have started long before then. But it hadn't, and now she was having trouble dealing with this unexplainable tension that had become her constant companion. The maddening part was that she just couldn't put her finger on the true source of the problem.

It all started with a simple get-away weekend. The travel section of the *Boston Globe* led them to New Westminster and the breathtaking scenic beauty that flowed across the hills of this charming, small community.

They had been walking down Main Street when Holly spotted it, wedged in between a candy store and Clare's Collectables. "Ian, look, a real-estate office."

"That's good, Holly. Now if you spot a restroom, we'll really be in business."

Holly's straight, dark brown hair matched her eyes perfectly, resting just on her shoulders. Not a beauty in the traditional sense, she had a natural beauty that seemed to flow from within. Her brown eyes were large and full of expression. Ian had told her more than once that her eyes could communicate all her feelings to him without her ever having to say anything. She wasn't tall, just a couple of inches over five feet, but her spirit was as bold as one could want. "Oh come on, let's go in."

"You're not serious?"

"Why not? We've talked about getting a place of our own, and New Westminster is beautiful," said Holly.

"I like it too, but Holly, we would be so far away from everything."

"Far away from what? Neither of us have family in Boston. You work out of our apartment as it is. Besides, things can't be nearly as expensive here as they are there. We'll get more for our money in a much nicer place."

Ian hesitated for a moment before giving in. "Alright, we'll go in, but if there's no restroom, we are out of there." He had never really been able to deny Holly very much. For him it had been love at first sight the day they met.

Their friends referred to them as Salt and Pepper. Although they blended well, they were as different as two people could be.

Holly never met a stranger, whereas Ian took some time to warm up to people and was much more comfortable with computers. Holly could come to a decision without hesitation. For Ian, big decisions, in particular, could drag on for weeks. His proposing to Holly took three separate dates before he was able to get the question out. It wasn't that he doubted his feelings for Holly; it was just that up until the third attempt he'd simply become overwhelmed by the whole idea. An inch shy of six feet tall, Ian was of medium build, with wiry, dark hair that never wanted to cooperate. Most of the time it gave people the impression that he'd just gotten out of bed. Nevertheless, Holly loved him, and couldn't imagine herself with anyone else.

Holly hugged his arm as they entered the real-estate office. Two metal desks dominated the small room. Pictures of houses on letter sized paper posters covered the far wall. The only person working appeared to be about their age. In his late twenties, maybe early thirties, he was terribly thin with sharp, pointed features. He kept his plain brown hair pulled back tightly into a sort of mini ponytail that under other circumstances would probably have made them laugh. The end result only served to make his face look even more gaunt.

The thin man was on the phone but smiled and motioned for them to sit down. He quickly wrapped up his call. "Hi, I'm Paul Lovett. How may I help you?" he asked as he came around the desk.

"I'm Holly Carpenter and this is my husband, Ian," she said as they both shook hands with Paul.

Ian was surprised at the strength in the smaller man's hand.

"Pleased to meet you," said Paul. "What brings you to New Westminster?"

"Actually we're just visiting for the weekend," answered Holly. "However, we've talked a great deal about getting our own home—this area is just beautiful—and so we thought we'd see what might be available in our price range."

Paul smiled. "Not a hard place to fall in love with is it? Let's do this. Let me get some information from you, and then we'll have a better feel as to what kind of home we should be looking for," he said as he sat back down behind his desk and pulled out a form.

Ian knew that this was going to take more time than his bladder could stand. "Paul, excuse me, but is there a restroom nearby?"

"Of course." Paul pointed to a door at the rear of his office. "Go through there and down the hall. It's your first door on the right. While you're doing that, Holly and I can get started."

* * *

It didn't take long before Paul had all the information he needed. He turned to his computer and began to see what New Westminster had to offer. While the computer completed its search, Paul asked, "So how would your family feel about you and Ian leaving Boston?"

"Ian and I don't have much in the way of family," said Holly. "Ian's parents both died before he graduated high school. I lost my dad when I was eight, and it was only my mother and I growing up. She never remarried. I don't think she has ever really gotten over losing Dad. Ian and I hope to start our own family soon."

"That must have been hard," said Paul. "Where is your mother now?"

"She lives just outside Lexington, Kentucky. That's where I grew up. She's lived around there all her life."

"Boston is quite a way from Kentucky. How did you end up there?"

Ian was just returning as Holly said, "Ian and I met at college. That was at Morehead State University in eastern Kentucky. We got married right after graduation, and then Ian got a job in Boston."

"Well, Boston's a good place to be," said Paul. "I get up there every so often. Nice thing about living here is that Boston's not that far away." Paul looked at Ian. "Holly tells me you are self-employed."

"That's right," said Ian. "Four months after we moved to Boston, the company I was with went under. Things got pretty tough there for a while. Most of the money we had, and that wasn't a great deal, we'd used in the move. Fortunately, I've always been pretty good with computers. Even though jobs were tight, I ended up working as a contractor for a couple of companies, with their IT groups. Anyway, a guy I knew helped me get set up as a consultant, and suddenly I had my own business. Frankly, it is probably the best thing that could have happened to us. I'm making more now than I ever would have at my old company."

"That is really good to hear, Ian. Congratulations. It always makes you feel good to hear stories like that. Now-a-days there are too many cases where things don't work out as well."

"Yes," said Holly. She reached over and held Ian's hand. "We are very blessed and we know it."

"Well, let's see what we can find for you in the way of a home. Ian, I personally would like to have you here in town so I can get you to help me figure out my own darn computer. I fight more with this crazy machine than I care to talk about," said Paul. "Course, truth be known, it is mostly pilot error."

Paul began to show them the various listings that were within their range. As expected, they were small homes, but none of them seemed very interesting. Holly's disappointment was evident, but then it had been a spur of the moment long shot. Paul leaned back and scratched his head. Then suddenly he seemed to remember something, sat up, and once again went to work on the computer. "Give me a minute here. We just may have something else."

He soon found what he was looking for. He explained that there was a piece of property—a small farm, actually—not too far out of town, on Hickory Hill Road that had recently come on the market. The family, Paul explained, lived out of state and had finally decided to sell. They were interested in moving the property fast and therefore had priced it pretty low. "If you have the time, I'd like to take you out there and show it to you. It is really very nice. A local man has been looking after the place, so it has been kept up pretty well."

Holly enjoyed the ride out to the farm. She and Ian had not been out this way, and the hills reminded her of Kentucky. Paul told them that the farm's twenty-five acres were already fenced. The water came from a well that tapped into a spring. They soon turned off onto the gravel drive that led up to the house. The driveway was little more than a twisting path, running across Shepard's Creek just after leaving the highway.

It snaked its way through the woods and emerged into a clearing that surrounded a small house with what looked like a work shed behind it. A huge oak tree next to the house towered above it. Both buildings were situated up the slope of the hill, providing a view from the front porch that was magnificent. The front of the house faced west, peering over the valley and on to the distant hills.

Paul parked beside the house and they followed him up on to the porch. Ian turned to admire the view. He noticed something at the bottom of the hill where the clearing met the trees. He turned to Paul and asked, “Is that an old road down there heading into the trees?”

Paul followed Ian’s gaze and saw what had prompted his question. “It’s really not much more than a path, but, on occasion, it is still used by the people who keep up the grounds for St. Thomas Church. Believe it or not, they manage to get a small pickup truck with their lawnmowers down that path all the way to the churchyard. Are you Catholic?”

“Yes, we are,” answered Holly.

“Well I think you’ll like St. Thomas. In fact, weather permitting, if you follow that path it’s really a very pretty walk. Very quiet and very peaceful,” said Paul, not missing a step with his not so subtle sales pitch.

At first the lock resisted Paul’s attempt to open the door, but after a moment, he had it and they went inside. The door opened into a small family room with a stone fireplace and hardwood floors. The kitchen shared space with the dining room, but there were several windows allowing the light to pour in. There were two bedrooms, the smaller of which could easily act as a nursery, and one and a half baths. Surprisingly, there was a basement, but it too was small and unfinished, with a dirt floor.

Paul stepped outside and told them to take their time. They stood in the kitchen, and Holly looked out the window while Ian continued to examine the appliances. Holly turned to him and asked, “Well, what do you think?”

“I think that it is hard to believe we can afford something like this. The house isn’t all that big, but that’s a lot of land.”

“Ian, I really love it here. It is everything we want and then some. As to the price, well, we just happened to be in the right place, at the right time.”

“It just doesn’t seem possible. I mean, it’s nice, but I’m just not sure,” said Ian. They were quiet for a moment. “Holly, I’ve never owned a home.”

They talked for close to an hour, trying to cover every aspect as to whether or not they should go for it. Finally, the point that won Ian over was the one that centered on their plans for having children.

"Do you really want to bring a baby home to our cramped apartment? An apartment that is, well, not in the best part of the city?" asked Holly.

Finally, as always, he went along with her and asked, "What do we do now?"

Paul took them back to his office and guided them through the mountain of paper work. After some discussion, they decided on their bid. Paul then worked with them on the necessary loan documents. One of the banks in the area, he explained, had a special program for first time homeowners that would greatly reduce the need for a large down payment. Paul promised to personally contact the bank president. Holly and Ian left New Westminster far later in the day than they had planned, and drove back to Boston with mixed emotions. They were both filled with the excitement of owning their own home, but at the same time came all the concerns of being attached to a mortgage.

They heard back from Paul the following Tuesday. Holly could tell by the tone of his voice that things had gone their way. Their bid, although under the asking price, had been accepted. Ian and Holly Carpenter had officially become part of the American dream.

From that point on, things moved quickly. They closed on the farm the first week in January and moved in two weeks later. Long hours were spent getting settled in their new home. Paul Lovett stopped by a couple of times to see if they needed anything, and dropped off a list of businesses, medical professionals, and emergency numbers that were in the area. It was Paul who recommended Dr. Ben Appleton, a recommendation that came in handy.

Their next piece of life-changing news came to them in February. Holly's appointment with Dr. Appleton that morning confirmed what she had already guessed. So, as she and Ian celebrated their first Valentine's dinner at home, Holly told him that he was going to be a father. This is what they had been praying for, and they both cried as they held each other. According to the doctor, the baby was due in mid to late October.

Spring came and went and the summer brought more pleasant surprises. The wildlife around them was abundant. Holly and Ian were amazed at how close the deer would come to the house. Holly kept a radio playing in the kitchen window and believed that the deer actually enjoyed the music. The raccoons, on the other hand, turned out to be downright aggressive. Soon Ian learned that he had to fasten the lids securely on their garbage cans.

Now autumn announced itself through the changing of the leaves, as Holly's pregnancy continued to progress nicely. It was now just a few months shy of a year since their first visit to New Westminster, a very full and fast-paced year.

"Where do you want me to set this?" asked Ian as he joined her on the porch.

"I'll take it," said Holly. She sipped the water and then set it down beside her chair. "I've been sitting here thinking about all that has happened to us—the move, our house, the baby. I like it here, Ian."

Ian sat next to her, holding her hand, something he did whenever he could. "Me too, honey, me too. I had my doubts, but moving to New Westminster has to be one of the best decisions we've ever made."

Holly cherished the closeness between them. She needed it, especially now. She wanted to talk to Ian, to open up to him and tell him that despite how good things had gone for them, something was eating at her. Something wasn't quite right. She could feel it. But feel what? Holly didn't know what it was; she didn't understand it and by opening up to him with this now would only serve to worry him. Maybe, she thought, it was the changes going on within her, the pregnancy. No, that wasn't it. This had started before then. No, the sad part was that this had truly started their first night in their new home, of that she was certain.

Holly sighed quietly to herself. She had decided that she would just have to find a way to deal with it; there was certainly no turning back now. It had taken every penny they had to move here and there was no one they could turn to for help.

The sun had almost dipped behind the ridge that ran across the valley from them. With Holly's due date drawing near, they were looking forward to what promised to be a glorious fall, and Holly wasn't about to let anything silly put a damper on things.

CHAPTER 4

Cori was based in the New York office, and MacBridan stopped by to see her after his meeting with Dolinski. Still assigned to the case, she would be in charge of his remote backup while in New Westminster, including everything from research, to managing reports, to sending in the cavalry if need be.

"So how's the man?" asked Cori. The investigative team referred to their boss as *the man*, unbeknownst to him, or so they believed.

"His usual loving, caring, demanding self."

"He should be pretty happy. It's my understanding that our client couldn't believe that we recovered the artifacts and didn't give up even one dollar of the ransom money."

MacBridan smiled at Cori. "Just how do you get all of your information? As much as I appreciate some of your finer qualities, I can't see those particular charms working on Ester King."

Cori dressed like a Wall Street executive in a cream-colored blouse, buttoned at the neck, which blended perfectly with the charcoal colored jacket and skirt. Although quite professional, the clothes couldn't hide Cori's curvaceous figure. While Hollywood's image of a lady detective was typically stereotyped as either a vamp or an overly made up model usually seen on a magazine cover, Dolinski demanded a neat, professional appearance from all his people.

"First, I will choose to overlook your borderline sexist remark," Cori retorted. "Second, may I point out that you seldom appreciate the full scope of my capabilities?"

"Alright," MacBridan laughed. "I stand corrected. Did your network of contacts tell you that the job isn't over?"

"Yes, but I didn't get too many details. Apparently our thief didn't have all of the items that were stolen."

"Right again. We have been retained to recover—are you ready—the Cross of St. Patrick." MacBridan brought Cori up to date and gave her copies of the files Dolinski had given to him.

"Do you think there's any chance of finding anything in New Westminster?" she asked.

"Not much, but on the other hand, we really don't have a great deal to choose from in the way of leads."

"How are you doing, Mac?"

MacBridan had anticipated, and dreaded, this question. He simply didn't want to talk to her about it. "I'm alright. Just wish I could remember more."

"Mac, we were there. You did everything right. Harry, Smithers, and I listened to the tape, and there's nothing else you could have done."

"Cori..." MacBridan hesitated. He was uncertain how far he should go. "I appreciate what you are saying, but there's more to it. There's no easy way to say this, but whatever happened down there scared me to death. I can't even explain it to myself."

"Mac, I've worked with you on some pretty tough cases, and I know you. You never quit. You'll find these people and then you'll have your answers."

MacBridan squeezed her hand, smiled and said, "Thanks, Cori, I appreciate that. I'll be in touch."

The long drive to New Westminster took more time than expected, but for MacBridan it acted as recuperative therapy. He needed the time alone, time to think things through. As he left the city behind and headed into the rural hills of Western Massachusetts it allowed him, both mentally and physically, to put some distance between him and that nightmarish event that he was still trying to come to grips with. His inability to understand how Vickers had been killed, to even be able to offer a reasonable guess as to what had happened, raised some serious doubts within himself.

He was concerned about the doubts he may have raised with his own team. Fortunately, Cori had been able to ease this concern before he left. But, on top of it all, it resurrected another nightmarish event that he still struggled with from time to time. It had happened years ago in another world, in another life. Although time had tempered the pain of the horrific event, it would forever haunt him and had raised its ugly head in that basement. Maria. For the briefest moment, when Cori had been trying to wake him up, it had sounded like Maria's voice calling to him in that basement. When Cori asked him about it, he'd been able to brush it off, but for MacBridan there was no escaping the guilt he felt and the betrayal of the one he'd been raised to trust in.

It had been a time of war and he and Maria had both been stationed in Baghdad. MacBridan, a young captain in the Marine Corps, and Maria, an army lieutenant, a linguistics officer working at headquarters. They had met there, and for MacBridan it had been love at first sight. Despite the horror of the war torn country surrounding them, their love blossomed and grew. Then, surprisingly, the impossible happened and they both secured a forty-eight hour pass. Before anyone could change their orders, they took off for a small hotel in the Green Zone that had become their private escape from the war. For two glorious days, they would be together, trying to imagine that they were anywhere else on the planet other than Iraq.

He remembered Maria walking out of the bathroom their first morning there, wrapped in just a towel. When she was close enough to the bed, he reached for her, but she pulled away from him, and smiled playfully, staying just out of his reach.

"Alright, what's going on with you?"

Maria moved over, sat next to him on the bed, and said, "Do you love me?"

"That cannot be a serious question," said MacBridan, but Maria's face had taken on a very serious look, a face filled with apprehension.

"Of course I love you; you should know that by now. What's going on?" asked MacBridan, sitting up in bed. "You've been acting weird since we got here."

Maria got up and walked to the window. After another moment's hesitation, she turned and looked at him. "I'm pregnant."

It was the last thing MacBridan had expected and he sat there in stunned silence. It wasn't that he didn't love Maria, but this was certainly not the time or the place.

"No response, nothing?" said Maria, her anger starting to rise.

"How did that happen?" said MacBridan, still trying to adjust to what she'd just told him.

She gave him a "how do you think it happened" look and he continued on. "How far along are you?"

"About eight weeks," she answered.

"Eight weeks," said MacBridan. "What are you going to do?"

"I'm going to have it; you don't have to worry about it."

MacBridan got up and went to her. She tried to pull away from him, but he wrapped his arms around her and wouldn't let her go. "That's not what I meant."

"What did you mean?" She asked, "I'm Catholic, just like you, and this is the most precious gift from God there is. When I finally get to leave this hell hole of a country with its blood thirsty people, I'll be taking this wonderful blessing with me and forgetting about the rest."

"I meant about your career. They'll send you stateside and unless I can get pregnant too, I doubt they'll let me go with you."

Maria turned to him. "Then this is okay with you? We'll still be together?"

"This is big news. You caught me completely off guard," said MacBridan. Pulling on his clothes he said, "I'll be right back. I'm going to go get us some coffee…well, at least get me some coffee. I'm guessing that from now on you're on a milk diet."

Maria hugged his neck as hard as she could and kissed him. When she pulled back, MacBridan could see the tears that had run down her face. "Go get us a table. We may as well get something to eat. I'll get cleaned up and will be right down."

MacBridan opened the door to leave, stopped and looked at her. "Of course we'll be together. I love you."

Fortunately, the small café across the street from their hotel had pretty decent food. As MacBridan walked towards the café, he bumped into an Iraqi man wearing an army jacket that was too heavy for the weather. MacBridan apologized, his mind was clearly elsewhere, and took a table outside. He nodded to one of the waiters he knew, and the man scampered off to get him some coffee.

MacBridan's world had completely changed. He loved Maria, of that he had no doubt, but he hadn't planned on starting a family now, and most certainly not in Baghdad. The waiter set down his coffee and moved off to another table. This brought MacBridan out of his reverie and he noticed a young mother with a baby at the table next to him. She was busy talking with another woman, while the baby scooped handfuls of cereal into its mouth. The baby made eye contact with MacBridan and they both stared at each other. All interest in the cereal was gone, and for no apparent reason, the child gave MacBridan a big, happy, toothless grin. MacBridan chuckled to himself and said, "I'm going to be a father. Imagine that."

***

Maria walked out of the hotel wearing brown army fatigues and looked for MacBridan. As he caught sight of her, he stood up and smiled, waving at her. His smile erased any doubts that might have been lingering in her mind and she smiled back at him. All was well between them. Suddenly, the Iraqi man MacBridan had bumped into earlier darted across the street to the hotel entrance, yelling something in Arabic.

***

MacBridan's recognized what was happening, but it was too late. Desperately he started to charge across the street, when the blast went off.

The force of the explosion lifted him off his feet and threw him back into the café. Maria was gone.

While his physical injuries took very little time to heal, the mental anguish was relentless. Why had he left her alone? Why had this happened? Why had God allowed this? From that day on, MacBridan's view of God changed dramatically. In time, he returned to active duty, but he returned deeply scarred and cynically hardened. That had been years ago and it had been a long time since he'd relived that terrible time in his mind.

Shaking his head to rid himself of the memory, he focused in on the present. MacBridan's spirits steadily recovered as the miles rolled by. The old state highway meandered its way through the hills—hills that were now coming alive with autumn color. MacBridan loved the fall. The sky remained nearly cloudless, and he found himself more relaxed than he had been in a while.

He hadn't mentioned the part about Dolinski's aunt to Cori, since MacBridan sensed that it was something Dolinski wanted to remain personal and private between the two men. Besides, the more he thought about it, the more contradictory it seemed, based on how Dolinski usually worked.

MacBridan knew Dolinski as well as anyone. Over the years, Dolinski had revealed very little about his personal life. In fact, Dolinski had often been openly critical of anyone mixing their personal problems with business. So for Dolinski to ask him to not only look into his aunt's problem, but to do so in conjunction with another case, while staying at her home, was completely out of character. Nothing about it made sense.

As he made his way into the town, his first impression of New Westminster was that of a quiet, stately community, nicely settled in the hills. Tall, white church steeples and the tree lined avenues offered a comfortable stability that promised a good place to raise a family. MacBridan took his time, driving slowly, taking in the atmosphere. This was where Gerald Vickers had grown up, and yet, based on what he knew of Vickers, the setting was not what one would have expected. The town was startlingly close to being Norman Rockwell picturesque. New Westminster presented a setting in which it was hard to imagine someone even jaywalking, much less being the springboard for a felon responsible for several robberies.

MacBridan continued on, following the directions he'd been given, and had no trouble finding the home of Dolinski's aunt. The house, located on the northern side of town, sat upon a ridge overlooking much of the community. A four-foot tall hedge that ran the length of the property guarded the front yard. MacBridan parked in the driveway, got out, and walked up to the porch.

The house was larger than he had anticipated. Although not an authority on architecture, it was easy for him to see that this two-story, red brick home was of colonial style. Sitting comfortably under massive trees, it exuded a quiet strength. Just as he reached the first step leading up to the large front porch, the front door opened and out stepped Katherine Chamberlin. She was slender, and taller than MacBridan expected. Her hair was completely white, but without any of the blue tones he had spotted on other women her age.

"Mr. MacBridan?" Her voice was surprisingly strong and clear. So far, everything was different from the mental picture MacBridan had created. Like the house, Katherine Chamberlin had presence. Although well up there in years, she was anything but frail and weak.

"Yes, you must be Mrs. Chamberlin."

"Please come in. Peter called and told me all about you. I was so pleased to hear that you'll be staying for a few days. And you must call me Katherine. Mrs. Chamberlin is much too formal, and besides, I feel old enough as it is. Hearing 'Mrs. Chamberlin' all the time just reminds me that I'm senior to just about everyone walking around."

She led MacBridan into the living room. Once again, he found things not to be as he'd envisioned. He had expected the stereotypical grandma's house—dark, filled with prehistoric furniture and the requisite musty, old smell. This room was bright, with somewhat modern furnishings. Rich cherry wood crown moldings and baseboards accented the off-white walls. MacBridan counted four vases placed around the room, all filled with roses and several other flowers he couldn't identify. A light tan leather sofa sat across from the fireplace, with two wingback chairs on either side.

"I appreciate you having me," said MacBridan. "I'm sure Peter explained that there is some business here in New Westminster I need to take care of, but it shouldn't take more than a couple of days. Hopefully I won't be too much in your way."

"Not to worry," Mrs. Chamberlin assured him. "I was just getting myself some tea. What can I get you?"

"That sounds great. You certainly have a beautiful home," said MacBridan as he followed her into the kitchen. With the exception of the large, six-burner gas stove, all of the appliances looked new. More flowers lay on the counter next to the sink. These had not yet been trimmed.

"Thank you. I have lived here for more years than I care to remember. I'm not sure how much Peter shared with you about New Westminster, but it is a wonderful place to live. Most would find it hard to believe that the thieves you are looking for are here."

Mrs. Chamberlin's knowledge of why he had come to New Westminster caught him completely off guard. Since when did Dolinski ever share details about their cases with anyone outside the company? Well, it was just one more little item he didn't understand to add to a rapidly growing list. MacBridan liked to think that he could keep a pretty good poker face in about any situation, but this time his surprise was evident.

Mrs. Chamberlin saw this and laughed. "Oh come on now," she said. "Did you really think my nephew would keep me in the dark as to what was going on? My dear young man, my late husband was in law enforcement for this very county, and he tangled with some pretty tough customers. A few small-time thieves stealing trinkets from the church is hardly going to upset me. In fact, I may be of help to you."

MacBridan smiled, "At this point, I'll take all the help I can get."

"You just let me know. I've been here most of my life and know most of the folks better than they'd like me to know them. It's a small town and not much goes on that someone doesn't see."

"That is probably the best offer I've had in a while. However, that's not my only reason for being here. I understand you have been having your own problems, someone watching the house."

Now it was Mrs. Chamberlin's turn to look surprised, and she almost seemed more than a little embarrassed. "Looks like my nephew isn't too good at keeping secrets from anyone, is he?"

"That makes us even," said MacBridan. "Seriously, though, Peter is very concerned, and we both want to help. He didn't give me a great deal of detail, but thought it would be better if I got the story straight from you."

Mrs. Chamberlin studied MacBridan for a moment. "Mr. MacBridan, I did not call my nephew asking for help. All I wanted was his opinion. Now I'm not sure why I wanted that. I've lived alone for some time now and I do very well."

"We all need help now and then," said MacBridan. He could see that she was ferociously independent and that this was hard for her. "Sometimes problems just come our way that are tough to handle. Please, I'd like to know more about what's been going on."

"For Peter to have confided in you with something this personal, it's obvious that you have his trust."

Mrs. Chamberlin rinsed her glass out, set it in the sink, and stood with her back to MacBridan as she stared out the window. MacBridan sat at the table sipping his tea. She needed time. He was in no rush.

"Very well," she said, turning to face him. "I won't pretend that I'm not relieved to have you here. It's been playing on my nerves more than it deserves. But, you are primarily here to work on the church's business. My problems can wait until dinner. Peter said you would never turn down a home cooked meal."

MacBridan smiled and said, "That would be very nice, but we really don't have to wait until then to talk."

"I do, Mr. MacBridan. I haven't really gone into the details of this with anyone, and I need to get my thoughts together. Now, tell me what I can do to help you."

"Okay. Well, for starters, I need talk with the sheriff. The Boston police have already talked with him, but I'd like to personally follow-up on their conversation and see if he can add anything to what he told them."

"His name is Frank Beninger," said Mrs. Chamberlin. "Let's get you settled first and then, if you need directions, I'll tell you how to find him."

They both walked out to MacBridan's car and he got his things out of the trunk. He then followed her around the side of the house to a small building that sat in the back of the yard, about twenty yards away, up against the tree line. Like the main house, it was made of brick and wood, and looked very old.

Mrs. Chamberlin handed him a key and then unlocked the door with a second key she kept on a small key chain. "When the house was first built this was used as a carriage house. It took us a while to get it finished—Jonathan, my husband, did most of the work in his spare time to convert it to a small guest cottage."

Inside, MacBridan found three rooms, all nicely furnished. The main area combined as a sitting room and bedroom. There was a bathroom, and a third room that acted as a kitchenette. It didn't take long for MacBridan to unpack his things and get set up.

"Frank Beninger has been sheriff now for nearly twelve years, and I've known him longer than that," said Mrs. Chamberlin as they walked back towards the house.

"He must be doing a pretty good job to have held the office for so long," said MacBridan.

"Oh, Frank's a pretty good man. He does okay, I guess, well enough to keep getting elected. He's actually the right kind of man for this county."

"How's that?"

"Slow. Frank has never been the kind of man who was overly self-motivated. Things move kind of slow around here and I guess that has allowed him to keep pace."

It was getting to be late in the afternoon, but MacBridan didn't want to wait until tomorrow to get started. He had an address for the sheriff's office, and before he left, Mrs. Chamberlin drew a map for him. Sheriff Frank Beninger's offices were about twenty miles outside New Westminster, over in Deacon's Mill.

MacBridan parked across the street from the sheriff's station. It was a long, one-story building that connected to a newer facility, which served as the jail. MacBridan went up three steps and through the double doors that had "Sheriff's Station" in large, black letters printed on them. He hoped that Beninger hadn't already left for the day.

The woman working the desk was on the phone when MacBridan came in. She wore a deputy's uniform, but it was hard to imagine her in that role. To put it kindly, she had an extremely robust figure, so much so, that the seams of her uniform were under constant strain. MacBridan did not want to be around when they finally let go. Her bleached-blonde hair had been carefully stacked on top of her head, and she had on enough eye shadow to last, MacBridan estimated, the next two months. The call ended and she immediately turned to the radio to send out instructions. *Multi-talented,* thought MacBridan, *receptionist and dispatcher.*

"May I help you?" she said in a loud, nasal voice.

MacBridan handed her his card. "I'm looking for Sheriff Beninger."

She studied MacBridan's card for longer than it should have taken. She then placed the card on the desk in front of her and looked up at him. "Is he expecting you?"

"No, I'm afraid not. Hopefully, that won't be a problem," MacBridan said as he leaned in, giving her one of his *you're special* smiles. This technique had, on more than one occasion, proven to be a lethal combination for the women he encountered.

Her resistance to him was admirable. The expression on her face never changed. She picked up his card and once again subjected it to intense study. MacBridan wondered which word she was stuck on.

"Have a seat. You'll have to wait." Her nasal voice raked across the walls. MacBridan watched as she got up and walked off down the hall. At best, it was a slow process. MacBridan thought back to Mrs. Chamberlin's comment earlier about the slow pace of the area.

She finally returned and said, "The sheriff will see you now. He's in the last office down the hall, on the right."

"Thank you for your help," MacBridan said. Once again, he gifted her with his patented *you're special* smile. Once again, she pretended not to notice and returned to her desk.

Beninger's office was of moderate size. The windows were large, and the early evening sun poured in. Sheriff Beninger remained seated as MacBridan entered his office. In his mid to late forties, Sheriff Beninger did not cut a very dashing figure. Although his hair hadn't yet started to turn gray, it had clearly begun to thin out. What he had lost in hair, though, he made up for in a stomach born of too many beers.

"Sheriff, thank you for seeing me this afternoon. I'm James MacBridan." MacBridan leaned across the desk, shook the sheriff's hand, and then sat down.

"The Hawthorne Group," said Sheriff Beninger, looking at MacBridan's card. "Can't say I ever heard of them. You a lawyer?"

"No, I'm not. It's actually frightening to think I look like one. I'm a private investigator in the firm's investigative division. I would like to talk to you about a case we are working on."

"Well, you sure look like a lawyer," Sheriff Beninger continued.

He was a slow talker, and MacBridan wondered if it was backed up by an equally slow mind. "What can I do for you?"

"The Hawthorne Group was asked to look into the thefts of several valuable artifacts that were taken from Catholic Churches in the New England area. About a week ago, one of the thieves surfaced and tried to ransom the artifacts back to the church. The thief's name was Gerald Vickers."

"Yeah, I remember that. Boston PD contacted us for information about him. As I understand it, he was killed during the exchange." Beninger's chair groaned under his effort to lean even farther back.

"That's right," said MacBridan. "I was running the operation; his death was unfortunate."

"So, you were there?"

"I was."

"What happened?"

"We're really not sure. He panicked and took off. I followed him into the basement of an abandoned building, and someone killed him," said MacBridan.

"You're a pretty big guy, you look fit enough. I imagine you could handle most situations, and yet this sounds like it got out of hand. Did you kill him, Mr...?" The sheriff picked up his card and looked at it again, "MacBridan?" It was the first time the Sheriff had made eye contact with him. MacBridan returned his stare.

"No. Whoever did it knocked me out and then killed Vickers."

"You must be a very lucky man, Mr. MacBridan. Wonder why you were so miraculously spared?"

MacBridan gave the sheriff a small smile. "You'll appreciate, I'm sure, and perhaps take comfort in knowing that I was part of a team. My backup was not far behind me, so the killer had very little time."

"I see. Well, that is one fascinating story, and it does fill in some of the gaps I had on the whole affair. The good news is that some of those artifacts that you recovered were taken from our church, St. Thomas, over in New Westminster. I never thought the good father would ever see them again. I'm sure the church was most grateful, as am I, but I'm still not sure what I can do for you."

"What can you tell me about Gerald Vickers?"

At last, Sheriff Beninger showed some sign of being a real cop, sitting up and extending his hand across the desk. "Before we go much further, I'd like to see your identification and your license. You do have an investigator's license, don't you, Mr. MacBridan?"

MacBridan ignored the taunt and gave him what he asked for. Beninger took down some notes and gave them back to him. "I'll tell you what little there is to tell," he said, resuming his relaxed slouch, "but first, I want to get one thing clear. I'm in charge here. It is peaceful, quiet, and that's how everyone likes it. You do your investigating, but you come across anything, anything at all, where you find the law is being broken, you stop and call me. I don't tolerate anyone coming in here and playing cowboy."

"Is that it, or do I have to be out of town by sunset?" asked MacBridan, a trace of a smile still on his face.

Beninger stared at MacBridan for a moment, trying to make up his mind about something, then grunted. "You've come a long way for nothing, MacBridan. Gerald Vickers was a nobody. His biggest accomplishment after dropping out of school was to go to work at a body shop. Even that was off and on. He lived in New Westminster and that's about it."

"Doesn't sound like a man who was involved in a successful string of burglaries," said MacBridan.

"Shoot, he couldn't figure out how to get through high school."

"Nevertheless, he ended up with the goods and tried to move them. That alone took a little imitative. Any close friends, relatives, girlfriend, anyone you think may know more about how he got mixed up in this?"

Beninger sat, lost in thought, or maybe just lost. "It's like I said, a waste of your time and mine. He never got into any real trouble around here, so I never paid much attention to him. His grandfather passed away a couple years ago and left him the house he was living in. It wasn't much, but it was about all Vickers had."

MacBridan put a picture of the missing cross and its description on Beninger's desk. "We've recovered most of what was taken. This cross, however, is worth more than the whole lot added together. Whoever recruited Vickers may be from this area. Any help you can give will be appreciated."

"I'll show it around," said Beninger. He didn't look at it and let it lie where MacBridan had set it down. "We come up with anything, you can count on my rushing to the phone and calling you first thing."

MacBridan enjoyed good sarcasm, no matter how poorly delivered. He got up and moved to the door. The relationship between private investigators and the police wasn't always as smooth as he would have liked it to be. Sometimes it was what MacBridan referred to as the Rodney Dangerfield Rule—PIs just don't get any respect, and it appeared that Beninger was intent on not being an exception to that rule. "Thank you for your time, Sheriff. My cell number is on my card."

"Oh, as I said, we'll get on this first thing," said Beninger. The sheriff remained seated, as MacBridan had found him. "You take care and remember our little talk."

"You have a very eloquent way with complete sentences. I cherished every word," said MacBridan and walked out.

CHAPTER 5

MacBridan's slow start on the case unfortunately reflected his expectations.

He left the sheriff's office and drove back to New Westminster. Stopping at a small gas station, he filled up and got directions to St. Thomas Catholic Church. St. Thomas had been the third church hit by the thieves, and, as Sheriff Beninger had reminded him, some of the artifacts that had been recovered belonged there. He hoped he'd fare better with the priest at St. Thomas than he had with the sheriff.

On the way to St. Thomas, MacBridan called Mrs. Chamberlin to let her know that he might be a little late in getting back. She assured him it was fine with her.

St. Thomas was easy to find. The church was large and appeared to be made from native stone. A magnificent structure, it sat on the banks of a broad but shallow stream. The sound of the water rushing over the rocks further enhanced the peacefulness of the setting. In the twilight, MacBridan spotted a footbridge, which crossed the stream and led to a vast cemetery. The church parking lot was empty, but he was pleasantly surprised to see lights on inside.

The front doors to St. Thomas were unlocked, and MacBridan went in. As with so many Catholic churches, the inside was a work of art. The

Stations of the Cross were made of sculpted marble, scenes from the New Testament covered the ceiling, and the altar itself, made of silver and a dark, carved wood, was breathtaking. Only the front of the church was lit, and it was there that MacBridan spotted the priest.

"Good evening," called MacBridan as he walked down the center aisle. He spoke only loud enough to get the priest's attention and not startle him.

The priest turned and smiled his greeting to MacBridan. As he got closer, he could see that the priest was a large man, well over six feet tall with broad shoulders. He had a stocky build and looked more like an aging athlete than a priest, but then, MacBridan remembered, no one looked like a priest anymore. The priest was completely bald on top, but the hair surrounding the sides of his head was thick with a salt and pepper mixture.

"Good evening to you, sir," said the priest. "Pray tell what brings you to St. Thomas this evening?"

Though not overwhelming, the soft lilt of his Irish accent was easy to pick out. "Father, my name is James MacBridan. If you're not too busy, I was wondering if I might have a word with you."

"And what might that be about?"

"Gerald Vickers. I'm looking into the circumstances surrounding his death."

"I see. It is always sad to hear of someone being struck down, but for someone so young to die, that adds to the loss. Give me a moment to finish up here, and we'll talk."

The priest went back to his work, and MacBridan watched him closely. He was easily in his fifties but showed no sign of slowing down. The priest did not wear glasses, and MacBridan had taken note of his eyes. It was not the bright shade of blue that had caught his attention. These were eyes that missed very little. The priest's gaze had been quite penetrating, summing up MacBridan rather quickly.

"There," said the priest, "now give me a moment to lock the doors, and we'll go some place where we can be a little more at ease."

Locking up took only a few minutes and the priest led MacBridan out of the sanctuary, through a side door. They followed a flagstone path a short distance to the rectory. Set back in the trees, it was difficult to see just how large the building was. The priest preceded him into a very comfortable living room. A fire already burned in the fireplace, and the priest added a couple of logs.

"May I get you something drink, Mr. MacBridan?"

"No thank you, Father, I won't be taking up much of your time."

"Are you sure, now? There's nothing like a nice glass of port to take the edge off a long day."

"Well, that is hard to argue with, but this evening I'll have to pass, thank you," said MacBridan. "I don't believe I caught your name."

"Forgive my rudeness. After a while, you just take some things for granted. I'm Father Collin Sheary. You wanted talk about Gerald Vickers."

"Yes. My firm, the Hawthorne Group," said MacBridan as he handed him his card, "has been retained to help in the recovery of artifacts that were stolen from St. Thomas, as well as from other Catholic churches."

"Archbishop Kerry called just yesterday and we discussed your company's involvement. I was most pleased to learn that you met with some success," said Father Collin.

"We did, to a point, but the exchange ended rather badly. Are you familiar with how Vickers died?"

The priest leaned back in his chair, bringing the tips of his fingers together forming a steeple. "Archbishop Kerry gave me what information he had, but I would very much like to hear your view of it, Mr. MacBridan."

MacBridan gave him an overview of what happened, leaving out many of the finer details. He especially did not share any of the details regarding the condition of Vickers's body. Those weren't the kind of things you told people unless you got some kind of sick joy out of making other people lose their cookies.

"So you never actually saw who it was that killed the boy."

"It all happened rather quickly and there wasn't much light. Believe me, I know how it sounds. The police weren't all too impressed with my story either," said MacBridan.

"I can imagine. Many of the policemen I've known see things strictly in black and white. It is a mindset that too often hinders their ability. I don't mean to dwell on this, Mr. MacBridan, but you were very fortunate to have survived. How were you rendered unconscious?"

MacBridan found the conversation homing in on the one area he wanted to avoid. What could he say? He hadn't been touched, and yet he went down hard. Had he fainted, as the police believed? Had he actually become so afraid that he had passed out? MacBridan couldn't accept that. He had been through far worse, had experienced extreme fear before, but had never been rendered helpless by it.

"That is somewhat hard to say, Father. The circumstances, to say the least, are rather odd."

"Mr. MacBridan, please, if you don't mind I would like to hear as much of this as you can tell me," Father Collin said, leaning forward in his chair. "It may even help give you a clearer perspective to talk it out."

Perspective. *Yes, Father, I believe I could use a different perspective.* He took a deep breath and started in. *After all, if you can't share with a priest...* "I'm not saying this makes sense, but it's what happened. The room became terribly cold, almost instantly. Vickers became terrified, but I don't know why. I didn't see anything. As I said, the light wasn't very good down in that basement, but, well it seemed like a darkness, a sheer black mass filled the door. I reached for my gun, but this weakness came over me and I couldn't pull the trigger. I was completely helpless. Next thing I know I'm on the floor and it's all over."

"Fascinating! Please forgive me, Mr. MacBridan," said Father Collin. "It is obvious that this causes you some distress. Rest assured that I am confident that you tried to defend yourself and Gerald Vickers the best you could. Remember that whatever did this struck with extreme violence. The fact that it first moved you out of its way is not so amazing."

Something the priest said stuck with MacBridan. He studied the priest carefully. "*It*, Father? Do you have some idea of what happened down there, something that you would like to share with me?"

"No, I'm sorry. I hope I didn't give that impression. It's just that I've been a priest for a long time and I've seen many things. Our worlds are very different. You deal in hard facts that have to be backed up with empirical evidence. In my world there are many things that can't be proven, and yet, are believed."

"Our worlds may not be all that dissimilar after all, Father. At the moment, faith is about all I've got going for me. Did you know Gerald Vickers?"

Father Collin settled back in to his chair. "New Westminster, by itself, is a rather small community. The parish, on the other hand, extends over most of the county and St. Thomas boasts a large and faithful congregation. Yes, I knew him, but I never spent any time with him to speak of. When I learned of his death, I was very surprised to find out that he had had anything to do with the thefts."

"Interesting. Why do you say that, Father?" asked MacBridan.

"Oh, it is not that he wasn't capable. He obviously did have some level of involvement. It is just that, well..." Father Collin hesitated, "Gerald could never have come up with this on his own. He wasn't very bright. I've given this a great deal of thought, and I can understand how he could have been easily influenced."

"Influenced by whom?" asked MacBridan.

"By just about anyone. Gerald was a loner. He didn't have any family and lived alone in a house out on Wolf Cave Road."

"I understand that he inherited the house from his grandfather."

"It was his grandfather who raised him. His father took off before he was born, and his mother died in an accident when he was four. After his grandfather passed away, he became very much on his own."

"For not having spent much time with him, you certainly seem to know a great deal about his life," MacBridan observed.

Father Collin smiled, shrugging his shoulders. "Pure hindsight, I assure you, nothing more. For better or worse, he was a member of St. Thomas. As soon as I learned of his death, I did some research to see if he had any family in the area, someone who might need help dealing with such a loss. I'm sorry to say that, prior to his passing, I knew little of him."

"Can you think of anyone else I could talk to who might be able to help me with this? Co-workers, girlfriend, buddies, anyone?"

"That's just it, Mr. MacBridan. There really isn't anyone else. He didn't get close to anyone that I could find."

"Well, thank you, Father. I appreciate your help," said MacBridan, rising from his chair.

Father Collin walked him to the door. "I've done very little to deserve your thanks, but I enjoyed talking with you. You shared a great deal of information about his death that I otherwise would never have learned. If you think of anything else I might be able to help with, remember that the door is always open."

They shook hands, and MacBridan made his way back to his car. Once again, he had come up empty. He put the car into gear and thought of Katherine. He hoped that he would be able to help her with her problems. That, at the very least, would keep the trip to New Westminster from being a total loss.

***

The man remained still, hidden in the shadows. He was tall, slender, with long, nearly ash blond hair. He watched as MacBridan got into his car and drove away, not wishing to be seen. He had been there when MacBridan arrived. He had closely watched the exchange between MacBridan and the priest. He did not interfere. No need to. Not yet. Even as MacBridan's car went around the corner and out of sight, he held his position. Then he turned, made his way to the front door of the rectory, and went in.

CHAPTER 6

The baby hadn't even arrived, but they had already racked up quite a few bills. To her credit, Holly had been doing as much as she could on her own. Taking advantage of many of the materials they had found stored in the shed behind the house, she had done a pretty good job of fixing up the nursery. Still, there were several items that needed to be purchased.

On the other hand, Ian's business was doing well. Recently, he'd picked up two new clients, and the extra money was keeping them ahead of the curve. When he wasn't working, he helped Holly with the nursery, as well as the hundred and one other things that demanded his attention around the house. With both of them starting each day early and finishing late, they finally decided that they desperately needed a rest. So Saturday, after lunch, they got in the car and headed out, taking a long overdue break.

They decided to take it easy and just drive around the area, further exploring their new home. Up until today, they'd never really taken the time to do this. The autumn foliage, now in full glory, was more spectacular than either of them could ever remember having seen before. They were almost to Deacon's Mill before deciding to turn back. It was late afternoon and the sun would soon start to set.

Since moving to New Westminster, they had driven past Furr's Antiques many times, but had never gone in. While neither had any particular interest in antiques, and they certainly didn't have the money for such things, it was a quaint shop and they decided that it would be fun to have a look. Plus, Holly had a new friend there.

Lucy, the owner of the shop, had become more than just an acquaintance of Holly's. They had met quite by accident at the post office and since then had run into each other in town several times, usually at the grocery store. Lucy was in her late forties, and although very pleasant, had a determined, speak your mind, air about her. Holly had become fond of Lucy. Every time they saw each other Lucy always asked about how things were going, truly interested in Holly's pregnancy and how their new home was coming along.

Lucy's face lit up as they came in, pleased to see Holly. She greeted the young couple and said, "I am so glad you finally came by! How are you?"

"Tired," said Holly as they hugged. "Tired, but good. We've both been working so hard, and we just had to get out of that house or go crazy."

Lucy laughed and said, "I understand, I understand. There is so much to do to prepare for a baby. But don't you worry; everything will work out just fine." Close to twenty years Holly's senior, Lucy stayed in pretty good shape. Her dark hair showed no sign of gray, but Holly wondered if it was perhaps color enhanced. She was taller than Holly by a few inches; making her nearly five foot seven. Her eyes curved slightly upwards, feline in their appearance. Their shape, along with their dark brown color, gave her face an exotic look.

"This is my husband, Ian."

"It is good to meet you, Ian. You have a very sweet wife here, which of course you know, and I am so happy the two of you decided to move to New Westminster."

Ian put his arm around Holly and squeezed. "Thank you. We are very happy to be here."

"Your shop is lovely," said Holly as she looked around. It was far larger than it looked from the outside, with several aisles of merchandise stretching back into a second room that appeared to be almost as large as the one she was in. "How long have you had it?"

"Long enough to know that I'll never willingly answer that question," said Lucy. "I'm afraid I'm beginning to look and feel like the antiques I sell."

Ian had left the two women and walked over to a display of old toys. "Holly, look at this. It is identical to the one I had as a child." He had opened an old train set and was on his knees going over every piece of it.

Lucy patted Holly's arm. "Ian is making himself at home, and I want you to relax and do the same. I'm going to go in the back and make you some of that special tea I've been telling you about."

"That is awfully kind, but please don't go to any trouble."

"Oh, nonsense. This tea is just the thing you need." With that, she turned and hurried off.

Holly watched the older woman as she walked away, smiled to herself and began to look around. The variety that the shop offered surprised Holly, and she was even more amazed to discover that there were several things she liked. Gradually she made her way into the back showroom, keeping an eye out for Lucy. The small windows of the back room, combined with the sun going down, left many of the items in the shadows.

The aisle on the far left displayed several old sets of china. Holly moved slowly along, admiring the delicate designs and the intricate patterns. Holly saw a picture at the end of the aisle, sitting on the floor. It was incased in an ornate frame, leaning against the wall. As she drew closer, she saw that it was a picture of a stand of trees. The trees were in various shades of gray, brown, and black. The limbs were bare and, in an unsettling way, resembled skeletal arms and hands reaching for the sky on what appeared to be a cloudy fall day. The dimness of the showroom only added to the somber mood of the picture. For some reason the scene looked familiar, some place she had seen before. Although it made Holly uncomfortable, she couldn't bring herself to look away.

The picture's allure was almost hypnotic. Finally, with some effort, she turned her back on it. It was then that she spotted a set of china that looked exactly like the stoneware her grandmother had kept in her kitchen years ago. She stopped beside the counter and picked up one of the old cups for a closer look.

The picture of the trees that had unsettled Holly's nerves rested only a few feet behind her. Its frame began to tremble ever so slightly, then went still. A couple of moments passed and it began to tremble again, more strongly this time, the right corner inching forward, making a small scraping sound as it dragged itself across the floor. Again, it went still. The trembling quickly returned, the entire frame quivering, loudly scraping across the wooden floor, drawing near to her.

Holly whirled around, her back against the counter, starring at the picture. Nothing else around the picture moved. The shaking continued, becoming increasingly violent. Holly stood frozen to the floor. She stared at it, unable to take her eyes away. Then, with tremendous force, the picture lunged out at her, away from the wall, and fell to the floor at her feet.

Holly gasped and gripped the counter behind her with both hands. She did not understand what she had just witnessed, pictures didn't move by themselves, but she knew what she felt. Instinctively, she knew the picture posed a threat to her. Worse, she knew it posed a threat to her unborn child. Her whole body shivered, but the fear also made her angry.

She took a deep breath, trying to steady her nerves. Taking strength from her anger, Holly tried to convince herself that she was being silly. What possible harm could a picture do? There was certainly some logical explanation. Perhaps a large truck passing by outside had caused it to fall. But nothing else had been affected. She knew she had to get a grip on her nerves. She stepped forward, and with some difficulty, knelt down to pick up the picture.

Miraculously, it had not been cracked or damaged in any way. As she attempted to lean it back against the wall, she noticed a small, weathered basket sitting on the floor behind the picture. Holly moved the basket out beside her, and then replaced the picture to its original position.

She stood back up, no easy task, and placed the basket on some open counter space. It was quite old and had a hinged top. It reminded her of the witch's basket in the *Wizard of Oz*. Intent on her discovery, she opened the top and inside found some papers, along with some odd shaped tools. The papers illustrated different designs, patterns of some kind she guessed, but the tools completely baffled her.

All of a sudden, Lucy was at her side. Holly jumped and gave a small cry. Her nerves had not yet fully recovered from the incident with the picture. This time her hands would not stop shaking.

"Oh, I startled you, I am so sorry," said Lucy. "I didn't realize that you hadn't heard me coming."

Once again, Holly supported herself against the counter. "I'm okay, just a little shook up, I guess. That picture over there fell, gave me a bit of a scare. When I went to put it back, I found this basket."

Lucy examined the picture and said, "No damage here. Now, it is nothing to worry about. Not the first time something's been knocked over in here."

"No! I didn't knock it over," Holly protested. "I wasn't even near it. I was right there looking at that china. I swear it moved all by itself!"

"That's odd," said Lucy. "Well, everything is alright now. Come on, let's you and I sit down over here and have some tea."

Holly gave one last glance at the picture. Once again, the same feeling of dread came over her, sending a chill down her spine. She picked up the basket and followed Lucy, grateful to get away from it. They didn't go far before Lucy stopped beside two comfortable rockers and they sat down. Holly was glad to be off her feet. Lucy poured the tea and handed a cup to Holly. "This blend has been handed down for generations. Many an expectant mother has been helped through some very trying times by this brew."

Holly raised the cup to her lips. Its strong aroma soothed her nerves, and Holly found it to be different from any tea she could remember. She sipped the hot drink, finding the tea's flavor as unique and as potent as the aroma. She took another sip and felt her entire body start to relax. The tea was wonderful! As if by magic, Holly could feel a mellowing warmth come over her and she continued to calm down.

"This is so good," said Holly, "but I can't quite place the flavor. It's familiar, and yet different all at the same time."

"Don't even try. It is truly a one of a kind. I've always found it to be quite pleasing," said Lucy. "I see you've held on to that basket."

"I guess I did," said Holly as she looked down at the basket beside her chair. "Lucy, you are going to have to tell me what all this is. I can't figure out what is inside here."

"Well, let's take a look and see what we have," said Lucy, picking up the basket. "My goodness, I haven't seen this for years. If you hadn't found it I wouldn't have even known we still had it."

Holly's mind drifted back to the moving picture and said, "I guess it kind of found me. What is it?"

"It is very old, and in a way, very timely."

"Timely?"

"Oh yes. We're close to Halloween and this is an old pumpkin carving kit from around the turn of the twentieth century. The patterns themselves, though, are much older." Lucy thumbed through them until she found the one she was looking for. "This particular one is a copy of a design that dates back to long before the Spanish Inquisition."

"That's amazing."

"Yes, and it is a design that, in its day, was very important. Your must remember, the people in those times, including the clergy, were very superstitious. This design, often carved into wood, or onto the side of a house, was used to ward off demons and other creatures of the night. It protected the home."

"How do you apply the design?"

"If I remember correctly, it's not hard at all," said Lucy. She began to explain the process to Holly, and although time consuming, it turned out to be rather simple. "Nowadays you see more and more of these kits in almost every store that carries Halloween merchandise."

"I doubt Ian and I will get too many trick or treaters out our way," said Holly. She felt so much better, the tea completely calmed her down.

"You are probably right," agreed Lucy, "but I have an idea. As my house-warming gift to the two of you, I want you to please accept this kit. Promise me that you'll carve this design on your new home's first Jack O'Lantern."

Holly laughed at the idea. "That is so nice, but I'm not all that talented in the art department."

"Believe me, you can do it. I know this because I have done it before, and they actually turn out pretty good. Oh wait, I'm forgetting something," said Lucy, and she picked up the basket once again and began to look through it.

"What are you looking for?" asked Holly.

"This," exclaimed Lucy as she held up a small piece of paper, yellowed with age. "You may not get any trick or treaters, but we just can't take any chances with the creatures of the night, especially at Halloween. I believe that the origins of this poem are Celtic. Nevertheless, the tradition is for the woman of the house to carve this design on to something, in our case it will be a pumpkin. Once finished you place a small candle inside and light it. Once that is done, the poem is read. The combination is guaranteed to ward off all spooks, as well as all other nasties, and bless the house."

Holly doubted her skill level with such a project, but agreed. "Very well, as you said, we can't take any chances. I'll do it on one condition."

"What is that?" asked Lucy.

"That you will come and visit. It would be so nice to have you over to just sit and talk."

"I would love to, and I'll bring you some more of this tea. As that special day gets closer, I know you'll need it more and more."

CHAPTER 7

MacBridan arrived back at Katherine's that evening just after seven to find dinner waiting for him. He couldn't remember the last time he'd had home cooked food that was this good. Everything down to the sweetbread tasted great. It was obvious that Mrs. Chamberlin took pride in her cooking. She explained, at some length, that everything she served was nutritious and pointed to her own good health as proof of what could come from eating right. By no means a health conscious eater, MacBridan finished everything on his plate and then went back for selected seconds. After all, he didn't want to hurt her feelings.

Their conversation remained casual throughout dinner, MacBridan continuing to learn more and more about the area. Afterwards, Katherine led him into the family room where, to his delight, an excellent brandy awaited them.

"I've always found that a touch of brandy could take the edge off any day," said Katherine.

"This is very nice," said MacBridan, sipping the liquor. "I do hope my being here isn't putting you to a lot of extra work."

"We have already covered that, Mr. MacBridan."

"Please, call me Mac."

"Of course. I know you are not here of your own choosing. Frankly, I feel I am the one who should be thanking you." Katherine displayed the same direct nature as her nephew. "As I said, normally I wouldn't have even bothered Peter with something like this. I've spent the whole afternoon trying to find the words to tell you about what has been going on, but no matter how hard I try, it still comes out sounding pretty ridiculous, even to me."

"Peter didn't find it ridiculous," said MacBridan. "Whatever it was you told him, he found it serious enough to ask me to look into it.

"Yes, I know that. My nephew can be rather protective when it comes to me," said Katherine. She stared at MacBridan for a moment, and then said, "This is very hard for me. I know how this is going to sound, but I can't help that. I have been alone now for over seven years, ever since the passing of my husband, Jonathan. Getting through that was the hardest thing I've ever had to endure. However, I did it, and I moved on. Today I enjoy my life and the friends that I have here in New Westminster. Now, though, for the first time in a long time, I may need some help. How much of my problem did Peter share with you?"

"Very little, actually," said MacBridan. He was halfway through his brandy and found himself starting to sink deeper into his chair. "He said that you had seen some things that had you concerned and that someone may be watching you."

"Did he tell you that I called that near worthless sheriff that you went to visit? Did he tell you that Frank Beninger talked to me like I was nine years old? Oh, he came out. He was most polite and even looked around. And even though he didn't say anything, it was plain as day that he thought I was just some senile old woman who needed reassuring. Well I don't, and he made me mad. This whole situation makes me mad." She leaned forward and looked MacBridan in the eye. "I'm afraid. Afraid in my own home, and that's not right."

MacBridan set his brandy down. "Fear is something I understand very well. Please, I'd really like for you to tell me what's going on."

"Very well. I think it will help if we go for a short walk," she said. She got up, went over to the coat rack, pulled a sweater down and put it on.

From the hall closet, she got some binoculars and led MacBridan out the front door.

"The ridge we are on overlooks the valley New Westminster sits in," she explained as they followed the flagstone path towards the guest cottage. They continued along the path around to the rear of the cottage and stopped where the land suddenly began to drop off. "The stream you hear below us is the same one that runs behind St. Thomas. If you look straight across from here you can see quite a bit of the churchyard."

Though faint, there was still enough light from the moon so that MacBridan could see pretty well. Away from the city, the star-filled sky provided enough illumination for MacBridan to make out the expansive churchyard. He'd had no idea that it was so immense. The trees, however, blocked their view of the church.

"I'll bet you never tire of this," MacBridan commented on the view.

"It was one of the main reasons we chose to live here. The view from my bedroom is even better, as I don't have as many trees in the way," said Katherine.

"That cemetery is huge," observed MacBridan. "It must be very old."

"It most certainly is. There are graves in there close to three hundred years old. Now if you look far to the right, past that stand of trees and a little ways up the hill, you can make out the ruins of the very first church that was built in this area," said Katherine as she handed him the binoculars.

It took MacBridan a few moments to find it. From where they were standing, he couldn't see it too clearly, but it appeared to be a small, stone structure. Most of the old church had fallen down. What remained was one of the walls, and surprisingly, the bell tower seemed to be still in tack.

"Of course it is difficult to see a great deal from here, but whoever decided to build the church on that spot picked a beautiful location," said MacBridan.

"It is pretty," agreed Katherine, "but scenic beauty had little to do with deciding the location of the church. The old church was built there to be close to Altar Rock."

"Altar Rock? What is that?"

"Just another of those unique, natural phenomenon that nature so often provides us. The first settlers believed that it was sacred, a sign from

God to settle here. Frankly, it's not hard to see why they felt that way. Altar Rock is a uniquely shaped piece of granite that sticks up out of the ground. It is unusual in a couple of ways. First, it stands alone and there is nothing else like it anywhere in the valley. But, more importantly, is its remarkable shape. Nature sculpted it in such a fashion that it looks exactly like a church altar. It stands about four feet tall, just over seven feet long and three feet across.

"Sounds like you've given this tour before," said MacBridan.

"Be happy I'm not charging you," she said as she gave a small laugh. "It's the only natural wonder we have around here. Anyone who lives here, and is old enough to talk, could give you the same statistics."

"It must be something to see," said MacBridan.

"It is. When the first settlers arrived, they saw that the land around it had been cleared. There were markings on the rock made by the Indians. Apparently they too thought it was sacred."

"Interesting," said MacBridan.

"People worshipped there long before the white man ever arrived."

"I take it that this has something to do with what you have seen."

"Yes, it does. It all started several weeks ago. It was late, and I had just turned out my light to go to sleep. Quite often, I'll sit by the window and watch the night sky. That particular night there was a new moon and the stars were brilliant. At first, I couldn't be sure, but I thought I saw a light coming from the churchyard. I got my binoculars and sure enough, there it was. It was weak, but it was there."

"Could you make out anything else about it?" asked MacBridan. "I mean, was it like what you would expect from a small flashlight? Perhaps someone passing through the churchyard?"

"No," said Mrs. Chamberlin, "it wasn't moving. It stayed still and seemed to be in the vicinity of Altar Rock. I don't know why I did it, but it was so unusual, so out of place, that I kept watching. After about twenty or twenty-five minutes the light went out and that was that."

"Go on," said MacBridan. Katherine turned and started back to the house.

"Well, the next day I called Father Collin and asked if he knew anything about it. Father Collin Sheary is the priest at St. Thomas," explained Katherine.

"I met him today after my talk with Sheriff Beninger."

Katherine smiled at MacBridan. "You have been busy. Father Collin is a delightful man. He knew nothing of the light, and it didn't seem to bother him. So that Sunday, after mass, I crossed the footbridge next to the church and walked out to the ruin to have a look around."

"Were you alone?"

"Oh yes, but the cemetery is maintained so well, and quite often I visit Jonathan's grave. It may sound silly, but, on occasion, I stand beside his grave and talk to him as if he were still with me. There are times I think he actually hears me. It brings me such peace. Anyway, the maintenance people keep a path clear all the way to the ruin, and even maintain the ground around Altar Rock. It is truly a beautiful place."

They went up the steps to the porch and back inside to the family room. "More brandy?"

"No, thank you," said MacBridan. "I'm good. Please continue."

"It is not unusual for people to go out there to enjoy the natural serenity and to just relax. So I went up to Altar Rock to examine it. On the surface of the rock I found candles, or what was left of them: Four, one on each corner."

"Could that have been the source of the light you saw?"

"I don't see how. Altar Rock sits down from the old church, and you can't see it from here due to the trees."

"I'm sure there are several explanations that could account for the candles," said MacBridan. "It sounds like something kids would do, go and tell ghost stories in the graveyard, doing their level best to scare themselves to death."

"That's possible," conceded Katherine. "I thought of that, but the candles were so very odd."

"How so?"

"They had burned down to almost nothing, but the wax that was left was black. Someone had burnt black candles, and they stank."

"What did they smell like?"

"That is hard to say, but the odor was very strong, putrid. It nearly made me sick to my stomach, and although I cannot explain why, I believe it was the smell that made me start to feel uneasy."

"What do you mean?" asked MacBridan.

"I do not have a nervous nature, never have. But for no good reason that odor put my nerves on edge. Something about it was very wrong. It was then I began to feel that someone was watching me."

"Did you see anyone?"

"No. I tried to shake the feeling off, told myself I was being childish. So, to try and take my mind off of how I was feeling, I tried to focus back on my original purpose. I reasoned that the only way that I could have seen a light coming from this area would have been if the light came from the old church ruins. Now the church fenced the ruin off years ago. There are signs warning people to stay out. As I'm sure you saw, time has taken its toll on the old structure. Nevertheless, I headed up to the ruin to see what I could find."

Katherine stopped long enough to sip her brandy. MacBridan could see that her hands shook a little and he knew that the brandy was helping her get through this. "The ruins are pretty close to Altar Rock," Katherine continued. "I'd guess not more than thirty yards away. I hadn't been able to shake the nervousness, and it became more intense the closer I got to the old church. About halfway there, I had to stop. I couldn't go one step further. Mac, I was terrified. Something was waiting in those old ruins, something that could hurt me, and yet I never did see or hear anything."

"At that point it didn't matter whether I could see anything or not. I turned around and got out of there as quickly as I could. The feeling of being watched was stronger than ever. Good thing I didn't run. At my age, I probably would have tripped and killed myself. The feeling of near panic stayed with me until I reached the footbridge. Once I got to the other side, the fear finally began to fade. I got into my car, locked the door, sat there and cried."

"The whole time you were there, you never saw anyone else?" asked MacBridan.

"No one."

They sat in silence; MacBridan waited for her to continue.

"After I got home, I got a bite to eat and kept going over the incident in my mind. By dinnertime I had pretty well convinced myself that I had simply fallen victim to an overactive imagination. Later that evening, though, as I was finishing up the dishes, I looked out the window over the sink. That was the first time I actually spotted the watcher."

"The light wasn't too good, but across the street, standing just inside the tree line, I could make out someone watching the house. Never did get a good look at him, but he was there for quite a while."

"Is there anything in particular you can tell me about this guy? What he had on, anything like that?"

"Please don't misunderstand me. Frankly, I don't know if it was a man or a woman. I never could get a clear enough look to say one way or the other."

"Did you call the sheriff?"

"Not that night," said Katherine. "Perhaps I should have, but I didn't really think that I had a serious enough problem to bother him. After a while, the watcher went away."

Katherine got up and walked to the mantle. "A few nights later the watcher returned. I caught sight of him because I'd been keeping a pretty close lookout. Once again it was dusk and I still couldn't get a clear view of him, but he was there, I am certain of it. Well, I do have a temper, once provoked, and what I did next was very foolish. I got my sweater and went outside to confront him."

"Katherine, that is the last thing you should—"

"I know, I know," Mrs. Chamberlin interrupted him. "There is nothing you can say to me that I haven't already said to myself, over and over again."

MacBridan smiled to himself. The more he observed Mrs. Chamberlin, the more similarities he saw with Dolinski, the same daring, reckless spirit.

"As I got close to the bushes that line the road," Katherine continued, "I called out to him. Whoever it was just turned and faded back into the trees. I never left my yard. It was then that it dawned on me just how foolish I was being. Then, all of a sudden, the same panicked feeling that I'd experienced at Altar Rock came over me, so I hurried back inside and locked the door. I even checked all the windows."

"Since then I have seen the lights in the steeple several times. I have no idea what is going on, or who is responsible, but here's an interesting point of fact. I've noticed that almost every evening when the lights appear in the steeple, the watcher shows up across the road."

"When did you call the sheriff and report this?" asked MacBridan.

"The same night I went out to confront the watcher. There are just too many crazies out there, and I was convinced that someone was sizing up the situation, getting ready to break in and rob me."

"That would certainly fit in with their behavior. What did Sheriff Beninger do?"

"To his credit he got here pretty fast. Must have been in the area. Brought a deputy with him, nice young fellow named Goodman."

"Goodman?" asked MacBridan.

"That's right, Larry Goodman. Can't be more than twenty-eight or twenty-nine, but like you, he is a pretty big man. Looks like he works out a lot."

"What happened then?"

"Well, they came in and I told them about the watcher, how I'd seen him twice and was certain that someone was planning to rob me. Sheriff Beninger and I stayed inside and talked while the deputy went out and looked around. I showed the Sheriff my view from the kitchen window. We could see the deputy's flashlight moving around over in the trees."

"Did they find anything?" asked MacBridan.

"Of course not. The sheriff never did look, and his deputy didn't spend all that long looking around either. He came back in; spoke with the sheriff for a moment, and then Frank Beninger started talking to me as if I'd lost it. Neither one of them believed me, and that's why I've never called them again."

"You never did mention seeing the lights in the churchyard to the sheriff, did you?"

"No," said Katherine, "and I'm glad I didn't. With their attitude that just would have made things worse. That is why I phoned Peter. I didn't know who else to turn to."

MacBridan smiled at the elderly lady, leaned forward and placed his hand on hers. "You have help now. I'll look around tomorrow and see what I can find. I'd also like to visit Altar Rock."

"Are you a Catholic, Mr. MacBridan?"

"Part time. Growing up I was full time, but over the years some things changed and I haven't been as consistent in my attendance as I guess I should be."

"What changed?"

"Let's just say there have been times in my life when it seemed like he wasn't there."

Katherine studied MacBridan's face for a moment. "Why don't you join me for mass tomorrow morning? We'll see if he's there." Katherine suggested. "Then afterwards I can take you to see Altar Rock."

MacBridan thought about it for a moment, then gave in. "That's an excellent idea," MacBridan said as he got up. "Now it's time I got some sleep. Let me give you my cell number. I'll leave my phone on. You see or hear anything, call me."

"That won't be necessary," said Katherine. "There is an intercom between the house and the cottage. I'll use that if I see anything."

"Good. You sleep well tonight," said MacBridan. "We will get to the bottom of this, I promise."

CHAPTER 8

For the second time that week, MacBridan found himself in church. Father Collin kept mass moving along, and MacBridan found the sermon more interesting than he'd expected. It had been a long time. Afterwards he and Katherine stopped and said hello to the priest. He seemed genuinely happy to see MacBridan again.

Once outside, Katherine took the lead and guided MacBridan across the parking lot. As they approached the footbridge, they came upon a young couple attempting to get into their car. The woman was having trouble walking, and it was all the young man could do to keep her from falling.

"Here, let me help," said MacBridan. Together they got the car door open and lowered the woman into the front seat.

"Thank you," she said. She was nearly breathless, and MacBridan could see that she was very pregnant.

"Are you alright Holly?" asked Katherine.

"Yes, thank you, just a little light headed. We're pretty close to my due date, and it is taking more and more out of me."

"Thank you for your help," said Ian as he shook MacBridan's hand.

"Let me introduce James MacBridan," said Katherine. "This is Ian and Holly Carpenter, two of New Westminster's newest residents."

"It's nice meeting both of you," said MacBridan. "How close are you?"

"According to Dr. Appleton," answered Holly, "we are a week, maybe two weeks away. But this is our first, so who knows. The doctor said it's not uncommon for the first baby to be late."

"My dear, you must get more rest, you are looking a little pale," said Katherine as she helped Holly get better settled in her seat.

"Lately it has been real off and on," explained Ian. "She'll be going along just fine and then, with no warning at all, this weakness hits her. We talked to Doctor Appleton about it, but he doesn't seem to be too worried."

"Every pregnancy is different, Ian," said Katherine. "I'm sure if it was significant, Dr. Appleton would have told you. I've known him for a long time and he is pretty thorough."

"Thank you again, Mr. MacBridan. I was afraid that Ian and I were going to end up spending the rest of the day with me stuck in the middle of the parking lot. We're headed home, and I plan to sit down and take it easy," said Holly. "It was nice seeing you, Mrs. Chamberlin."

"You take care, dear. You have my number. Night or day, don't hesitate to use it. I'd be happy to help in any way I can," said Katherine.

"We may take you up on that," said Ian. "Bye."

Katherine and MacBridan watched them drive away and then continued on toward the footbridge. The bridge's design gave it the appearance of being older than its true age. While strictly for pedestrian traffic, the arched bridge was quite wide and, like the church, made from native rock. The bridge, the stream and the surrounding woods blended into a charming, peaceful setting, appropriate for a place of eternal rest.

The churchyard was enormous, with paved trails leading off in several directions, making access easy. They followed the main path, which gently wound its way through the cemetery. Massive oaks and maples were evenly mixed with several tall fir trees. As Katherine had said, the grounds were very well kept.

MacBridan harbored a fascination for old graveyards. A bit of a history buff, he had learned at an early age that there was much to be gained in studying such places. The headstones varied greatly—many large, with beautifully detailed sculptures. There were also several family crypts, one so large that it rivaled many small chapels. Time, however, had had its effect on many of the monuments, eroding the engraved words and dates to the point where some were barely legible.

Katherine explained that the oldest graves were in the very back, close to the old church and Altar Rock. At one point, she showed MacBridan the path that led to her husband's grave. MacBridan was impressed at the brisk pace his septuagenarian companion maintained and still it took almost half an hour to cover the cemetery.

Eventually they left the churchyard behind, the path changing from a paved walkway to a simple dirt trail, but continued on, taking them into the woods. Farther in, the trees began to crowd the path, blocking out much of the daylight. They became so dense that at one point the intertwining branches created a natural tunnel. The path made a hard turn to the right, angled down a gentle slope, then opened into a broad clearing. Although he couldn't see it, MacBridan could hear the very stream they had first crossed over, now on the far side of the clearing, hidden amongst the trees.

In the center of the clearing stood Altar Rock. MacBridan was taken aback by the close resemblance the massive rock actually had to a church altar. Imagination was not required. The natural formation struck MacBridan as unnatural. The top was perfectly flat, uniform in width. The sides beveled in before broadening at the base.

"Impressive, isn't it?" said Katherine.

"Very," answered MacBridan. "Easy to see why the early settlers were so awed by such a stone."

Up from Altar Rock stood the ruins of the old church, its roof completely gone. Closer now, MacBridan could see that his first assessment of the structure from the previous evening had been correct. All but one of the walls had collapsed. Although the bell tower looked worse for wear, it still claimed a commanding stance over the clearing, the very top of the tower having partially fallen away. The tower, however, was much taller than it had looked from a distance. The overall setting, though tranquil on the surface, projected an aura of sadness. MacBridan realized it was a grave of sorts, although larger than any of the others they had just passed by. Worse, he thought, it was an open grave where one could view the decaying remains of the corpse. He easily understood how Katherine could have gotten spooked.

"Why don't we take a closer look at Altar Rock?" suggested MacBridan.

Up close, the monument was even more impressive. Cool to the touch, the top had been worn smooth by centuries of exposure to the elements. MacBridan began to examine it, and only at the third corner of the rock did he find traces of candle wax. "Just here."

"I don't understand it," said Katherine. "There was wax on all four corners last time I was out here, and far more than is here now."

"Well, maybe someone is being a little more careful now," said MacBridan as he scraped off as much of the wax as he could into a small, plastic bag. "They know you are aware of them, so they're probably being cautious."

"But why? I really can't really see anything."

MacBridan stepped back and began to examine the base. He stopped at one end and squatted down to get a closer look. Seven letter-like symbols had recently been etched into the stone near the ground. "This took some effort," said MacBridan. Taking out his cell phone, he took a few pictures of them.

"What are they?" asked Katherine.

"I don't know, but they haven't been here long. That's why I noticed them in the first place. These cuts in the stone are pretty fresh, and because of their newness, they stand out. Have you seen these before?"

"No, but then I could have missed them last time I was out here," said Katherine.

MacBridan continued to walk around Altar Rock. "There's more here," he said as he got to the other end. Once again, there were seven letter-like symbols. While similar in style they were different from the seven he had already photographed.

The gentle fall breeze that had first accompanied them on their way to Altar Rock steadily grew in its intensity, ushering in dark, brooding clouds, which now covered the sky, blocking the sun. MacBridan slipped his cell phone back into his pocket and said, "Let's head on up to the ruins. I want to look them over and if we don't hurry, we may get wet."

They quickly made their way up to the old church. MacBridan looked around to ensure they were the only ones out there. "Where does that lead?" asked MacBridan, pointing to dirt road that emptied out of the trees, just down the hill a little ways from the ruins.

"The crews that keep the grounds use that. I believe that it eventually empties out somewhere up on Hickory Hill Road."

MacBridan eyed the fence surrounding the ruin and climbed over it. This simple act reminded him of his boyhood and the same sense of satisfaction he got every time he climbed over the back fence of the stadium to watch the ball game. Good to keep the inner child alive. "This won't take long," he assured Katherine. "If you see anyone, sing out."

There was nothing left of the front door to the old church which had fallen away long ago. The walls to the entrance had also been eroded over time, rising to the level of MacBridan's waist. He noticed that much of the grass leading up to the door had been trampled down. Obviously, there had been a fair amount of traffic through here recently, further substantiating Katherine's story.

Once inside the old church, MacBridan headed straight to the bell tower. A multitude of vines and plants competed for space on its walls. The doorway into the tower was arched and quite narrow. The stairs inside leading up to the top were just as narrow. The age and condition of the tower and its tight slit of a stairwell concerned MacBridan. It wasn't really a question of being claustrophobic; it was more a question of just how stable the old tower really was.

"Oh well, in for a penny..." MacBridan muttered to himself. The stairwell turned out to be more confining than he anticipated. The entire structure was made of stone and the low ceiling forced him to stay stooped over as he worked his way up. More than once the gun he had holstered on his belt dug into the small of his back as he negotiated the many tight turns. Several times, he felt stones move under him as he put his full weight on them. There were no windows. What little light there was came from small holes where some of the stone and mortar had crumbled away. The only good thing, if he could count this as a positive, is that he ran into very few spider webs. MacBridan hated spiders. On the other hand, the fact that there weren't many told him that someone else had been up the stairs pretty recently.

Finally, he came to the top of the stairs, which ended at a small, square opening. Slowly he climbed out on to a stone platform atop the tower. Here too, over time, the elements had eaten away at the old church, and most of the stone that had originally supported the bell was gone. MacBridan stood on the platform and stretched. It felt good to be able to stand up straight again.

What was left of the walls that had once acted as a railing around the platform were now little more than knee high. Standing just above the treetops, MacBridan had a clear view of Altar Rock, the creek and a large part of the churchyard. His gaze carried across the creek and up to the distant ridge. He tried, but could not locate Katherine's home.

"You made it," a voice called from below.

He looked down and waved to Katherine. "Wasn't sure I would," he said. "I'm going to look around for just a moment and then I'll be down."

It was easy to see that someone, perhaps even more than one person, had recently been up here. He found residue from numerous candles. There clearly hadn't been the effort here to clean up the melted wax as there had been at Altar Rock. He took out a second plastic bag and started taking more samples. This time there was enough left that he could smell it. If anything, Katherine had understated the terrible odor. It nearly gagged him.

The odor was so pervasive that it clung to him. Its pungency reminded MacBridan of another case from several years ago. MacBridan had been hired to find a missing person, an elderly gentleman who lived alone in a small house. It didn't take long before MacBridan discovered that the old man had crawled under his small home, apparently to work on a pipe, had suffered a heart attack and died. He'd been under that house seven days, baking in ninety-degree temperatures, before MacBridan located him. In fact, it was the stink that had led MacBridan to the body. He put the memory out of his mind and worked as quickly as he could, sealing the bag filled with wax, and put it in his pocket.

Nothing else of interest appeared to MacBridan so he turned to head back down the stairs. Just as he was about to start down, something shiny caught his eye. He stopped and moved back out onto the platform. Getting down on all fours, he examined the stones and he soon found the object. Taking out his penknife, he gradually worked it free from the crack where it had lodged between two stones.

It was a medallion, about the size of a Liberty Head silver dollar, with several symbols engraved on both sides. They appeared to match some of the ones he had found etched on Altar Rock. He slipped it into another plastic bag. He then started back down the stairs. Going down was almost harder than the climb up had been, so he had to move slowly.

About a third of the way down, MacBridan became wedged the wrong way at one of the turns, forcing him to stop. Carefully, he took a step back up the stairs, and by twisting his shoulders at the same time, freed himself up. At that moment, ever so faintly, he heard something scuff across a stone on one of the steps above him. He was no longer alone. Someone else was on the stairs. MacBridan froze, listening, waiting. Nothing. A cold chill settled over him. He held his breath, listening as hard as he could. Silence. Nothing but the wind whistling as it blew through holes in the tower.

He quickly considered his position. It wasn't good. If someone did come at him, he was in much too tight quarters to make any kind of winning defense. But, where had they come from? This just wasn't possible.

MacBridan slowly began to edge his way down the steps. He wanted to go as fast as possible but couldn't risk getting stuck again, or worse, falling. Again, he stopped and peered into the darkness above him. Whoever was behind him took a couple more steps, and then stopped. They had gained on him, moving closer. MacBridan wanted to believe that it was just an echo, but he knew it wasn't.

Fighting every impulse in his body, he continued his slow descent. He had to get out of that tower. His mind raced for explanations, but the answers that his imagination came back with nearly panicked him. At last, he made it to the doorway and lunged through it. He gasped in air, like a swimmer breaking the surface of the water after having been under too long. Sweat stood out across his forehead. He turned and quickly took up position next to the door, ready now for whoever had been following him. Other than the wind moving through the trees, all remained silent.

It could not have been just his imagination, but, on the other hand, he certainly had no plans to go back in there and look for them. He glanced at the sky and saw that the weather was getting worse, so he stepped away from the tower.

Katherine was waiting for him as he came out of the church and crossed back over the fence. "Did you find anything?" she asked.

"Several things, actually," he answered. "But I'm not sure what they all mean. This has been a busy place lately."

"Then I'm not imagining it all?" asked Katherine.

MacBridan smiled at her, gently touching her arm. "By no means. There was quite a bit of that candle wax up there, and you're right—it stinks. I also found this," he said as he handed her the bag with the medallion. As Katherine examined it, MacBridan looked over his shoulder, back towards the tower.

"What is it?" she asked, turning it over in her hand.

"I don't know," said MacBridan, "but I'll wager that whoever dropped it has something to do with the markings I found on Altar Rock." Once again, he turned and looked at the ruins. Still, no one appeared, but the feeling of being watched bore down on him.

"You feel it, too. It's here, watching us, and just like before I haven't seen anyone," said Katherine as she stepped closer to MacBridan.

The same sense of no longer being alone, the extreme nervousness that started as he came down the tower stairs was even stronger now. The sensation grew, and as it did, it became more and more menacing. "Come on," he said. "I think we've accomplished all we can here."

They quickly entered the woods. It was all that he could do to keep from breaking into a dead run. Neither of them talked. They moved at a steady pace, with MacBridan keeping a close watch behind them.

The sky darkened even more, deepening the shadows that filled the graveyard. The wind blew much harder, making a screeching noise as it whipped through the branches in trees and tore around the headstones. Katherine tripped, but MacBridan caught her before she could fall.

"It's okay," he shouted above the wind. "We can slow down. I don't see anyone."

"No, please, I want to get out of here. Just let me hold your arm."

They pushed on, but MacBridan did slow down. He was also struggling with another problem. He was embarrassed. His own fear had once again nearly taken control of him. MacBridan had no idea as to who, or what, he was up against, but he did know this: whatever it was, it scared him to death.

CHAPTER 9

"I'll put you through, Mr. MacBridan."

He had been holding for a little more than ten minutes. After the first five minutes had passed, he'd been ready to hang up, but he knew he was on Dolinski time, so he waited. Now even the cold, unemotional tones of Ester King's voice were a welcome relief.

The clock beside the bed showed that it was a little past nine in the morning. He had slept surprisingly well. MacBridan found the guest cottage to be more than comfortable. Under different circumstances, he would have enjoyed his time here, a nice, relaxing get-a-way. But that was not the case. Things here were becoming tense.

Dolinski answered after the first ring. "Mac, sorry to have kept you waiting. How are things in New Westminster?"

"Pretty close to what I expected, but the day is young."

"You've made quite an impression on my aunt. I warned her that you are a bit of a charmer."

"Your aunt is a very lovely lady. At times I find it hard to believe you're actually related."

"Yeah, well, other than completely pulling the wool over her eyes, what have you accomplished?" asked Dolinski.

"Very little I'm afraid," reported MacBridan. "Gerald Vickers was what we surmised, a nobody. He has no living relatives, and so far, no close acquaintances that I can find."

"I take it the local authorities weren't of any help."

"Not yet, anyway. Sheriff Beninger knew Vickers but really didn't have anything to add. Vickers was never in any serious trouble. Frankly, the sheriff was surprised to find that he'd even had the initiative to have been mixed up in something like this."

"So Frank Beninger is still sheriff. That's remarkable in itself. What did you think of him?"

"Kind of hard to tell. He doesn't seem to be the most action-oriented sort of guy, but based on our one meeting, he seemed pretty average. Do you know him?"

"Not really," answered Dolinski. "Most of what I know comes from my aunt. However, it appears he's sharp enough to continue to survive small town politics. You might want to press him a little."

MacBridan continued, "I also stopped by St. Thomas and spoke with the priest there, but like the sheriff, he didn't know that much about Vickers. Most of what he knew he learned after Vickers died. He had wanted to reach out and help any family Vickers might have left behind. Turns out there weren't any."

"That's odd. After all the years he's been there, you would think Father Henry would have known his own flock a little better," mused Dolinski.

"I didn't speak with a Father Henry," said MacBridan, looking at his notes. "The priest I talked to was Father Collin Sheary."

"Interesting. Wonder what became of Father Henry? He was getting up in age. Guess he earned his retirement. Anything else?"

MacBridan knew that Dolinski wanted to know if he'd made any progress regarding his aunt. He also knew that he wouldn't ask him directly. "I've talked with your aunt. There are some ruins of an old church that she can see from her bedroom window. She has spotted lights there at night on numerous occasions, but not much else. Frankly, it could be kids fooling around, but I'm not sure yet."

"She told me she was being watched."

"She told me that as well. It seems that whoever is watching the house, their activities started around the time the lights appeared at the ruins. She had the sheriff out, but he didn't find anything. Apparently he didn't take her too seriously."

"Mac, I have a great deal of respect for Aunt Katherine. If she says someone's there, then they are."

MacBridan hesitated, and then said, "So far I haven't seen anyone, but I'm not finished."

"Very well," said Dolinski. The disappointment he felt blended poorly with the irritation in his voice. "I'm expecting more from you, Mac. Stay close to this."

"Yes sir, I understand. It's just that I felt you needed to know that I haven't really come up with anything, and at this point there's not too much more to go on."

"Stay in touch," snapped Dolinski as the line went dead.

MacBridan sighed as he hung up the phone. He really hadn't expected the call to go too well. After all, he was zero for two on an assignment that, for Dolinski, was both professional and personal.

He picked up the phone and put a call into Cori Hopkins. "Hi, Cori, it's Mac."

"I was wondering when I'd hear from you. How are things going?"

"Great. Ranks right up there with root canal. That's why I called. Need your help."

"You don't sound so good," said Cori. "What's up?"

"I'm no closer on this than when I left New York. In fact, I think I'm even a few points behind, if that's possible. Anyway, there are a couple of things I need you to look into."

"Okay, go ahead. I'm ready."

"See what you can find regarding thefts and break-ins in the New Westminster area. I'm curious if this place is actually as peaceful as it looks."

"That won't be hard," said Cori. "I should be able to turn that around pretty quick."

"Good. There's one more thing. I found some markings on a medallion that I can't identify. It looks like some kind of language, but I don't even have a good guess as to what it might be. I also found similar markings on a local landmark. I'm going to text some pictures of these markings to you."

"Are they connected to the missing artifact?" asked Cori.

"I rather doubt it, but I'd still like to know what they are. In regards to this, I have a name I want you to take down, Dr. Emerick Wilson. He's a local and apparently is into all things mystical, at least he was growing up. He's now a professor of ancient cultures and civilizations at Clark University. Katherine knows him and thinks that he might be able to translate the symbols for us if we ask him nicely. See what you can come up with, okay?"

"As soon as you get them to me, I'll reach out to the good professor. I'll even ask him nicely. Listen, are you alright? I could join you up there if you need me."

MacBridan gave a small laugh. It was the first time he'd really smiled all day. "Thank you for that most tempting offer. No, I just think I'm wasting my time here, and it is beginning to eat away at me. Call as soon as you have something."

MacBridan then left Katherine's and drove to the post office in New Westminster. He hadn't mentioned to Cori the wax samples he had taken at the ruin. He just didn't want to talk to her about his activities yesterday at the ruin, so he wrote her a brief note asking her to have them analyzed. He sent them overnight for morning delivery. He wasn't surprised that Cori had picked up on his mood. Try as he might, he just couldn't shake it. And he certainly didn't feel ready to talk to anyone about all that was going on in his head. In the past few days, an overwhelming fear had started to show up on a semi regular basis, and in his line of work that was not good. *At least I haven't started wetting the bed,* he kidded himself.

MacBridan was beginning to doubt himself again. Maybe that was too strong a statement, but he definitely had concerns about his nerve. He couldn't get away from the fact that he had passed out in that damned basement. *Why? Did I really faint from fear?* He couldn't accept that, but then there was yesterday. *Yesterday was another stunning performance. I nearly ran through the graveyard dragging poor Katherine behind me. It has to be more than just fear, but what else could this devastating feeling be? I know this, though. Whatever followed me down the bell tower was real, we both felt it and once again, just like the incident in the basement, I didn't see anything.*

A car horn pulled him out of his stupor.

MacBridan got back in his car and thought about what he should do next. There weren't that many options available so he decided to drive back out to the sheriff's office.

The same woman who had been both receptionist and dispatcher the last time he came by was on duty again. It had only been a couple of days, but MacBridan would swear she had put on weight. He was confident that the uniform manufacturer had never envisioned buttons being tested at such a high stress levels.

"Hello again," said MacBridan. "I'd like to speak with Sheriff Beninger. Is he in?"

She stared at MacBridan for a moment, deciding if his query merited a response. "May I have your name, sir?"

"James MacBridan. You remember, I was in the day before yesterday, met with the sheriff."

She continued to stare at him, then slowly shook her head. "You did?"

"Late in the day, maybe five, five-thirty," prompted MacBridan, looking for some glimpse of recognition.

Nothing registered with her, the blank expression permanently in place. MacBridan wondered if this was merely nepotism in action, or the effects, over time, of an over indulgent application of cosmetics. Perhaps she had lost the ability to alter her facial expressions? After all, chemicals are chemicals. Slowly she shook her head and said, "He's not in. Got called out about thirty minutes ago."

"Any idea when he'll be back?"

"No, he didn't say." The look on her face remained unchanged, confirming his suspicions.

Yeah, she is definitely family to someone around here. MacBridan thanked her and headed back out to his car.

Halfway across the parking lot a cruiser pulled in. The young officer getting out matched the description Katherine had given of the deputy that had accompanied the sheriff out to her place. He was a little over six feet tall, dark hair, young, and obviously spent a fair amount of time at the gym. His uniform was immaculate.

MacBridan started toward him. "Excuse me. Are you Deputy Goodman?"

"Yes, I am. How may I help you?" Goodman looked MacBridan over carefully. His right hand eased back toward his holster ever so slightly.

MacBridan handed him his card and introduced himself. "Oh yeah," said Goodman, "Sheriff Beninger mentioned that you'd been in. Said you're working on those church robberies."

"That's right. With St. Thomas having been one of the churches hit, and Vickers being from the area, it seemed a good place to start. Did you know Gerald Vickers?"

Goodman shrugged, "Wasn't much to know. Guy was a zero."

"That seems to be the consensus," said MacBridan.

"Wish I could help you, but there just isn't anything to add. But if there were, the sheriff would be the one to know. He's spent his whole life here, and I'll swear he has the scoop on just about everyone."

"Well, it looks like I just missed him," said MacBridan.

"That's not a problem. I heard the call on the radio. It didn't sound like much of an emergency. Be happy to give you directions. You come up with something?"

"Maybe, not sure really. Have a couple of more questions I hope the sheriff can help me with."

Deputy Goodman gave him directions to state highway 1202. About five miles outside of town there was an old railroad bridge. That's where he would find Beninger.

"Deputy, it was nice meeting you. I appreciate your help."

"Not at all, glad to do it. You're staying out at the Chamberlin place, aren't you?"

"Word travels fast."

Goodman smiled, "Small town. She's a sweet old lady. How's she getting along?"

"Just fine. Why do you ask?"

"She called us a few weeks ago. It was Saturday, September twenty-second, around eleven at night. Said she'd spotted a burglar. We got out there pretty quick, but there wasn't anyone there. I looked around for about ten minutes, but couldn't find a thing. It's a shame the tricks age can play on a person."

"You must have a pretty good memory, Deputy. To remember the exact date and time."

Goodman looked down and gave an almost sheepish smile. He didn't blush, but it was close. "Like I said, small town. There's not enough going on around here that requires a great deal of memory. It's really pretty quiet."

"That's what everyone says."

"Course, I can't complain. It's a good thing, and I wouldn't want it any other way."

MacBridan thanked him again and headed out of Deacon's Mill in search of the sheriff. Goodman's instructions were on the mark, and he didn't have any trouble locating highway 1202. MacBridan enjoyed the fall, perhaps his favorite time of year. The leaves on the trees around him created a virtual rainbow of autumn colors. It was a warm day and MacBridan had the windows down, taking full advantage of the good weather. The air was rich with autumn scents, and MacBridan's spirits began to rise.

It was actually rare for MacBridan to be down for any significant period of time. He wasn't sure he had ever truly been depressed. He just didn't have the patience for it. Usually, whatever was eating at him and trying to pull him down ended up infuriating him and he would fight back. So far, this odd formula had served him well.

He had been on highway 1202 for about fifteen minutes when he spotted the railroad bridge. Whatever was going on had attracted a crowd. MacBridan slid his car in next to the sheriff's. There was a deputy's car parked a little further down, with an ambulance and an old Ford pickup truck off to the side of the road.

MacBridan started across the field to the trees where everyone had gathered. Two teenage boys were sitting on the ground by themselves, and out of the way. One had his head down in his hands. The other was staring aimlessly into space. His face was pale, so pale that he looked as if he was going to be sick.

Beninger and another deputy were going over what had been a campsite. The two men from the ambulance were standing next to something on the ground. They had covered it with a blanket.

"Stay where you are, MacBridan. There's already been enough people tromping through here to qualify as a parade ground," said Beninger. He said something to his deputy then walked over to him. "Didn't think I'd see you again."

"I'm just following your instructions, Sheriff."

"What instructions?"

"You told me to report to you immediately if I found something, so here I am."

"Well, I must say I'm surprised. What do you got?"

"Nothing," said MacBridan, "at least not yet."

"Some detective."

"My boss wasn't very taken with my performance either."

"So you drove out here to report nothing."

"I wanted you to rest assured that I'd keep you updated," said MacBridan. "Plus, I have another question for you."

"Look, I don't have time for this, MacBridan. This is far more serious than some damn missing church relic."

"What happened?" asked MacBridan.

"Those two boys over there were doing a little rabbit hunting. They came across this campsite and found a body, or at least what was left of it."

"How long's he been dead?"

Beninger stopped, made eye contact with MacBridan and said, "I shouldn't be telling any of this to you." Beninger looked back at the body covered on the ground. "It's just that it's the strangest thing I've seen in a while."

"Fair is fair, Sheriff. You haven't charged me for all your help. I won't charge you for mine."

Beninger thought that over for a moment and grunted. MacBridan took it to be an affirmative grunt. "Guess you had to have had a little experience to get your job. Whoever this guy was, he died, I'm guessing, twenty-four to forty-eight hours ago. I don't know how he died, but something got to him."

"You mean animals, dogs?"

"I don't know, maybe. It's a mess. The throat and neck were mauled and the face is all but gone."

"A pack of strays could have done that," said MacBridan. "That wouldn't be all that unusual. I came across a body once that rats had gotten to. It wasn't pretty."

"No, that's not it, that's not what bothers me. Only the neck and face were mauled. He wasn't wearing a shirt, but there are absolutely no other injuries that we can find. Nothing. Not a scratch. None on his arms, hands, his chest, his back, nothing. Animals wouldn't have been that targeted."

"Did he have any ID on him?"

"No," said Beninger. "Which leads me to believe he was probably a vagrant. We found his stuff over by that tree, and he'd used a couple of blankets to lay out a bed. He had a watch on. A cheap one, but it's still working. I also found a little money in his pack. So whatever happened, it wasn't robbery."

MacBridan looked around, taking several deep breaths. He circled the body, studying the ground. "That's odd," he murmured.

"What's odd?"

"You estimate that this guy's been here for a day or two, yet this place really doesn't smell all that bad. I mean, for all the blood this guy had to have lost, this place should reek." MacBridan knew that most people really didn't have any idea just how bad a mutilated body smelled.

"There isn't much blood," Beninger said, shaking his head in disbelief. "I caught that too. My first thought was that he'd been killed somewhere else, but there's no sign of that. No, unless I'm wrong, he was killed right here."

"Have you found anything else that would help?" asked MacBridan.

"Not a thing. There is no sign of a struggle, no defensive injuries, and no tracks other than the two boys. Yet, when you look at the victim, it was clearly a violent death. There should be signs of some kind of struggle and there should be tracks, or at least some sign of what did this." The sheriff seemed almost to be talking to himself.

"How old of a guy was he?"

"No way of telling, at the moment," answered Beninger. "State boys are coming to help go over the crime scene. We'll know more in a couple of days." Beninger turned and looked at MacBridan. "Now what exactly was so important that you just had to ask me?"

"I was hoping you could tell me more about Gerald Vickers," said MacBridan.

"You really ought to give this up. There is nothing about Gerald Vickers worth finding out."

"Wish I could disagree with you. But for better or worse, he played a hand in this, and he's all we've got."

"Well if those are all the cards you're holding, you're about at the end of the game."

"Come on, Sheriff, he had to have had some friends, someone," said MacBridan. "Where did he hang out? What did he do to kill time around here?"

"MacBridan, I have no idea," said Sheriff Beninger. He started to turn away, then stopped. "No, maybe there is someone. Seems to me there was one guy that he hung out with from time to time. Another real zero. Macy. That's it. Carl Macy."

"Where can I find this guy?" asked MacBridan.

Beninger gave a small laugh and said, "You may not want to. Macy is a bad guy. I've seen the results of guys who have crossed him in the past."

"Careful now, I scare easily. On the other hand, I am quite touched at the level of concern you have for my well-being. That said, I still want to talk to him."

"Yeah, I forgot, you're a real tough guy up from the city. Okay, MacBridan, do what you want, but I already warned you. I don't want any trouble coming from you."

"Sheriff, you got all the trouble you need lying right over there. I'm just going to have a friendly, get acquainted talk with Mr. Macy. How do I find him?"

"Macy usually hangs out at the Box Car Bar. It's out by the old railway station, just south of New Westminster. Railway station's been closed for years, but the bar has hung on. It's a tough crowd out there, and Macy's one of the meanest."

"Thank you, Sheriff. I knew you wouldn't let me down," MacBridan said. He turned and started back to his car.

"MacBridan," called Beninger, "watch your back. All I need is another mess to clean up."

CHAPTER 10

As she walked across the campus of Clark University, Cori thought back on some of the professors she'd known, both as an undergrad and while working on her master's program. Although she couldn't quite put her finger on it, there was something that separated them from normal people. This was not to say that they were abnormal, though a couple of them had most certainly been quite eccentric. It just seemed that the whole collegiate environment changed the people who chose to live within its ivy-covered walls. For them the real world didn't exist, or at best, they refused to acknowledge it and they had a tendency to look down on everyone else. That difference had been all too apparent during her call with Professor Emerick Wilson.

To be fair, he'd been very nice, carefully listening while she explained the situation, and then, before she could ask, insisted on offering his help. In fact, his excitement on seeing the symbols Mac had found bordered on giddiness. But despite his cooperative attitude, there'd still been that unique difference, a subtle variance in how he'd phrased his words. In short, she'd felt like a student again. Here was the good professor, most willing to help, yet his tone contained that mildly veiled, condescending patience for the student who just couldn't grasp the obvious solution.

He'd given her very good directions and she quickly found his office in the Anthropology building. She was anxious to put a face with the voice. The door was partially open, but she knocked anyway.

"Come in."

Cori stepped into an office that would have driven Dolinski to madness. It looked like a tornado had blown through. Tall bookshelves lined both walls, each shelf sagging with the weight of all that had been haphazardly crammed into them. His desk was littered with even more books, topped off by piles of papers waiting to be graded. There were two chairs in front of his desk, one of which held a layer of books while balancing a coffee maker with a long extension cord.

"Dr. Wilson?" asked Cori.

"Yes, do come in. You must be Cori. Delighted to meet you! Please, do sit down, we have much to discuss." Dr. Emerick Wilson appeared to be in his sixties, was of medium height and modestly over weight. He was nearly bald, but a few tuffs of hair still held on here and there. His glasses were large with very sturdy frames and his face had the reddish tones of someone who is more than a casual drinker. He was wearing a green and blue plaid jacket, with a dark brown shirt, and a dull, gold colored tie decorated with more than one food stain.

"I appreciate you meeting with me on such short notice," said Cori. "I hope you've had an opportunity to look at the symbols that I emailed to you."

"Oh yes, and I must say they are quite extraordinary. You say that your man found these in New Westminster. That's probably the last place I would have expected them to turn up."

"Then you recognize them," said Cori.

"I most certainly do. Never thought I'd see them outside of a manuscript, but yes, I recognize them," said Professor Wilson. He had the symbols up on his computer screen.

"Would you mind if I record our conversation?" asked Cori. "I want to make sure I don't miss anything."

"Of course, that's just fine. I can't tell you how surprised I was when I opened your email."

"Please go on, I'm all yours," said Cori.

"Turns out these markings are symbols from an ancient language, one that dates back nearly as far as the days of the legendary King Arthur, possibly even earlier. As far as anyone knows, this language was first used by a small, fanatical band of druid priests, and is tied to a very old religion."

"Interesting," mused Cori. "They were found carved into the side of a religious monument, of sorts."

Dr. Wilson continued, "Have you ever heard of grimoires?"

Cori smiled at him. "I have no idea what you just said."

"It's okay, most people haven't. Let me explain. As I said, these symbols are letters, an old alphabet, if you will. This language turned up in written form as early as the twelfth century in what are called grimoires, all part of the practice of witchcraft."

"What exactly are grimoires?" asked Cori.

"Books of magic, and they date back to ancient times. They were used to conjure and, if successful, to control demons. Many of the grimoires are supposed to be quite detailed, providing precise instructions as to how to go perform spells and such. It is interesting to note that quite often these instructions coincide with astrological events. Is any of this making sense?"

"I'm with you, but it all sounds a little farfetched," said Cori.

"Be patient, it's important that I fill you in on the rest. While I certainly don't believe in this sort of nonsense, there are those that do. Based on what you sent me, your man may be dealing with a group that is pretty far out there. They may even be dangerous."

"What makes you think that?" asked Cori.

"I've been able to loosely translate the symbols, although I have to admit that, on one or two of them, I'm still guessing a little. The first set of seven symbols is a blessing, of sorts. It was used to designate, or claim, an area as being sacred to one of the worst, and most feared, of the old pagan gods. This god was pure evil, and it was believed that just saying his name could bring on ruin and damnation."

"So what you're telling me is that this group is taking what has been holy ground and is now claiming it for their god."

"Good versus evil, God against devil. This would be consistent with the instructions laid out in the grimoires. Conjuring, it seems, is quite an involved process."

"Alright, assuming it's not kids doing this, I would guess that we are probably not talking about pillars of the community, but I still don't see what makes you think they may be dangerous."

"Give me a moment. That brings us to the second set of seven symbols," Dr. Wilson continued. "Again, loosely translated they say *red dragon*."

"So you think it may be some kind of gang doing this?"

"No. The symbols representing *red dragon* refer to a specific grimoire."

"Is that bad?" asked Cori.

"Yes, it's bad. The *Red Dragon Grimoire* is very old, and is feared today by people who really believe in witchcraft. It is black magic in its most evil form. This specific grimoire outlines, in vivid detail, what needs to be done to perform necromancy."

"Necromancy?" asked Cori.

"Necromancy is raising someone from the grave, possibly even bringing a demon out of the pit."

"This is crazy, said Cori. "There are people who actually buy into all this?

"Sadly there are. I've studied paranormal activities and their role in various cultures for years. Witchcraft is alive and doing well, even here in the United States. When you've lived as long as I have, Ms. Hopkins, you find that the line between what is crazy and what is sane starts to narrow."

Cori nodded. "What else can you tell me about this?"

"No matter what you believe, you need to warn your colleague. Only the worst, the most dangerous, the most criminally insane would even try this grimoire. That alone speaks to their fanaticism. That's why I believe things could get pretty rough for anyone who gets in their way."

"I'm not sure what I was expecting, but I can tell you it certainly wasn't this," said Cori.

"May I ask you a question?" asked Dr. Wilson. Cori nodded her answer.

"What they really need, in order to permanently raise the demon, is some important Christian artifact that they can desecrate during the ceremony. Are you aware of anything that they might have for that purpose?"

Cori paused before answering. While this was all too fantastic to believe, Mac had to know what he was up against. With that in mind she said, "The cross of St. Patrick. It's missing."

"Oh my, that is exactly the kind of thing they would need. Do you have any leads on where it might be?"

"That's one of the items our investigator is looking into in New Westminster. He's very good at what he does."

"By all means, let me know if you find it, or I if can be of any help," said Professor Wilson. Leaning back in his chair he looked at the ceiling for a moment, deep in thought. He then reached for a paper lying on top of some books. "One last thing. The pictures of the medallion were clear, but the symbols were harder to decipher. As best I can tell, it serves as a blessing or a charm. It's probably to protect the one doing the conjuring if things should go bad."

"You've been of tremendous help, Dr. Wilson," said Cori. "Thank you."

"It's been my pleasure. You should know that the run of the mill person dabbling in witchcraft wouldn't have this kind of knowledge and would never think of using the *Red Dragon Grimoire*. I can't put this in strong enough terms, this is pure evil. I'd be careful if I were you. These kinds of people are lethal."

CHAPTER 11

It felt so good to relax. Holly leaned back and rested her head against the rocking chair. Of all the things she had come to love about their new home, she absolutely loved the view from their porch, with the quiet peacefulness of the surrounding woods, all colored by the soft light of dusk. It had been a lovely day with one glaring exception. Ian, once again, had left on business. Other than that, she felt good, at least for the moment. In truth, though, her health had her worried.

Something was draining her strength. Holly found herself getting weaker and weaker as time went on. Most days she felt all right, but when the weak spells hit, they were nearly debilitating. So much so, that she found herself leaving the house less and less. Being tied to the house created several difficulties for her, especially with her doctor.

Dr. Appleton's office was a long way from their home, all the way over in Deacon's Mill, and it took nearly an hour to get there. The long drive itself usually seemed to trigger a weak spell. These spells would come on quickly, aggravating the drive to the doctor's to the point of actual physical pain. Fortunately for Holly, Dr. Appleton, unlike the vast majority of doctors, had not done away with the practice of making house calls. Without his understanding, she really didn't know what she would have done.

Lucy, who had become a frequent visitor, had seconded the recommendation given by Paul Lovett to get Dr. Appleton as their doctor. His practice was well established in Deacon's Mill and New Westminster.

Holly looked over at the pumpkin that sat next to the door and smiled. Lucy had brought it to her earlier that day. They were becoming quite close, and Lucy's visits eased the isolation that Holly had started to feel. She had also brought more of her special tea.

Lucy's visit had been quite unexpected. She'd knocked on the door just after lunch, "Hello! Anyone home?"

Holly had been back in the bedroom folding some laundry. "Back here. I'll be right there." As Holly approached the door, she spotted the pumpkin.

"They told me at the store that this pumpkin is one of their best, absolutely prime for carving, so here it is," said Lucy.

"Well, I don't know how it will turn out," said Holly, "but I did promise to give it a try."

Lucy put the pumpkin down on the porch, came in and sat down at the kitchen table. "You sure will. A promise is a promise. This is the first Halloween in your new home, and we want to make sure you do it right. Besides, when else can you really make use of my house warming gift?"

"You got me there," laughed Holly. "Would you like something to drink?"

"I'll take some soda if you have some. Which reminds me; I brought you some more tea."

"Oh, thank you. Lucy, the tea is wonderful! Lately I have been feeling so terribly weak and that tea seems to be the only thing that helps. It actually revives me."

"I'm so glad," said Lucy. "Have you talked to Dr. Appleton about the weak spells?"

"Yes, in fact Ian brought it up to him before I did. He really couldn't explain it, but told me not to worry. He said I'm as healthy as can be, and that every pregnancy has its own challenges. So, I guess I'll just have to ride it out."

"Well, at least the doctor's not worried. That's good. Speaking of Ian, where is that cute husband of yours? He's been gone a lot lately," said Lucy. "Is everything all right?"

"That's the problem; things are going almost too well. One of his newest clients has been sending a great deal of work his way, but wants him in Boston as often as he can get him there. I really don't mind too much, but I am getting so close to my delivery date and it worries me not having him here."

"Will he be gone long this time?" asked Lucy.

"No, thank goodness, just a couple of days."

"That's not that long," said Lucy.

"It's really not, I suppose, and the extra money sure has come in handy."

Lucy leaned across the table and patted her hand. "Things will work out just fine. If you need anything at all, you just gave me a call, and I'll be here. You're not alone so long as I'm around."

Thinking back over their conversation helped Holly feel safe. She bowed her head to once again thank God for the many blessings that he had sent to her and Ian. Dr. Appleton being in Deacon's Mill, the growing friendship with her new friend Lucy, Ian's business picking up, and, most of all, their baby.

The sky had started to cloud over. Holly could hear thunder off in the distance as the wind started to pick up. *So much for relaxing on the porch*, she thought. She worked her way out of the rocker, carefully picked up the pumpkin, and went inside. After filling the kettle for tea, she went to the hall closet and got the basket down that held the pumpkin carving kit.

Halloween always brought several special memories back to her. As a little girl, Holly and her father would always carve their pumpkin together. No matter how it turned out, her dad always assured her that it was the best one in the neighborhood. Carving pumpkins had been easy and fun to do back then. It had never been nearly as complex as the pattern she was now holding in her hand.

Following the directions, Holly attached the pattern to the pumpkin with tape. She then took one of the sharp, pointed tools from the basket and began to punch holes into the pumpkin, following the lines on the pattern. By doing this, she transferred the pattern onto the pumpkin so she could eventually carve it out. It took several minutes, and as she worked, the storm slowly drew closer; the lightning and thunder more threatening.

The teakettle started to whistle, and Holly fixed a cup of Lucy's tea. She settled back down at the table and continued to punch out holes along the lines of the pattern. The cool, smooth surface of the pumpkin felt good to the touch. Twenty minutes later, she finished step one. Now came the gooey part.

She had never enjoyed reaching inside a pumpkin and cleaning out the seeds. In second grade, the little boy who sat next to her—whose likeness was destined to grace the post office's wall—said that it was all pumpkin snot. For some reason that "pleasant" thought had stayed with her. She wasted no time gutting the pumpkin—"gutting" being one of Ian's terms. That chore completed, she finally got started on the part of the process she enjoyed the most, carving the pumpkin.

Holly soon realized just how long this would take. She worked slowly, closely following the pattern. It was important to her that it turn out well. She wanted it ready for Lucy's next visit and took extra care to make sure it looked good.

The storm finally arrived, and the rain began to fall. Night had come on quickly, or so Holly thought. She could feel the strong wind as it buffeted against the house, rattling many of the windows. She stopped, put the knife down, and made sure all the windows throughout the house were tightly fastened shut. She locked the door and stood there watching the intensity of the storm as it lashed out against the countryside. Lightning came in frequent bursts, illuminating the yard all the way to the edge of the woods that surrounded the house.

Just as she started to turn away, the lightning flashed again. Holly stopped and turned back to the window. At the point where the driveway entered the woods, something had moved. At least she thought it had. She'd only glimpsed it out of the corner of her eye and it was probably nothing, but she wanted to be sure.

Her eyes tried to penetrate the pitch-black night as she waited for the lightning to give her another look. She didn't have to wait long. As the lightning lit up the sky once again, she saw it. There stood a dog. An enormous black dog, standing in the middle of the driveway at the tree line, staring up at the house. The light in the sky reflected in its eyes, giving them a reddish glow. In that brief glance, she saw that the dog's stance was one of defiance, oblivious to storm around it.

Holly couldn't remember having seen this dog before. It was huge. Her hand moved to the deadbolt on the door, reassuring her that it was fastened tight. She stayed at the door, continuing to peer into the night. What if it came closer? Where had it come from? Would it try to get in?

The next burst of lightning seemed even brighter than the last. Her eyes had already started to adjust to the dark when the bright flash stung them. The dog was gone. She wanted to feel relieved, but the dog's disappearance had the opposite effect. Where had it gone? Why did its appearance bother her so much?

Holly kept watch for another ten minutes, but didn't see anything else. She finally turned away, her stomach reminding her that it was time to eat. She busied herself making soup and turned on some music. The music was Celtic, something she and Ian both liked. She found it soothing. As soon as she finished eating, she made herself another cup of the tea. She felt much better now and the nervousness over the dog, for the most part, had passed.

The storm, however, hadn't. It thundered on with a sustained strength, but it didn't bother Holly as much now. She tried to turn her focus back to the pumpkin. The pattern gradually began to take on form, piece by piece. It was a face. A hideous face. Holly remembered her talk with Lucy back at the antique shop. The custom of carving these had begun as an effort to ward off evil spirits. The gruesome thing was supposed to work for her, protect her house; instead, she found that it frightened her. It frightened her a great deal.

Holly felt a little silly and she tried to shrug it off, yet she couldn't completely rid herself of the nervousness that had taken up residence in the pit of her stomach. On the other hand, she really couldn't put all the blame upon herself. *After all,* she reasoned, *I'm alone. It's night. There is a storm that's trying to knock the house down, and let's not forget the hound from Hell I spotted.* The image of the hound still lingered in the back of her mind. And to complete the ghoulish atmosphere, she was carving an image meant to ward off evil spirits. Anyone would have felt a little nervous.

Holly rummaged through the kitchen drawer that served as a catchall. She found the candle she was looking for and carefully placed it in the pumpkin. Using one of the long matches they'd purchased for lighting fires in the fireplace, she lit the candle, put the lid of the pumpkin in place, and stepped back.

A chill settled over Holly as she stared at her creation. It was even more hideous with the candle burning inside. So much so, that she turned her eyes away from it. She had done a remarkably good job, but that really didn't matter much at the moment. The horrible thing scared her. She quickly came to a decision. She would show it to Lucy, and then get rid of it.

She leaned over to blow out the candle, but stopped, remembering the poem. *This is ridiculous*, she thought. *Lucy will never know*. But that thought sent her to the basket in search of the old verse. As small a thing as it would have been, Holly did not want to lie to her friend, not even about something so inconsequential.

The instructions directed that the poem should be spoken just as the first candle was lit. It wasn't too late, Holly thought, *after all this is the first candle and it hasn't been burning all that long.*

Holly stood before the pumpkin. The poem was on a separate piece of paper, written in a cryptic language. Neither she nor Lucy had been able to figure out which language it was. Lucy had looked, but couldn't find a translation. "Some things just can't be translated," Lucy finally conceded. They agreed that when the time came, Holly would sound it out as best she could.

The rain came down in torrents, pounding on the roof harder than before. The pumpkin glared at her from the table, seeming to take offense that she would dare to stand before it. Her hand shook as she began to sound out the poem, her voice trembling, "*Eko Eko Azarak, Eko Eko Zomelak, Eko Eko Cernunnos, Eko Eko Aradia…*" Something inside told her that this wasn't right, to stop, but she did her best, continuing to sound out the strange language. The harshness of the sounds that came out of her mouth surprised her, compounding the dread that had already begun to spread within her.

Just as the final sound left her mouth, lightning struck near the house. A split second later, the thunder cracked so loud that it shook the entire structure to its foundation. The lights flickered and went out leaving her in utter darkness. Holly screamed. The poem fell from her hand; the paper floated down to rest on the floor beneath the stove. The only light left came from the pumpkin. With no other light to compete with, its evil presence grew to fill the room.

Holly couldn't move. The face, so hideous, held her stare with a power she couldn't understand. She tried, but couldn't look away. The storm continued to rage around her. The pumpkin now began to glow brighter and brighter. Fire erupted from the eyes, its hellish light dancing off the walls.

It took all the strength she could find to start to back away from the table. She had to get away. She was in danger, she knew it, but still couldn't take her eyes off the terrible thing.

Her heel caught on the rug. She fell backwards, her arms flailing outward. Her left hand hit the counter, gripped it briefly, but couldn't hold on. She landed on her side, hurting her arm and nearly knocking her breath out. Holly rolled onto her back, holding her arm to her, pain lancing through her shoulder. As she lay on her back, gasping for breath, all thought of pain left as another sound even more threatening assaulted her.

Something was clawing at the door to the porch, trying to get into the kitchen. The hound had returned. It barked and growled furiously, frantically trying to get through the door. Her eyes left the door as a worse horror presented itself—the pumpkin moved. It moved again, proceeding to glide to the edge of the table.

Holly could not believe her own eyes as her creation began to rise from the table. The room suddenly grew cold, terribly cold, engulfing her as if someone had pulled a blanket of ice across her. The hound's attack on the door had become frantic, desperate in its effort to get inside. The pumpkin hovered above, staring directly down at her. Fire now burst from the eyes and the mouth. Holly screamed one last time, finally escaping into the depths of unconsciousness.

CHAPTER 12

MacBridan rolled over to the side of the bed, his fingers blindly fumbled around trying to find the watch that he'd left on the end table. His eyes took a few moments to adjust to the luminescent dial, but finally focused in on the fact that it was nearly five in the morning. The storm had kept him awake most of the night. In the last half hour, the lightning and thunder had lessened somewhat, but the rain continued to pour down.

His mind wandered as he dozed in and out of sleep. MacBridan remembered his trepidation and fascination with storms as a child. Back then, the storm striking New Westminster would have terrified him. Twice, the lightning and thunder had been so intense that they had startled him awake. Some remnants from his childhood fears still held on, creating just enough tension to keep him from falling into a restful sleep. Then, of course, there was the monster that used to live under his bed. Now there was something he hadn't thought about for a long time. Back then, though, he had an older sister just down the hall to comfort and take care of him. *I doubt that Katherine would understand my jumping into bed with her and pulling the covers over my head*, he thought.

He lay there, not asleep, yet not entirely awake. Then, from the darkness, a voice, small and distant, spoke his name. His eyes flashed open. Had he really heard something or had he dreamed it? The disembodied voice spoke his name again, this time more forcefully. He sat up quickly, looking for the intruder.

"Mr. MacBridan, are you there?"

The intercom. It was Katherine trying to reach him on the intercom.

"You have got to get a hold on yourself," he muttered as he reached over and turned on the light. The intercom was mounted on the wall to the left of his bed. He got up and pressed the button labeled talk.

"I'm here, Katherine. Are you alright?"

"I need you to come to the house. Quickly. Come in through the back door and be as quiet as you can."

"What is it? What's the problem?"

"The watcher has returned."

"Be right there."

MacBridan turned the light off in his room. If the mystery watcher had returned, he didn't want to warn whoever it was that they'd been spotted. He quickly dressed, fastened his gun to his belt, and put on a waist length jacket that was supposed to be waterproof. This night would certainly put that to the test.

The storm easily covered any noise he might have made as he left the carriage house and made his way quietly across the yard to the main house.

Katherine was waiting for him in the kitchen. "I'm so sorry to wake you, but he's back. I need to prove to you that I'm not crazy."

"That thought has never crossed my mind," MacBridan assured her.

MacBridan followed her as she headed upstairs. "The storm's done a good job of keeping me awake tonight. Every time I started to doze off, the thunder would wake me up. One crack of thunder was so loud that I got up and looked out the window to see if anything nearby had been struck," she explained.

They entered her bedroom and moved to the far window. "As I was looking to see if anything had been damaged, I caught sight of something else. I wasn't sure at first because the rain made it even harder to see than usual, but after awhile I saw it again, and this time I was certain."

"What did you see?"

"Light from the old church tower."

"You could see a light in the tower in this storm?"

"The storm's kept it hidden from view most of the time, but it was there. In the past, whenever the lights have appeared, the watcher has also appeared. Tonight is no exception."

"Where did you spot him?" asked MacBridan.

Katherine went over to the window on the other side of her room. "Let's be careful. Whoever it is, he's still there."

They stood to the side of the drapes that framed the window. "From here I can see part of the front yard and also where the road curves around," Katherine said. "The watcher is in those trees across the road. Right across from the end of the hedge."

MacBridan watched for a moment, but even with the intermittent flashes of lightning, he couldn't see anyone. Normally, with anyone else, he would have had his doubts. But considering all that he had recently experienced, in addition to his high regard for Katherine, he believed all that she said.

"Alright, let's see who this is and what he is up to," said MacBridan.

"You shouldn't go out there alone. Wait, I'll call the sheriff," said Katherine as she turned to the phone.

"No, we'll keep him out of this for now. Besides, he had his chance and blew it. Now it's our turn."

She started to follow him as he went to the door.

"Katherine, I need you to stay here," MacBridan instructed. "If anyone other than me tries to come in this house, that's when I'll want you to call the sheriff."

"You are a very imposing man, and I'm sure quite capable, but going out there alone is just plain crazy."

"Not at all," said MacBridan as he smiled at her. "All I'm going to do is find whoever it is and have them explain to me exactly what he or she finds so fascinating about your house, so fascinating that they would stand out there, in the dark, in a storm."

MacBridan went back down the stairs, through the kitchen, and out the back door. He carefully worked his way around to the front of the house, staying in the shadows, ignoring the rain. He stopped near the corner of the front porch, positioning himself behind a tree and waited.

The rain continued to pound down and soon lightning lit up the yard. Nothing. MacBridan crouched down and quickly made his way to the far end of the hedge, away from the watcher. Once again, he waited, but still couldn't see anyone. As quickly as he could, he crossed the road before the lightning would give him away.

MacBridan stepped into the trees that bordered the road. Fortunately, there was very little underbrush. He moved forward carefully, one step at a time, approaching the spot that Katherine had pointed out to him. About twenty feet in front of him something moved. It looked pretty large, but he hadn't gotten enough of a glimpse to figure out what, or who, was there. MacBridan froze, waiting for the next bolt of lightning. "I'm going to feel pretty ridiculous if this turns out to be a bear," MacBridan whispered to himself. MacBridan tried to keep in mind that the woods always tended to amplify things, especially one's imagination, especially at night.

Lightning soon rewarded MacBridan with an extra long flash. There he was. A man, partially concealed by a tree, just as Katherine had said. But, before MacBridan could get any closer, the watcher left the trees and dashed across the road. MacBridan watched as his quarry hid in the hedge surrounding the house.

MacBridan stayed hidden in the trees, continuing to make his way to the spot the watcher had just vacated. He estimated that he was now about twenty to twenty-five feet away from his quarry. However, with the road once again between them, there wasn't any kind of cover to help MacBridan hide his approach. He decided to rush the intruder on the next burst of lightning.

MacBridan raced across the road just as the sky lit up, but by the time he got to the hedge, the watcher was gone. He froze, looking from side to side but couldn't spot anyone in the downpour.

Some kind of instinct, or sixth sense, told him that his quarry was behind him. Quickly he spun around, raising his arms to ward off the blow he knew was coming. The club caught him high on his left shoulder, instantly numbing his arm and glancing off his head. The impact of the blow hurled him into the hedge.

Even though he had deflected most of it with his shoulder, it took MacBridan a few seconds to clear his head. He struggled to get to his feet, but the hedge held on to him with an unnatural grip. He fought his way free of the hedge just as a shotgun blast went off behind him.

MacBridan turned, dropped to one knee and brought his gun to bear, searching for his target. Katherine stood before him on the front porch. She held the shotgun with both hands, the second barrel ready. MacBridan looked around, but they were alone. The watcher had vanished.

CHAPTER 13

MacBridan sat by the fire in the living room, across from his hostess, slowly sipping some brandy. His arm and shoulder ached, but, as best he could tell, nothing was broken. The small cut above his ear hadn't bled much and now had stopped altogether.

A knock at the door startled both of them. "I'll get it," said Katherine, rising from her chair. She too had been nursing a brandy.

MacBridan followed her into the hall to find Deputy Goodman on the porch. He wore a black poncho to help protect him from the rain that continued to fall. The sky had lightened considerably with the dawn, but there were no visible breaks in the clouds.

"Morning, Mrs. Chamberlin, Mr. MacBridan. I got here as fast as I could."

"Good to see you, Deputy," said MacBridan. "It's been quite a night."

"Won't you come in, Deputy?" said Katherine, opening the screen door for him.

"Thank you. Is everyone alright?"

"Pretty much," answered MacBridan. "I had a brief run in with someone watching the house. Unfortunately he got away."

Deputy Goodman took out a small notepad and pen and began to make some notes. "When did this happen?"

"I'd say around five-fifteen, five-thirty. Mrs. Chamberlin spotted him and called me." MacBridan continued on, giving the deputy what little detail he had.

"So you never got a good look at him?"

"No, not really. He appeared to be a fairly good-sized guy, but I can't be certain. Just as I got knocked into the bushes, Katherine rescued me."

She gave a small smile at that and said, "Oh, nothing quite so dramatic. I was watching from the door here and when I saw Mr. MacBridan run across the street I thought he might need some help."

"That was mighty brave of you, Mrs. Chamberlin," said Deputy Goodman, obviously impressed. "I think I'll go outside and look around a bit."

"I'll go with you," said MacBridan. "It's considerably lighter now, and I'd like to take a look myself."

MacBridan led the deputy to the spot where he'd been hit, and then across the street to the place where the watcher had been standing. The rain had already taken care of any signs of who might have been there. After a few minutes, they returned to the front porch.

"You need somebody to check out that arm?"

"No, it's okay. Just wish I'd gotten a hold of the guy."

"Yeah," nodded Goodman, "that would have been nice. Well, I'll file my report and talk this over with the sheriff. I'm sure he'll step up the patrols out here for awhile."

"Thanks, I'll tell that to Mrs. Chamberlin."

MacBridan went back inside to find Katherine busy in the kitchen fixing breakfast. "The deputy said he'd talk with Beninger and make sure they patrol this area more often."

"Well, it's about time. I just wish I could be there when they talk. I'd give Frank Beninger a piece of my mind. If he'd done his job the first time I called him this never would have happened!"

MacBridan sat at the table and smiled at her. "Katherine, you are a remarkable lady. You make a great partner, and I want to thank you again for what you did."

"You're making too much of this. I really didn't do that much," she said, setting a plate of bacon and eggs down in front of him. The smell of the food, mixed with the aroma of fresh brewed coffee, stirred life back into MacBridan.

"Truth is, I couldn't see a thing."

"Well, that's understandable, it was dark out there," said MacBridan.

"No, that's not it. The darkness didn't have a thing to do with it. The whole thing had me pretty rattled. As I went out on to the porch, the wind carried the rain straight into my face. This was just as you were crossing the street. So I took my glasses off to wipe the rain off of them, but only had one hand to do this, because I had the shotgun in the other. Anyway, I wasn't making much progress with my glasses, and then I heard the struggle and the sound of someone falling. That frightened me, and my glasses fell out of my hand. All I wanted to do was scare whoever you were fighting with, so I fired the shotgun into the air."

MacBridan laughed, "Well, as shots in the dark go, you did alright."

The phone rang and Katherine went to answer it. "I'll bet that's Frank Beninger. At least I hope it is," she said as she left the room.

MacBridan refilled his cup and stared out the window at the rain. Katherine's home was indeed being watched; he knew that for certain now. Was someone waiting for the right time to break in? He didn't think so. *No one stands in the rain watching a house that, if Katherine is right, has already been under surveillance several times already. Is the watcher really tied to the lights at the old ruin? And if so, why?* MacBridan wondered.

Here too, MacBridan had little to go on. Other than a bruised arm and a small cut on the side of his head, he had nothing to show for his efforts. In the morning light, New Westminster looked about as tranquil as a small town could. Everyone he'd talked with so far further underscored just how quiet a place this was. But MacBridan knew just how deceiving appearances could be. His experience told him that there was clearly something going on here. Something, MacBridan felt, if left unchecked, could turn far more serious.

"It's your office on the phone. A Ms. Hopkins."

MacBridan looked at his watch. It was just after seven. "Looks like everyone is getting started early this morning. Thank you, Katherine."

MacBridan went into the living room and sat down in the winged back chair beside the phone. "Cori?"

"Morning, Mac. Couldn't reach you on your cell phone. Hope I didn't wake you."

"Not hardly. What's got you going so early this morning?"

"Case reviews," said Cori. "I've got two of them starting at eight. One's internal, but the other one is with the client. I don't know how long they'll run, and I wanted to make sure I got a hold of you first thing this morning."

"You must have found something."

"You tell me. Personally, it's a little strange, but it's what you asked for. Ready?"

"I'm all yours." MacBridan liked Cori more than he cared to admit. She was a pro, and, second to Dolinski, was one of the most detail-oriented people he knew. Plus, she had great legs, which never hurt.

"Other than what was taken from St. Thomas Church, there has been very little going on in New Westminster in the way of thefts. However, two months prior to the theft at the church, a bicycle was reported stolen from the middle school."

"A bicycle?"

"Yes, but I don't want to get you too excited, Mac. It was returned the next day. Apparently, it had been taken by accident. Case closed."

MacBridan waited patiently. Nothing followed. "And that's it?"

"That's it."

"I'm not buying it, Cori. Quit holding back and tell me whatever else it is you've found."

"There isn't anything else theft related, but as to the markings you found, that is a whole different story."

"How so?" asked MacBridan.

"I met with Emerick Wilson, that professor you asked me to talk to. It turns out the markings you found are very unique. In fact, to say that they are rare is an understatement.

"And…?"

Cori was quiet for a few seconds before asking, "Mac, is this on the level? Did you really find those symbols there or has this been another one of your weak attempts at humor? I mean, we are rather close to Halloween and you have been known to pull practical jokes before."

"Cori, I'm not fooling around. I believe these symbols are tied into what Mrs. Chamberlin has been able to see from her window. I also believe that it may help to explain why she's being watched."

"She's actually being watched? You've confirmed that?"

"Yeah, the hard way, but I'll tell you about that later. First tell me what you've learned about these symbols."

"Okay, here goes, but this really gets weird. As I said, I met with Professor Wilson at Clark University. Turns out he's an expert in this area." Cori then proceeded to tell MacBridan all she'd learned from the professor. "Does any of this help?"

"Yeah, it just might. My first guess had been kids telling ghost stories in the graveyard at night. However, after Mrs. Chamberlin and I visited Altar Rock, I suspected that it might be far more. What you're telling me confirms that. Sounds like some of the good citizens of New Westminster are engaging in the age-old art of witchcraft. If true, that would certainly go a long way to explaining what I found," said MacBridan.

MacBridan was quiet for a moment, going over all that Cori had told him. It not only confirmed many of his suspicions, but also, after this morning's incident, convinced him that Katherine may be in real danger.

"You still there?" asked Cori.

"Yes, this just changes things. Cori, I need you to dig deeper into this. Find out all that you can, especially anything that might help lead me to these people."

"What are you going to do?" asked Cori.

"I'm not sure, but let me tell you what has been going on here." MacBridan quickly brought her up to date, concluding with the run-in he had with the watcher. "One more question, what about the black wax that I found?"

"Oh yes, I forgot to thank you for telling me about that in advance. I swear I've washed my hands a dozen times, but I cannot get rid of the odor. You also found that at Altar Rock?"

"Some of it. Most of what I sent you came from the ruin of the old church, up on top of the old bell tower," explained MacBridan.

"Well, next time warn me when you're sending a stink bomb. It's still at the lab, but I'll put a rush on it. You have any guesses as to what we'll find?"

"Not really, but my bet is that it too ties to witchcraft. Push on this, Cori. Whoever has been meeting in the graveyard has been at it for some time now. If they are as bad as you think, Katherine could turn out to be a target, which would explain why she's being watched."

MacBridan thanked Cori and hung up. He'd brief Dolinski on this later, but first he had some questions for Katherine. As bizarre a twist as things had taken, it felt good to finally begin to get a grasp on what might be going on. He had been fighting shadows long enough. Now, to some degree, he had a tangible target.

As he made his way back to the kitchen, he wondered if all this could somehow tie into the missing Cross of St. Patrick. After all, the similarities between the way Vickers had been killed and the injuries to the body found by the boys that Sheriff Beninger was investigating were almost too much to be just a coincidence. Had Vickers been one of the people practicing ancient rituals in the graveyard? But if so, who had killed him? How had they gotten in and out of that basement so quickly, so quietly? MacBridan worried over his own experience. What had he seen in that basement that had so affected him that he lost consciousness?

"Is everything alright?" asked Katherine.

"Just fine," answered MacBridan. "Cori was following up with me on the markings we found at Altar Rock. We may have a theory as to what's going on there."

"Can you tell me?"

"Of course, but before I do, I'd like to go over a couple of things with you. Please take your time with this, as it could be rather important. The lights you've seen at night, the people watching your house, your experience at Altar Rock, what you felt there and the black, smelly wax, all of this, who have you talked to about these things?"

"Mr. MacBridan, we have been over all of this before," said Katherine.

"Yes, I know, but I need for you to go over it in your mind one more time. Again, please understand, I wouldn't ask you to do this if it wasn't important."

For a moment, Katherine stared at MacBridan. She then leaned back in her chair, her eyes resting on the cup of coffee in front of her. A couple of moments passed before she said, "Well, as you know, I talked with Peter about all of this. Sheriff Beninger knows about the watcher, but I didn't tell him about the lights in the churchyard. The opposite is true with Father Collin. I told him about the lights, but not the watcher." She remained focused on her coffee cup.

"Anyone else?" asked MacBridan. "A friend perhaps, someone at church, anyone at all?"

"It is not my way, James. I do not like to burden others with my problems. Especially when it is something that could make me sound like a foolish old woman."

"Okay, that's good. That is very helpful," said MacBridan. "Now let me tell you what we've got. The symbols we found, and probably the wax, may tie to the practice of witchcraft. Your professor Wilson was most helpful with this regarding the symbols. Whoever's doing this, I believe, is also responsible for your house being watched."

"I find that somewhat unsettling to think about." She was quiet for a moment before saying, "Then, although you haven't said it, you believe that I may actually be in trouble." She suddenly looked older, smaller, drawing in to herself, trying to distance herself from a fear that up to now she had been trying to deny.

"We certainly can't rule that out, Katherine. For some reason they are keeping a close watch on your house, so we won't take any chances. Going forward, we will have to start taking some added precautions.

"What kind of precautions?"

"We'll work those out. For now, even though I know this is upsetting, there is actually a good side to it all. We may have some idea as to why you are being watched and what is going on in the churchyard. Now we become the watcher. Once we identify these people, it won't be hard to stop them," said MacBridan.

"But will we be able to identify them?"

"For some reason they seem to be tied to Altar Rock and the ruin of the old church. That's good, because from your room we have an excellent vantage point. We can see their lights; letting us know each time they're there. Because of that, we'll find a way to identify them. Each and every one of them."

CHAPTER 14

Holly didn't know where she was, but she did know that she was lying down, on something soft, but for some reason she couldn't see. Oddly, though, this didn't panic her. Lately she had been so tired, so worn down, but now she was warm, comfortable, and she welcomed the peace and rest. Then in a rush, it all came back to her. All of it came flooding back into her mind in a terrible collage of images—the storm, the dog, and worst of all, the pumpkin—that horrible, horrible pumpkin.

Holly tried to sit up, but just as she started to rise, the nausea hit her. She dropped back down again, bringing her hands to her head. In addition to the nausea, her head began to ache terribly. Her hands discovered a damp cloth lying across her eyes and forehead. Holly lay still, fighting her stomach's sudden urge to purge itself. She hadn't felt this sick since the passing of her first trimester.

It was then she noticed the voices. They were calm, quiet, two people having a normal conversation. But she had been alone. Who was there with her? What had happened to her? All too vividly, she remembered reading the poem and all that had followed. The pumpkin had come at her. There was no mistaking that. And the dog, where had it come from? Why had it tried to get at her?

The voices were clearer now, a man and a woman. The man's voice was familiar, but she was having trouble placing it. She couldn't hear the woman's voice as well. As she lay there waiting for her stomach to settle down, she tried to focus in on what they were saying. Words became clearer, and she realized that they were talking about her.

"Oh, she may have suffered a bruise or two, but otherwise she seems to be alright. All things considered, she was very fortunate. A fall like that could have produced far more severe consequences," the man said. His voice was steady, comforting, his tone reassuring.

"The baby, what about the baby? Are you sure it's not in danger?" asked the woman, her voice stern, almost harsh, demanding. Holly knew this voice too, but couldn't figure out who the woman was.

"Yes, as I said, I don't believe the baby was hurt in anyway." Holly heard them walk toward her. She felt someone sit down next to her. "Let's see how our patient is doing," said the man as he touched her wrist. Holly pulled the cloth from her eyes and watched Dr. Appleton take her pulse.

He smiled at her and said, "Hello there. I don't want you to worry. Everything's fine now. It appears you fell and struck your head hard enough to cause you to black out. How do you feel?"

"My head hurts, and I'm very sick to my stomach," said Holly as she looked around. She was in her bedroom, and it was morning. Through the window, she could see that clouds still filled the sky, but the rain had stopped. "How did you get here?"

"For that you have to thank your guardian angel," said Dr. Appleton, looking over his shoulder at the woman behind him. He got up and moved to the dresser that stood beside the door. Holly noticed his medical bag sitting atop the dresser.

Lucy sat down on the bed, taking Holly's hand in hers. "You gave us quite a scare. My poor dear, what happened to you?"

Holly suddenly found herself fighting to hold back the tears. A lump rose in her throat, making it hard for her to talk. "It was so horrible. The storm, it was so loud, and…but wait, how did you find me?"

"I knew Ian was out of town, so I called to see how you were doing. The storm was pretty rough, and for some reason I was worried about you," explained Lucy.

"I don't remember you calling," said Holly.

"You never answered the phone. I had an operator check the line and when she told me that it was in working order, I got in my car and drove out here as fast as the roads would let me."

"Holly, you have no idea just how lucky you were," added Dr. Appleton. "It wasn't an hour later that the phone lines did go down. For that matter they're still out."

"Anyway, just as I started knocking on the door, I saw you lying on the floor. The door was locked, but the window next to it hadn't been latched and I was able to get it open. I knew I couldn't move you all by myself, so I called Dr. Appleton and he got here as quickly as he could."

"Holly, you don't seem to have hurt yourself too badly, although I do expect you to be sore in places for the next few days," said Dr. Appleton, looking up from some notes he had been jotting down. "However, I do want you to come by my office later today, tomorrow at the latest, and we'll run a few tests just to make sure."

"My baby," Holly choked out, "is my baby alright?"

"Yes, I believe so. Actually, I'm more concerned about you at the moment, but rest assured, we will check you out from head to toe."

"Holly, what happened?" asked Lucy. "Do you remember falling?"

"Yes, oh yes, I remember." She could no longer hold back the tears that flooded her eyes, and she began to sob quietly. Lucy leaned over and held her, gently patting her arm.

"There, there, things are fine now, no need to cry," said Lucy.

"No, things are not fine. I'm so scared. Why am I so weak lately? I'm eating the right foods, I'm not doing nearly as much around the house as I use to. Poor Ian has to do it all, but I just keep getting more and more… I don't know, frail. What is happening to me?" Holly sobbed through the tears, her voice a mixture of fear and frustration at her condition.

Dr. Appleton took Lucy's place next to Holly on the bed. He handed her a tissue. "Now we've talked about this before. I know it worries you, but you've got to stop that and let it go. I'll be the first to let you know if there is something to be concerned about. What you are going through is natural. You are very close to delivering what I believe is going to be a beautiful, healthy child, and it is simply taking more and more out of you."

"But what if I become too weak, what if something is wrong?" Holly pleaded.

"Holly, this last month will be the hardest. Every patient I've ever had has gone through this, to one degree or another. Once the baby is born and things begin to get back to normal for you, the tired spells will go away. I'm pretty confident of that," said Dr. Appleton.

Holly shut her eyes and took a deep breath, trying to get control of herself. "Thank you, Doctor. I'm sorry, I'm not usually such a wimp."

"You're hardly a wimp, Holly," said Doctor Appleton as he got up and moved back to the dresser. "You're pregnant, that's all. Now, can I expect to see you soon?"

"Ian is out of town, doctor," explained Lucy. "I'll help Holly, and we'll get her in to see you."

"Good. Now Holly, you get some rest and take comfort in knowing that you have friends here that are going to help take care of you."

Holly lay there and listened as Lucy followed Doctor Appleton to the door. They talked some more, but she couldn't hear what they were saying. Eventually she heard his car start and pull away from the house, heading down their drive, into the woods. Lucy was doing something in the kitchen and she soon stuck her head back in Holly's room. "I going to make us both some tea, and then we can talk," said Lucy.

Holly smiled her response and closed her eyes. She missed Ian, missed him so much. She needed him now, but also knew that it had been important for him to leave. She quietly prayed, thanking God for sending Lucy to her. What would she have done without her? What if they had never met and had not become friends? What if she had been more seriously injured in her fall, and had no one to help her? No, she knew how blessed she was to have such a friend.

It didn't take Lucy long, and she soon returned with a tray. She had already poured the tea, and she had also brought a plate of crackers for Holly. "We need to get something in your stomach to help settle things down. Here, let me help you to sit up."

Lucy helped Holly up to a sitting position, propped up with pillows, so that she could drink and eat, but still rest. "Lucy, when you found me, was I alone?" Holly asked.

"Heavens yes, you were alone. Why, was someone else here?"

"No, I'm sorry. I mean, was anything wrong, you know, not where it should be?"

Lucy studied Holly for a moment, trying to understand what Holly was driving at. "I don't think so. I'm guessing that when you fell you knocked the pumpkin off the table. I'm saying this because it was on the floor, but I didn't notice anything else."

Holly's face paled, "The pumpkin was on the floor?"

"I'm afraid it didn't fare nearly as well as you did. It broke apart, but not to worry, I've already cleaned everything up," Lucy assured her.

Holly sipped her tea, but both hands trembled. "Lucy, I'm really scared."

"Oh honey, I know this has been very frightening for you, I understand that, but you're alright. Even Dr. Appleton thinks that you are going to be just fine."

"It's more than that. At times, I become so weak. Just sitting up is almost more of an effort than I can muster. But last night, last night was terrible and I'm not sure what to do."

"Last night was an accident, wasn't it Holly?" asked Lucy.

"Lucy, please, I know you are going to think I'm losing it, but I was attacked last night. That is what caused me to fall."

Lucy sat up straight; concern etched across her face. "Attacked? By whom?"

Holly tried to drink more of her tea, but her hands were shaking so much that Lucy took the cup out of her hand and placed it on the bedside table. "What I am about to tell you is the truth. As crazy as it is going to sound, it happened, and I don't know what to do. I have to reach Ian. We've got to do something. He and I can't stay here."

"Holly, please calm down and talk to me. Who attacked you?"

Holly didn't know what to do. She wanted to tell Lucy, but she also didn't want her friend thinking that she had flipped out. The terrifying events she had experienced were not just the symptomatic imaginings of a hormonal, pregnant woman. They were real, but how could they be? Holly realized that they were so fantastic that even she had trouble believing what had happened. "Lucy, you've got to help me, I have to get in touch with Ian."

"We will, we will, I promise. Now Holly, please let me help, tell me what happened."

Holly lay back on the pillows. She told Lucy of how she had gone inside as the storm began moving in. She told her how she started to work on the pumpkin, about looking out the door and seeing the dog near the trees. Then she told Lucy of the final horror. She explained how she lit the candle and read the poem, just as they had discussed. Her voice broke a couple of times as she relived the moments when the lights went out and the pumpkin rose off the table, fire shooting from it, the dog attacking the door. "I knew I had to get away, but I couldn't take my eyes off of it. As I backed away from the table, I tripped on something and that is when I fell. Oh Lucy, I looked up and the pumpkin moved all by itself. It floated directly above me. I've never been so scared in my life. I must have fainted then, that's all I can remember."

Holly watched Lucy's face carefully, looking for any sign of doubt, or worse, of total disbelief. Lucy's eyes never left Holly's. Finally, she reached over and once again held Holly's hand. "I don't know what to say. It is hard to believe, and yet, I do believe you."

"What am I going to do?" Holly asked, desperation filling her voice.

"Well, let's take this a piece at a time. The storm is gone. Now, as to the dog, well, that may have just been coincidence."

"Coincidence?"

"Yes, you know," said Lucy, trying to comfort the younger woman. "Let's face it, the storm was absolutely terrible, one of the worst we've had around here in a long time. There are several strays in the area, and my guess is that one of them was nearby when the weather landed on us. I imagine that poor creature was simply terrified out of its mind. A dog I once had couldn't stand storms. I'll bet that wretched animal was just trying to get inside. He wasn't attacking you; he just wanted to escape the storm. Then, to top everything off, the storm knocked the power out."

"I wish I could accept that, Lucy, but you didn't see that animal. The first time I saw him he wasn't acting scared at all. In fact, he stood completely still, staring at the house. And his eyes, they were terrible, they weren't right. Despite the darkness I could still see them because they were red."

"That could have been the light from the storm, or even from your house. You've seen deer, even dogs at night when they step out in front of a car, their eyes always light up."

"You don't believe me?" asked Holly.

"Honey, I believe you, I already said that, I'm just beginning to wonder if maybe several things could have come together all at the same time, making them look far worse than they really were."

Holly closed her eyes and thought about what Lucy was saying. Had much of what happened been colored by her imagination? Had the storm, with Ian being gone, set her nerves on edge enough to do all this? She had already been worried about the weak spells she was having. Could her anxiety over that have set her up for such a scare? Maybe, but that alone couldn't explain the pumpkin.

"What about the pumpkin, Lucy? I didn't imagine that. That happened. You yourself found it shattered on the floor beside me."

"I know I did, and again, I believe you, but let's talk about it just a little bit more. You were alone, with a terrible storm going on outside. You weren't feeling well, and that stupid dog would be enough to terrify anyone. The pumpkin was just the icing on the cake and for that I'm sorry."

"You're sorry? Why? What did you do?" asked Holly.

"It has to be the dumbest house warming gift ever. What could I have been thinking?"

"Lucy, I liked it. My dad and I used to carve pumpkins when I was a kid, and I thought it a very special gift."

"Well, still, the pattern we picked out for you ended up scaring you half to death and I feel badly about that. But I do have an idea what may have happened. Now hear me out on this. You were scared, the storm, the dog, everything. Then, just as you light the candle in the pumpkin, the lights go out. Holly, that would do it for anyone."

"But it moved; it came at me," said Holly, her voice softer now, almost a whisper. Could Lucy be right? Had she let her imagination run wild? "Fire shot from its eyes; it wasn't right."

"I understand, but I've been thinking about that too. The problem might have been with the candle. I've had candles do exactly what you are describing, especially new ones. Did you use a new candle?"

Holly thought for a moment and said, "Yes, it hadn't been used before."

"Then I'll bet that's it. There was probably too much wick, or something, and for a few moments it flared, burning far brighter than it normally would. My poor child, I'm not surprised you passed out. All of that would have certainly done me in."

Holly didn't know what to think. All that Lucy said made sense. And yet, it had all seemed so real, so different from the explanations Lucy was suggesting to her.

"You may be right, Lucy. I don't know what to think anymore. I guess in the dark, I may have accidentally knocked it over, or somehow pulled it toward me. Heaven knows I've been clumsy enough lately with everything else around here. This isn't like me at all. What is happening?"

"My dear you are in the last stages of your first pregnancy. You've never experienced any of this before, and it must be quite overwhelming. You've got to remember that Doctor Appleton says you are doing just wonderfully and, believe me, he is a very thorough man. When is Ian coming home?"

"He should be back late tomorrow afternoon. Oh how I wish he was here."

"Well, by then you'll be feeling much better and this little incident will be behind you."

Holly shut her eyes and tried to relax. She wanted to believe that Lucy was right, that she'd blown everything out of proportion. *Guess I'm just another crazy pregnant lady*, she thought to herself. *When Ian gets back things will be better, the baby will arrive and things will get back to normal.* With that thought in mind, Holly eventually drifted off to sleep.

CHAPTER 15

The next morning MacBridan made it out of bed just after seven, well rested after all the excitement of the previous day. His arm ached; still tender to the touch, but he felt certain that he'd acquired nothing more than a bad bruise. For close to an hour he performed stretching exercises in the small guest cottage, trying to work the soreness out of his arm.

As soon as he finished, he put on some sweats and went for a run. He covered nearly five miles and it felt good. Giving him the cardio workout he needed, the run also allowed him to familiarize himself with the surrounding area. He discovered that there weren't many other homes on the ridge near Katherine's house, not much traffic either. The pleasant, private home on the ridge was an isolated, vulnerable target.

By nine-thirty he had showered, dressed and was on his way into town. Before leaving, he spoke briefly with Katherine, letting her know his plans. She assured him that she'd be all right, and that if anything happened, she'd call him on his cell phone.

Late yesterday evening he had brought Dolinski up to date on the events. Dolinski had always believed his aunt; still it hit him pretty hard when MacBridan confirmed that she was indeed being watched. Dolinski became more upset when he learned that things had turned violent.

"It doesn't make sense, Mac. Why would anyone be after her?" mused Dolinski.

"At this point we really don't know that they are after her, or who we are dealing with, or what they're up to. After last night, they may not even come back. Either way, we're on to them, and that gives us the advantage," stated MacBridan.

"Advantage? What advantage?" Dolinski barked.

"They're no longer invisible, we know they're there. Plus, we have a sheriff's department that is mildly embarrassed and has promised to beef up their patrols out here. Our position has clearly strengthened and changed for the better."

"Don't try talking to me like I'm some naive client. That's awfully thin, Mac."

"Perhaps, but it's better than nothing," replied MacBridan.

"What are your plans?"

"I think it is time for another visit with our local parish priest, as well as the good sheriff," answered MacBridan.

"Mac, I can get some people up there to help if you need it," offered Dolinski.

"Thanks, but that would be premature. I'll let you know," said MacBridan.

***

MacBridan pulled into the parking lot at St. Thomas Church, parked and headed up the steps to the front door. The church doors were locked, so MacBridan went back down the steps and made his way around to the side door that he and Father Collin had used the first evening they met. It too was locked. That left only one other place to look, so MacBridan walked into the trees to the rectory.

The daylight allowed MacBridan to see that the rectory was actually larger than it had first appeared. He knocked on the large, oak door and waited. The sounds coming from the stream behind the rectory, rushing, and gurgling over and around the rocks, were relaxing, almost to the point of being hypnotic. A couple of minutes passed. He leaned in closer to the door, listened, but couldn't hear anyone inside. He looked for the doorbell, rang it, but still didn't get any response. Strike three. MacBridan left the rectory and walked back to his car. It wasn't unusual for the priest not to be there, MacBridan reasoned. He might be visiting the sick, or doing other priestly duties. Still, MacBridan wanted to talk with Father Collin, and he was disappointed that he'd missed him. As he was opening the door to his car, he spotted Father Collin crossing the footbridge, returning from the churchyard. The priest seemed lost in thought, and didn't notice MacBridan leaning against his car until he was almost upon him.

"Good morning, Father," said MacBridan.

"Mr. MacBridan, always a pleasant surprise." The words were right, but didn't match the expression on his face, which displayed a grim, almost worried look.

"Hope I'm not interrupting."

"No, no, not at all," said Father Collin. "I often like to stroll through the churchyard. It is so quiet there, so peaceful. I often think out loud, and it's rare for any of the residents there to give me an argument."

"I was hoping that I could ask you a couple more questions," said MacBridan. "If you have the time."

"Of course, but I'm not sure what more I can tell you. I trust all is well with Mrs. Chamberlin?"

"She's doing well, Father. I'll let her know you asked about her."

"A remarkable woman, Mrs. Chamberlin. It is a pity that time has not allowed us to get to know each other better."

"Father, have you noticed anyone in the churchyard late at night? Kids perhaps, anyone?" asked MacBridan, bringing the focus back to business at hand.

"No, but then I'm not really in a position to see who might go there late at night. Why do you ask?"

"I've been wondering if you've had any problems with vandalism."

"Vandalism? Heaven and saints preserve us, no, whatever has led you to think that that might be going on?"

"No one else has said anything to you? Maybe noticed something they thought was odd, or perhaps looked out of place?"

"I really have no idea what you are getting at. Why don't you tell me what you think is going on? I'm afraid at this rate, we're not going to make much progress."

MacBridan was annoyed that Father Collin kept answering his questions with more questions. Still, he was determined not to let Father Collin divert the conversation and take control, like he had the last time. "What about at Altar Rock?" MacBridan persisted. "Have there been any problems there?"

Father Collin locked his gaze on MacBridan, attempting to discern what was behind MacBridan's questions. The wind moved through the trees around them, competing with the sounds of the stream. The combined chorus of natural music nicely filled the pause in their conversation. "We often have people go out to Altar Rock. They visit at various times throughout the week. It is very beautiful there. But other than some occasional litter, there haven't been any real problems to speak of, at least none that I'm aware of."

"Father, when was the last time you visited Altar Rock?"

"I'm not sure I remember."

"Were you out there today?"

Color appeared in Father Collin's face, his body stiffened but his gazed never faltered. "No, I would have remembered if I'd been there today. Mr. MacBridan, I do not appreciate being interrogated like this. If you will kindly tell me what it is you are trying to find out, I'll help you all I can. It is unpleasant to think that you are insinuating that I am being less than truthful."

"It's just that I noticed the mud on your shoes, Father, which is interesting since all the paths in the churchyard are paved. However, the path out to Altar Rock isn't, therefore, I thought that perhaps you might have been out there this morning."

"Always the detective, Mr. MacBridan, and most observant too, I see now. No, not this morning. As I'm sure you heard, we had quite a storm pass through here. I did stop a few times on my walk this morning to remove branches that the wind had blown down onto some of the headstones. In doing so, I must have stepped in some mud. Is there something going on out there I should know about?"

"There just may be," said MacBridan. "I walked out to Altar Rock last Sunday after mass. As you say, it is very nice there and seeing Altar Rock for the first time is, well, pretty impressive. I was intrigued, though, by some markings I saw etched into the stone at the base of Altar Rock."

A look passed over the priest's face. It passed so quickly, though, that MacBridan nearly missed it and wasn't sure what it meant if anything. "Markings? What kind of markings?" asked Father Collin.

"Nothing I could recognize, which is why I wanted to ask you. Have you seen them, Father?"

Father Collin hesitated before answering. He appeared almost uncertain as to what to do. "I'm not sure. I may have noticed them, but if I did, I don't remember paying much attention to them. What is your interest in them, Mr. MacBridan?"

MacBridan had to fight to keep from laughing out loud. The priest's answer had been masterful: evasive, yet truthful. How many times had he watched attorneys at the Hawthorne Group coach their clients for such answers as they prepared them for depositions? Once again, the priest responded with a question, again attempting to turn the flow of the conversation to where he'd receive the information rather than give.

"They are most unusual, different from anything I've ever seen, and I'm not sure they belong there, Father. Are you sure you haven't noticed them?"

Father Collin didn't respond. MacBridan felt confident that Father Collin knew all about the markings. It was becoming pretty clear to him that Father Collin did not want to discuss them, or for that matter, pursue their conversation any further.

"Father, have you heard anything about the possibility of some people in the area practicing witchcraft? Performing their rituals in the churchyard?"

"This is getting a little bit ridiculous Mr. MacBridan. I thought you were here investigating the thefts of the artifacts taken from the church. Of course, I'm not aware of any such activity. There isn't any! Why would you suggest such a disgusting idea as witchcraft?" Father Collin was visibly angry now, stepping in closer to MacBridan.

"My search for the Cross of St. Patrick has taken some interesting turns. You may want to swing by Altar Rock on your next walk. Take a real close look. Believe me, Father, there's a great deal going on here in New Westminster."

"I'll do that, Mr. MacBridan," said Father Collin, trying to hold rein on his temper. "I appreciate you bringing this to my attention. Our talk has been most informative. But I caution you not to jump to conclusions or be too quick to accuse."

MacBridan smiled at the priest, which appeared to push Father Collin closer to the edge. MacBridan did not want the priest's anger to pass. People often made mistakes when they were angry and it was clear that Father Collin wasn't telling him everything he knew. "You forget, Father, my profession is based on fact, not faith. I don't jump to conclusions. I just go where the facts lead me. Understand this, Father, nothing is off limits to me, and I'll follow the facts no matter where they may go."

"It's been good talking with you, Mr. MacBridan. May I wish you a good day and God's blessing." Without waiting for a response, Father Collin brushed by MacBridan and headed towards the rectory.

"Good day, Father," MacBridan said to the priest's back. It surprised and disappointed MacBridan that Father Collin had not been more forthcoming. He liked the man. He didn't want to believe a priest could actually be mixed up in any of this. *More than likely*, thought MacBridan, *Father Collin was probably embarrassed that this kind of thing could be happening right under his nose*. Nevertheless, Father Collin knew more than he had shared, and that opened new lines of consideration for MacBridan.

MacBridan got into his car and pulled out of the parking lot. Hopefully, he'd be able to find Sheriff Beninger and get something more tangible out of him. He thought about his brief talk with Father Collin. Although the priest had not directly given him any new information, he had indirectly told him a great deal. Unfortunately, though, this also meant that Father Collin deserved a closer look.

As he got closer to the sheriff's station, he realized that he was not up for another stimulating conversation with Beninger's dispatcher. MacBridan called information, got the number, and called instead.

"Sheriff's office, may I help you?" It was her.

MacBridan didn't even try to disguise his voice. He was pretty sure, based on his previous encounters, that he, as well as his voice, had already been forgotten. "Need to speak to Sheriff Beninger, please."

"Sheriff's not in. Can I take a message?"

MacBridan barely stifled the groan that formed in his throat. This was not going to be easy. So far this morning nothing had been easy. "This is Bob Minter over at the DA's office. Got some papers I need to have Sheriff Beninger sign and we need to get this done pretty quick. Any idea where I might find him?"

The line went quiet. MacBridan patiently waited for her response. He could visualize her being deep in thought over this amazingly complex question. Finally, she said, "Bob Minter? I don't recall no Bob Minter at the DA's office."

"Well I've been here for nearly three years. Course, this is my first criminal case, usually I handle civil matters," bluffed MacBridan. She didn't say anything so MacBridan continued. "I'm under some pressure here to get these signed, and I'd really appreciate your help."

The dead air, didn't last as long this time. "Sheriff Beninger went over to get some lunch at the Pine Cove Diner, but he don't much like people bothering him at lunch."

"Wouldn't dream of it. I'll come by later. Thanks," said MacBridan and hung up. If nothing else, that had felt good. "James MacBridan, master of deception," he chuckled.

The Pine Cove Diner sat on the left side of the road, a half-mile before the sheriff's station. MacBridan had seen it before and pulled in next to Sheriff Beninger's cruiser. It was still a little early for the lunch crowd and there were only two other cars in the lot. The Pine Cove Diner wasn't that large, with tables spaced around all three sides of a horseshoe shaped lunch counter. Sheriff Beninger was seated next to the window near the back of the diner. MacBridan smiled as he approached his table.

"How did you know I was here?" asked Sheriff Beninger.

"I'm highly trained detective, remember?" MacBridan answered as he sat down across from the sheriff.

"Oh yeah, hard to tell sometimes. To what do I owe the pleasure of your company?"

"Have you talked with Deputy Goodman?" asked MacBridan.

Beninger moved his coffee cup out of the way as the waitress brought out his sandwich, a generous portion of chips on the side. MacBridan ordered coffee. "As a matter fact, I have. Sounds like you had a bit of excitement last night. Course, I was a little disappointed with my deputy for not arresting Mrs. Chamberlin. I can't have citizens going around discharging firearms in the city. But then we talked, and we both agreed that it was probably best that Mrs. Chamberlin did what she did. After all, how would it look if we let some big city detective get his ass kicked while visiting here?"

MacBridan stirred his coffee, mixing in the cream he'd added. "Always good to know that the local government officials have a moderately developed sense of humor."

"Well, next time that mean old Peeping Tom comes around, you call us. We'll take care of it. Besides," said Beninger, his tone turning serious, "you did promise that you would call me if you found anything. I'm guessing that in all the excitement that little item just happened to slip your mind?"

"Let's just say that Mrs. Chamberlin wasn't all that impressed with your performance the last time she called you for help. The way she tells it, you came up empty."

"Yeah," Beninger grunted quietly. He put the sandwich down, pushing the plate aside. "We missed on that one. It's been bothering me all morning. I plan to stop by and talk with her this afternoon." The sheriff looked MacBridan in the eye and said, "We weren't careless, but then, we didn't take her as seriously as we should have either. Believe me, I won't make that mistake again."

"It happens. I'm sure she'll appreciate you coming by," said MacBridan.

"You got any idea who might have been out there watching the house last night?"

"Not specifically, no, but I am working on a couple of things and it just may tie to them."

"What things?" asked Beninger.

"That's where I need your help again. How are you doing with your investigation regarding the body those boys found?"

"First, that's none of your business. Second, what could that possibly have to do with what went on out at Mrs. Chamberlin's?"

"I'd like to get a copy of the medical examiner's report and get it back to my people. I'm going to ask them to compare it to the report that was filled out on Gerald Vickers. The way Vickers died closely matches the injuries you found on the John Doe, and that's just too much of a coincidence for me."

"You think they're connected?" Beninger gave a small laugh. "Well you must be holding one heck of a lot back because that sounds like quite a stretch to me."

"I'll know more after we get a chance to go over the report, but here's what I do know. Vickers died by the same means as your victim, the throat mutilated with very little blood in the immediate area. You and I both know that a wound like that should have sprayed blood around everywhere. For that matter, they didn't even find much blood left in Vickers' body, which begs the question, where did it go? Both men had some connection to New Westminster, and both men died within a couple of weeks of each other."

Beninger shook his head. "I'll admit that there are some similarities, and I too would be interested in a comparison once you get it, but I still don't see how they could be connected."

MacBridan took a deep breath, anxious to see how Beninger would react. "It's my theory that the murder of Vickers, as well as the death of your John Doe, may have been the result of ritual killings. I hope to know more later today, but that fits in with some things I've found."

"What exactly are you saying, MacBridan?"

"My guess is that there is a cult, or coven, or whatever you want to call them, here in the area. If I'm right, they are involved with the practice of witchcraft, black witchcraft to be specific. Your case and mine could be tied together with both men being victims of this group."

"That kind of talk can scare a hell a lot of people and do a great deal of damage, especially when it's not true. Do you have any facts to back this up?" demanded Sheriff Beninger.

"Not as many as I'd like, but as I was saying, later today—"

"So you have nothing."

"Nothing confirmed that ties it all together but things that are pointing in that direction."

"Pointing in that direction? Guess your client must be pushing you pretty hard, but I really don't care. Feed whatever you like to the sap that hired you, but unless you have rock solid evidence, I don't want you stirring anything up around here that eventually I'll have to straighten out. This is a quiet, peaceful community, and I don't need you scaring the hell out of everybody just so you can collect your fee."

"Yes, quiet and peaceful, I remember you telling me that the day I met you. That was just before those boys found that man who was murdered out by the railroad tracks."

"The cause of death has not been determined," Beninger snapped, glaring at MacBridan.

"And just before that nonexistent Peeping Tom, the one you and your deputy couldn't find, hit me over the head. This place gets any more peaceful you're going to need to expand the morgue."

"Slow it down, MacBridan. You've got nothing that even remotely ties to a cult, nothing at all."

"But I will later today. Sheriff, I'm trying to tell you that I have found some evidence that points to this, and you can't just ignore it. I've sent this evidence off to my office and, by this afternoon, their analysis should be complete. That will tell us even more of what we're up against."

Beninger slammed the flat of his hand down on the table, his face turning red. "Well until you do confirm your facts, MacBridan, keep your mouth shut. I won't allow that kind of talk scaring people and creating all kinds of unnecessary trouble. You be real sure of your facts before you breathe a word of this again, and when you do, it better be me you're talking to. We clear on that?"

"Crystal, but I'm still going to need a copy of the medical examiner's report. You may not like the idea, Sheriff, but it doesn't mean I'm wrong."

Beninger got up and tossed some money down beside the uneaten sandwich. "You can pick up the report from my office later today, but I've just about reached my limit with you MacBridan."

Beninger strode out of the diner, slamming the door behind him. MacBridan stayed where he was, sipping his coffee. It hadn't been a pleasant morning but, on the other hand, it had been pretty interesting. The reactions to the idea of witchcraft from Father Collin and Sheriff Beninger had been far from what he'd expected. MacBridan had expected Father Collin to simply dismiss the idea and not take it too seriously. As to Sheriff Beninger, MacBridan had been all but certain that he'd get laughed at for even suggesting such a thing. Instead, both had become angry. In fact, the more he thought about it, he wasn't sure that either of them had even been surprised. All this added to the picture that was steadily beginning to develop. He had plenty to work on. Now if he could only figure out what it all meant.

CHAPTER 16

The Box Car Bar had not been hard to find. After MacBridan left the diner, he drove back to New Westminster, stopping for lunch at a small hamburger joint downtown. The guy who had waited on him told MacBridan how to get to the Box Car Bar, but added to the warnings he'd already received against going. "Nothing good ever happens out there. They especially don't like strangers," advised the young waiter.

MacBridan thanked him and drove off. It's not that he looked forward to walking into a hornet's nest, but he needed to talk to Carl Macy, and the bar was the only place he knew to look for him. Macy had been identified as the only individual who had actually socialized with Gerald Vickers. Even though Sheriff Beninger had been the first to warn him about Macy, it was actually Macy's reputation for being a low life that, in a way, encouraged him. Vickers had clearly been involved in the church thefts. If he and Macy had indeed hung out together, then it stood to reason that there was a good chance that Macy was either involved in the thefts, or would at least have some idea who Vickers was working with. Despite Macy's reputation, MacBridan was confident that he would be able to "charm" the information out of him.

The old train station stood next to the tracks, its physical condition having deteriorated to a point of extreme despair. Yet in its time, it had obviously been a grand building, probably the focal point of the surrounding community. But time had moved on, the train replaced by other, more rapid, forms of transportation, leaving the old station behind to fend for itself, slowly withering away. For some reason, this saddened MacBridan. From the look of things, this faint remnant of a more vibrant past wouldn't be there much longer, then it too would be lost.

A railroad spur turned away from the main track at the far end of the old station. At its end, a lone boxcar rested, rusted to the track. The end of the old boxcar had been connected to a one-story, cinder block building, with a corrugated steel roof. Both the boxcar and the building had been painted a dull shade of gray, a long time ago. MacBridan couldn't locate a sign, but he knew he was looking at the "world famous" Box Car Bar.

Two pickup trucks and a beat-up ford station wagon were the only vehicles in the gravel parking lot. Parked next to the door were three motorcycles. One, surprisingly, looked to be a rather expensive Harley Davidson. "And who says crime doesn't pay?" MacBridan laughed.

The bar didn't have any windows that MacBridan could see from his vantage point. The mild exception, one too small to count, turned out to be part of the front door. The door, made of broad, oak panels, had a small, rectangular window at eye level, the glass deeply tinted. The parking lot, littered with several beer cans and a fair amount of broken glass, crunched under his feet as he approached the door. The sound of the old country music song "Your Cheatin Heart" greeted him as he opened the door and went inside. MacBridan had never been a fan of country music.

His eyes took a few moments to adjust to the dim interior, but the Box Car Bar didn't look all that much better on the inside. It was made up of one large room, with a smaller one off to the right of the entrance. The smaller room had two pool tables, both in use. The actual bar itself was large, stretching across the length of the wall directly in front of MacBridan. Other than the guys shooting pool, the only other patron sat slumped over on a stool at one end of the bar. His drink rested in front of him, held firmly with both hands. MacBridan reasoned that this was to insure that no one would take it away from him during his power nap.

MacBridan made his way through the scattered tables and took his place on a stool at the center of the bar. The bartender had closely watched

MacBridan from the moment he'd entered. He was a short man, very heavy, with a round, puffy, red face. His nose and cheeks were laced with veins, open testimony to his frequent and longstanding drinking habit. His blue shirt was stained and looked to be on its third day of use. He stared at MacBridan for a few moments more then walked over and asked, "What can I get you, buddy?"

"I'll take whatever you've got on tap," answered MacBridan in a low, level tone, his face set in a hard, stern look. He returned the same scrutiny the bartender had given him.

The bartender poured the beer and set the glass in front of MacBridan, foam running down one side and onto the bar. "That'll be a buck." The close proximity of the bartender brought with it an odor that told MacBridan that he'd misjudged things. The shirt was definitely on its fifth day of use.

MacBridan reached into his jacket and brought out a money clip, displaying a large wad of bills. The bartender's eyes immediately focused in on the money. MacBridan slowly took out a fifty, put the money clip away, and then slide the bill across the bar. The bartender reached for the bill, but MacBridan didn't move his hand away, holding it firmly to the bar.

The bartender looked up and their eyes locked. "One more thing," said MacBridan. "I need to talk to Carl Macy."

Even though the bar separated them, the bartender stepped back from MacBridan, reevaluating this new customer. Knowing Macy's reputation, MacBridan figured that not many people came looking for him, unless they were either crazy or cops. Although MacBridan didn't believe he looked like a cop, he felt he could potentially meet the requirements of the first qualification.

"Look buddy, I just pour the drinks. I don't know where nobody is."

MacBridan continued to stare at him, then gave a small smile. But the smile only deepened the severe look on his face. The bartender, no stranger to trouble, swallowed hard. Finally, MacBridan said, "It is important to both of us that I talk to him. In fact, I'm sure Carl will be most appreciative of your help."

The little man didn't budge, his eyes darting back and forth between MacBridan and the fifty-dollar bill in front of him.

MacBridan stood up, towering over the bartender. "I'm a patient man, a fair man, and I believe in paying people for their trouble. Now I'm going to take a seat at one of those tables, relax, and enjoy my beer. You locate Carl for me, and you can keep the change. We'll call it a finder's fee."

The bartender studied MacBridan for a moment, and then seemed to come to a conclusion that not only satisfied him, but resulted in a mild amount of backbone. "Macy, huh? Okay, sure, I'll see what I can do. Yeah, you sit and relax. Course, I'm not positive I'll be able to locate him, he's not all easy to—"

MacBridan held up his hand, cutting him off and releasing the fifty at the same time. "It's okay, buddy, I'm sure you'll find a way."

MacBridan picked up his drink and took a table against the wall, one table over from a dimly lit exit door. It was as clean a table as any there, with a large, metal ashtray nearly overflowing with ashes and butts adorning its center. It gave him easy view of both doors, the bar, and the poolroom.

The bartender stayed where he was until MacBridan sat down. Then he picked up the fifty, slowly folded it and put it in his pocket. He then turned and moved down to the far end of the bar where his other customer still sat motionless, hunched over his drink. There was a phone there, and the bartender quickly put it to use.

MacBridan leaned back and waited. He'd stirred the pot. Now it was just a question of time. He had little doubt that the bartender would be able to get a hold of Macy. The guy was a well-known thug and was most probably a big cheese here at the Box Car Bar.

On what appeared to be his third call, the bartender finally reached someone. The conversation didn't last long. MacBridan couldn't help but notice the change in the bartender's attitude after he'd hung up. There was a certain air of confidence, a smugness in the man. He'd definitely reached someone. Someone the bartender believed would properly take care of MacBridan, and he couldn't wait for the fun to start.

Time passed. As it turned out, there just wasn't very much going on to distract MacBridan while he waited. At different times, two of the guys playing pool had come out for drinks. Having a great deal of experience in the area of beer drinking, MacBridan set his mind to figuring out which one of them would have to pee first. Would it be Mr. Overalls, with the extended beer belly, or his bearded friend in the *Dead Head* t-shirt who looked to be about ten to fifteen years older? It was a tough call, but MacBridan finally placed his money on Mr. Overalls. It wasn't the greatest of intellectual exercises, he admitted to himself, but it was something to do.

It had been about forty minutes since MacBridan arrived when the front door opened and two men came in. Both were about six feet tall, but the guy in front easily outweighed his companion by a good sixty pounds. He had a stocky, though not quite muscular, build, dark hair, and a moustache that spread around both corners of his mouth. His outfit included a black leather jacket, jeans, and what appeared to be high top work shoes. He crossed straight to the bar and began to talk with the bartender.

The other guy waited by the door, looking around the bar. He had long brown hair that hadn't been washed in weeks. His blue jean jacket was open, revealing a silver chain with a death's head medallion hanging from it. He too had on jeans. His cowboy boots gave him extra height. A smirk spread across his face as he spotted MacBridan.

The discussion at the bar ended quickly. Leather Jacket turned and looked at MacBridan.

"Hey buddy, here's your man. Thanks for the tip," said the bartender. He clearly thought that his remark was about the cleverest thing ever, and burst out laughing. His laugh was phony though, and far too loud. As no one else laughed with him, he stopped almost as quickly as he'd started, scurrying back down by the phone. He knew what was coming and wanted to make sure he was well out of the way.

Both men headed towards MacBridan's table. MacBridan watched them, casually taking a sip of his drink as they approached. Neither man sat down, but flanked the table on either side. MacBridan pushed the large, nearly full ashtray forward and set his drink down.

"You better not be what I think you are," said Leather Jacket, "cause that'll buy you one world of hurt."

"Name's James MacBridan, and unless you're Carl Macy, we've got nothing to talk about."

Leather Jacket stared down at MacBridan. His friend brought out a small chain and began to twirl it around so that it wrapped around his hand one way, then the other. It was probably meant to be intimidating, but MacBridan saw it as a tell, a nervous tell. The guy was a bit edgy. Good to know.

"Don't have much use for cops, MacBridan. Why don't you show us what kind of badge you're carrying? See if I want to add it to my collection."

MacBridan smiled at this. "You're a collector, too. So am I. But, as I just said, unless you're Carl Macy, we have nothing to discuss."

"I'm Macy, but I don't think I like you," he said as he leaned forward, placing both of his fists on the table.

"He's a cop, Carl, I can feel it," his friend squawked, his voice surprisingly high for a man.

"Is that right, MacBridan? You a cop?"

MacBridan picked up his beer and took another sip. "As I said, I'm a collector. But before we get into that, we're going to have to stop trying so hard to impress each other. Now we can either do some business, in which case we both come out ahead, or one of us can get hurt. Your call."

Macy straightened up, his eyes never leaving MacBridan. He snorted out a short laugh, pulled a chair around and plopped into it. "Okay, MacBridan, I'll hear you out, but it better be good. You're a long way from the door."

"What I have to say is for you and you alone. We don't need your friend."

"You don't give the orders around here, MacBridan; I do. He stays. Now you're running out of time. Say what you got to say while you still can," said Macy, tilting his chair back on two legs.

Macy had lived up to all of MacBridan's expectations. MacBridan could see how his tough guy act would be pretty effective here in a small barnyard, but unfortunately for Macy, it had given him far more confidence than he deserved.

"I want to talk about a friend of yours, Gerald Vickers."

"What about him?"

"Gerald tried moving some rather rare merchandise, but, unfortunately for him, the deal didn't turn out all that well. The people I represent are very interested in the same kind of merchandise that Vickers was selling."

"You're not fooling anybody; you are a cop."

"I'm a collector, Macy, and I'm getting tired of having to repeat myself. The people I work for pay very well for the things they want. Now, you and your friend are beginning to bore me, so let's cut to the chase. I'm here to buy ancient, religious artifacts. If you have access to the same source as Vickers, then we can do some business. If not, I'm wasting my time."

"Vickers got himself killed," said Macy. "He was stupid. You don't cross the kind of people he was tied into and live to tell about it. You're right, MacBridan, you are wasting your time here."

"I don't think I am," countered MacBridan. He reached into his pocket and brought out a picture of the Cross of St. Patrick. "We're very interested in this particular artifact. If you are able to get this specific item for us, we would be willing to pay ten grand, in cash, no questions asked."

The expression on Macy's face told MacBridan that the offer of ten thousand dollars hit a nerve. He studied the picture. Then he looked at MacBridan and slowly shook his head. "Sorry, can't help you. Even if I could, I just don't believe you are who you say you are."

"Sure, but keep the picture anyway," said MacBridan. "My number is on the back. You're a big man around here, Carl, and I have faith in you. You call me, anytime, and I'll follow whatever terms you lay out for the exchange. It's important for you to understand that my employer is a private collector. Very private and we would prefer to handle this quietly."

At this point Jean Jacket decided that it was time for him to insert himself into the conversation. Mimicking Macy, he slipped the chain into his pocket and placed both hands, palm down, on the table. He leaned over, sticking his face as close to MacBridan's as he could. "Maybe you can't hear so good. We can't help you."

The death head's medallion nearly touched the table. His face hung just above the ashtray. His high voice just wasn't scary, and MacBridan almost felt sorry for him. On the other hand, his breath was probably the most intimidating thing about him. Up close MacBridan could see that his face had been scarred from a bad case of acne years ago.

MacBridan smiled at Jean Jacket, inhaling deeply at the same time. Then, without warning, blew as hard as he could into the ashtray, spraying its contents into Jean Jacket's eyes. MacBridan's right hand shot out, grabbed the chain around Jean Jacket's neck, and pulled him across the table. The heel of MacBridan's left hand smashed into Jean Jacket's oncoming face. The crack of his nose cartilage made a loud, sickening sound.

Before Jean Jacket even hit the floor, MacBridan was out of his chair. All of this had caught Macy completely off guard and he was slow to respond. Macy came up swinging; looping a right handed roundhouse punch at MacBridan's head. MacBridan easily sidestepped the punch, grabbed Macy's arm, and taking advantage of Macy's own momentum, twisted his arm painfully up and behind his back. Macy cried out, unable to pull away. MacBridan had Macy off balance. He gripped Macy's shoulder with his left hand and easily forced him back down into his chair. He increased the pressure on Macy's arm, forcing it further up behind him.

"Shit! Stop it, man; you're breaking my arm," cried Macy. The fight had all gone out of him. The poolroom had quickly emptied to watch, but no one joined in. The fight ended almost before it started.

Jean Jacket lay on the floor moaning, his face covered in blood from his broken nose. The bar was quiet except for the seemingly never-ending drone of country music. Everyone watched, waiting to see what would happen next.

MacBridan kept the pressure on Macy's arm. "Your friend is an idiot," MacBridan said quietly to Macy. "My offer still stands. You get me that cross, and you get the ten grand—but lose your partner. Also, and this is important, you ever take a run at me again, and I'll tear your arm off. We clear on this?"

"Yeah, we're clear," muttered Macy between clenched teeth.

MacBridan released his grip on Macy's arm. Remarkably, MacBridan's drink had survived the brief struggle. He looked down at both men, picked up his drink, and took one more sip. "This is a one time offer, Macy. Don't let somebody else beat you to it," he said, turned and left the bar.

CHAPTER 17

All things considered, MacBridan felt that the meeting with Macy had gone pretty well. He'd made contact, so to speak, and had planted the seed of greed that would hopefully inspire Macy to lead him to the missing artifact.

On the way back from the Box Car Bar, MacBridan stopped off at the sheriff's station. True to his word, Beninger had left a copy of the medical examiner's report on the John Doe he was investigating with the dispatcher. MacBridan read through the report. He'd have Cori and their people compare it with the report on Vickers, but he felt reasonably certain as to how that comparison would turn out. He stopped at a UPS store on Main Street and overnighted the report to her.

By late afternoon MacBridan had returned to Katherine's. She was glad to see him and reported that her day had been quiet and most uneventful, which was good to hear. MacBridan returned to the guest cottage to get cleaned up. He also needed to get a hold of Cori. Things were finally beginning to move, but to what end, MacBridan had no idea. What he did know is that he needed additional information, and Cori was the one to get it for him.

"So how are you and Aunt Bea getting along?" asked Cori. "Enjoying your vacation in Mayberry?"

"Don't even try to convince me of the peace, quiet, and serenity of small town life. This place is turning more and more disturbing by the minute, with its own unique collection of oddballs."

"Hopefully that means you're making progress," said Cori. "Has your night stalker returned?"

"No, but it has been an interesting day." MacBridan brought Cori up to date, telling her of his talks with Father Collin and Sheriff Beninger. Neither man had reacted as he'd expected, and that raised some questions that needed answering. He also told her of his encounter, and "business" offer, with Carl Macy.

"Mac, be careful. Don't underestimate these people. They've already killed once, maybe twice, if your theory is correct, and have executed a series of successful thefts," cautioned Cori.

"Not the people I've been dealing with. Vickers, at best, was a bottom level flunky, and Macy isn't much further up the evolutionary ladder. No, we still haven't found the brains behind all this, but I do believe we're getting closer."

"Still, going into that bar alone and confronting him there was taking a pretty big chance."

"Cori, I didn't have many options. Macy is the only one I know of still breathing that had a connection to Vickers. I'm just hoping that the ten thousand dollars will be enough to draw him out, or maybe even flush out his employer."

"And if it's not?"

"Then I go back and up the ante."

"Well, watch yourself, okay? You have no backup, and we can't expect Mrs. Chamberlin to save you every time you get into trouble."

MacBridan wondered if Cori might somehow be in league with Beninger. Why did everyone find that particular event so darn funny? He chose to ignore the jibe. "Here's what I need. Find out all you can on Sheriff Beninger. Family background, are there any large, unexplainable bank accounts, anything that might show some connection to the wrong people."

"Okay, that shouldn't be too hard."

"Good. I also want you to find out as much as you can about the priest, Father Collin Sheary. He's hiding something, and I need to know what it is. He wouldn't be the first man of the cloth to be tempted."

"That's a touch cynical," commented Cori.

"Perhaps, but let's look and see what's there anyway."

"That it?"

"Just one more," said MacBridan. "Get all you can on my future business partner, Carl Macy. It'll be interesting to see exactly what his background is and who he might be tied in to."

"Will do. Now I have something for you. The report came back on that candle wax you sent me. It's not good."

"Tell me about it," said MacBridan.

"As we suspected, they are black candles, similar to those commonly used by satanic groups, so really no surprise there. However, the samples you sent in were composed of more than wax and black dye. I trust you remember how bad they smelled?"

"Of course, they were disgusting," said MacBridan. He remembered the clingy odor all too well.

"Well, hang on to your stomach. Combined with the wax were traces of human blood, along with human remains."

"Human remains?"

"Yes, body fat, melted down and mixed in with the wax. Mac, whoever made those candles is very sick and very dangerous."

"And is that why they smelled so bad?"

"Yes," continued Cori. "As the candles age, the human ingredients continue to decay. Mac, I've been through the *Red Dragon Grimmoire* from beginning to end. These candles, with their special ingredients, are only part of what they need to be successful. They'll need other victims. Human sacrifice plays a critical role for them to be successful." Cori walked him through the *Grimoire*, letting MacBridan know all that the group would need.

MacBridan didn't know what to say. This went well beyond anything he could have imagined. "Could the lab date the candles? I mean as to when they might have been made?"

"I asked the same question," said Cori. "They estimate that they were made ten to twelve weeks ago."

"Dolinski know about this?"

"Not yet, I wanted to tell you first."

"Thanks, I appreciate that. Go ahead and get him a copy of the report. It'll save me some time later when I talk to him."

"Mac, please watch yourself. These people appear to be without any kind of moral base."

"Thanks, Cori, I'll be careful. Let me know as soon as you have anything."

Katherine called MacBridan on the intercom to let him know dinner would be ready at seven. He'd showered, changed clothes, and was surprised to discover just how hungry he felt.

Once again, Katherine had outdone herself in the kitchen. As soon as he entered the house, his appetite went into overdrive. The wonderfully enticing aroma of pot roast filled every room, escalating the demands of his stomach.

Although he didn't go into a great amount of detail with her, MacBridan shared the highlights of his day with Mrs. Chamberlin, from his talks with Father Collin and Sheriff Beninger, to his meeting with Carl Macy. He did not, however, tell her what Cori had reported regarding the candles. He was having enough trouble with that one himself, and, other than needlessly scaring her out of her mind, he could not come up with a good reason to share the information.

"I don't know Carl Macy," said Katherine, "but from stories I've heard about the Box Car Bar, I'm surprised that he even talked with you."

"Usually stories about places like that tend to be exaggerated," said MacBridan. "Macy wasn't really all that hard to draw out. It's all a matter of knowing how much pressure to apply."

"Do you really believe he will call you back?"

"Yes, in all probability he will. It's my belief that I'll hear back from him for one of two reasons, if not both. I'm betting on the old stanza of no honor among thieves and that his mercenary soul will look out for number one and go for the money."

"And the second reason?"

"If the lure of money doesn't work, then he, and whomever else he is working with, will probably want to know more about me. They'll also want more details as to whom I am working for. That information will help them to see if they can shake me down for more than the ten grand that's presently on the table," explained MacBridan. *Not to mention Macy getting the chance to extract a little revenge for the incident in the bar*, but MacBridan didn't share that thought.

"And you believe that all of this is tied into the events going on in the churchyard?"

"Strangely enough, yes, I'm beginning to believe that more and more. We're pretty certain that someone in the area is practicing witchcraft and using Altar Rock as their focal point. Based on the markings that you and I found there, we have a pretty good idea as to the rituals they are performing. These specific rituals help to explain their need for the artifacts, which gives us a different motive for the thefts than we first expected, as well as explaining why they chose Altar Rock."

"Why?" asked Mrs. Chamberlin. "What is so special about Altar Rock?"

"Altar Rock, as well as the artifacts, are all important symbols of the Christian faith. If we're right, then our coven of witches, if you will, has to desecrate holy ground in order to be successful. We believe they'll also need to attempt to use the artifacts in some perverted fashion in order to successfully complete their rituals."

"But I still don't understand why. I mean, what are they after? There has to be some kind of goal in all this," said Katherine.

MacBridan smiled at her and said, "I'm afraid we have now exhausted the limits of my knowledge on this. I have no idea what they're doing or why. If I were to guess, I would imagine that they could be doing all this to recruit new members, trying to show off some kind of imaginary power. Or maybe they believe that they can cast spells on people they don't like, you know. It makes them feel good, getting even with people. Now if it were me, I'd be trying to divine a way of coming up with the correct six numbers for the lottery."

The sun had set about an hour earlier and MacBridan was trying to lighten the mood. Katherine, however, still had more questions. "This doesn't explain why they are watching me. What did I do?"

"At this point all I can offer is a little speculation. These people are something of a private club, and they don't want to draw attention to themselves. With that thought in mind, you not only spotted their activity in the churchyard, but you went out there to look around. Your curiosity into their actions may be the motivation for having someone watch you on the nights they hold their rituals."

"But what could I do? I can't see how I could possibly be of any threat to them."

"Not all of these people—as illustrated by Gerald Vickers—are the sharpest tacks in the drawer. They probably thought that they could scare you into keeping quiet. Instead, you called the Sheriff, and now I'm here. Because of you, their anonymity is now in danger."

"So what do we do?" she asked.

"Exactly what we've been doing. Talking to people, asking questions, all in an effort to either find them, or draw them out. I have to be up front with you; I thought my trip to New Westminster would lead to a dead end. I could not have been more mistaken."

"Well, you have no idea how happy I am that you are here. Last night I actually slept all the way through. It's been a long time since that has happened," said Katherine.

They continued talking as MacBridan helped to clear the table. Against Katherine's protest, MacBridan also helped to clean up the kitchen. "Are you kidding? And let word get back to your nephew that I just sat on my can and let you wait on me? No thanks." They both laughed at this and MacBridan told her goodnight, returning to the guest cottage.

He tried calling Dolinski but couldn't reach him, so MacBridan left a message that he had called. That done, MacBridan settled back on the couch, trying to relax. It had been a full day. Although he felt good with how things had progressed, it now became a waiting game. What would Macy's next move be? Would Macy call him back, and if he did, would it be for the money, or would he be working with the others to lure him into a trap? MacBridan's only real fear was that nothing would happen and he'd be stuck.

Hours passed and eventually MacBridan dozed off. The ringing of his cell phone startled him. He looked at his watch. It was almost eleven. He'd slept for nearly two hours. The phone rang again. *Oh well, my fault for leaving a message*, thought MacBridan. *Why didn't I wait until morning?*

He grabbed his phone and fumbled for the button. "MacBridan," he answered.

"We need to talk," the voice said. MacBridan sat up. He thought he recognized the voice but he couldn't be certain.

"Who's this?"

The response wasn't immediate. "We met this afternoon. You remember."

"We going to do some business?" asked MacBridan.

"I'm not sure yet. You had no right to sucker punch Benny the way you did. You got lucky. We owe you for that, MacBridan."

"Takes you awhile to catch on, doesn't it? That wasn't luck with Benny. My kid sister could handle that loser. I came there to talk with you, not your friend. He insisted on sticking his nose in. I just showed him what happens to people who do that."

"Who are you really, MacBridan?"

"I'm the man with the money. That's all you need to know."

"You still haven't caught on, have you?" Macy nearly shouted. "In case you haven't noticed, there are people involved in this who kill when they're crossed. Vickers crossed them, and you know what happened to him."

The memory of that night caused MacBridan to shudder. He remembered it far more vividly than he wanted to. "Okay, I'm not a cop. I don't work for the police. Let's just say I work for an organization that's in competition with the people Vickers was tied into."

"Competition? What do you mean?"

"I mean that we are interested in the same merchandise. Do you have the cross?"

"I can easily lay my hands on it, but we're not done talking," said Macy.

"I'm waiting."

"Yeah, well look, the ten grand you offered won't cut it. We do this, I'm going to have to get out of here. They killed Vickers, and they'll try to kill me too. I don't plan on hanging around and waiting for that to happen."

"Perhaps I should deal directly with them, keep you out of it," offered MacBridan. "I'd pay you for setting it up, then I'll complete the transaction with them, and that way you stay in the clear."

Macy's laugh was harsh and laced with sarcasm. "MacBridan, you're not as tough, or as bright, as you like to think you are. These people are unlike anything I've ever seen. They'll kill me just for making this call if they find out. No, the only chance you have of getting that cross is through me."

"Alright then, tell me how you want to do this. The offer I made still stands."

"The price is twenty grand, not ten. Take it or leave it. It's like you told me, MacBridan, this is a one time offer."

"That's ridiculous. I'm in no hurry, Macy. Maybe I'll just hang around a few more days, find the people you seem to be so afraid of, the people who actually have the cross, and work something out with them."

"That's so rich. Let me fill you in on some things," said Macy. "They already know who you are. They've been keeping an eye on you, but so far, you haven't done anything to cause them any serious concern. But all that will change the minute you get your hands on that cross. At that point, they'll be coming after you and you won't stand a chance. I'm no coward, MacBridan, but these are the scariest people I've ever known. The price is twenty grand, and for that you get your precious cross from me and a death sentence from them. So what's it going to be?"

It wasn't the threat to his life that bothered MacBridan as he considered the source. What did strike him as remarkable was the fear in Macy's voice. He truly was afraid of these people. Who were they and what had they done to instill such fear? Macy, to the best of MacBridan's knowledge, had always been involved with a tough crowd. What would these people have to be like to put someone who had been around violence all his life in such a state?

"I'll need to examine the cross, Macy. For the kind of money you're asking, I'm going to have to make certain that it is the genuine article."

"All I want is the money," said Macy, "and then I'm outta here. What you do is up to you, but I'd suggest you not stick around. Believe me, MacBridan, they will kill you and there is no stopping them."

"All right, twenty grand. When do I get the cross?"

"Tonight. I'll meet you at the high school."

"I'm not sure I know where that is," said MacBridan.

"The New Westminster High School. It's right across from St. Thomas Church. You'll find it. It's set back from the street. Drive around to the backside of the school. The doors in the center of the school building will be open. I'll be waiting for you inside."

"What time?" asked MacBridan.

"Midnight works for me. Can you get the money?"

"My end is covered. Will you be able to get the cross?"

"Don't worry about it, you just come alone and bring the money, every penny. MacBridan, I'll be ready for you this time. You try anything cute and I'll cut you real good."

The call ended. MacBridan wasn't sure if Macy's offer was on the level or not, but as it was the only offer on the table, he would be there. Should it turn out that Macy was telling the truth, which he felt was unlikely, and brought the cross with him, then his assignment would be complete and the Hawthorne Group would have a happy client. *On the other hand, if it is a trap, then, at least I'll finally find out who is behind all this,* he reasoned.

The most promising sign in their conversation was that Macy had demanded more money. That point alone encouraged him to believe that Macy might be going out on the ledge to pull off his own private deal. Had he just accepted MacBridan's original offer, then the whole thing would have been far more suspect.

Nevertheless, MacBridan prepared for a trap. These people were killers and, based on what he knew, were reasonably smart. On that much, he and Cori agreed. He dressed in jeans, gym shoes, and a thick flannel shirt. He holstered his gun on his belt, and placed it behind him at the small of his back. The black leather pilot's jacket he wore would not only keep him warm, but covered the gun and would help to protect him if things got rough.

He called Katherine on the intercom system to let her know that he was leaving.

Fortunately, she was not yet asleep. He asked her to make sure that all the doors were locked. If anything happened while he was gone, he wanted her to make two calls if she could—the sheriff's office, as well as the state police. He quickly explained that Macy had agreed to the exchange, and he was off to meet with him. She too asked him to be careful. He promised to call and let her know how things had gone just as soon as he could.

As he left the guest cottage, he briefly considered calling Sheriff Beninger. Unfortunately, he just wasn't sure who he could and couldn't trust, which is why he had told Katherine to also call the state police. At the same time, he felt pretty certain that he could handle whatever Macy had planned for him. All it all, it promised to be an interesting night.

CHAPTER 18

The gothic-styled New Westminster High School had been built using 1950s architecture. The large, rambling brick structure stood three stories tall, with several large windows, complete with window ledges and a fine, ornate trim framing them. The L-shaped building stood alone in the center of a small forest of tall oaks and maples, set back a good fifty yards from the street. A low wall ran next to the street, bordering the front of the school grounds.

MacBridan sat in his car, studying the empty building as best he could from across the street in the parking lot of St. Thomas Church. He scanned the old school using a pair of night finder binoculars. Even with their help, the school's darkened windows revealed no signs of life anywhere. For that matter, MacBridan noted, the church and the rectory behind him were also dark.

Aside from the tension gripping the muscles in his neck and shoulders, it was actually a rather comfortable night, at least weather wise. MacBridan estimated the temperature to be in the low fifties, with an overcast sky that blocked whatever help the moonlight might have offered him.

MacBridan drove slowly out of the church parking lot and eased his car into the driveway leading up to the front of the school. As instructed, he veered to the left and made his way to the rear of the building. The driveway emptied into a large, blacktop parking area with tennis courts at the far end. MacBridan pulled into a spot near the center of the school, next to a flight of stone steps leading up to two large doors. MacBridan did not get out right away, but sat there with his window down for a couple of minutes, listening, continuing to study the school and the grounds. It was nearly midnight. Things didn't feel quite right to MacBridan, and it was more than just nervous tension. There was an unnatural quiet to the place.

Finally, he stepped out onto the pavement, locking his car. Once again, he waited, listening, but other than the wind gently blowing through the treetops, nothing else made its presence known. There simply were no lights on anywhere, not even streetlights. This too struck MacBridan as being rather unusual. He carried a long handled, six cell flashlight, but kept it turned off as he made his way up the stone flight of steps. He had no intention of making an easy target of himself.

Of the two doors, the one on the right had been left slightly ajar by a couple of inches. The explanation for this, a hole punched through the glass portion of the door, made itself quite evident. It swung open easily at MacBridan's touch, but made far more noise than he expected or wanted. Quickly he stepped inside, broken glass crackling underfoot.

Moving to his right, MacBridan pressed his back to the wall. With the exception of the door having been broken open, there were no signs of anyone else being there. MacBridan waited, standing perfectly still in the dark stairwell. The door slowly swung shut behind him, its lock snapping into place. The silence blanketing the school grounds was amplified in the cavernous old building, the only exception being the occasional creaking sounds, common in old buildings. His nerves were stretched to the max, waiting for the unexpected to lunge at him out of the darkness.

Making as little noise as possible, MacBridan moved into the school. He immediately came upon two more doors, both securely locked, keeping him in the stairwell. Only two choices were now available to him. He could go down the steps into the gaping jaws of what appeared to be an absolute black hole, or try his luck going up the stairs to the second floor. It was not all that hard a decision for him.

MacBridan climbed the two flights of stairs to the second floor. This brought him to a long hallway running left and right. Directly across the hall was a door and he could just barely make out the number twenty-two above it. Like the back door to the school, it too was partially open. MacBridan waited for a moment, then crossed the hall, and pushed it open, switching the flashlight on at the same time. The classroom was empty, but brought back many memories. There were twenty desks, lined up in four rows, facing the teacher's desk. Besides the blackboard, maps of all sizes covered the walls. History or geography, guessed MacBridan. He preferred history.

MacBridan turned the flashlight off, stepped back into the hall, and waited for his eyes to once again adjust to the near pitch-black hallways of the old school. Standing there, he realized that his breath was coming in short, rapid gasps, almost to the point of hyperventilation; he focused on trying to calm himself down. At this point, MacBridan didn't care what Sheriff Beninger and Cori thought, the idea of having Katherine with him right now sounded pretty darned good.

"MacBridan."

The disembodied voice sounded so loud against the silent backdrop of the school that MacBridan's entire body clenched. He answered, but his voice came across more angrily than he'd wanted it to. "Quit playing games, Macy, I'm in no mood. Where the hell are you?"

Macy chuckled and said, "Take it easy tough guy. Come on back out into the stairwell."

MacBridan cautiously walked back to the second floor landing. He quickly spotted Macy's silhouette above him on the landing halfway between the second and third floor.

"Didn't know if you'd show up or not," said Macy.

"Macy, normally I appreciate a good sense of the dramatic, but don't you think this is a little ridiculous? Why go to all the trouble of breaking into a school when we could have just as easily completed our business outside?"

"Because I'm not taking any chances, MacBridan. You see, I don't trust you, not one little bit. So I had to make sure you came alone. As to the school, I'm not stupid enough to do this out in the open. These people see everything, and we really don't want that."

"Right, I forgot, they're omnipotent."

"They're what?"

"Forget it. Let's see the cross, Macy, that's why we're here."

"Don't rush me, MacBridan. We're going to do things my way. You got the cash?"

MacBridan patted the left breast of his jacket. "It's all here."

"Good, good, that's real nice. Now you wait right there, MacBridan, and I mean don't move an inch. I'm going to get the cross out of safekeeping. Then we'll make our little trade."

Without waiting for a response, Macy turned and went up the remaining steps to the third floor, disappearing from sight. MacBridan quietly moved over to the wall of the stairwell, positioning himself as best he could to keep an eye on the stairs and the hallway. He didn't believe for a minute that Macy was going to play it straight. His right hand checked his gun, loosening it in its holster. He could hear Macy, or someone, moving around in a room at the top of the stairs.

Outside MacBridan could hear the wind as it suddenly began to pick up, rapidly accelerating to a near impossible level. Howling in its intensity, it slammed into the school. The trees became the wind's accomplice, their branches clawing at the windows, in an effort to break through the fragile glass. Below him the wind screeched through the door's broken window, as it struggled to find its way in to the old building. The wind so dominated everything that MacBridan could hear nothing else, losing all track of Macy.

But above it all, he did hear the scream. A scream so filled with anguish that it temporarily froze MacBridan to the spot where he stood. The second scream rivaled the first in its desperation. As best as he could determine, it had come from the third floor, exactly where Macy had disappeared.

Drawing his gun MacBridan raced up the stairs. He could hear Macy more clearly now, screaming, "No, please, no! Get it away from me!"

A door slammed. MacBridan, halfway up, could hear what sounded like desks being thrown across a room, but the wind made it impossible for him to be sure. "Help me, no—" Macy's anguished plea cut off midstream.

MacBridan reached the third floor landing. Nothing moved. Then, everything suddenly went silent. The wind that had risen to near gale force levels in mere moments simply stopped. The change, so abrupt, startled MacBridan. Reactively, he dropped to one knee, both hands leveling his weapon in a defensive posture. MacBridan strained his ears, but everything had gone deathly still.

He waited, but nothing happened. "Macy," called MacBridan, his voice echoing off the walls of the empty hallway. Silence.

Everything had happened too quickly. The wind's violent appearance, coming out of nowhere like a malignant force, made MacBridan wonder if its purpose had actually been to attack the school, attack them. Trying to keep a grip on his nerves, he shrugged the thought off as being ridiculous. How could that be, and where was Macy?

"Macy," shouted MacBridan. He switched on the flashlight, casting its beam up and down the hall, looking in both directions. Nothing. The door across from him hung by one hinge, and MacBridan aimed the bright light into the room. It was another classroom, but it had been utterly demolished.

MacBridan peered through the door. From his vantage point, it appeared as if the windstorm that had struck the school had vented its entire fury in this one room. He couldn't believe his eyes.

All the desks had been swept into one corner, most of them splintered and cracked. Only the blackboard remained hanging on the wall, and it hung precariously so, with just one corner still attached. Paper, and other school supplies, littered the floor. In the center of it all, lay Macy's crumpled body.

MacBridan once again checked the hall behind him. He entered the classroom, moving the flashlight around in a complete circle. He and Macy were alone. Macy lay face down on the floor, but from the twisted angle of the head, MacBridan knew he was dead. He knelt next to Macy, examining him more closely. The throat and neck had been mauled, so much so that MacBridan couldn't tell whether or not the head was even still attached to the body.

Once again, MacBridan looked around the room. He'd missed it when he came in, but near the door, next to the wall, was a dark green canvas bag.

MacBridan moved over to the bag, set his flashlight on the floor and carefully opened it. Inside was a bundle of purple silk. He removed the bundle and laid it on the floor beside the bag. Then, for the first time that night, MacBridan smiled. Much to his delight, wrapped in the delicate fabric, was the Cross of St. Patrick.

"Well I'll be," MacBridan said to himself. "Looks like I misjudged you, Macy."

He quickly rewrapped the cross, putting it back in its bag. Whoever had killed Macy couldn't have gone far. MacBridan felt certain that they had no intention of letting him waltz out of there with the cross in hand. He went back to the door, switched off the flashlight, and waited.

His eyes took longer to adjust; the school remained impossibly silent. Time was against him for he knew he had to get out of there as quickly as possible. All he had to do was go back down to the first floor, out the back of the school, down the last flight of steps and get into his car. A short distance, one that under normal circumstances would have taken him less than a minute or so to cover, but not tonight. Tonight a killer stood between him and the outside. To MacBridan his car seemed a hundred miles away.

He held the canvas bag and his flashlight in one hand, the other gripping his nine-millimeter automatic. The rough texture of the gun's handle reassured him, nothing had ever felt so good. Cautiously he moved out of the doorway and was halfway across the hall when it hit.

For the second time that night, the wind besieged the school. MacBridan froze, frantically looking up and down the hall, but still couldn't see anything. No, something was there. He looked to his right again. At the far end of the hall, his personal nightmare had returned. The dark mass, blacker than pitch, the one he'd first seen in that basement with Vickers, filled the end of the hallway.

It took everything he had to keep from collapsing. The blood rushed to his head, roaring in his ears. He felt completely numb, choking on the nausea that swept over him in a nearly debilitating wave.

Then the thing began to move. This time it appeared to have taken an almost human form but was immense, grotesque in size. MacBridan turned the flashlight directly on it, but the powerful beam of light was of no use. The entity absorbed the light, allowing nothing of itself to be revealed. Two red slits burned where eyes should have been. It was the only thing close to being a feature that MacBridan could make out. It continued its advance towards him, slowly gliding across the floor.

The wind's relentless assault on the school continued, rattling the windows with such force that they were approaching the point of implosion. The temperature in the hallway plummeted. Summoning all his will power, MacBridan forced himself into the stairwell. His movements were mechanical, fear nearly incapacitating him as he moved down the stairs. He was only one step away from the landing between the second and third floor when the cold enveloped him, far more intense than ever.

He chanced a quick glance over his shoulder. The thing was close, too close, standing at the top of the stairs, exactly where he had been only moments before. It was too fast for him! The realization that he would not be able to outrun this thing coursed through his body, chilling him with the knowledge that his death was at hand.

His mind was rapidly reaching the limits that it could tolerate, bordering on panic, losing what little focus remained. His glance back at the creature turned disastrous, causing him to trip over the last step. The canvas bag, the flashlight, his gun, all went flying as he sprawled across the hard surface. He landed hard, nearly knocking the breath out of him. A strength deep inside took over and forced him to roll over on his back, forcing him to watch the final horror.

But the creature had only moved down a couple of steps, stopping in its advance. For some inexplicable reason, it stayed there, hovering on the stairs. Its eyes, though, continued to bore into MacBridan, holding him with hatred beyond anything he could have imagined.

The creature stayed where it was, not moving. MacBridan willed himself to take advantage of the thing's hesitation, trying to catch his breath and trying to understand why it did not finish him off. Only then did he notice the soft, blue white light near his head. Where was that coming from? He wanted to look, but the thought of taking his eyes off that thing for even a moment was out of the question.

Slowly he moved his left hand up above his head, his fingers searching the landing for the source of the light. Something soft lay near his head.

Gently he pulled it to him. He guessed that it was the purple silk that had been wrapped around the cross, which had evidently spilled out of the canvas bag when he fell.

Although his eyes remained fixed on the abomination in front of him, he noticed that the more he pulled the cloth towards him, the more it caused the bluish light to move as well. He had no idea where the light was coming from, nor did he care. All he knew was that he needed some kind of weapon, and the cross would work out just fine until he could get his gun back.

Gradually he edged it closer to him, trying to get his hand on the cross, when the cloth snagged on something. It wouldn't move. He pulled a little harder, but whatever it had caught on held fast. MacBridan tightened his grip on the slick cloth and jerked it as hard as he could. The cloth tore free, but the cross didn't come with it and he heard it clatter to the floor, falling from its protective garments.

The soft blue light now burst forth with a startling brilliance that hurt his eyes. The creature hissed out a pain filled groan and drew back, retreating into the hallway above him with inhuman speed. It disappeared from MacBridan's sight, and stayed out of the direct rays of the light. MacBridan forced himself to sit up and looked behind him.

The Cross of St. Patrick lay on the landing next to him. It didn't make sense, it wasn't possible, but he found the cross to be the source of the light that now filled the stairwell. *That's okay,* MacBridan told himself. *Nothing else is making any sense tonight, why should this?* His gun had slid all the way across the landing. MacBridan picked it up, constantly checking for any movement by the creature lurking in the shadows.

He knelt down next to the cross. He could feel the power of the blue white light that radiated from every part of the ornately carved artifact. After all this, MacBridan certainly couldn't leave it behind, but at the same time, he wasn't sure whether or not he should even try to touch it.

MacBridan briefly caught sight of the creature's eyes. Outside the wind continued to rage against the school. He didn't understand what was holding the creature back, but he had no intention of sticking around to find out.

His gun held at the ready, MacBridan reached out, barely touching the cross with the tip of his finger. He expected it to be hot. Something that bright, that radiant, had to be. Worse case, he figured, he'd try to slide it with his foot back into the canvas bag. Hopefully, that way he'd be able to carry it.

However, much to his surprise, the cross was actually cool to the touch. Not wanting to waste time, he carefully picked it up. The light continued to shine brightly from the cross. MacBridan, one step at a time, began to work his way down the stairs. The creature cried out in frustration. It followed him, but kept its distance, staying out of the light.

The wind nearly knocked MacBridan down as he stepped outside. Putting his gun away, he gripped the railing and made his way down the steps to the parking lot. The wind lashed at his face, stinging him again and again. He saw that a large branch had fallen not far from his car. The cross had dimmed somewhat, but still provided all the light that he needed.

The panic that had nearly seized him inside the school returned as he got close to his car. All four windows had been smashed in, broken glass coating the seats, the tires slashed. At that moment, the doors of the school exploded outward. Glass shards and chunks of wood showered down around him. A large piece struck MacBridan just above the right eye, dazing him, sending him to the pavement.

The creature rushed from the school, glaring at MacBridan from the top of the stone steps. It's eyes burned into him, their color the deep red of molten steel. Miraculously, he'd held on to the cross, and its light blazed again in defiance of the creature. Blood from the cut over his eye partially blinded him. Remembering how the creature had reacted inside, he held the cross up in front of him like a shield.

Again, the creature retreated into the darkness. The angry, wailing moan that erupted from it chilled MacBridan to the core.

Despite the wind battling against him and the injury to his forehead, he made it back to his feet. He had to get away from there, but how, where? With nowhere else to go, MacBridan started down the driveway, mustering a half run. As best he could, he tried keeping the cross between him and the thing that was pursing him.

It became harder to see as the driveway entered the trees, but the cross continued to light his way. The density of the trees caused MacBridan to lose sight of the creature. The wind battled against him, forcing him to slow down. Where was the creature? Where had it gone? The light from the cross created strange shadows causing MacBridan more than once to jump at things that his strained nerves mistakenly took for the creature.

He stumbled and almost went down as he made it to the end of the driveway. He leaned against the low wall for support, all of his strength nearly drained from him. The wall was all that kept him from falling as the creature emerged from the trees, a mere twenty feet away from him. The thing had run a parallel course, flanking him down the driveway. MacBridan cried out in desperation. He feared it more than anything he'd ever known.

He had to keep moving, to stop was to die. Although they hadn't been on earlier, warm, welcome lights now glowed from the windows of St. Thomas. Refuge! Sanctuary! He somehow knew he had to get to the church, his last hope.

Strengthening his hold on the cross, MacBridan stepped into the street. The wind, impossibly sensing his plan to reach St. Thomas, descended on him with even greater force than before. For MacBridan, each step became a struggle. He leaned into the wind, slowly making his way to the church. Between the blood covering his face and the ceaseless assault by the wind, MacBridan could hardly see a thing.

The air around him turned bitterly cold, signaling MacBridan that the creature was near. MacBridan stopped and whirled around. The creature had glided up behind him and was as close now as it had been in the stairwell. The cross had dropped to his side and again he raised it out in front of him. The creature spat out its wailing scream, fleeing off into the darkness.

He was close now. Head down, he continued to inch his way towards the church. Small stones and twigs filled the air, lashing his face and hands. Not ten feet from salvation, disaster struck. Exhausted and battered from the ordeal, MacBridan's feet became tangled up in a branch the wind had blown against his legs and he went down, smacking the pavement. The impact of the fall caused the cross to fly from his hand, leaving him utterly defenseless.

MacBridan looked up at the creature. It sensed his vulnerability. The thing loomed over the parking lot, gloating down at him, oblivious to the wind swirling around it. MacBridan struggled to get to his feet, and with one last effort lunged forward, throwing himself up the few steps that lead to the church's doors. The intense cold spread across him as the creature charged.

MacBridan's shoulder struck the church doors dead center, flinging both of them open. He landed on the cold marble of the church's foyer. Behind him, the creature's wailing scream filled his ears. Then, all went quiet. The wind stopped. The cold that always accompanied the creature disappeared. MacBridan dragged himself a few feet further into the church, collapsing on his back. He was too weak to even call for help.

As he laid there, his eyes closed, MacBridan sensed someone standing over him. *Good. If there was ever a time when I needed a priest, this is it,* he thought. *Besides,* MacBridan reasoned, *Father Collin is probably the only one who might, at least in part, believe what just happened to me.* He also hoped that once he got done telling the events to the priest, that Father Collin would have an explanation. His exhausted body ached and his mind was reeling, but he fought to remain conscious. He had to, at least long enough to warn Father Collin not to go outside.

His eyes slowly opened, but the figure standing over him was not Father Collin. He blinked his eyes several times, trying to clear his head, but despite his efforts, Father Collin did not appear. The man standing over MacBridan was tall, a few inches over six feet, with a slender, athletic build. His hair, ash blonde, was long and tied in a ponytail. The eyes were a pale, watery blue set in a face of Slavic heritage. MacBridan knew this man. He knew that at one time he had been extremely dangerous, a killer of the first magnitude. He also knew that over two years ago, he had died. This, on top of everything else, was more than MacBridan could take. Finally, peacefully, his mind turned off, slipping away into darkness.

CHAPTER 19

Only an hour had passed since MacBridan burst into St. Thomas, but during that time, the area surrounding the high school and the church had become a beehive of activity. MacBridan rested in a chair in Father Collin's office, near the back of the church. An EMS technician had examined the cut over his eye, cleaned the wound and bandaged it. MacBridan dismissed the idea that he should go with them to the hospital so that a doctor could further examine him.

He leaned back, closed his eyes, and took full advantage of the quiet. He was alone, but knew that would not last. His mind continued to go over all that had taken place in the school, as well as his desperate race to the church. He found himself incapable of understanding what had happened, what had killed Macy, and what had pursued him. The only explanation he could come up with that was even remotely logical was that he was losing his mind. MacBridan smiled to himself at the idea that he was going crazy, even though Cori had accused him of this many times before. Funny to think she might have been right all along.

Putting aside his potentially deranged state of mind, he took stock of his physical condition. The Advil he'd been given had not done anything to ease the pounding in his head. The EMS tech had argued with MacBridan that he needed stitches to properly close the cut over his eye, but they had eventually compromised on a butterfly dressing. He had also received some other small scratches on his face and hands. Last, but not least, to top it all off, his right shoulder throbbed.

This was the same shoulder he'd hurt in the confrontation with the stalker in front of Katherine's house. When he hit the doors of the church, it was his right shoulder that had led the way. Nothing was broken, but it had already been sore to the touch and he'd succeeded in bruising it all over again. In short, mind and body, he was a mess.

The door to the office had been left open and he heard footsteps coming down the center isle of the church. He listened carefully but couldn't make out if there were two or three people approaching the office. He didn't care.

"Wake up, MacBridan. We've got a lot of questions for you." MacBridan opened his eyes to find Sheriff Beninger standing in front of him. A deputy he didn't know leaned against the doorframe of the church office.

"You'll understand if I don't get up," said MacBridan.

"Don't try being cute, MacBridan. You're not looking too good on this thing."

"You can't be serious. You actually believe I killed Macy? Come on, Sheriff, that's a reach for even a rookie cop."

Beninger sat down on a corner of the priest's desk. "Well let's take a look at this from my point of view. You come into town looking for a stolen cross, a cross you failed to recover during a ransom exchange with Gerald Vickers. A confrontation, I might add, that Vickers didn't survive."

"You know I was cleared of that, Beninger. There were witnesses, remember?"

"Witnesses that work with you. Witnesses being paid by the same client with the same deep pockets that you continue to represent. Yeah, I remember. It's never left my mind."

"So you come into town," continued Beninger, "trying to find who, if anyone, might have been in on the robberies with Vickers. So I give you Macy's name as someone who hung out with him."

"Your contributions have been invaluable," said MacBridan.

"Shut up, MacBridan. So you go and see Macy, which resulted in a fight between the two of you at the Box Car Bar."

"That's not entirely accurate, but like they say, close enough for government work."

Beninger glared at MacBridan. "And now, not twenty-four hours later, Macy turns up dead, the result of yet another ransom exchange—with you—that went bad. Cause of death: injuries very similar to those that Gerald Vickers sustained when he met his death. Pretty darned coincidental, wouldn't you say?"

"More than that, I'd say there's a pattern emerging, but you're going off in the wrong direction," answered MacBridan.

"Well MacBridan, you're just going to have to help me get back on track. If I understand your story, Macy called wanting to sell you the cross and told you to meet him at the school. Following his directions, you were able to get into the school, thanks to Macy having broken open the back door. He goes to get you the cross and someone unknown kills him. You grab the cross, find your car has been vandalized, and barely make it to the church because whoever killed Macy then went after you. Is that about it?"

"You know, Sheriff, if the next election doesn't work out, there's a career in writing *Cliffs Notes* just waiting for you."

"MacBridan, they're just going to love your sense of humor in prison."

"Where's the weapon?" asked the deputy. "What'd you use on that guy anyway?"

MacBridan stared at him for a moment, then looked at Sheriff Beninger and said, "I'll do you one better. Forget the weapon. Where's the blood?"

"What are you talking about?" asked Sheriff Beninger.

"From what I could tell, Macy nearly had his head torn off. We've been through this before, Sheriff. Where was the blood? I didn't see much, and an injury like that would have coated that room in gore."

Before Beninger could respond, the deputy chimed in again. "That's not hard. You killed Macy somewhere else, brought his body to the school and dumped it. But, as you were leaving, you ran into some of his buddies and you barely escaped to the church. We may be a small department, but that doesn't make us idiots."

"Yes, well, I'd say the jury's still out on that one," said MacBridan.

The deputy straightened up and started toward MacBridan, but Sheriff Beninger held up his hand, stopping him.

"The coroner has come to some of the same conclusions as the deputy," said Sheriff Beninger. "Due to the fact that there was so little blood at the crime scene, he suggested the body might have been moved."

It took some effort on his part, but MacBridan smiled at the Sheriff. "Okay, let's follow that line of thought. I run Macy's throat through a mulching machine. I then put his body in my car, drive to the school and break in. Not content with the first floor, I carry him up multiple flights of stairs and then dump his body in the first classroom I find. Being filled with abundant energy, I decide to stick around and tear the place up. Needing an alibi, I then destroy my car, hit myself in the head, and for added effect, pass out in the church."

No one said anything, so MacBridan continued. "But we still have the same problem. Where's the blood? You're not going to find any on me. There's not any in my car, nor is there any on the steps leading up to that classroom. It doesn't hold up. It doesn't hold up because that's not what happened."

Sheriff Beninger thought for a moment, then shook his head and said, "I hear you, MacBridan, but the problem is that I know you're still not telling me everything. For that matter, your own argument could actually work against you. What did become of the blood? If he had died in that classroom, like you say he did, then you're right, it should have been a mess in there. No, I'm sorry, but it's your story that doesn't hold up."

MacBridan leaned his head back on the chair; the pounding in his head wasn't getting any better. "I don't know. I can't explain it either, but it's what I was referring to earlier. There's a pattern here, and it's real, but it doesn't make any sense."

"What pattern?" asked Sheriff Beninger.

"By my count, we have three unexplained deaths," answered MacBridan. "There's Vickers, the John Doe out by the railroad tracks that you're investigating, and now Macy. All of them from New Westminster, or perhaps, in the case of your John Doe, just passing through, and all three killed in the same manner. And, perhaps the most significant point, at all three crime scenes there was far less blood than there should have been."

"My John Doe was killed by animals," challenged Beninger.

"Oh really? What animal?" asked MacBridan. "What animal did they identify as having killed that guy?"

"They found teeth marks on some of the vertebrae, fangs from an animal."

"What kind of animal?" MacBridan persisted.

Beninger stood there, staring at MacBridan, his face nearly devoid of expression. "They don't know," he said quietly. "So far they haven't been able to identify it."

"The same with Vickers," said MacBridan. "The only bright spot, if you can call it that, is if we find that the teeth marks in all three deaths match up, we'll be one step closer."

Deputy Goodman entered the office and went over to Sheriff Beninger. "Sheriff, I've been over that parking lot several times, but it's not out there."

"You sure?" asked Sheriff Beninger.

"I even checked the shrubs around the front of the church. Nothing."

Sheriff Beninger directed his gaze at MacBridan. "You claim that someone chased you out of the school. Finding your car disabled, you made a run for the church, fell out in the parking lot, and at that point, you lost the cross. Is that right?"

"Yes," sighed MacBridan. "That's right."

"We couldn't find it, MacBridan. Deputy Goodman searched the entire area, but it's not there."

"I'm not surprised," said MacBridan. "They may have failed to get me, but they got the cross back."

"MacBridan, give it up. We have no evidence of anyone else being there except for you and Macy. There is also no evidence of this cross you claim he brought to sell to you."

"You didn't find anything? Not the canvas bag? Nothing?"

"We found the bag," answered Sheriff Beninger, "but so what? It doesn't prove anything. You're either holding out on me, again, or you're just plain lying. Either way there are too many things here that just don't fit. Looks like I'm going to have to take you in, MacBridan."

"God bless all here," the familiar Irish lilt interrupted. They all turned to find Father Collin standing in the doorway.

"How long you been standing there?" Beninger asked.

"Not all that long, and I didn't want to interrupt, but I believe I may be able to provide some assistance."

"How so, Father?" asked Sheriff Beninger.

"As it turns out, I'm a witness to some of Mr. MacBridan's story. Based on what I saw, I believe he is telling you the truth."

Beninger gave the priest a hard look and said, "What exactly did you see, Father?"

"Some unfinished business brought me back to the church. I was here in my office when that terrible wind storm started."

"Working rather late, weren't you, Father?" The Sheriff's tone held a trace of skepticism.

"I'm afraid it was something I couldn't get off my mind, and I knew the only way to put it to rest was to get it done."

"All right, go ahead, Father, what did you see?"

"As I said, I was here in my office when the wind came up; its intensity startled me. It was so strong that after a few minutes I thought I had better take a look around; make sure that everything was okay. One tree in particular was pounding against the side of the church. So I stepped outside and walked around to try and see if it was doing any damage."

"Exactly what were you planning to do, Father?" asked Sheriff Beninger.

"The stained glass windows here at St. Thomas are very old, true works of art. My thoughts were to call the fire department if I felt the tree might damage one of them."

"The fire department?"

Father Collin smiled, mildly embarrassed. "Yes, it sounds silly, I know, but at the time they were the only ones I could think of who might have been able to help me. My thoughts were to have them cut the tree down before it could do its worst."

"I see," said Sheriff Beninger, staring at the priest. "That's all very interesting Father, but I fail to see what that has to do with backing up MacBridan's story."

"I do run on so," said Father Collin. "Let me get to the point. As I stood there trying to figure out if the tree was doing any harm, I saw something move out of the corner of my eye. A man ran out of the trees, away from the school. He crossed the road and came toward the church. At first I had no idea who it was, but as he got closer I could see that it was Mr. MacBridan."

"Was he alone? Did you see anyone else?"

"No, not at first. Actually, seeing anyone out so late at night, in the middle of that storm, took me quite by surprise, and I stood there awestruck, rooted to the ground, watching. Then I saw a second person come out of the trees close to the same place where Mr. MacBridan had been, and it was obvious to me that this man was chasing him."

"Did you recognize the other man?" asked Sheriff Beninger.

"No, I didn't, and I've been giving that a great deal of thought. I'm afraid I never got a good look at him."

Sheriff Beninger considered that for a moment. "Okay, then what happened?"

"Finally my senses returned to me, and I realized that Mr. MacBridan needed help. I started toward the front of the church, but it was dark where I was, so I couldn't move too quickly. I made it to the parking lot in time to see Mr. MacBridan fall. The other man continued to charge forward, but Mr. MacBridan was able to pull himself up and seemed to dive into the church. At that point, I yelled out. I'm surprised the other man heard me over the wind. My being there must have surprised him because he stopped, looked at me, turned and ran away."

"MacBridan said he had a cross with him. Did you see the cross Father?"

"Not clearly, no. However, when Mr. MacBridan fell, I did see something fly from his hand, but my focus was on his assailant."

"What did you do next?" asked Sheriff Beninger.

"I ran to the door and found him lying on the floor. He was unconscious, and I could see that he'd been hurt. I didn't want to move him, but I had to get him further inside. I then locked the doors and called your office."

"Did MacBridan tell you what had happened?"

"Poor Mr. MacBridan didn't come to until the medical people brought him around. I had no idea what had taken place until I heard him tell you about that unfortunate man at the high school. I left Mr. MacBridan here in my office as he was being taken care of, and followed you and your people across the street."

Beninger turned and looked at MacBridan. "This changes things somewhat."

MacBridan smiled and said, "Now that is what you call the luck of the Irish. No offense, Father."

Father Collin didn't respond, but walked over behind his desk and sat down, a trace of a smile played at the corners of his mouth.

"Father, it may be necessary to have you make a formal statement to what you just told us."

"As always, it's my pleasure to help."

Sheriff Beninger stood directly in front of MacBridan. "At this time I don't have enough to hold you on, but you make sure you stick around and don't wander off. This is far from being over."

"I'm not going anywhere. I want these people as much as you do," said MacBridan.

"Come on, MacBridan. I'll have Deputy Goodman drop you off at Mrs. Chamberlin's," said Sheriff Beninger.

"That's all right, Sheriff," said Father Collin. "Mr. MacBridan's been through a great deal. Let's let him rest some more, then I'll take him back."

Beninger nodded. "Take care of yourself, MacBridan; you look like something the cat dragged in." With that, he and his deputies left the office. Father Collin followed after them, and MacBridan could hear what sounded like the priest locking the front doors.

As Father Collin walked back through the office door, MacBridan looked at him and said, "Forgive us, Father, for we have sinned."

"Now whatever are you talking about? Let me help you, and we'll go over to the rectory. It is far more comfortable, and we could both do with something stronger than water."

MacBridan was none too steady on his feet. However, with the priest's help they left the church and followed the path to the rectory. It impressed

MacBridan how easily the priest held his 220 pound frame up, quietly demonstrating a surprising degree of physical strength.

Father Collin deposited MacBridan into the same chair he'd occupied during their first visit. He left, but quickly returned, placing a blanket over MacBridan's shoulders. The priest then went out to the kitchen, returning with two glasses and a bottle of Jamison.

The whiskey tasted good. MacBridan could feel its warmth begin to spread throughout him. Both men sat quietly. "I want to thank you for all you've done, Father, especially that story you told about watching me run to the church. Not to put too fine a point on it, but you lied to our good sheriff. Why?"

"Now isn't that the pot calling the kettle black? It seems to me we'll both have something to bring up in confession. Mr. MacBridan. I feel it's time we were a little more open with each other, wouldn't you agree?"

"Perhaps you could set the example for us, Father."

"Very well. You are very good at what you do, to have found so much in so little time. You're right, of course, there is a coven here in New Westminster worshiping the devil. I didn't think too much of it at first. Every community has its fringe, and I thought it was harmless, but that soon changed."

"How so?"

"Altar Rock seems to be where they perform many of their rituals. Twice now, I've found blood on it, and on the ground around it. Not much, mind you, but enough to raise my level of concern. In fact, even then I never really considered them a threat to anyone until they carved those symbols you saw on the base of the rock."

"The blood wasn't enough?"

"My heavens, no," chuckled the priest. "The simple practice of animals being sacrificed is not unusual. The symbols, though, now that was quite a shock, they changed everything. Do you know what they are, what they mean, Mr. MacBridan?"

"We've translated them as best we can. We believe that they relate to a spell, or ritual, to bring the dead back to life."

Father Collin stared into the glass he was holding, swirling the whiskey around the bottom. "That's near enough, I suppose, but this specific ritual is very old, very dangerous. That is what has had me so worried lately. To our knowledge there are very few people alive who have knowledge of rituals such as this."

"Father, I don't want to upset you any more than you already are, but this information is out there for anyone who wants it. There are books that have been published on it, not to mention what's available on the Internet."

"Oh please, Mr. MacBridan, I'm not a complete idiot. Yes, there is a great deal of published material available, but it is all very general knowledge, worthless for all intents and purposes. No, in this case there is one amongst this coven who knows the ancient secrets, the intimate details necessary to complete this terrible spell."

"How do you know this?"

"It is my business; it is what I do. The church has battled this evil for centuries, and the fight continues to this day." Father Collin leaned forward in his chair looking directly into MacBridan's eyes. "You ask me how I know this. Tell me, Mr. MacBridan, what was it that killed Macy tonight? What was it that chased you from the school? But most importantly, what was it that saved you tonight?"

"I have no idea what that was, Father, but I can tell you this. I have never known the kind of gut wrenching fear that I feel for that thing. This is hard for me to say, but you don't know how hard I fought just to keep from giving in to sheer panic."

"Now there you are wrong. I do know how you felt, and I know why. Whether you are aware of it or not, much of your fear was instinctive, and not based on just being afraid of losing your life. Tonight your very soul was at risk."

"I'm not following you, Father, slow it down."

"I can help you, Mr. MacBridan, but first I need for you to tell me what happened in that school. Tell me everything, every detail and not the piece parts that you gave to Sheriff Beninger. I believe your story to him was perhaps as inventive as my own."

MacBridan hesitated at first but was soon deep into the details. He had not opened up to anyone regarding this monster, and it was something he wanted to do, something he needed to do. He had to get it out to someone who wouldn't immediately think he'd lost it. Father Collin asked several questions, especially regarding the cross and the light it gave off. When he finally finished, Father Collin poured them each another drink.

"You were very fortunate to have had the Cross of St. Patrick with you this evening, Mr. MacBridan. Whether you can understand this or not, having it there saved you and would have saved Macy too, if he'd just taken it out of the bag."

"I'll be honest with you, Father, if I hadn't been there, I'd have a hard time believing any of this. But the light, where did it come from? Why did that thing back off?"

"Good versus evil. It is the simplest explanation that I can give. I'm not trying to preach to you, but tonight you witnessed the power of God. Through that holy relic he reached out and saved you." The priest stopped talking and settled back in his chair, deep in thought.

After a while MacBridan said, "That's the second time I've seen that thing, Father, the first was in the basement of that building with Vickers. Unless I'm mistaken, that's what killed him. It appeared to have a more definitive form tonight, but it was the same creature. What I don't understand is that I didn't have the cross with me when I met with Vickers. Why didn't it kill me then?"

"Because it wasn't directed to kill you. I'm sure they didn't even know anybody else would be there with Vickers. Tonight was different, tonight it was sent to destroy you and Macy. Each time it kills, it gets stronger, and—as you saw—begins to take on a more definitive form. It is growing, and so is their ability to control it."

MacBridan mulled that over then shook his head. "This is too impossible to believe."

"Believe it, Mr. MacBridan. It is what we are up against. You've been very blessed, twice now, but even your good fortune may not come through a third time."

"I'm trying, but this is beyond anything I've ever experienced," said MacBridan. "While we're at it, I have one more thing to discuss with you, Father. Before I passed out, someone came and stood over me. I had expected to see you, but it wasn't."

"Who was it?"

"The man who stood over me is dead, or at least he's supposed to be. He died in Europe a couple of years ago."

"This man, he was a friend of yours?"

"Not hardly. He was an East German assassin named Ubel Obermann. Now how do you explain that, Father?"

"This man, Obermann, you feared him?"

"Father, anyone who knew of this guy feared him. He was a merciless killer of the worst kind."

"The worst kind?"

"Yes," said MacBridan, "he enjoyed it."

"Mr. MacBridan, tonight you faced death, barely escaping. By the time you made it to the church, you had reached the limits of your endurance. Your mind was deeply affected by the fear you had experienced. Despite who you think you saw, I was the one who pulled you into the church. Me, not some phantom from years ago."

MacBridan was beginning to fade fast. Exhaustion, extreme nervous tension, and the flat out beating he'd taken were all finally beginning to take their toll. "If you say so. I think I need to lie down."

"Of course, how thoughtless of me, we can talk more tomorrow. Please, let me help you to my car."

The priest's car was parked under the trees near the church.

As they drove to Katherine's house MacBridan said, "Father, you never did tell me what that thing is. Do you know?"

"I'm pretty sure I know the grimoire that this coven is working. That creature is not of this world. It has been brought straight out of the pit, at the coven's bidding, and will continue to be brought forward as they continue working this grimoire through to its end. Had it reached you, nothing could have saved you."

"Please, Father, I'm really tired. 'Out of the pit'? I'm just not understanding what you're telling me."

"A demon, Mr. MacBridan, a demon from the deepest pits of Hell, a very dangerous entity capable of a fate truly worse than death. As I said, the Catholic Church has encountered creatures like this before. This thing not only takes its victims life, but it consumes their soul, condemning its victims to eternal damnation."

MacBridan continued to stare at the priest. "You're serious, aren't you?"

"Yes, unfortunately so for all of us."

CHAPTER 20

Katherine stood next to his bed, shaking his shoulder. "Mr. MacBridan, you need to wake up. You have a call."

With a great deal of effort, MacBridan opened his eyes and tried to sit up, but his body wasn't quite ready to obey. His shoulder ached and the cut above his eye continued to throb. "Good morning," he said, his voice little more than a raspy whisper.

"I didn't want to disturb you," explained Mrs. Chamberlin, "but your assistant, Cori, she's on the phone. Said she needed to talk to you right away. I tried to raise you over the intercom. When you didn't respond I thought I'd better come right over."

"Thanks," said MacBridan, this time successfully making it to a sitting position. Thankfully, before the covers fell back he realized he wasn't wearing anything. MacBridan saw that his clothes had been piled in a chair across the room. He didn't remember undressing. Shoot, for that matter he didn't even remember getting back to the cottage. "Seems I owe someone a thank you. Did you help me last night, Katherine?"

"No, all I did was unlock the door. Father Collin came and got me, and together we brought you here. He undressed you and helped you into bed. I suggested calling Dr. Appleton, but Father didn't think that was necessary."

"Well, thank you. It turned out to be quite a night."

"Father Collin said you'd had a run in with that gang. He told me Macy is dead and that you barely escaped. Can I get you anything? You poor man, you look terrible."

"It's my hair," said MacBridan. "I always have a bad case of morning hair, makes me look worse than I feel."

"You don't have to make light of this on my account."

"Of course not," said MacBridan, managing to get out a small smile without wincing. "Some Advil would be most appreciated."

"Very good, I'll be right back. Don't forget your assistant, she's still waiting."

MacBridan waited until Katherine left and then got up. He was a little unsteady at first, but managed to put on his pants and throw on a shirt. He walked over to the couch, sat down and picked up the phone. "Cori?"

"Well it's about time. You going to live?"

"Hard to tell at this point, but I'll get back to you."

"Mr. MacBridan?" The voice was Katherine's. "I'll hang up now."

"Thank you," said MacBridan, as he heard the click of the phone at the house.

"You know, in Mrs. Chamberlin you have quite a guardian angel. If things keep going the way they have been you may have to hire her on full time."

"Yeah, I've got to hand it to her, she's an amazing lady."

"Did she tell you she called Dolinski?" asked Cori.

MacBridan let his head drop down on the back of the couch. "No, she failed to mention that little detail."

"After the priest brought you back, she called him and told him what had happened."

"I'm guessing, coming from her, that he didn't take the update all that well."

"No, not at all," said Cori. "He called me and told me to meet him here at the office at seven. He's been on the phone with Beninger twice already, and he should be joining us in just a moment."

"What did he learn from the sheriff?"

"It seems your charm has failed to work its magic on Sheriff Beninger. Right now you're at the top of his list as possible suspects in the death of Macy."

"I didn't kill him, Cori," said MacBridan.

"I know that. Dolinski told him the idea was absurd."

"What else did the sheriff have to say?"

"Not a great deal. He said that you claimed to be trying to work an exchange with Macy, someone else intervened, and things got rough."

"He had it, Cori. The Cross of St. Patrick, he actually had it. As hard as it is to believe, New Westminster actually holds the answers to Vickers's death, the thefts of the artifacts, everything that's been going on."

"Sheriff Beninger also said you'd been hurt. How are you, James?"

"I'm okay, just scuffed up here and there. Did he tell Dolinski how Macy died?"

"On that, he went into some detail. It's sickening."

"Ring any bells?" asked MacBridan.

"You know it did. The similarities between his death and Vickers weren't lost on Dolinski or me."

"Don't forget to add the John Doe that Beninger is investigating to our list. That makes three men to die in the same way in a very short period of time, all with ties to New Westminster."

"Mac, do you know who's doing this?"

MacBridan considered how to answer her. He really didn't know who was responsible, but that wasn't the problem. The hard part was that, even though he had seen it twice, he couldn't even identify what was actually doing the killing. "Not yet, I haven't gotten a good look at them either time."

"Hold on," said Cori, "Dolinski wants me to conference him in."

MacBridan waited while Cori worked the phones. He wasn't comfortable with the position that circumstances had placed him in. He wanted to tell them what was going on but also realized that he could only go so far. MacBridan wasn't ready to believe in killer demons himself, much less even consider offering that up as a possibility to Dolinski. On the other hand, he knew the time had come to ask for backup. Things had progressed to a point where it would not be possible for him to stay after these people and protect Katherine at the same time.

"Mac, you still with us?" Dolinski's loud voice shot from the phone.

"Good morning," answered MacBridan.

"It appears that things have escalated on your end. Fill me in. What's happening up there?"

MacBridan began his narrative with the call from Macy and their agreement to meet at the school. He gave them as much detail as he could, but left out the role the cross had played, as well as Father Collin's explanation of what it was that had attacked him. He explained to Dolinski that even though he hadn't gotten a good look at his attacker, he felt certain that it was the same "person" who had killed Vickers. For now, it was the closest he dared to get to the truth of the matter. He finished up his report with the interrogation by the sheriff.

Dolinski didn't respond for a few moments, then asked, "So what is your plan from here?"

"I have to keep the pressure on them. Hopefully, they'll now believe that I'm too much of a liability to keep alive and come after me. That said, I'm not just going to sit around and wait for them to act. I'm going to backtrack on Macy. Who were his friends? Did he live with anyone? Where did he work? New Westminster is too small a town, and unlike Vickers, Macy was a bit of a local hotshot. Someone will know something because we now know that there are definitely others in the area who are involved."

"I'm sure you realize the people watching my aunt's home are somehow tied into this," stated Dolinski.

"Yes, I am, but at the same time, I can't leave either. Macy told me that they know I'm staying here, and I don't want that to change. If I don't find them first, then maybe they'll come looking for me. Either way we learn who they are."

"What about Mrs. Chamberlin?" asked Cori. "Let's not forget that we've managed to put her right in the middle of things."

"Cori, she's been in the middle of things from the start," said MacBridan. "But you're right; she can't stay here any longer. I suggest that one of our people pick her up and take her somewhere safe until this is over."

"Fat chance of that happening. You obviously don't know my aunt that well, MacBridan," said Dolinski. "She'll be highly offended even at the suggestion of letting someone run her out of her own house."

"Then I'm going to need backup. We all know there's a good chance they might go after her to get at me. She may not like it, but we need to move some of our people in with her."

"Agreed. I'll have them on their way within the hour. Unless you hear otherwise, expect Smithers and Harry to join you sometime late this morning."

"Would you like me to talk with her? Tell her that she'll be having some of our people staying with her for the next couple of days?" offered MacBridan.

"No," said Dolinski, "I'll do it. This will not be an easy negotiation, and I'd rather keep you on her good side."

"Then I'll wait until after you've talked with her before I say anything," said MacBridan. "I've been as open with her as I can and I think she understands how serious this is."

"Very well," said Dolinski. "You know what is at stake here. Anything Mac, anything at all, you let us know and you got it," said Dolinski, then dropped off the call.

No one said anything and MacBridan wondered if they'd both hung up. "Cori?"

"I'm here. Are you sure they're all the backup you'll need?"

"You're not losing confidence in me, are you? Look, I really wouldn't need them, but I can't leave Mrs. Chamberlin alone. Come on, Cori, I've been in far tighter spots than this before."

"Yes, but this is different."

"How?"

Cori didn't answer at first. "This is the first time I've ever known you to hold out on us. I don't know why, but I know you're not telling us everything, and that scares me."

That she had seen through his story didn't really surprise MacBridan, as Cori knew him all too well. Truth was, he wanted to tell her everything but also knew she wouldn't believe it any more than he did, and he'd witnessed everything first hand.

"Cori, last night was pretty tough. There were a couple of times I wasn't sure I was going to make it. I'm just tired, and frankly hurting in more places than I care to think about. That's all."

"You can trust me, Mac, with anything, you know that," said Cori.

"I do trust you, Cori, there's nothing to worry about," he said as he heard a light tapping on the door. Katherine stepped inside, smiled at him and set two Advil down in front of him along with a glass of water. She slipped out as quietly as she'd entered, closing the door behind her. Maybe Cori was right, maybe he should consider hiring her. "Were you able to find anything on Macy or the sheriff?"

"Some, but I don't know how much it will help," said Cori. "Macy was a small time hood with a long history of run-ins with the police, but never anything too serious. Like Vickers, he didn't have any immediate family that we could find, even though he did grow up near New Westminster."

"What did he do for money?" asked MacBridan.

"According to the tax records we accessed, for the past couple of years he's been working at Furr's Antiques. It has a New Westminster address."

"Anything else?"

"That's about it. Sheriff Beninger's information is almost as lightweight. Like Macy, he's lived in the area his whole life. He went into the military right after high school, the Army, and became an MP. He's served as sheriff there for the past seventeen years and as best we can tell, runs a pretty clean shop. In fact, at least until you hit town, the crime rate in New Westminster had almost been nonexistent."

"Thanks, Cori. Just keep feeding me those little confidence boosters," said MacBridan.

"My pleasure."

"Not much to go on is there?" asked MacBridan. He went over everything Cori had told him and it added up to precious little. Outside of stopping by the antique shop, he really didn't have anywhere else to look, no one else to talk to. And this time, he certainly couldn't drop by and see what Sheriff Beninger knew.

"Perk up, it's not all that bad. I've left the most interesting news for last."

"I'm too tired for perky. What have you got?"

"It turns out that our true man of mystery is none other than Father Collin," reported Cori.

"Really?" mused MacBridan. "What did you find out about him?"

"Almost nothing and as you know, that in itself is nearly impossible. Everyone has a past, but not this guy. The only thing we could confirm is that he is a priest. Dolinski called Archbishop Kerry and asked if he could help us. The Archbishop tried but didn't get any further than we did. He even called Rome but hit a wall of secrecy. Yes, he's a priest, they acknowledge that, but anyone who might know anything more can't be reached."

"What about his educational background? Where did he attend seminary?"

"That's just it, this guy's file, assuming there even is one, is blank. He exists, but not on paper or the internet. There are no written records on him that gives us anything more."

"Now that is interesting. I mean, even people placed in the witness protection program have backgrounds. They're fake, of course, but they have them all the same, just in case someone does decide to look," said MacBridan.

"It frustrated me that we couldn't find anything," Cori continued. "So I thought about it and decided to check out his present position a little more, see if that might shed some light on things. What I found is most intriguing. Prior to Father Collin's arrival, Monsignor Henry had been the priest at St. Thomas for fourteen years."

"Yes, Father Henry. Dolinski mentioned his name to me. I remember Dolinski being surprised when I told him that the priest at St. Thomas was Father Collin. He speculated that Father Henry had probably retired."

"He didn't retire," said Cori. "Monsignor Henry died in a freak accident earlier this year, May fourteenth to be exact."

"What kind of accident?" asked MacBridan. Here was yet another death all tied to New Westminster.

"He died in a car wreck. The accident report stated that, for no apparent reason, his car ran off the road and flipped over, breaking his neck."

"Were there any signs of foul play?"

"None what so ever," said Cori. "A priest was then sent up from Boston to temporarily take over St. Thomas until a new priest could be assigned. Father Collin arrived to fill the position early in July."

"So he's only been here for about four months. Odd, he never mentioned that. Quite the opposite actually. He almost tried to make it appear that he'd been here for a while."

"His arrival, if you think about it, nearly coincides with the time that the thefts of the relics began. It would be the perfect cover, and he would certainly bring a great deal of inside information with him as to what relics are where, and how to get at them. Taking that one step further, by having a few relics stolen from St. Thomas, he could further divert any possible suspicion."

"A fallen priest," said MacBridan, thinking out loud. "It is possible. Certainly wouldn't be the first time, and it would go a long way in helping to explain his actions last night."

"I thought you said he helped you?" asked Cori.

"He did, or at least that's how it looked at the time. When Sheriff Beninger was getting ready to arrest me and lock me up, Father Collin stepped in, validating some of my story. On his word, he helped to firm up the fact that there had been someone else at the crime scene, other than just Macy and me. Thing is, he lied. He couldn't have possibly seen the things that he claimed he saw," explained MacBridan.

"Okay, but that doesn't make sense. If he were the bad guy, why would he have saved you? With you under arrest and out of the way, he and his band of goons could continue on with whatever it is they're doing."

MacBridan thought that over for a moment. "Cori, he couldn't afford to have me locked up."

"Why not?"

"Can't believe I didn't see through this sooner. Guess I got hit on the head harder than I thought. He couldn't let me go with Beninger for two reasons. First, he needed to find out just how much I knew. Unbelievable! I actually opened up and told him everything."

"That's a little out of character for you," commented Cori.

"Cori, I was hurt, mentally drained, trying to make sense of all that had happened. So I reached out to what I believed was a friendly face."

"Okay, I understand that, but why not let the Sheriff put you away, effectively taking you out of things, then just visit you to find out what you knew?"

"Because, and here's the second reason, he couldn't risk my being alone with Beninger. He couldn't risk that I might actually convince Beninger that I was telling the truth and point him in the right direction. A direction that would eventually lead right back to him."

"It does seem to add up. I hate this," said Cori. "It's almost like discovering a cop who's dirty. But, why are you still alive? Once he found out everything, why not just kill you and be done with it?"

"He's too smart for that. My death would have brought Beninger back with more questions than he wants asked. No, by bringing me home, it puts him in the clear. He's even got Mrs. Chamberlin as a witness that I was alive when he left. Now if I meet an untimely end, the suspicion will fall on Macy's friends."

"So what do we do?"

"We know that there is a coven here practicing some kind of satanic rituals. We believe they stole the artifacts because they were needed to complete these rituals. They are not afraid to kill to accomplish their goal, having killed two of their own to protect whatever it is they're trying to do. Difference now is that we have two of their group available to us at any time."

"I think we're back to your being hit pretty hard on the head. If you're referring to Vickers and Macy. It's a good bet that they won't be doing any talking," said Cori.

"It's all in the question you want answered," said MacBridan. "I don't know much about covens or cults or groups like this, but check with the coroners. Let's see if there are any physical similarities that we may have missed."

"Such as?"

"Something on the bodies, cuts perhaps, where they bled themselves for the rituals. Ask about tattoos, scars, a severed appendage, something that is the same for both of them. We find the common link on Vickers and Macy, and it may help us to connect them to Father Collin. So far, every time I've been with Father Collin, only his hands and face have been visible, and it is reasonable to assume that if he's part of the coven, then he'd have the same, or at least similar, kind of mark on him that they do."

"I'll get right on it. In the meantime, what are you going to do?" asked Cori.

"I've got to get a little more rest and then something to eat. But then, I'm going to go and see Father Collin. If we're right, and I think we are, then there's a good chance the cross is hidden somewhere in the church, or even the rectory. For that matter, he could simply have it sitting out in plain sight. Who would notice another cross in a Catholic church?"

"Maybe you should take one of our people with you," cautioned Cori.

"I think I can handle Father Collin," said MacBridan, looking forward to the confrontation. "I'm sure, if need be, that with a little friendly persuasion, he'll talk. After all, look how cooperative Macy was."

"Oh yes, real cooperative."

"Cori, put a rush on this and call me back."

"Will do," said Cori. "I'll also reach out to Professor Wilson, to see if I can get any insight from him as to what they may do next, now that they have the cross back."

"It would be nice to anticipate what's coming."

"Alright, I'll call back soon. Mac, please be careful."

"Cori, wait, one more thing. This may seem a little out of place, but I also need you to pull up the file on Ubel Obermann. I'd like to know the date and details surrounding his death."

"On Obermann? Now where did this come from?"

MacBridan hesitated, then said, "Try to keep an open mind on this, but last night, before I blacked out in the church, there was someone standing over me. At first, I was sure that it was Father Collin, but when I opened my eyes and looked up, I'll swear it was Obermann. Later on, I asked Father Collin about it, and he tried to assure me that it had been him and that my overwrought mind had imagined the whole thing. All things considered, his assurances no longer carry much weight."

"Mac, on this one I'd have to agree with the priest. If memory serves, Obermann's been dead for quite a while now."

"I know, and I'm asking that you keep this to yourself. It's one of those things, crazy as it sounds, that I feel I need to check on—you know, to put my mind at rest," said MacBridan.

Cori promised to get back with him as soon as she could and hung up.

MacBridan lay down on the bed, but couldn't go back to sleep as his mind refused to turn off. Who was Father Collin? Was he the coven leader? If so, then he had to be stopped, but MacBridan needed more evidence. Had they killed Monsignor Henry? It stood to reason that they must have, as MacBridan just couldn't buy into such a convenient accident. But what were they after that justified so many deaths? And what was that horrible creature that had been unleashed to do their bidding?

He lay there for an hour, then forced himself out of bed and took as hot a shower as he could stand. The heat not only helped his shoulder but all the other little aches and pains that had shown up. He shaved, got dressed, and changed the dressing on his forehead. The bruised area had darkened around his eye. He glared at the mirror, but quickly determined that it was going to be harder for him to be intimidating when it looked like someone had dragged him back and forth across a gravel road a few times.

It was almost eleven when he went up to Katherine's house. About twenty minutes earlier, she had checked on him, via the intercom, and had a hot breakfast waiting.

"How are you feeling?" she asked.

"Much better, thank you. In a day or two, I'll be as good as new. Have you heard from Peter?"

"He called me right after he hung up from you. I am so glad to hear that he is sending you the help you asked for. No one should have to face such danger alone."

MacBridan looked harder at her, puzzled by her reaction. Then it began to dawn on him what had happened, and he tried to keep the smile off his face. He had finally found the one person who Dolinski was afraid to cross. "Yes, that will be good. I want to talk to you about this also, but, at the same time, I don't want to be completely redundant. Why don't you tell me all that Peter shared with you?"

"Just that two of his men would be joining you, and that if it's not too much trouble, to have them stay here at the house with me. He said that the idea is to keep them out of sight so that this gang won't know that you have any help. That way, should they come after you, these men will be ready and waiting to surprise them. At first, I objected. I don't like the idea of you just sitting out there like some kind of bait."

"I appreciate your concern, Mrs. Chamberlin," said MacBridan. "What did he say to that?"

"Peter assured me that it was all right, that you are paid to take those kind of risks and that you are perfectly capable of taking care of yourself. He has great confidence in you."

"Well, you don't know how good it makes me feel to hear that," said MacBridan. So good old Peter "give it to them straight" Dolinski had bailed when it came to telling his aunt the truth; that in reality he was sending people not to help him but to baby-sit her. He couldn't wait to tell Cori about this.

"Mrs. Chamberlin, let me change channels on you for a moment. I need some more information about St. Thomas, and I'm hoping you can help me. It is my understanding that Father Collin hasn't been here all that long."

"No, he hasn't, but he is such a dear man. He helped so many of us to get through the passing of Father Henry. Father Henry was like family. He'd been here for years. He died in a terrible car accident, shocking all of us."

"Do you know where Father Collin came from? I mean, had he been a priest at another church here in the area?" asked MacBridan.

Katherine sat down across from him. "No, I don't think so. To tell you the truth I don't know where he was before this. I think I remember someone saying that he'd been sent up from Boston. Why do you ask?"

"I too have become rather impressed with Father Collin. Did he know Father Henry?"

"I don't think so, but he did say that he was familiar with all that Father Henry had accomplished in the parish, spoke very highly of him. Many times he stated that the church was sad to have lost such a good man."

"What can you tell me about Father Henry?" asked MacBridan.

"He was a kind old gentleman, always ready to help. He wasn't afraid to get his hands dirty, if you know what I mean. Although many of us thought that he might retire soon, we weren't expecting that to happen for at least two or three more years. He shouldn't have been driving anyway."

"Why do you say that?"

"Well, he was getting up there in years. Not that old people can't drive—in fact, we're more careful than most. But Father Henry had seemed, I don't know, distracted in the weeks leading up to his death."

"Was he sick?"

"I don't think so. He just seemed to be on edge a great deal of the time, very nervous. Whatever was bothering him kept him so preoccupied that he even got confused a couple of times during mass, actually lost his place. Many of us asked him if there was anything we could help him with. He would just laugh and ask us to be patient with an old man. I miss him so much. I'm afraid there's not much more to add. Does any of this help you?"

"Yes, I think it does," said MacBridan. Katherine's input on Father Henry fit in all too well. MacBridan figured that it was a good guess that Father Henry had discovered the coven's activities. That being the case, he wondered what Father Henry had experienced that had strained his nerves to the point of distraction. Had he feared for his life too? Had he encountered that creature on the highway, causing the accident that led to his death? A sudden anger coursed through MacBridan, adding fuel to the desire to strike back that already burned within him. Although he would never admit it, not even to Cori, this had become personal. Since that night in the basement with Vickers, circumstances had forced him to question his nerve, his capabilities. MacBridan was finally beginning to accept the idea that he was facing an enemy that, even in his worst nightmares, he'd never for a moment could have believed existed. He checked his watch, anxious for his backup to arrive. He wanted to find Father Collin and get the truth out of him now more than ever.

CHAPTER 21

Dolinski's men arrived shortly after noon. MacBridan handled the introductions and helped the two men to get settled in. Although Cori had given them a thorough briefing, MacBridan provided them with additional details as to all that had happened up to now. Katherine welcomed Smithers and Harry to her home and put together a quick lunch of soup and sandwiches for all of them. The soup was homemade, and as MacBridan was getting ready to leave, Katherine and Harry entered into a rather animated discussion on the preparation of cream based soups. MacBridan smiled to himself. *So, Harry is a cook, who knew?*

MacBridan took Harry's car and drove straight to St. Thomas Church, wasting no time in getting there. As it was, he was getting started far later in the day than he'd wanted. The cut over his eye still hurt, but Katherine had armed him with plenty of Advil to take along.

He pulled into the parking lot of St. Thomas and parked next to the only other car there. He got out and looked around, but as best he could tell, Father Collin's car was gone. MacBridan went up to the front doors of the church and just as he reached for the handle, the door swung open, almost hitting him.

"Well that was close," said the man MacBridan had nearly collided with. "Good morning, or should I say, good afternoon?"

"Good afternoon," said MacBridan as he stepped aside to make room for the man to pass.

But the man didn't pass by. Instead, he stopped and stared at MacBridan, taking particular notice of the bandage over MacBridan's eye. He appeared to be in his late fifties, thin, just over six feet tall, with a full head of grayish white hair. "Excuse me, but are you James MacBridan?"

"Yes, but I must apologize, I don't remember our having met."

"We haven't. I'm Doctor Appleton. I ran into Officer Goodman this morning, and he mentioned that there'd been some excitement out here last night. He said that you'd taken a pretty good crack on the head, and it's plain to see that he wasn't exaggerating."

"Yes, well, it's a good thing I have a hard head. Fortunately it's not as bad as it looks," said MacBridan.

"If you like, I'd be happy to take a peek at that for you," offered Dr. Appleton. "You can't be too careful with a head injury."

"Thank you, Doctor, but that won't be necessary."

"Odd my running into you like this. I'd come out here to see Father Collin, make sure he was okay, but he doesn't seem to be around."

"Now that's disappointing. I wanted to talk with him also."

"Yes, I imagine so. Officer Goodman said that Father Collin helped you a great deal last night."

"Sounds like Officer Goodman should have his own news talk show," said MacBridan.

Dr. Appleton chuckled at that. "He probably should be somewhat more discrete, but you see I've treated him since he was a baby. We talk quite often, and, frankly, last night… Well, it easily ranks up there in the top ten of the most exciting things that have ever happened in New Westminster. Normally this is a pretty sedate community."

"That is the party line."

"Well, if you change your mind, drop by my office and we'll see how things are healing. It was nice meeting you," said Doctor Appleton. They shook hands, and the doctor walked out to his car.

MacBridan entered St. Thomas and waited in the vestibule as the door clicked shut behind him. He stayed where he was, waiting for Dr. Appleton to drive off. The sound of the doctor's car quickly faded and things became still. MacBridan checked his gun, then quietly made his way down the aisle on the far left hand side of the church. Up until now, he'd never noticed how many areas of a church remained in shadow even during the day. Despite his best efforts to be quiet, the minor creakings of the floorboards echoed throughout the chamber, as if trying to alert those present of MacBridan's approach. The hollow stare from the statues of the various saints followed MacBridan as he passed by. There was no sign, no sound of Father Collin, or of anyone else.

The church office was also empty. MacBridan didn't waste any time, and began to look for the Cross of St. Patrick. His search went uninterrupted and thirty minutes later, he finished, coming up empty. To have found the cross sitting out in the open, even hidden somewhere in the church, would have been almost too easy. On the other hand, he couldn't overlook the possibility that Father Collin might have gotten careless. MacBridan left the church and walked over to the rectory. He glanced back at the parking lot, but Father Collin had not returned.

MacBridan knocked on the door several times, listened closely, but didn't hear any movement inside. He tried the door, but unlike the church, it was locked tight. For a moment, he considered letting himself in but quickly decided against the idea. His current status with the New Westminster law enforcement community was somewhat tenuous, and adding a charge of breaking and entering to it just wouldn't help to advance his cause.

MacBridan returned to his car, disappointed to have missed the priest, and began the drive out to Furr's Antique Shop. As much as he had wanted to talk with Father Collin, he was just as anxious to find out as much as he could about Macy. Katherine had already given him directions to the shop, which was located out on Hickory Hill road. According to Cori, Macy had recently been working there, and MacBridan hoped that someone would be able to provide him information that would lead to others in the coven. It was about the only lead he had left.

The sign in the window of the antique shop said open, but the darkened windows made MacBridan question its accuracy. He parked near the front door and went up on to the broad porch that extended across the entire front of the building. He didn't see anyone but could faintly hear music coming from somewhere inside the shop. He tried the door and stepped inside.

Either the antique shop was deceptively large, or they had made exceptionally good use of the available space. Whatever the case, its size surprised him. Several tables and shelves, tightly packed with collectables, greeted MacBridan. Soft lighting filled the room, accounting for the darkened windows, and helped to create a homey atmosphere, further enhancing the assumed value of the various items on display from times past. A man emerged from a back room, hesitated, and then approached MacBridan. He was of medium build, nearly six feet tall, easily in his early thirties. Completely bald, he wore an earring in his right ear. The earring accentuated the long scar that ran along the jawline from his right ear to his chin. He had on jeans and work shoes, his t-shirt a skin tight fit over a well-muscled torso.

MacBridan pretended to be interested in an old book. The man asked, "You need something?"

"You certainly have some wonderful books here," answered MacBridan, hoping that a complimentary approach, brimming with charm would help to get the ball rolling. "I collect first editions."

The man didn't respond. The expression on his face remained neutral. Time passed. Finally, he impatiently shifted his weight from his left leg to his right, but his eyes never left MacBridan. MacBridan accepted that as his cue to continue. He realized that it was going to take more than his everyday wit and personality to win Scar Face over.

"Are these all the books you have?' asked MacBridan. "I'd hate to leave and not get the chance to peruse your entire inventory."

"I'm not sure," said Scar Face. "Not my area of the business. Maybe you could come back some other time."

"If only I could, but that may not be possible. Is your manager in? Lucy, isn't it? Perhaps I could talk with her." Katherine, MacBridan's new "full-time" New Westminster operative, had told him about Lucy at the same time she had given him the directions to the shop.

"She's not here," he said. "Like I said, it'd be best if you come back some other time." For Scar Face the conversation was over. He turned away from MacBridan and started to return to the back of the store.

"That's odd. I called yesterday, and she told me she'd be in this afternoon. Will she be gone long?"

Scar Face stared at MacBridan; his expression began to shift from neutral to one of annoyance. Working with customers was clearly not his strong suit. "Look, all I can tell you is what I told the other guy. She's visiting a sick friend, some pregnant lady, and she may not be back until late today."

"You wouldn't happen to know the lady's name would you? Look, I hate to be pushy, but Lucy promised to hold a couple of rare books back for me. If you know her friend's name, I could give Lucy a call and set up another time for us to get together."

Scar Face thought about that for a moment and said, "Don't know her name, Holly something or other. Sorry, can't help you out." Again, Scar Face turned to leave.

MacBridan anticipated the move, reached out and took the man's arm. Scar Face tensed up, looked at MacBridan's hand on his arm, and then glared into MacBridan's eyes. "You got a problem?" he said, his voice taking on a menacing edge.

"This may work out well for both of us. Before I spoke with Lucy, I talked to another guy here at the store named Macy. You know him?" asked MacBridan, releasing Scar Face's arm.

"Yeah, I know him. What about him?"

"Lucy said she'd make sure Macy set them aside for me. Now, I'm sorry your manager isn't here, but I really want those books. Why don't you ask Macy where he put them, get them for me, and I'll make it worth your time, Macy's too. Lucy doesn't even need to know I came by."

"Macy's not here either."

"You know how to reach him?"

Scar Face grunted, gave a small laugh and said, "That ain't possible."

"Well, do you know where he might have put them? I mean, if he's not here, then there's no need to cut him in on this. What do you say?"

Scar Face stepped in close to MacBridan, their faces separated only by inches. "Macy was a friend of mine. I don't cheat friends. You gotta lot of nerve asking me to do that and I really think it's time you left."

"All right, I'm sorry, but one last question," MacBridan persisted. "You said 'the other guy.' What other guy are you referring to? I'm sure this all sounds a little paranoid, but there are some other book collectors shopping the area and I really don't want to lose out to them."

"You are a real piece of work," said Scar Face, shaking his head in disgust. "You've got nothing to worry about. The other guy's a priest and he didn't say anything about any stupid books." With that, he walked away, disappearing into the back room.

MacBridan set the book down and went back outside. It was interesting to learn that he was following the same path as Father Collin. MacBridan guessed that the pregnant lady Scar Face mentioned was the same one he'd met with Katherine a few days ago in the church parking lot. He remembered that her name had also been Holly. Had Scar Face shared Lucy's whereabouts with Father Collin? MacBridan started to go back inside, thought better of it, and got in his car. He called Katherine.

"Katherine, hi, this is Mac."

"How did things go with Lucy?" she asked.

"She's not here at the moment. One of the people who work here thinks that she might be visiting a friend of hers, Holly, who's expecting. They didn't know Holly's last name, and I was wondering if you might know whom they're talking about. Could it be the same lady you and I met after church?"

"I'm sure it is. Her name is Holly Carpenter."

"It's rather important I talk with Lucy. Do you know where Holly lives?"

"Are you still at the antique shop?"

"Yes, I am," said MacBridan.

"Good, then it's not very far from where you are. Poor dear, her pregnancy has been giving her such fits. She's been so weak. According to Dr. Appleton, she's due any time now."

It seemed that Dr. Appleton was just a wealth of information and was willing to share it with whomever would listen. MacBridan decided that the next time he found himself in a small, rural community, he'd save everyone a great deal of time and aggravation and go directly to the local doctor.

"I'm sorry to hear she's having problems. How do I find her house?"

Katherine gave him directions. He thanked her and headed further out Hickory Hill Road. Katherine told him that Holly and her husband Ian lived in a small house, set on a hillside overlooking the valley. Normally it would have been a perfectly charming location, but considering all that was going on in New Westminster, the loneliness of the location, for some reason, bothered MacBridan.

MacBridan nearly missed the turn off, just catching sight of their mailbox as he went by. He backed up and turned off onto the gravel lane. Crossing Shepard's Creek, he followed the narrow lane through the trees, which soon emerged into a clearing. The house was exactly as Katherine had described it, sitting up the hill to his left.

He parked in front of the house behind a station wagon that had "Furr's Antiques" stenciled across its back window. MacBridan went up the steps to the front porch just as the front door opened. The screen door, however, remained closed. He estimated the woman facing him to be in her mid to late forties.

"Good afternoon," she said. Her voice had a cautious tone to it, and she studied MacBridan closely. He understood her concern. He was a pretty big guy, a stranger to her, and his face looked far worse for wear.

"My name's James MacBridan. Are you Lucy?"

"Yes," she answered, the concern more evident now as she learned that this stranger somehow knew her name.

"I stopped by the antique shop and they told me I might find you here. I hope I'm not disturbing Holly."

A look of recognition crossed her face as she suddenly realized who he was, and the tension went out of her face. "Of course, Mr. MacBridan. Holly's mentioned meeting you at St. Thomas."

"That's right," said MacBridan. He flashed her one of his most alluring smiles, a real ice melter.

"I heard about what happened last night at the high school. That must have been so terrible for you," Lucy said.

"I see you've been talking with Dr. Appleton."

"Why yes I have. How did you know?"

"Just a lucky guess," said MacBridan.

"I suppose you'd like to talk about Carl Macy."

"Very much so."

"Sheriff Beninger said that you might come by the shop. He also said that I didn't have to talk with you."

MacBridan flashed her his killer smile again, realizing that it was a completely unfair tactic. "Nothing like a positive reference from the local sheriff. Please understand, my company has been investigating the thefts of several religious artifacts. Some of the stolen artifacts were taken from St. Thomas. We know that Gerald Vickers and Carl Macy were involved in the thefts. All we're trying to do is to find the people who helped them to steal the artifacts and to recover those that are still missing. Nevertheless, Sheriff Beninger is right. You don't have to talk with me, but whatever help you could give would be greatly appreciated."

"I don't mind at all. In fact it would be my pleasure, but I don't know how much I'll be able to help."

"When did you talk with Dr. Appleton?" asked MacBridan.

"He called here this morning, checking up on Holly," she answered.

"You've been here all day?"

"Yes, you see—"

A voice from inside interrupted Lucy. "Lucy, please ask Mr. MacBridan in."

At first, Lucy seemed reluctant to do so, but then opened the screen door and let MacBridan step inside. Holly lay on the couch, propped up with several pillows. Her appearance shocked MacBridan. He thought that she actually looked worse than he did. Dark circles had taken up residence, carving deep lines under her eyes, her cheeks were sunken, and her skin had taken on a deathly pallor.

MacBridan's smile never wavered, and he walked over and took the hand she had extended to him. Her grip was almost nonexistent, underscoring Katherine's comments on her weakened condition. He sat down on the chair next to her. "How have you been? I understand that that special time is pretty close."

"It is good to see you. We don't get many visitors out this way. Yes, as you can tell," she said, patting her stomach, "the baby's due any minute now."

"We're keeping a close eye on her," said Lucy.

"It must be a very exciting time for you and Ian," said MacBridan.

Holly had not let go of his hand. At the mention of Ian's name, a sudden burst of strength surged through her and her grip noticeably tightened. "Mr. MacBridan, maybe you can help me. I am so worried about Ian. Three days ago, he went to Boston. He was only supposed to be gone one night, but he hasn't come back and he hasn't even called. That's not like him."

"Have you called the people he went to meet with?"

"I did from the shop," interjected Lucy. "Ever since the storm the other night, Holly's phone has been off more than it's been on. I've tried the number in Boston repeatedly, but I never get an answer."

"Mr. MacBridan, I'm so scared that something may have happened to him. I don't know who else to call."

"Holly, even though that does sound unusual, sometimes people get caught up in things. If you like, I'll make some calls, see what I can find and get back to you as soon as I can. In the mean time, try not to worry and just focus on that baby. We'll find him. I'm sure he's all right," said MacBridan, trying to reassure her. He wished he felt as positive about it as he was trying to sound.

Silent tears ran down her face. "Thank you. Oh thank you so much! You have no idea how much that means to me. And Lucy, she's been such a godsend. I've been so run down lately that I don't know what I would have done without her."

"I'm just glad that I've been able to help. Holly sleeps a great deal of the time, but Dr. Appleton comes out regularly and believes that everything is progressing along quite well," said Lucy.

MacBridan looked at Holly and smiled. "Well, if you have managed to get a doctor to come all the way out here to make regular house calls, then I'd say you have pulled off quite a remarkable accomplishment."

"Everyone's been so kind, but I can't get my mind off of Ian and, of course, the baby. Mr. MacBridan, what will I do if something has happened to him? And on top of that, I am so tired all of the time, my strength is draining away and I worry that I won't be strong enough to deliver the baby. Or worse, what if something has happened to Ian and I'm so weak that I don't make it through the birth? What will become of my child?"

"Now Holly, hush that nonsense," said Lucy. "You're going to be all right, we're not going to let anything happen to you. Mr. MacBridan just said he's going to find Ian. Everything is going to be fine, you'll see."

"Please help me, Mr. MacBridan," said Holly, still gripping his hand. "You're my only hope."

MacBridan got up, leaned over and hugged the young girl. "Holly, you have my word, we'll find him. Here's my card and my cell number is on there. Night or day, you need me, use that number. Now, do you have a phone number, or an address, for the people Ian was going to meet with?"

Holly let go of his hand and reached into a pocket of the sweater she had on. She handed him a crumpled up piece of paper. "I got this off of his computer. You can keep that. I also have it written down beside the phone. Thank you again, Mr. MacBridan."

"I'll be out to see you again real soon," said MacBridan. "You can count on it."

Lucy got up and followed him outside. Neither of them said anything until they reached his car. "I too was concerned about Holly's health, but Dr. Appleton keeps giving us his assurances that she's okay. He's watching her quite closely and that has really helped to give her a little peace of mind. The problem is she's just so worried about her husband," said Lucy.

"Do you have any idea where he is?"

"No, Ian and I didn't get to talk before he left, but he's such a nice young man and he adores Holly. I would never say this to her, but his not coming back, not even calling to let her know what's going on, isn't right."

"I agree," said MacBridan. "That doesn't seem to fit the picture, does it?"

"I'm glad that you're going to look into it. Holly did call the Sheriff's department, but we haven't heard anything back from them."

"Before I go, I'd like to know what you can tell me about Carl Macy," said MacBridan, turning the conversation back to his original objective.

"His death came as quite a shock to me, especially when the sheriff told me that he'd been murdered. That kind of violence is pretty rare around here."

"What did Carl do for you at the antique shop?"

"Carl and I never really talked all that much. He helped clean up, inside and outside. Pretty much all he did was manual labor, you know, pick-ups, deliveries, that kind of thing."

"Who did he hang out with? Was he close to anyone at the shop?"

"To be honest, I never really paid any attention to him. People like Carl tend to come and go. He did what I asked of him and never did anything to cause a problem," explained Lucy.

"I spoke to another one of your employees before coming out here today. A man with a long scar on his face."

"Oh yes, that would be Frank. He's been with me for quite awhile."

"Were Frank and Carl friends?"

"They could have been, I really wouldn't know. However, Frank has never come across as being all that sociable."

"Did anyone ever visit Carl at the shop? Did he get any personal calls that you can remember?"

Lucy thought for a moment and then began to slowly shake her head. "I'm sorry Mr. MacBridan, I'm not being much help to you at all. He may have, I just don't know."

"Well that's all right," said MacBridan. "I appreciate your trying. If something does come to mind, anything at all, please give me a call."

"I will," promised Lucy. "I need to get back inside with Holly, but it has been so nice meeting you. You've given Holly hope."

"Thank you," said MacBridan. "I'm sure we'll see each other again."

MacBridan got in his car, watching Lucy as she went up the steps and back into the house. Having seen Holly's condition, he was glad that she wasn't going through this alone. Her husband's disappearance, though, did not sound good, and he planned to get Cori on to that immediately. He started the car and began to pull away when he caught something out of the corner of his eye.

He stopped and studied the house. Then he saw it. On the bottom step, coming down from the porch, nearly hidden by the overhang from the step above it, something had been carved into the wooden plank. He studied the scrawled markings and a chill swept over him as he realized that he was looking at symbols just like the ones he'd found at Altar Rock.

MacBridan had not expected this turn of events, but he also realized that someone might be watching him. MacBridan picked up his cell phone and pretended to be making a call as he sat there studying the symbols. As best he could, he took a couple of pictures of them. Two of the symbols were identical to those he'd already emailed to Cori. Finishing his pretend call, he put his cell phone down and drove back to the main highway.

The symbols had not been there long, which was the only reason he'd spotted them. Having been freshly cut into the wood, they stood out against its weathered surface. He also recognized that they had been written in such a place that, under normal use of the stairs, no one, in all probability, would have ever noticed them.

Events surrounding Ian and Holly now took on a far more ominous tone. Who had put the symbols on the Carpenters' house, and for that matter, why? How did their being there tie into the rituals being held at Altar Rock? Considering how recent events had taken a violent turn, he wondered if Holly and Lucy were in any danger. He also wondered now if Ian's disappearance might be the result of deliberate action on the part of someone wanting to get him out of the way, actually isolating Holly. And if that were true, why? Bottom line, finding those symbols where he did was not a good thing, and it drew Holly and Ian into the middle of it all.

As MacBridan drove back into town, he went over his talk with Holly. Up until a few minutes ago, he had been willing to accept that the pregnancy had been sapping her strength, but now he wasn't so sure. The look of her eyes, the sluggishness of her voice, was it truly the pregnancy affecting her so drastically, or was it something else? Was she being drugged? If so, why and by whom? Dr. Appleton? There were simply too many unanswered questions, and he couldn't see how they all tied in together.

He put in a call to Cori to find that she was out but was expected to return any minute. He left her a voicemail to call him. He also left word for her to start the hunt for Ian Carpenter, leaving her the number and the address Holly had given him. MacBridan planned to talk to Katherine regarding Holly. Based on what he'd just found, he was giving serious thought to the idea of moving Holly over to her house.

His sense of urgency in finding Father Collin increased. MacBridan felt himself beginning to get a little desperate. He still didn't understand the end game, the purpose behind the thefts and the killings. This worried him because without that he really had no idea how to protect everyone involved. He had confirmed that Katherine was at risk, and now he had to add Holly into the same equation. However, he was just as positive that Father Collin held the answers and was equally as confident that he would be able to get the truth out of him.

CHAPTER 22

Although he'd participated in several of them over years, and clearly understood their value, MacBridan simply hated stakeouts. Bottom line, it was the waiting, the mind numbing, time stretching inactivity that ate away at him. But MacBridan knew he had to find Father Collin and, one way or another, get some straight answers from him. Problem was, the only place he knew to look was at St. Thomas Church, and so there he sat.

On most stakeouts, MacBridan usually found ways to occupy his mind, but this afternoon it wasn't happening. There was absolutely zero going on at the church. This was aggravated by the fact that he hurt in multiple places and, try as he might, finding a comfortable position in the car turned out to be impossible.

He'd parked under a large oak tree across the street from the church in the same driveway that led to the high school he'd driven up the previous night. It was a good location for observing the church, as it was situated directly across the street from the main entrance to St. Thomas's parking lot. A five-foot statue of the church's namesake stood at the entrance to the parking lot, its arms open in welcome, staring back at MacBridan. Finally, he became so bored, that he rolled down the window and engaged the statue of the saint in a staring contest. It was now ten till six, and MacBridan was losing, having only taken one out of three rounds.

His cell phone began to ring, bringing a welcome break to the monotony. It was Cori. "Where are you?"

"Parked across from St. Thomas, praying for Father Collin to return. I haven't been able to locate him all day."

"Sorry to hear that, but it's been an interesting day for me. I'm about twenty minutes from the office. It would be good to talk with you on a land line." As unlikely as it seemed, they knew how easy it was to intercept a call to a cell phone, and with the recent escalation of events in New Westminster, they'd decided not to take any chances. Cori's statement signaled MacBridan that she had some sensitive information to pass along and wanted to insure that they wouldn't be overheard. "You going to be there much longer?" she asked.

"No, I don't think so. Not for lack of trying, but I'm not accomplishing much of anything here. By the time you get back to the office, I'll be at Katherine's."

"Sounds good. I'll talk with you soon," said Cori and hung up.

MacBridan straightened up, started the car, and pulled out onto main road. As he drove by, MacBridan nodded to the statue of St. Thomas, silently acknowledging his defeat. Not much more than twenty minutes later, he pulled into Katherine's driveway. Harry answered his knock at the front door.

"How are things going?" asked MacBridan.

"Quiet as can be," answered Harry. "We've been taking turns watching from an upstairs window, but there's not a great deal of traffic out this way. Sheriff's department has rolled by a couple of times, but that's about it."

"Glad to hear you two have been working," MacBridan said as they entered the living room. "Based on the way things were going when I left, I figured I'd find you in the kitchen swapping recipes with Katherine."

"Laugh if you want to, but that old girl knows her way around the ladle. That delightful aroma you're enjoying now is the beef stew she's fixing us for dinner."

"'Delightful aroma,'" mimicked MacBridan. "Who are you and what have you done with Harry?"

Before Harry could respond to MacBridan's jibe, Katherine came into the room. "Oh good, Mac, I'm so glad you made it back in time for dinner. How are you feeling? That eye of yours doesn't look good at all."

"The Advil you gave me did the job," answered MacBridan. Truth was he still ached all over. "Thank you for asking."

"Could I get you something to drink? Some hot tea perhaps? Dinner isn't going to be ready for a few minutes, I'm afraid," she offered.

"No, I think I'm all right for now," said MacBridan as the phone began to ring. "That's probably Cori. I'm expecting her call."

Katherine answered the phone, and then handed it to MacBridan. "If you need me, I'll be in the kitchen," she said and walked off with Harry, her dutiful pupil, in tow.

"So you never did find Father Collin," Cori said matter-of-factly. "That's disappointing."

"No, I didn't, but I did come across some other things that have me concerned. I'll tell you about that in a few minutes. So what do you have that merits a land line?"

Cori ignored the question and asked. "You doing okay? How's the head? I know you won't agree with this, but I still believe you should be checked by a doctor."

"I'm fine, Mom. You know me, a couple of Advil, a few minutes of rest, a clean cape and I'm ready for action."

"Your making light of it doesn't change the facts. Smithers said your face looked like someone had left you outside during a hail storm."

"Let it go, Cori, I'm all right."

"Well no one else believes that."

"If you're trying to make me feel better, it's not working. Now do you mind if we get back to business and focus on what you've found? You remember, the investigation, the reason we're all here?"

"You know, Mac, there are times that you can be a real…"

"Sure."

The line remained quiet for a moment. Finally, Cori said, "All right, never mind then. Most of my day has been spent with the state police. It was their medical examiner that did the autopsies on Macy, as well as Beninger's John Doe. I had the Boston ME's report, as well as pictures from Vickers's autopsy with me, following up on your idea that there may be some kind of common mark or feature, on Macy and Vickers. By the way, what made you think of that?"

"It really wasn't all that clever," said MacBridan. "It's pretty common with gangs to have some kind of identifying mark, be it a special tattoo, certain kinds of clothing, gang colors, that kind of thing. So, even though this is a coven we're dealing with, it struck me that it was just another type of gang. I take it that I was on target."

"Yes, surprisingly, you were," said Cori. MacBridan let the sarcasm pass. "Both Macy and Vickers had one, but it wasn't a tattoo. Both men had been branded."

"Are you sure?"

"We missed it on Vickers for a couple of reasons. First, we weren't looking for anything like that, and second, the brand itself is quite small. In fact, at first glance it looks a great deal like a small mole. Both men had had this mark placed directly between their shoulders blades."

"Could you make out what the mark is?"

"Keep in mind that this thing is about the same size as a cigarette burn, but yes, we could. It matches one of the symbols you found at Altar Rock."

"Good, good, that's what we needed. Now if we can just take one of these guys alive, it'll be easy to see if they're part of the coven. Good work, Cori."

"Thank you," said Cori. "And I take back what I was thinking earlier. You're not a complete moron, only partial."

"I'm so relieved," said MacBridan.

"Have you ever met Detective Sergeant Barry Mills? He's with the Massachusetts State Police Homicide Division."

"No, I don't believe I have."

"Well Sergeant Mills spent a great deal of time with me today. We really owe him one. Once we'd finished up with the Medical Examiner's Office, I filled him in on our investigation. Although he preferred the word cult, as opposed to coven, he pretty much agreed with our assumptions. However, what intrigued him the most, was the fact that all three of our victims had seemingly been killed in the same manner, and that no one has been able to identify what kind of animal has been doing the killing."

"Believe me, Cori, it's the one thing in this entire case that has me the most troubled, and it bothers me more than you'll ever know," said MacBridan. He continued to struggle with accepting Father Collin's explanation of an evil entity.

"Sergeant Mills suggested that we broaden our search area for similar kinds of crimes. Our early research found that the New Westminster area had been pretty quiet up until recently. What Sergeant Mills caught, and frankly I failed to take into consideration, was the actual geographic location of New Westminster."

"Not sure I'm following you on this," said MacBridan.

"New Westminster sits in the far Northwestern corner of Massachusetts, bordering New York and Vermont, creating one large, contiguous, rural area. Following his suggestion, we used the State Police computers and were able to query a fifty mile radius out from New Westminster, taking in all three states, which is exactly what I should have done in the first place."

"Keep going, you've got my undivided attention."

"Up to now we believed that we were dealing with the deaths of only three men—Vickers, the John Doe, and Macy, all killed in the same way. Mac, whatever's going on up there is far worse than we knew. Our search turned up five additional deaths, two in New York and three more in Vermont. All were men, all died in the same manner as Vickers and Macy, with their throats being torn out, ravaged. Four of the five were vagrants, just like Beninger's John Doe. Lastly, in all but one of the reports, on-scene investigators commented on the surprising lack of blood at the crime scene."

"Vagrants wouldn't be missed by anyone, so there'd be no one pressing the police for an investigation," mused MacBridan.

"Exactly. In all five cases their deaths were attributed to animal attacks, the wounds being that savage, but as to the specific animal responsible, again, no positive identification."

"Did any of the victims have teeth marks on their bodies that were clear enough to help us with an identification?"

"Two of them had distinct teeth marks on their neck vertebrate, but they weren't of any help. No one's been able to match them to a specific animal. We're having copies of all five autopsy reports sent over for comparison."

"Who was the fifth victim?"

"An elderly gentleman, retired military, lived in a small cabin just over the state line in Vermont. The only way he fits in, if you're looking for a pattern, is that like the vagrants, he didn't have any family that anyone could find."

MacBridan let this new information sink in then said, "Cori, eight people have been killed by this monster, but why? The coven carefully targeted and stole specific artifacts, artifacts that they needed, with absolutely no intent of selling them on the black market as everyone first suspected. The fact that the two members of the coven that tried to ransom the artifacts were killed for their efforts confirms that the coven didn't want to give them up. They've had a very specific purpose for stealing them. Based on what we've been able to piece together, it is reasonable to assume that these artifacts were needed in order to carry out the ritual they've been performing at Altar Rock. But why? Why this particular ritual? Are they really trying to bring someone back from the dead? Is that their goal; is that what all this is building up to? And if so, how do all the other killings fit in? And, just as puzzling, if not more so, is how in heaven's name are they doing it? What is it that is killing all of these people?"

"There's one other interesting point he added to the mix," said Cori. "In this same geographic area, taking in all three states, over the last twenty-five years there has been only one homicide. There's been a couple of hunting accidents, but that's been the extent of it. Now, in roughly the last four months, there have been seven deaths, homicides if we decide to discount the theory that they were killed by animals. Vickers, of course, was killed elsewhere."

"Four months," said MacBridan. "This, of course, also coincides with the arrival of Father Collin. Believe in coincidence, Cori?"

"No more than you do."

"Well this is just wonderful. We've managed to uncover a group of mass murderers running around terrorizing the countryside, but we don't know who they are, why they're doing it, or even how they're doing the actual killing. Pretty impressive. Maybe we should go out and hire a real detective to figure all of this out."

"We could have you take over the cooking and let Mrs. Chamberlin wrap up the investigation," suggested Cori.

"Don't think the thought hasn't crossed my mind."

"You mentioned that you'd found something today that has you concerned. What was it?"

MacBridan told Cori about his trip to the antique shop and his talk with Scar Face. Although MacBridan couldn't account for why he had been there, it was interesting to learn that Father Collin had been in earlier, also asking for Lucy. He then told Cori of his talk with Lucy and Holly, and how hard the pregnancy seemed to be affecting Holly. But, most disconcerting of all, was the finding of the symbols carved into the lower step that led up to Holly's porch.

"I couldn't get real close to them, but I was close enough to tell that they hadn't been there that long. I don't know how, but this definitely connects Ian and Holly into everything else that has been going on. It also bothers me that their house isn't close to anything. They'd be nearly defenseless out there, even if Ian was here. But with him having disappeared like he has, I'm planning to bring Holly over to Mrs. Chamberlin's."

"Mac, I'm sorry, I should have told you sooner. We found the husband."

"Oh no," said MacBridan. "Tell me he's not dead?"

"He's not, but he's also not in very good shape, and things could still go either way. He was the apparent victim of a hit and run driver. They took him to Baptist General and they still have him in intensive care. The problem was that when he was brought in he didn't have any identification on him, so the hospital had no idea who to contact. We started looking for him this morning, and during our check of the hospitals, he matched the age and description you'd given us. We then contacted the police and worked with them. It didn't take long for the DMV to provide a picture, as well as other information, enabling us to make a positive ID."

MacBridan was on his feet. "Cori, I've been a little too arrogant. Macy tried to tell me that these people were omnipotent, and I laughed at him. Now I'm beginning to believe he was right. I'm going to call Beninger and fill him in on what we know. Hopefully I'll be able to motivate him to get out there and pick Holly up as soon as possible."

"What? You're not going to go out there and get her yourself?" asked Cori, surprised to find MacBridan handing something this important off to someone else.

"Cori, don't misunderstand me. I want to protect that girl as much as you do, but I think it is perhaps more important that we first find Father Collin. St. Thomas is on the way to Holly's home. On my way out there, I'll swing by the church and see if Father Collin has returned. If not, I'll keep on going and head straight out to Holly's. However, if he is there, and I can neutralize his participation in all this, then we will have potentially cut the head off the snake. At this point, it is reasonable to assume that he's their leader. Hopefully, by stopping him we'll stop the killing. On the other hand, we don't know what may have already been set in motion, and I don't want to leave Holly at risk any longer than is necessary. Hence my need to send Sheriff Beninger out after her."

"What about Harry and Smithers? Why can't they help?"

"Can't do that, Cori. I need them where they are. Mrs. Chamberlin's been on this group's radar screen for a long time. All of us believe that they'll take a run at her sooner or later, which is why I want to keep both of them right here with her. Plus, Holly's house wasn't all that easy to find in the daylight. With the sun going down, it's going to be hard even for me, and I've already been there once. I'm going to ask Beninger to bring Holly here, leaving both women with Harry and Smithers. It's the best we can do."

"Mac, what can I do?"

"Get some men over to that hospital, post a guard on Ian. Also, I need you to brief Dolinski and bring him up to speed on all that's happened."

"I'll do that, then I'm coming up there," said Cori.

"No!" MacBridan nearly shouted into the phone. "No, Cori, I don't want you to do that."

"What is the matter with you?"

"Cori, please listen to me carefully. There's one more thing I need you to do. There's no explaining this, but I have a feeling that we don't have much time left. If I'm right about this, then the coven will be all the more dangerous."

"Left before what? You're not making any sense."

"Before their final act, before they complete whatever it is they're up to. They may even strike at Ian again. I firmly believe they meant to kill him the first time."

"All right, I'll get some men over to the hospital, but that won't take me all that long. What do you want me to do then? I'm not going to just sit by quietly and watch when I know I could be helping."

MacBridan inhaled deeply, held it for a moment, then slowly let it out. *Here goes*, he thought, *the moment I've been putting off for far too long. Either she'll go with it or beat a path to Dolinski to let him know that I'm certifiable.* "As quickly as you can, I need for you to get two crucifixes. Get over to that hospital and put one around Ian's neck. The second one is for you, Cori. Put it on and don't take it off for anything. Do you understand?"

Cori didn't respond at first, then quietly asked, "What are you saying?"

"You're going to have to trust me on this, Cori, no matter how out there it sounds. Your life, as well as Ian's, may depend on it. I'm going to have to make this quick, but here it is. Cori, I've seen this thing, this monster, twice now, and both times, it has killed, quickly and with extreme violence. Despite the fact that I've been face to face with this creature, I can't even tell you what it looks like. It is something unnatural and I have no idea what it is, but its power is absolutely terrifying."

"Okay, I understand all that, but why the crucifixes? Are you putting me on?"

"Please believe me because I know how this sounds. I'm still having trouble with it, but the only reason I'm alive today is because the night I encountered it at the high school, I had the Cross of St. Patrick with me. Cori, that cross saved my life. I don't know how. I hardly believe it myself, but it kept that monster at bay, kept it from attacking me. Please Cori, as fantastic as this sounds, I am telling you the truth."

"I knew you were holding out on me, but I never imagined anything even close to this."

Neither of them said anything. MacBridan finally broke the silence and said, "Cori, this is real. It's terrifying—it's completely unbelievable—but it's real. For your own protection, for Ian's, you have to trust me on this."

"Mac, I'm trying to, but there has to be some other explanation."

"Cori, this is tearing me apart, but stop and consider the facts. The symbols found at Altar Rock reference a grimoire that is considered fanatical even by those who believe in this kind of thing. All of the deaths have had the same MO, and none of the highly trained forensic experts who have investigated the bodies can identify the kind of creature that is killing them. Why is that? Because it's not an animal, Cori, and it's not a madman."

"So what's that leave, Mac? This is crazy!"

"It leaves things that I don't understand, things I've never encountered, or even heard of before. Father Collin may have just been trying to scare me worse than I already am, but the night I escaped from that monster at the high school, he told me that the creature was actually a demon. He said that this coven is trying to bring a demon out of Hell, that they control it, and that that's what's killing these people."

Again, the line remained quiet. MacBridan feared he'd made a mistake in telling her. "You really believe this, don't you, Mac?" asked Cori.

"Cori, I know what I've seen, what I've experienced. Believe me, I, more than anyone, want there to be another explanation. I've tried my hardest to come up with one, but there just isn't any. And that, in itself, leaves us in an impossible spot. We find ourselves having to defend against something that the rational part of our mind tells us isn't possible, while the spiritual side of us fears, and prays, it isn't happening."

MacBridan waited for Cori to respond.

"I can't tell you that I believe all of this, Mac, but I don't have anything to refute it with either," said Cori, her voice a combination of disbelief, shock and concern. "I'll do what you ask, for now."

"What does that mean?"

"It means that I'm trying, and that's the best I can offer you at the moment. Come on, Mac, give me a break. You throw this impossible story at me and expect me to just take it on faith and believe it?"

"Yeah, I understand. Like I said, it's hard for me too, and I've seen this thing up close and personal."

"Are you wearing a crucifix?" asked Cori.

"My plan is to get one before I leave here tonight. I've got to go now, Cori. I've got to get a hold of Beninger and find that damned priest." He paused, then said, "Thanks, Cori, this means a lot to me."

"Be careful, Mac. Whatever it turns out to be, we know what it can do, and you know what they say—third time's the charm."

"Not exactly the words of encouragement I was looking for, but they'll do. You be careful too, Cori. This monster doesn't seem to be hindered by geography, or much else for that matter."

MacBridan hung up the phone and made a mental list of all that he had to do. He quickly put in a call to the sheriff's office, but Beninger wasn't there. MacBridan left word that it was urgent that he speak with the sheriff and gave them his cell number. Then he got up and headed out to the kitchen to talk with Katherine. It was going to be a busy night.

CHAPTER 23

After MacBridan hung up from talking with Cori, the realization came to him. *I'm actually beginning to believe that this killer is not human*, he thought. This brought on a numbing sensation that quickly spread throughout his body. Early on, he'd entertained the possibility that he was losing his nerve, but now he faced a far worse possibility. Was he losing his mind? Was that it? Was all this just him slowly cracking up? No, he had to stop thinking like that. Losing his self-confidence at this juncture would be fatal. The coven he was up against had killed too many times and had to be stopped. Besides, he didn't really have to worry about his sanity. At this point, he was reasonably confident that Cori was planning a thorough psychiatric examination for him as soon as he returned.

He paused before entering the kitchen to make sure he had his strategy well prepared. His goal was not an easy one. How would he be able to get Harry and Smithers to wear crucifixes and at the same time not believe that he was completely off his nut? Obviously, he now faced one of those times when honesty was simply not the best policy. Falling back on the creativity that he repeatedly demonstrated when writing expense reports, he stepped into the kitchen.

Harry sat at the table talking with Katherine, who was busy cleaning the sink and counter area. "Have you changed your mind about that tea?" she asked.

"Actually I need to talk with Harry and Smithers for a moment. Time those two did some work around here."

"They have been most attentive," said Katherine, rising to their defense, "and Harry has been so helpful in the kitchen."

This made MacBridan smile. "Alright, I promise not to keep him too long," he said.

Harry followed MacBridan out of the kitchen and both men went upstairs to the front bedroom. Smithers sat there in the dark, staring out the window watching the yard outside through a night scope. He turned as both men came in.

"How close are we to eating?" he asked. "I'm tired, bored and starving."

"I'm guessing you haven't spotted anything of interest outside," said MacBridan.

"Absolute zero," answered Smithers. "I've spent the past hour watching some damn squirrel on that tall maple across the street. I think he's bored too."

"I just finished talking with Cori. It appears that this thing is larger in scope than we knew." MacBridan brought them up to date with all that Cori had discovered. Both were surprised to learn of the number of deaths that were being attributed to this coven. MacBridan also pointed out his concerns regarding Father Collin, his inability to find him, and what he had found during his visit to Ian and Holly's house.

"How do you think the symbols you saw on their porch steps tie in to those at Altar Rock?" asked Smithers.

"It's pretty obvious that the same people put them there. The good news is that neither Ian nor Holly fit the profile of any of the victims that we're aware of. But finding the symbols there, along with the attempt to murder Ian, leaves us with something we can't ignore."

"That does have a real bad smell to it," agreed Harry. "We going to go get her?"

"I've got a call into Sheriff Beninger. I'm going to see if he can go and pick her up. If that doesn't work out, then yes, I will go and get her."

"Wish I'd known you were trying to reach him. Sheriff's car just passed by here again not thirty minutes ago. They sure are keeping a close eye on this place," said Smithers.

"That's good to know." *But not all that surprising*, thought MacBridan, remembering back on the lecture Katherine had given to Beninger. "With you two here and their stepped up patrols, we should be able to protect both Holly and Katherine."

"You really think they're going to come after these women?" asked Harry.

"I can't be certain, but my guess is yes. They'd started watching the house long before I arrived. Since I got here, I've done my level best to get in their way and disrupt their plans, which has put even more focus on Katherine. They know I'm staying here. Since their attempt to kill me at the high school failed, grabbing Katherine and using her as leverage against me makes a great deal of sense. As for Holly, I have no idea what's going on there, but I now know she's connected. Keep in mind, her house has been marked, her husband's been attacked, and she has no way of defending herself."

"So what do we do?" asked Smithers.

"I'm going to leave and see if Father Collin has returned to St. Thomas. Hopefully he has, and I'll finally be able to press him and determine just what his involvement is in all of this."

"I think one of us ought to go with you," said Harry.

"Normally I'd welcome you along, but you're needed right here. If things go the way I think, and they do come after Katherine, believe me, you two will have your hands full."

"What are you going to do if you can't reach the sheriff?" asked Harry.

"If I don't hear from him soon, then I'll go and get Holly myself and bring her back here." MacBridan hesitated, gathering his thoughts. "There's also one other thing I want you guys to do. Mrs. Chamberlin talked to me about this a couple of times before, and I think it would make her feel better."

"What are you talking about?" asked Harry.

"Katherine is a devout practicing Catholic. The whole idea of a coven of witches creeping around the woods has not been easy on her. I'm sure you've noticed the crucifix she wears around her neck."

"Yes, a small, gold one, what about it?" asked Harry.

"She has asked if we would mind wearing crucifixes while we're here. To her way of thinking, the devil is stalking the streets of New Westminster. The point is she actually has our well being in mind, and I believe it would make her feel better it if we would wear them. Think of it as a comforting gesture on our part for her."

Both men looked at each other and shrugged. "Don't think it'll do much good, but I don't mind," said Smithers.

"Be happy to," Harry said, agreeing with Smithers. "If it'll make her feel better then I'm all for it. Wonder why she's never said anything about it to us? She's so direct about everything else and we've talked all day."

"It's probably nothing more than I've been here longer," said MacBridan. "She probably didn't want to risk offending anyone."

"So you're heading out before dinner?" asked Harry. "Mrs. Chamberlin certainly won't like that."

"Afraid I have to," said MacBridan. "We don't have any time to waste, and it really bothers me that Father Collin has seemingly dropped out of sight. I'll go and let her know what I'm doing. Why don't you give me a couple of minutes alone with her?"

Smithers and Harry smiled at the idea of Dolinski's aunt arguing with MacBridan. Harry said, "Sure, but let her know that your leaving is okay with us and that we'll happily eat your share."

"It's what I like about you, Harry," MacBridan said as he left the room. "Always ready to take one for the team."

MacBridan quickly went back downstairs and found Katherine setting the table in the kitchen.

"Everything all right?" she asked.

"Yes, but I need to talk with you about a couple of items. Things have heated up, and I have to leave."

"Certainly you have time for some dinner. Everything's ready. Mac, you have to eat."

"Katherine, please sit down for a moment," he said and then took the chair catty-cornered to hers. "Today my search for Father Collin took me out to Holly Carpenter's home. While there, I found symbols carved into her porch steps, symbols just like those you and I found at Altar Rock. This really has me worried. She's out there all alone. If it is all right with you, I'd like to bring her here."

"Of course it's all right, she's a sweet child and is welcome here anytime, but where is her husband?"

"That's one of the things Cori called me about. Ian went to Boston on business and was the victim of a hit and run driver. He's in the hospital, and he's in pretty bad shape."

"That's horrible! Do they know who did it?"

"No. The police are still investigating, but we're pretty certain that it somehow ties into the thefts we're looking in to, as well as the activities going on at Altar Rock. Holly didn't look good at all when I talked to her today. She's very weak, so much so that she could hardly get off the couch. If Lucy hadn't been there helping her I'm not sure how she'd have gotten by."

"Lucy from the antique shop?"

"Yes," answered MacBridan. "She and Holly seem to be pretty good friends. How well do you know her?"

"Lucy? Not all that well. I've seen around town, we've spoken a few times, but I can't say I know her. I had no idea that she and Holly were that close."

"Well, the antique shop is not far from Holly's house, maybe Holly met her there, or they got to know each other at church. Lucy's being there seems to surprise you. Why?"

"I don't know, it's probably nothing, but she just doesn't seem to be the type to help out like that."

"What makes you say that?" asked MacBridan, intrigued by her reaction.

"I'm not trying to say anything bad about her, but she's always been somewhat standoffish in the past. Her reaching out to Holly like this just struck me as being a little out of character for her. And they certainly didn't meet at church. Lucy doesn't go to church. Of course, both of them are new to New Westminster. Perhaps that was the common bond that drew them together."

"How long has Lucy lived in New Westminster?"

"Let me see," said Katherine. She leaned back, closed her eyes and thought for a moment. "If memory serves, Ian and Holly moved in about ten months ago. I'm guessing Lucy has been here about a year and a half, maybe two years. She took the old Butler place and turned it into a shop and a home. From what I hear she's done alright."

"Hopefully Lucy's still out there with Holly," said MacBridan. "Now that we've talked, the plan is to pick Holly up this evening and bring her here."

"You do that and I'll get a place ready for her. I may have to ask your men to move out of the spare room."

"I'm sure they won't mind," MacBridan assured her. "One more thing and then I have to go. We're getting close on this, and I want you to keep an extra sharp eye out. Stay inside and keep everything locked tight."

"Then you think I may be in even more danger than before," said Katherine.

"We're dealing with some very dangerous people. At this point, we are all somewhat at risk. That's why I want to bring Holly here. Harry and Smithers are quite good at what they do, and by bringing everyone under one roof, we can better minimize the risk."

"I know you're doing everything you can. You have no idea how grateful I am to have all of you here."

"Thank you. There is something else you can do to help me. Do you have any extra crucifixes that we can borrow?"

"Crucifixes? Yes, I've collected several over the years. What do you need?"

"All we need is one for each of us—Harry, Smithers and me. Cori spoke with a behavioral psychologist that sometimes works with us, creates profiles of the people we are up against. It was his suggestion that we all wear them. Because we are dealing with a group that is practicing witchcraft, he believes that the symbol of Christ might actually help to protect us. In their minds, they think of themselves as true witches.

Therefore, in order to live up to that self image, they might actually shy away from the sign of the cross."

"Yes, I see," said Katherine. "Let me get them for you right now."

"Thank you, Katherine, that'll be a big help."

Smithers had stayed at his post, and MacBridan found Harry waiting for him in the living room. "Everything go alright?" asked Harry.

"Yes, she's going to get the crucifixes now."

"I figured as much. She shot past me like a woman on a mission."

"I'll stay in touch via my cell phone. Let me know if anything happens here."

"Got it," said Harry. "Watch your back."

Katherine came in and gave MacBridan a crucifix. He thanked her then headed out to his car. As he got behind the wheel, he took the crucifix and put it around his neck. More of a recovering Catholic than anything, MacBridan was surprised by the amount of comfort the crucifix immediately brought to him.

As he pulled out on the road, Beninger returned his call. "Unless you called to confess, we don't have much to talk about," said the sheriff.

MacBridan pulled off onto the shoulder and stopped. "Then I guess I need to confess. Sheriff. I may have held out on you a little."

"Gee, I'm shocked."

"We've come across some information that you need to know. I also need your help."

"You are absolutely amazing. You never quit, MacBridan, I'll give you that. All right, let's have it. Even though I know that this is going to be just one more of your never ending lines of bull, tell me what you want."

MacBridan took Beninger through everything Cori had found, giving him names and numbers in the event he wanted to verify what MacBridan was telling him. "Here's the bottom line," said MacBridan. "New Westminster is the base of operations for the people who stole the artifacts that I was hired to recover. We believe that they're all members of a coven and needed the artifacts to help them with the satanic rituals they are performing out at Altar Rock."

"You've got no proof of that, MacBridan."

"We think we do. We think this coven is responsible for all of the killings that have taken place in the area surrounding New Westminster and that there is every reason to believe that they'll kill again. Here's where I need your help."

MacBridan told him of his visit to Holly's house, of the symbols he found on her steps, her physical condition, and the attempted murder of her husband in Boston.

Beninger was quiet for a few moments then said, "What would be the coven's interest in Ian and Holly?"

"We have no idea, but I'm real worried with her being out there by herself."

"Yeah, that I agree with."

"Sheriff, two men that work with me are at Katherine's guarding her. I need you to pick up Holly and take her to the house. She'll be safe there, and Mrs. Chamberlin will take care of her until the baby arrives."

"Any other errands I can run for you? Not that I mind getting her to a safer location, but while I'm out picking up Holly, may I ask what you'll be doing?"

"I'm going to try and find Father Collin. He knows far more about all that's been going on with this coven than he's told me."

"There's a lot of that going around," said Beninger. "I have to say that I find it rather interesting that you'd impugn the very man who supplied you with an alibi."

"Guess it's time for the rest of my confession," said MacBridan. "He lied."

"He lied about what?"

"He lied about all that he claimed to be doing at the church while I was at the high school, and especially about all that he claimed to have seen. I was there and the good Father was nowhere in sight."

"Why would he lie for you?" asked Beninger.

"That's a very good question. If our suspicions are correct, and he is somehow connected to this coven, then he lied to keep me away from you, to keep me from being locked up in a cell. It would have been harder for the coven to get at me if I'd taken up residence in your fine facility. By providing me with an alibi, he kept me where he and his group of looney tunes could get to me whenever they wanted to."

"So who was in the high school with you and Macy? If you didn't kill him, who did?"

"The same killer that murdered Vickers and the other victims that this coven has taken out."

"But who is it? Can't you identify who's doing all this?"

"In all honesty, no. That night at the high school was the second time I've come up against this killer, but I've never managed to get a clear look at him."

"All right, MacBridan, here's the deal. I'll head out now to get Holly and I agree that taking her to Mrs. Chamberlin's home is probably the best place for her. But I expect to find you there when I arrive. I want to see this proof you think you have. I just can't help but believe that you're still holding something else back from me."

MacBridan frowned into the phone. To a mild degree, this bothered him. Cori had picked up on his holding out on her earlier, but at least she had the edge of having known him for years, had something to compare with. The problem he had with Beninger was that the sheriff had only known him for a few days, and now he too had managed to pick up on the same thing. *Got to work on that,* thought MacBridan, *I used to lie so much better.*

"Not a problem. It's time you know everything."

"I'll see you real soon," said Beninger and hung up.

MacBridan felt better as he pulled back out onto the road. Beninger would get Holly and leave her in the capable hands of Harry and Smithers. Cori was with Ian, watching over him, and hopefully far enough away from New Westminster to be safe. It was time to bring Beninger into the loop. Now if he could find Father Collin and nail down his role in all this he would be much closer to putting these people out of business. Based on the coven's history, MacBridan knew they would not go down without a fight. MacBridan's cell phone stared to ring again and he could see that it was Cori calling him.

"Hi, what's up?"

"I'm at the hospital with Ian. Dolinski is sending two more men over to back me up. Where are you?" asked Cori.

"I'm on my way to the church. Hopefully Father Collin will have returned. Sheriff Beninger is on his way out to pick up Holly."

"Well, it may not be necessary," said Cori. "I just got off the phone from Professor Wilson. A couple of days ago he shared the pictures of the symbols you took at Altar Rock with a colleague of his. He told this guy how you found them and that we were trying to recover an old artifact."

"Okay, how does this change things?"

"Professor Wilson just got a call from him and immediately called to let me know what he'd learned. His friend is visiting his son in New Haven and yesterday evening, while walking the dog, found more of these symbols that had recently been scrawled on the side of an old church. According to Professor Wilson the symbols indicate that whatever is going to happen, it's going to be tonight, but in New Haven, not New Westminster," explained Cori.

"Is he sure about this? Almost everything else has happened in the New Westminster area."

"I asked the same question. According to Professor Wilson, this is not uncommon. We just didn't have all the information before, but now we do."

"Alright, I'll get back with you. Hopefully Father Collin can fill in the rest of the missing pieces."

As MacBridan approached St. Thomas, he saw that the lights were on. *Good. Finally.*

MacBridan turned his headlights off, and just before turning into the church parking lot cut the engine. The car coasted to a stop not twenty feet from the front doors of the church. MacBridan had his windows down, studying the church, listening. Thunder rumbled off in the distance, hinting at another storm approaching the town. He stepped out of his car and quietly closed the door. Pulling his gun, he chambered a round in the nine-millimeter automatic. He looked around one last time, then started up the steps.

***

MacBridan hadn't been gone more than ten minutes when another car pulled into Katherine's driveway, its wheels crunching on the gravel as it pulled to a stop. The driver casually got out of the car and made his way up on to the front porch. He knocked twice on the door, then stepped back a couple of paces. With all that had been going on he wanted to be sure that Katherine could easily identify her evening caller.

Katherine opened the door, smiling at her visitor. Harry stood a couple of feet behind her.

"Well this is a pleasant surprise. Won't you come in?"

He pulled open the screen door and stepped inside. "I won't be staying long," he said, "but I was out your way and I thought I'd drop by to see how things are going."

"That was awfully thoughtful of you," said Katherine. "I'm afraid you just missed Mr. MacBridan, but this is his associate Harry."

The two men shook hands. "Good to meet you. Welcome to New Westminster," said the visitor.

"Thank you, we're enjoying our visit," replied Harry.

The visitor looked up the stairs and at the man standing there looking down at him.

"Hello. I'm Kurt Smithers."

"Oh I'm so sorry," said Katherine. "I didn't see you."

"Good evening," said the visitor, nodding at Smithers.

"Would you join us for a cup of coffee? We were just getting ready to sit down and relax a little," offered Katherine.

"I really don't have a lot of time, but it'd be hard for me to turn coffee down."

"Excellent," said Katherine and she turned to lead the two men into the living room.

The visitor stepped forward and, with a smooth, casual motion, reached around behind him, under his jacket in a manner that suggested that he was adjusting his belt. Harry didn't see the gun the man pulled from his waistline. The visitor brought his hand back around and in an arching blow brought the gun down hard on to Harry's head. The attack caught Harry completely by surprise, sending him flying into a small table in the hallway.

Quickly the visitor stepped back to the foot of the stairs. The noise of Harry hitting the table brought Smithers rushing back to the head of the stairs.

"What was th—"

The two shots echoed loudly in the stairwell. Their impact picked Smithers up, hurling him into the wall. Slowly he slid down the wall to a sitting position, trailing a broad smear of blood.

Katherine stood rooted to the floor, staring at Harry's motionless body. The sudden and unexpected violence left her in stunned disbelief. Her eyes finally left Harry and turned to the visitor.

"Why?" The one word trembled out, so low that it was nearly inaudible.

"Let's go, Mrs. Chamberlin. Time for church."

CHAPTER 24

MacBridan paused before going into the church, his eyes searching the surrounding area for movement of any kind. Nothing but a gentle breeze wove its way through the treetops as it slowly ushered in the distant storm. He focused his gaze on the rectory, but there was no sign of light from any of its windows. He moved to the doors, reaching for them with his left hand, his right firmly holding his gun close to his side. The door to his right was unlocked. He opened it with as little noise as he could manage.

He quickly stepped inside, closing the door behind him. He stood completely still, listening, waiting for his eyes to adjust to the near pitch-blackness of the entryway. He could smell the soft, aromatic odor of candles burning. Dim light came from the front of the church, and he could hear faint noises of someone moving about.

MacBridan cautiously made his way through the vestibule and peered into the sanctuary. Numerous candles were burning on the altar, along with several ornate, golden candelabras lined up on either side. Father Collin, with his back to MacBridan, stood at the altar; busy with something MacBridan couldn't see. The priest's attention was so focused that he did not seem to be aware that someone else had entered the church.

Veering away from the center aisle, MacBridan crossed over to the left hand side of the church and silently worked his way forward towards the priest. Twice floorboards creaked loudly, but Father Collin, oblivious to all that was going on, did not turn around. MacBridan halted his approach directly in front of the confessional booths that stood recessed into the wall, to the side of the front pew. From this vantage point, he could see a small black bag on the altar. Father Collin continued to inspect several items, gently placing them in the bag one at a time. He then took a small vile of water, poured in on the blades of three swords and began to pray over them.

"Good evening. Those wouldn't just happen to be church artifacts that you're packing away there, would they, Father?" asked MacBridan.

Surprisingly the priest did not jump or act startled in any way at the sound of MacBridan's voice. He kept his back to him and said, "Mr. MacBridan, I was hoping that you would come by."

He turned to face MacBridan; a pleasant smile on his face and a small caliber automatic in his hand, pointed directly at MacBridan's stomach. "Now be a good lad and remain still. I'll use this if I have to, but I think you'll agree that it's in neither of our interests for that to happen."

Silently MacBridan cursed himself for being so stupid. Despite his suspicions, he'd underestimated the priest, allowing himself to be lulled into a bad situation. He knew that he could get a shot off. He was ready. He was also reasonably confident that he would hit the priest. The problem was that Father Collin's gun was already leveled at him at point blank range. Although he was certainly in the right place for heavenly intervention, he realized it would take nothing short of a minor miracle for the priest to miss him. But, before MacBridan got the chance to decide on his next move, the decision was taken away from him.

The hard nose of a gun barrel jutted into the small of his back. Someone had been hiding in the confessional booth. They'd been waiting for him. "Easy. Do not move," the harsh, raspy, voice commanded. Traces of a Slavic accent coated each word. A strong hand slid down his right arm, relieving him of his weapon.

"That's better," commented Father Collin, his gun still aimed a MacBridan's mid-section. "Please, won't you be seated? You'll find it almost like new—so few people ever sit in the front pew."

MacBridan stepped forward and sat down in front of Father Collin as directed.

"I believe you know my associate," said Father Collin, nodding in the direction of the man who had disarmed MacBridan.

MacBridan turned and looked into the face of Ubel Obermann, the German assassin MacBridan had seen in the church the night he'd been attacked at the high school. A twisted trace of a smile etched its way across the lean face. His cold, watery blue eyes stared intently at MacBridan.

"You look pretty healthy for a dead guy," said MacBridan. "On the other hand, you've got to be the ugliest altar boy I've ever seen."

"Please don't disappoint me, Mr. MacBridan," said Father Collin. "We have so much to discuss and so little time."

***

"So what is the phone company saying?" demanded Beninger as he drove out on Hickory Hill road to pick up Holly.

"They're just not sure, Sheriff," answered the dispatcher. "They haven't had any trouble reports turned in on the line, but at the same time they can't get through either. Unfortunately they don't have anyone in our area and probably can't get anyone out there to take a look until morning."

Beninger had tried to reach Holly by phone to let her know that he was coming out to get her. Each time he called it sounded like the call was going through, but no one answered. So Beninger had radioed his dispatcher to contact the phone company and see if there was a problem. Phone lines in rural communities went down far more often than most people realized. There were many reasons for this ranging from a tree branch falling and knocking a line down to some dim-witted animal literally chewing it in half. Disappointingly, it now appeared as if no one was going to get through to her tonight.

"Okay, thanks for trying."

"What do you want me to tell the phone company?"

"Tell them to get it fixed," snapped Beninger and hung up. Normally he wouldn't have thought twice about a phone line being out, but this time was different. Considering all that MacBridan had told him, not being able to reach the young girl bothered him considerably.

Even though it had been some time since he'd been out this way, he knew the area well. He'd hunted these woods many times, starting when he had been just a boy. He easily found the turn off and followed the twisting lane through the woods. Soon he came to the clearing where the house stood. It had been a moonless night to begin with, but the night sky had filled with clouds casting a shroud of darkness over the house and the valley, making it almost as dark as it had been along the wooded lane. In the far distance lightning danced across the horizon.

Beninger let the cruiser coast to a stop next to the porch steps. The house was completely dark. It had a bad feel to it. Why wasn't the area light on? If memory served, it was attached to the telephone pole beside the house. Was there a problem with the electricity as well as the phone? Anxious to verify some of what MacBridan had told him, he turned his flashlight on the steps before getting out. It took only a moment to find the symbols etched into the wood planking. He switched the hand held light off and got out of his car.

Strange sounds of the night from the surrounding woods greeted him. He stared up at the front door, then walked along side his car to the corner of the house and aimed his flashlight up towards the top of the telephone pole. Beninger really didn't expect to be able to figure out what the problem might be with her phone, but the area light not being on nagged at him. The strong beam of his flashlight quickly located the light's casing. The entire lamp had been shattered. From his vantage point, it appeared as if someone had shot it out.

Beninger hurried back and quickly opened the door to his car, sliding across the seat. He picked up the radio, "This is Beninger. Patch me through to Officer Goodman."

While he waited for Goodman, Beninger kept a close watch on the house and the yard around him, but the dark countryside held its secrets close.

Static burst through the radio. “This is Goodman.”

“What’s your twenty?” asked Beninger.

“I’m about a mile outside New Westminster on Highway 1421.”

“Get out to the Carpenter place as fast as you can. I think I may need back-up.” Beninger told him where to look for the lane leading to the house and was pleased to hear that Goodman already knew where it was.

Beninger got back out of his car and carefully made his way up the porch steps, unsnapping the leather strap that held his gun in its holster. He peered through the glass in the door with his flashlight but couldn’t see anyone. Carefully he tried the doorknob. It turned easily, and he went inside.

“Mrs. Carpenter, don’t be afraid, it’s Sheriff Beninger,” he called. “Are you all right?”

Silence answered him. Suddenly a vague form emerged from the darkness of the hallway that led to the bedroom. With his nerves already on edge, this sudden movement startled Beninger, and he jerked his flashlight toward it. “Mrs. Carpenter?” he nearly shouted.

“Sheriff, please, you’re hurting my eyes,” said Lucy, trying to shield them from the powerful beam with her hand.

“I’m sorry,” muttered Beninger, lowering the light back down to the floor. “Where is Mrs. Carpenter? Is she all right?”

***

Concealed in the shadows and unseen by Beninger, he had been waiting in the kitchen, out of sight from anyone looking in from the outside. As Beninger entered the house, he’d remained utterly still, hardly breathing. Lucy coming out of the bedroom provided the necessary distraction he’d been waiting for. Quickly he closed the short distance between him and Beninger, striking the sheriff a vicious blow across the side of his head.

The attack came without warning, accomplishing its goal as Beninger crumpled to the floor. He stood over his victim, ready to strike again.

“How is he?” asked Lucy, looking down at Beninger’s still form.

Scar Face, pleased with himself, put the leather sap he'd used in his hip pocket. "He took that full force across the temple. He may never go anywhere again."

***

MacBridan watched Obermann carefully. Of the two men he faced, Obermann was by far the more dangerous. The fact that this remorseless killer was actually alive and here brought things to another whole level.

Two years ago, MacBridan had been part of a team trying to catch Obermann. The Hawthorne Group had been engaged to protect a former US Ambassador to Germany. The ambassador had been retained to fly to Paris to help negotiate new trade agreements between the United States and Germany, and MacBridan had been assigned to go with him. Prior to their arrival in Paris the FBI learned that parties, opposed to the new trade agreements, had hired Obermann to assassinate the ambassador. Obermann's reputation as a skilled and cunning assassin was well known within the law enforcement community, especially before the unification. Coordinating with French Security Services, a phony location for the negotiations was leaked. MacBridan stayed close to the ambassador, supervising the security immediately around him.

As planned, Obermann got wind of the leak and made his attempt to penetrate the phony location. Finding it to be a trap, he shot and killed a French security officer then stole the man's car. The French security team chased Obermann for nearly five miles, firing at him at every chance they got. The chase ended when Obermann crashed through a guardrail, plunging forty feet into a ravine. His car burst into flames, burning the upper portion of his body beyond recognition. Items belonging to Obermann were found on the body, and it was believed he'd been killed. In the two years that followed this event, Obermann never surfaced, reinforcing the belief that he had died.

"Does Rome know the true identity of your acolyte?" asked MacBridan.

"As always, an astute question," answered Father Collin. "I would have to say that very few in Rome would know that, but then there are some.

They are in fact, the same individuals who intercepted your inquiry into my background and shut it down. However, I must say that I was pleased to learn of your effort to find out more about me. You were quite thorough, the mark of a true professional."

"Thank you," said MacBridan. "I'll have to use you as a reference sometime."

Despite the circumstances, Father Collin actually chuckled. "If only we had more time, but I'm afraid we don't."

"Why? Is there another meeting at Altar Rock tonight? Will you be leading your flock, as it were, through the *Red Dragon Grimoire*? Don't want to ruin your evening, but there's a storm approaching, or does it matter if it rains?"

"You do think the worst of me, don't you?" said Father Collin. "Yes, I guess from your point of view I could very easily be one of them. Admittedly, I didn't tell you everything, but I too had to determine who you were and whose side you were on. Happily, we fight a common enemy."

MacBridan glanced at Obermann. He hadn't moved, his gun still aimed at him. "All things considered, you'll understand if I find that a little hard to accept."

"Yes, I see your point," said Father Collin. He placed his gun into the black bag on the altar, and then sat down to the right of MacBridan, keeping him between the two men with Obermann maintaining a clear shot. "I'll explain this as well as I can, but stay with me. As I said, we have little time."

"I'll do my best," said MacBridan.

"I am a priest and my name is Collin Sheary. I'm proud of my Irish heritage and it may interest you to know that in Ireland the name Sheary means 'peace from God.'"

"As interesting as that is, I'm hoping there's more of a point to this."

"Most assuredly," smiled Father Collin. "I am not the first of my family to take up the cloth, but am, perhaps, one of the more unlikely to enter the priesthood. Much of my youth, I'm afraid, was ill spent and without going into a great deal of detail, I was most involved in the IRA. So you see, a significant part of my past is similar to that of Mr. Obermann."

"Well you'll have to invite me over some evening when the two of you are swapping stories."

Father Collin smiled patiently at MacBridan. "The events that led to my conversion and my decision to devote my life to Christ and His church are a story that one day I do hope to share with you. However, for our purposes here, it is important for you to know that I came to the church with a checkered past. A great uncle of mine, also a priest, knew how a man like me with my background, my special skill set as it were, could best serve God. So the church took me in and placed me in an order that to this day remains cloaked in secrecy. It is an old order dating back several hundred years. An old order with a violent history."

"What are you saying? Am I to believe that the Catholic Church has an order for semi-reformed killers?"

"No, not at all. The church continues to teach the Word of God, bringing as many to salvation as possible. But, at the same time, we recognize that we face a powerful enemy. An enemy, who never sleeps, never rests and will work to spread its absolute corruption among men until the final day. Mine is the Order of the Cross and Sword. An order dedicated to battling Satan and his minions wherever they are found. We are sent to investigate attacks upon the church, black witchcraft, not Wicca, mind you, but actual Satan worshipers, and all kinds of paranormal activities, possession being the worst of these."

Two weeks ago, MacBridan would have laughed at the priest, dismissing the whole story as ridiculous. But that was two weeks ago. Since then he had personally experienced too much and found himself intrigued by the priest's story.

"So why were you sent to New Westminster? What's going on here?"

"The theft of the artifacts, though valuable and important to the church, would not have been enough to involve my order. However, Father Henry, the previous priest here at St. Thomas, had reported to his bishop that a satanic coven was busy recruiting new members in and around his parish."

"That kind of thing can't be all that unusual, can it?" asked MacBridan. "I mean there are so many strange people out there doing all kinds of bizarre things, deluding themselves into believing they can become all powerful. What was it that made you take notice of this particular group?"

"The symbols," answered Father Collin. "The very ones you found at Altar Rock and confronted me with. Father Henry had also discovered them and sent copies to us. You and your people did well to decipher them so quickly. As you discovered, they are part of an old language, centuries old, that very few know of today. The combination of the thefts, Father Henry's report, and the symbols led us to believe that something very serious might be shaping up in New Westminster. Regrettably we did not arrive in time to prevent Father Henry's murder."

"According to the police report, Father Henry died in a car accident," challenged MacBridan.

Father Collin shook his head. "The church took Father Henry's body and had a private autopsy performed. It revealed that Father Henry's neck had been broken long before the accident. We'll probably never know exactly what happened, but he was a brave man. He wouldn't stop, wouldn't wait for us to get here. The idea of allowing a cancer such as that coven to grow in his own backyard was despicable to him."

"If their goal was to remain anonymous, to keep their presence concealed, then why steal the artifacts in the first place and risk being found out?" asked MacBridan.

"Simple, they needed them. Apparently, Father Henry got too close. They couldn't afford any exposure at that time, so they killed him. We searched the church and the rectory, but someone had beaten us to it, already having removed any journals, records, or evidence on the coven that Father Henry may have collected. But the symbols on Altar Rock, as well as those we have found in three other locations around New Westminster, confirmed our worst fears. Someone with rare knowledge is attempting to perform the *Red Dragon Grimoire*. Hence their need for the artifacts, especially the Cross of St. Patrick."

"I still don't understand. What exactly do they need the artifacts for?"

"My order has in its possession ancient texts where it is written that, if performed correctly, the *Red Dragon Grimoire* can 'open the grave.'"

"Are you saying that it can bring someone back from the dead?"

"Not exactly. We believe it has a broader meaning and that in this particular case their goal may actually be something far worse. Based on what we've learned from the various marked sites, we're pretty certain that their plan is to open an actual portal into Hell, summoning a dark angel, a very powerful demon, out of the pit and into this world."

"Hold on. Sorry, Father, but this is getting a little too crazy for me. True, I can't explain everything I've seen in the past couple of weeks, but please tell me that you really don't believe all this nonsense you're feeding me."

"Nonsense, Mr. MacBridan? To accomplish what they're trying to do takes time and is very dangerous, even for them. They have already opened the portal several times, and they are growing in their knowledge of how to control this creature. You've seen it! You have come face to face with it twice now, and the very fact that you're still alive is nothing short of a miracle!" said Father Collin.

"Demons and miracles, guess I don't see things the way you do," said MacBridan, trying his best to remain cavalier.

"Then open your eyes, man, and see what is right in front of you. Tell me what happened to you that night in the high school? I'll tell you what happened. God saved you. Through His sacred symbol of the cross, He repelled the demon that had been sent to kill you as well as Macy. There it is, Mr. MacBridan, a miracle, a true miracle. You asked me why they stole the artifacts. In order to complete the grimoire, it must be performed on sacred ground that has been defiled by sacrifice, hence their use of Altar Rock. They must also defile the very symbols of God's church, using them for their own vile needs. The Cross of St. Patrick was perhaps their greatest triumph," explained Father Collin, "for it is said to contain a fragment of the true cross. They will invert that cross during the final phase of the ritual to bring the creature out of the pit. We are almost certain that the final phase will be performed tonight.

"Fortunately a couple of things have worked in our favor," continued Father Collin. "First is time. The *Red Dragon Grimoire* takes a great deal of time if it is to be successfully completed, and it is a very complex process. The coven took its greatest risk during the first couple of times they opened the portal between our world and Hell, beckoning the demon to them.

They must have a strong, knowledgeable leader to have kept them focused during this time, for they were releasing a creature filled with pure hatred for everything in our world. Its malevolence and strength are beyond anything we can understand and will lash out with an unquenchable thirst for human souls. But it cannot survive for very long in our world in its own form; it needs time to acclimate if it is to survive here. My guess is that its first victims, human victims, were bound to Altar Rock where it feasted on them."

"The bodies I've seen weren't eaten," said MacBridan, "although they were mutilated in and around the throat."

"Yes, and each time one of the questions that couldn't be answered was what became of the blood. That is what it feeds on; blood is what is needed to acclimate it to our world. Over time, two things happen. The creature finally gets enough human blood in it that it is in a constant state of agony. It is no longer a true denizen of Hell but is now part of both worlds, yet belonging to neither. In its torment, the coven takes full control, finally being able to direct its actions toward specific targets. The creature, at this point, is almost dependent on them, not so very different from the relationship between an addict and its pusher."

"But why? What's the point?" asked MacBridan. "If it can't survive in our world, are they planning to just continue to use this thing as a killing machine that they can direct?"

"Frankly there are many fearsome possibilities, some too dreadful to think about."

Both men sat quietly, MacBridan fighting between the beliefs he'd held for most of his adult life and a hellish potential that threatened his sanity. "You said that two things worked in our favor. Time was one. What was the other?"

"Greed. It's amazing if you think about it. When you consider all that the members of this coven have witnessed, the horror, the violence, a world revealed to them that so few really even believe exist, and yet the power of greed overcame all of this. Though it cost them their lives, Vickers and Macy bought us valuable time."

MacBridan slowly shook his head. He looked Father Collin in the eye and said in a quiet, level voice, "I'm sure you believe all that you've told me. I find myself closer to believing you than I care to admit, but no matter how these people are doing it, there's nothing special about them. They're just criminals playing at some sick game. As to the rest of what you've told me, perhaps you do belong to an order that targets this kind of activity, but the Catholic Church that I know doesn't have assassins on its payroll."

Father Collin got up and returned to the altar, continuing to carefully place items into the black bag.

"We're out of time," said Obermann, his voice low, strong, cold.

"I know," said Father Collin, "we have much to do tonight. Regarding Ubel, I'll put this as succinctly as I can. He obviously did not die in that car crash in France, but he was grievously wounded."

"Then whose body was it that burnt up in the car?"

Ubel answered before the priest could. "The man worked for me. I needed someone who knew the area well, someone who could get me out of there quickly once I'd made the kill. As it turned out, the French security man I shot also shot me. I made it back to my associate and told him to take the security man's car and lead the authorities away from me. He accomplished his task far better than I could have ever dreamed. I took our car and escaped into the French countryside."

"I see. Of course, he just happened to be wearing your coat, with your passport sewn in the lining. Most convenient."

"An old ruse," shrugged Obermann, "one that I have used many times before. Earlier that evening I had given him the coat to wear, giving him the look of a high priced chauffer. Unbeknownst to him were the complete contents of the coat. The idea was that should something go wrong and he be captured, the papers, as well as the other articles on him, would confuse the police long enough to help secure my escape." Ubel's smug smile chilled MacBridan.

"Ubel made it to a small monastery not far from the site of the shooting," said Father Collin, picking up the story. "Before collapsing from his injuries he asked for sanctuary." He closed the black bag and then turned, facing MacBridan.

"I nearly died," said Obermann. "The monks were very good to me and during my recovery I had, how shall I put this, a life altering experience?

I spoke to the abbot about it many times and he led me in prayer. A few weeks later Father Collin came to see me."

"Let me guess," said MacBridan, "you're a priest, too."

"No," answered Father Collin, "but he has been brought into our order, and he works with us, helping us while continuing to pray for forgiveness."

"Didn't think it could be done, but that story actually tops the one about the demon," said MacBridan, shaking his head. "In fact I find your demon theory more plausible than Ubel Obermann repenting and turning over a new leaf."

"Be that as it may, Mr. MacBridan, the time has come for me to leave and you have a choice to make." Father Collin extended his hand to Obermann who gave him MacBridan's gun. Obermann then holstered his own weapon under the waist length jacket he wore.

Father Collin walked up to MacBridan and handed him his weapon. "Here," he said. "We need your help, and we need it now. I really don't care what you believe. However, I think we all agree that this coven must be destroyed. We're leaving. Are you with us or not?"

Unexpectedly events had taken a 180-degree turn. He checked his gun, a little surprised to find it still fully loaded. He looked at Obermann. The man held his stare. He then looked back at the priest and said, "So, where are we going?"Father Collin went back up to the altar, picked up one of the swords and handed it to MacBridan. "Your gun will work on any human foes we encounter, but you may need this, especially if the coven is successful. The blade has been coated with holy water and is one of the few weapons that will take down a demon. It's time."

CHAPTER 25

MacBridan and Father Collin made their way up the aisle of the sanctuary of St. Thomas with Obermann following close behind. The thunder continued to increase in its frequency, its low growl penetrating the ornate walls of the old church. All the candles had been extinguished, their thick fragrance now mingling with the smoke spiraling from the wicks. The light guiding them came from Obermann's flashlight.

"In answer to your question," said Father Collin, "we are on our way to Altar Rock. Tonight is when they'll try and complete the *Red Dragon Grimoire*, bringing their pet demon out of Hell. Our fear is that their ultimate goal is to complete the creature's transition, enabling it to live in our world. If they can pull this off, they will control an entity, a power if you will, more lethal to our existence than anything we've known. Its thirst can never be quenched, and we cannot allow this to happen."

They stepped into the parking lot and once the church doors were locked, Obermann extinguished his light. The cool night breeze felt good to MacBridan, but the air was filled with the heavy scent of rain. They were definitely going to get wet before the night was out.

"What is their interest in Holly Carpenter?" asked MacBridan.

His question stopped the priest in mid stride. He stared intently at MacBridan. "Why do you ask that?"

"There are symbols carved into the front steps leading up to her porch. You didn't know that did you?"

"No," answered the priest. "I did not."

"I saw her earlier today, and she is not only close to delivering that baby, but she is very weak and very alone."

"Alone? Where's Ian? Isn't he with her?"

"Someone tried to kill Ian three days ago in Boston. They ran him down with a car."

Father Collin bowed his head and crossed himself. "Holy Mother of God, this cannot be happening."

"Sheriff Beninger is on his way to get Holly now. He and I talked about thirty minutes ago. The plan is for him to pick her up and take her to Mrs. Chamberlin's. I have men with Mrs. Chamberlin, guarding her."

At the mention of Beninger's name, Father Collin shot a look at Obermann. "That may not have been the wisest move," said Father Collin.

"I assure you the two men I have there are quite capable," said MacBridan.

Father Collin shook his head. "That's not what I was referring to. We're not clear on where Beninger stands in all of this."

"I'll be the first to admit that he's perhaps not the most motivated law enforcement officer I've come across, but I certainly don't see him being mixed up in this."

"We asked Sheriff Beninger to reopen the investigation into Father Henry's death. He refused."

"Did you show him the autopsy report?"

"Yes, but he said that because it had been done by a private physician and not an authorized legal authority that the report didn't hold much weight. He told us that one of his best men had investigated the wreck, and he agreed with his officer that it had been just a tragic accident. This belief was further validated by Dr. Appleton, the county medical examiner, who ruled it accidental."

"That may have been frustrating, but it doesn't make him a bad guy."

"We also asked him for help with the activities going on at night out at Altar Rock. We explained that we were concerned about vandalism. He said he'd look into it."

"Did he?"

"I really don't think it registered as a high priority for him. Once again, a few days later, I got the tired old line that one of his best men had looked into it and hadn't found anything. He was content to write it off as just kids being kids."

That sounded familiar and MacBridan reflected on his short association with the sheriff. Could he have so completely misjudged Beninger? In addition to all that, the priest had just laid out, Beninger, and *one of his best men*, hadn't been all that effective in finding the jerk who had been watching Katherine's house either. Still, he had trouble accepting the idea that Beninger was dirty. He also didn't believe Beninger to be as inept as all this made him look. Something didn't make sense.

"Nevertheless, what about Holly Carpenter? What would they want with her?"

"The baby," answered the priest grimly as they rapidly crossed the parking lot. The rushing water of Shepard's Creek grew in volume as they neared the footbridge. "They'll need one more sacrifice. Can you think of anything more innocent, more pure than a newborn child?"

Anger surged through MacBridan at the very thought of that possibility. "Then we damn well better make sure that doesn't happen. Obermann and I can easily handle the locals. I just hope you're ready to stop that thing, whatever it is. When you were packing your little black bag, I trust you remembered to bring along a couple of wooden stakes?"

Father Collin hesitated, his hand resting on the handrail of the footbridge. "The coven has probably already started the ceremony to open the portal. The process is very involved and cannot be rushed. Because of that, once we cross the stream and enter the churchyard, we are going to find that things have changed. You're going to see things. Do as I say, when I say it, or all of us may die tonight."

He looked directly into MacBridan's eyes. "There are no wooden stakes in this bag, no garlic, nor anything else for that matter that you will find laced throughout the fictional stories you grew up with. They were just that, fiction. Leave the folklore and the wives' tales on this side of the bridge. Very few people alive today really understand what we are about to face. There's no time to prepare you, and I'm sorry for that, but you are about witness a reality more terrifying than any ghost story you've ever heard. Stay close to me and let's hurry or we will be too late."

***

He couldn't move, but considering that, his head felt like it wanted to part down the middle, moving wasn't all that attractive an option. "Where are we going?"

It was a woman's voice, faint, the words slightly slurred.

"We are taking you to Altar Rock, Holly," another woman's voice answered. "Our leader is already there waiting for you. Tonight he will present you to the true lord. We will all pray to your baby."

"I can't," protested the first woman. "I'm so tired…"

Beninger felt them pass by him. The sound of the door hitting the wall as they flung it open reverberated through his head. He tried to open his eyes but couldn't. He still couldn't move. The pain from his head traveled down his neck and spread into his stomach causing a wave of nausea to wash over him.

Outside he heard what sounded like doors being shut. Then a car engine started, and he listened as they drove away. All was quiet now. He knew he was alone. The blow to the head had caught him higher up than his attacker had guessed, missing his temple by a fraction. He was hurt, no doubt about that, but not dead yet. He had to get up even though his head wanted to argue the point. The pain throbbed and sent a sharp, piercing jolt shooting down his neck and across his shoulders.

He tried moving again and this time succeeded, the side of his face pulling away from the pool of blood that had become a sticky mess, nearly gluing him to the linoleum. As he rolled onto his side, his head continued to protest violently. The pain lanced through him, once again racing across his shoulders and down his spine. He was going to be sick, there was no stopping it. He got his arm under him and rose up just in time, adding the contents of his stomach to the bloody mess already spread across the floor.

Only his left eye would open. His right eye had swollen shut, and the welt on the side of his head felt like it was the size of golf ball. He tried to make sense of what had happened. They had taken Holly. Wasn't he supposed to have picked her up? They were taking her to Altar Rock. Why? Beninger couldn't figure out who *they* were.

Carefully he brought himself up to a sitting position. The pain was beyond anything he'd experienced. With his hand he lightly touched his head, quickly pulling it away as a new wave of misery rocketed through him, rewarding him for his effort. Finally, the throbbing began to subside a little, and he tried to remember where he was. It took a moment before it all came back to him. Beninger needed help and realized he needed it badly.

An inch at a time Beninger crawled through the open door, making his way out onto the porch. The crisp autumn air acted like smelling salts, helping to further revive him. His car. He had to get to his car.

His trip down the porch steps was agonizing, and he had a great deal of trouble opening the door to the cruiser. The pain—combined with the nausea and the loss of blood—nearly defeated him, but he managed to pull himself into the driver's seat. Gently he leaned his head back against the seat cushion.

Focus, he needed to retain focus. Beninger's first goal was to get help. His fingers discovered the handset of his radio lying on the seat where he'd left it, but something was wrong. With great care, he slowly turned his head so that his one good eye could examine it. The wire connecting the handset had been cut.

Waves of pain came and went with nearly overwhelming force, but he'd recovered to a point where he could now at least sit up straight. The keys he'd left in the ignition were gone, but the spare key he kept over the sun visor was thankfully still there. They had broken the radio. Had they also disabled the car? To his relief the engine turned over on his first try. He gripped the wheel with both hands, fighting the sickness in his stomach that threatened to erupt again. As it passed, he reached to his belt for his cell phone but it wasn't there. Hard to tell what had happened to it, and he certainly was in no condition to go looking for it. At least they hadn't removed the gun from his holster.

Beninger didn't know what to do. He couldn't reach anyone to let them know what was happening. He felt certain he could drive, but knew it would be a slow process and that he would not get to Altar Rock in time enough to be of any help to anyone. He then remembered the old dirt road that had originally taken people to the church at Altar Rock crossed the Carpenter property. Today it was still used, but only as a maintenance road. As the crow flies, he wasn't all that far away from Altar Rock, but even if he did make it, what then? Beninger half smiled and figured he'd worry about that when he got there, if he got there. The way he felt it'd be a minor miracle if he could even find the old road.

He put the car into gear and began to slowly move down the hill toward the tree line. Each bump caused his head to ache as if it were about to burst. He guided the car parallel to the trees and finally found it. Slowly he began his way down the old lane, entering the woods.

* * *

The churchyard lay quiet before them, the constant babble of Shepard's Creek nearly drowning out all other sounds. MacBridan could see very little. The whole area this side of the creek was practically pitch-black. Obermann turned his flashlight back on, handing MacBridan one just like it. With both lights guiding them, they stepped away from the footbridge, leaving it behind.

All at once, a low roar rose up downstream from them, making itself known, rapidly building in volume. They stopped and listened. Try as he might, MacBridan could not identify the sound. However, one thing was clear, it was coming at them and coming fast, with the force of a locomotive. Treetops began to sway violently as the screaming torrent of wind swept in. It quickly grew in intensity, descending like a wave breaking on the shore, launching its assault against the three men.

The wind ripped through the churchyard, whirling around them, making it nearly impossible for them to talk to each other. It hit with such ferocity that they had to brace themselves to keep from being knocked off their feet. MacBridan looked at Father Collin. He watched the priest as he knelt down and pulled a large silver cross from the bag. MacBridan knew enough to recognize the cross's Celtic design. Father Collin bowed his head, prayed, and then held the cross up before them. Obermann picked up the black bag, maintaining his position just a step behind the priest. MacBridan moved closer to Father Collin, but could barely hear him as he began to chant. Miraculously the force of the wind lessened considerably, and the wind screamed its protest as it tore away from them, lashing out in anger against the monuments. MacBridan could hear better now and recognized some of the Latin coming from Father Collin as he continued to chant.

The churchyard had quite a different aspect to it compared to how it had been on his previous visit with Katherine. The peaceful, well-groomed haven of eternal rest had turned into a menacing collection of twisting paths, all leading to unknown horrors within the necropolis. The wind continued to tear around the three men but no longer posed a threat. They walked on, untouched, in the eye of the storm that raged all around them. MacBridan felt off balance carrying the heavy sword and a flashlight, so he tucked the sword away under his belt, freeing up one of his hands. He had zero experience with swords and knew he'd be next to useless if it came down to his having to use it.

Then the wind changed tactics, breathing life into many of the large fir trees that lined the path they were following. Branches frantically tried to reach Father Collin, but struck MacBridan and Obermann instead as they shielded the priest.

Flashes of lightning offered brief glimpses of the numerous graves and the old, weathered stones that marked them, but it also revealed something else. MacBridan caught sight of something moving amongst the monuments, circling, getting closer. He watched as closely as he could and realized that there were several of them, on both sides of the path. Each time the sky lit up MacBridan could see them quickly dart behind headstones or drop down behind a bush or tree, a seemingly futile attempt to conceal their approach. But something was wrong, terribly wrong. Their silhouettes were misshapen, grotesque in their form. MacBridan tried shining his light on them, but could not get a clear look. The notion that these beings had them surrounded worried him, but at the same time, he couldn't understand how they kept disappearing. Most of the gravestones were too small to conceal anyone, as were many of the bushes.

"What are those things?" shouted MacBridan. "They're all around us!"

"Demon shades," Obermann yelled back. "We stay in the light, we're safe. They catch up with us without any light…" Obermann grimaced and moved on. The path they followed came upon a private family mausoleum, set back from the path, standing just to the left of them. Its door, framed by marble columns and topped by sculpted angels, shuddered under the constant impact from a force within the large structure. A dull green light could be seen glowing beneath the doorframe. It oozed its way out from under the door of the mausoleum and flowed upwards, encasing the statutes that stood atop the columns. MacBridan watched in fascinated horror as the heads of the angels turned in unison, glaring at him. Their eyes filled with the cold, green light and their gentle faces changed into contorted masks of rage.

"What is happening?" yelled MacBridan, desperately trying to keep a grip on his rapidly fraying nerves. He didn't remember pulling his gun, but he had it at his side, ready.

"Keep moving," shouted the priest. "The gates to the pit are opening, and Hell is beckoning forth its disciples. There is little time left. We have to make it to Altar Rock."

Father Collin never faltered, leading them along the winding path. The dull green light they had seen at the mausoleum could now be seen seeping from various graves scattered throughout the churchyard.

Suddenly the grave next to MacBridan began to move. The earth covering the grave started to boil, green light erupting through the cracks in the ground. An almost overpowering stench of decay and filth struck MacBridan in the face, with nearly as much force as the wind that had first assaulted them. Lightning flashed and in that brief moment, MacBridan could see a gnarled, withered hand reaching up from the grave, clawing at the earth. He jumped back from it, nearly knocking Father Collin down.

MacBridan pointed his light at the monstrous hand by way of explanation. He tried to shout some kind of warning, but his voice failed him. Father Collin saw what was happening and stepped toward it, directing the face of the cross at the grave. He knelt beside it and once again bowed his head in prayer. A blue white light steadily grew in brilliance to the point MacBridan could not look directly at it. Then, as suddenly as it had appeared, the light was gone. MacBridan trained his light back on the grave to find that the hand had retreated back into the ground, the green light vanquished. The earth around the grave trembled, then collapsed inward, leaving a low, sunken area over the top of the grave.

Father Collin stood up and squeezed MacBridan's arm. The gesture, although small, reassured him and gave him a surprising amount of comfort. The priest started to chant again and, holding up the cross, continued along the path. MacBridan briefly made eye contact with Obermann, embarrassed by his weak reaction, expecting condemnation from the other man. Obermann, however, met his gaze and merely nodded, letting MacBridan know that he understood.

MacBridan's hand holding the flashlight shook, but fortunately, due to the pace they were keeping, only he was aware of it. His other hand still held his gun, his grip on it so tight that his knuckles had turned white.

MacBridan found himself thrust into the middle of a living nightmare from which he could see no escape, fearing that if he fell he would end up at the mercy of the abominations that dogged their every step. He pressed on; he would not give in to the madness that threatened to send his mind into a blind panic. MacBridan fought desperately with every step to hang on.

The wind continued its assault, but still could not reach them. The path took a hard turn to the right, passing through several tall evergreens and then straightened out for several yards, more of the private mausoleums now on either side of them. They were able to increase their pace a little and MacBridan recognized where they were. They had nearly made it through. The vast churchyard would soon be behind them. MacBridan began to feel a sense of relief, knowing that in just a few minutes he would be away from the terrors that inhabited the cemetery.

His elation was premature.

Out of the corner of his eye, MacBridan caught sight of something as it moved beside one of the mausoleums on the left nearest Obermann. Both men reacted as one, MacBridan bringing his gun up, Obermann raising the sword before him. They stopped as a man walked out onto the path, blocking their advance. MacBridan quickly stepped in front of the priest, shielding him. Obermann moved in closer to Father Collin, also watching to see that nothing came up from behind them.

A flash of lightning allowed MacBridan a closer look at their antagonist and his remaining resolve nearly crumbled. The man seemed to glow with the same pale green light that had haunted many of the graves. His eyes, like those of the statuettes on the mausoleum, were filled with the green light, glowering at them, emanating hatred. The stench coming from the specter filled the air around them. Much of the man's neck had been torn away, leaving strips of withered flesh hanging from his jaw and shoulder. The man stood close enough to them that they could see swarms of maggots eating away at the open wound. It was Carl Macy.

"MacBridan," hissed the creature. The sound of his own name forced MacBridan back a step. "This time things will be different. Tonight I will feast upon you in my grave." Macy reached for him and MacBridan fired.

The bullet struck Macy in the center of his chest, tearing a hole in the man, but to MacBridan's astonishment did not knock him down. The impact of the nine millimeter bullet at that range should have sent him flying, but it only caused Macy to stagger back a couple of steps. Macy felt where the bullet had entered with his hand. A maniacal smile crawled across his face and once again, he raised his arms, reaching for MacBridan.

Father Collin had managed to get around MacBridan, and met Macy's advance with his sword. The blue white light that MacBridan had seen emanate from the cross dance along the blade. Continuing to chant his prayers, he advanced on the creature. Macy charged at them and Father Collin plunged the sword into his heart. A low moaning scream started to force its way from Macy's mangled throat, a scream that bore no resemblance to anything human. Macy's chest seemed to explode from within and he fell to the side of the path.

"Come," he shouted, "they have done their worst and God has vanquished them, but we cannot stop. We must hurry."

MacBridan kept pace with the other two men, but his mind continued its struggle to comprehend all he had witnessed. Then the ground under him shifted, nearly tripping him. He looked down and found that the paved path had ended, putting them on the dirt path that would take them the rest of the way to Altar Rock. The trees standing at the edge of the woods loomed in front of them.

Father Collin stopped briefly and turned to MacBridan. "We are about to face our most difficult challenge. This time we will be up against human foes, as well as supernatural. You have done well, better than I could have hoped, but you will now have to reach deep inside and give even more."

"Don't stop now, Father. Give me time to think about all that just happened, and I may decide I've had all the fun I can take."

Father Collin reached into the bag and brought out a container of water. He prayed before each of them and drew the sign of the cross on their foreheads with the water.

"Holy water," said Father Collin, answering MacBridan's question before he could get it out. "It may not keep you alive, but I pray that it will protect your immortal soul."

"How do you want to do this?" asked Obermann.

"Get me to the rock," said the priest. "It'll be up to you and MacBridan to save their final sacrifice." He looked at MacBridan and said, "It very well may turn out to be Holly, but whoever it is, get them out of there."

"Saving that person may not be practical, all things considered," said Obermann. "It'd probably be better for me to just go ahead and kill their sacrifice right off. Doing that may throw them off balance, bettering our odds of destroying them."

"Forget it," said MacBridan before Father Collin could respond. "That may be the way you operate, but not me. I don't really care what you do to the members of the coven, but so long as I can help it, no one else is going to suffer because of them." MacBridan looked at the priest. "Where does Rome stand in all this?"

"I agree, Mr. MacBridan," said Father Collin. "That is not what any of us want. Ubel was merely pointing out that contingency as an option."

"Well it's not an option for me," said MacBridan.

Obermann looked at MacBridan with no discernible expression. He shrugged his acceptance, but MacBridan was nowhere near convinced that Obermann wouldn't carry out his suggested contingency at the first opportunity.

"Come along, there is no time to argue. The only way to thwart them is to take away their sacrifice, the creature's final meal, if you will, and get me the time to sanctify the ground they are using. People are going to die tonight; there is no way around that. But so long as one of us is alive, we cannot allow them to complete the grimoire. May God be with us." With that, he turned and headed into the woods.

CHAPTER 26

The ride down the old, dirt lane leading to Altar Rock was one of constant torment for Beninger. Over the years, the narrow lane had not been well maintained, and its surface consisted of holes, rocks and small branches that had fallen from the trees that arched overhead. His head and shoulders ached terribly, the ever-persistent pain causing him to cry out each time his car connected with one of the deeper holes. Beninger had no idea how long he had been driving, his entire focus was targeted on getting to Altar Rock and not colliding with a tree in the process.

He had not given much thought to what he would be able to do once he arrived and was only concerned with the fact that he had to get there. Holly Carpenter was in danger, and, as far as he knew, he was the only one who could help her.

For most of the way the lane kept angling down the slope of the hill, but now it turned sharply left, heading up a steep grade. Remarkably, Beninger had had enough presence of mind to keep his lights on low beam. Even though he realized that anyone watching would see his lights, putting them on high would have exacerbated the problem, further advertising his approach.

The cruiser easily topped the small grade, and Beninger slowly began to make his way around a curve that angled sharply to the right. Suddenly, without warning, another car appeared directly in front of him. The dense woods, with their thick undergrowth, had kept the other car well hidden. Beninger slammed on his brakes, barely avoiding running into it, but the jerking movement and the sudden stop enflamed the wound to his head.

He gripped the wheel as if hanging on for dear life, waiting for this new spasm of pure torment to pass. Finally, his vision cleared and he studied the car in front of him. It faced away from him, an old station wagon, and yet, for some reason, it looked vaguely familiar. There didn't seem to be anyone inside. Beninger turned his lights off and, after a moment, cut the engine. He couldn't imagine why anyone would have left a car literally in the middle of nowhere. He figured that the people who had taken Holly must have left it here. The good news was that this probably meant that he was close to Altar Rock. The downside, however, presented a potentially impossible task. From this point on, he would have to make it on foot.

Beninger rested for a few moments, opened the door, but struggled getting out of the cruiser. He held on to the side of his car for support as he moved forward, continuing this process with the other car to keep him steady. He looked into its windows, confirming that it was empty.

The station wagon was parked at the base of another steep incline, this one more than twice the distance of the one he'd just driven up. Beninger took a deep breath, released the grip he had on the front of the station wagon and started up the hill. But with nothing to hold onto, he only managed a couple of steps before the dizziness sent him to his knees.

Beninger knew that if he went all the way down he'd never make it back up again. He had to keep going. Despite the constant pain punishing his entire body, Beninger started a slow crawl up the hill.

* * *

MacBridan remembered that the path twisted through a small patch of woods before it reached the clearing that held Altar Rock. What concerned him was just how vulnerable they would be once they entered the trees. The dark night, blending with the thick growth that bordered both sides of the path, would keep an enemy well hidden until it was too late.

MacBridan gripped Father Collin's arm, stopping him. "Father, I think I'll lead for a while. It'll be best if you stay between us."

"I understand, thank you."

With that, MacBridan turned and entered the woods. His nerves were raw, but the thought of Holly being murdered so that her unborn child could be used as a sacrifice drove him on. Despite everything he had just witnessed, he dreaded more than ever, what might be waiting for them at Altar Rock.

They had just entered the woods when things took a dramatic turn. The wind stopped. It wasn't that the trees had just slowed it down, lessening its impact—it literally stopped. Everything was utterly still as if the world had instantly been frozen in time. But it was more than that. The woods around them were completely silent. Every sound that typically filled a wooded area at night was gone. The world had become mute.

"What is it?" asked MacBridan. They had stopped, expecting something to come at them, but nothing did. All was still.

"The time is upon us," said Father Collin. "Keep moving, we're almost there."

The path seemed narrower than MacBridan remembered it. He held his breath with each step, expecting something to lunge at him out of the darkness. The total lack of sound and movement was as unnerving as anything else that had gone on that night. The heavy breathing from the two men behind him betrayed their nervousness, sounding abnormally loud. The path finally turned one last time, dropping down steeply and opening up on the clearing.

"Wait," whispered Father Collin, but in the absolute silence that draped across the landscape, his voice carried as if he had shouted the command.

They stood at the edge of the clearing, having turned their flashlights off just before stepping out from the relative shelter of the trees. The darkness was so complete that they could only vaguely see Altar Rock, the skeletal ruins of the old church but a dim silhouette against the tree line. The memory of the creatures Obermann had called demon shades flashed back into MacBridan's mind. He struggled with the desperate urge to turn his light back on. His companions, however, didn't seem to be worried about the lack of light, and he found himself praying that the demon shades no longer posed a threat. It had been a long time since he'd prayed.

Father Collin opened the black bag, withdrew a priest's robe and quickly put it on. He then brought out a broad stole that, as best MacBridan could make out, was covered with intricate patterns. The priest prayed over it and then placed it around his neck, allowing both ends to hang down in front of him, the ends reaching down to his knees. With the black bag in one hand, his sword secured under his robe, and the cross in the other, he began to walk across the clearing, directly towards Altar Rock.

"Come along," he said. MacBridan and Obermann closely followed, flanking the priest.

They had not gone more than six or seven paces when the landscape altered, taking on an unreal aura. From the center of the clearing, emanating from Altar Rock, the dull, green light shot forth and raced across the grass, covering everything with its sickly glow. The trees, the ruins, everything was bathed in the unholy light.

"The sky, look at the sky," whispered Obermann.

Even the clouds radiated the same green light that covered the land. As stunning a sight as this was, the fact that the sky itself was also absolutely motionless awed MacBridan. His stomach revolted against the thick, pungent odor of decay that permeated the air, adding to the near claustrophobic dread that rushed over him. He felt like they'd been moved inside a vast crypt with images of clouds painted on the immense ceiling far above them, a distorted line of trees similarly painted on the surrounding walls.

"Move quickly," said Father Collin. "We stand between earth and Hell. The portal will open any moment now."

They started to run toward Altar Rock and it was then, thanks to the green light, that they saw the bodies. One lay atop Altar Rock, the other sprawled across the grass at its base. MacBridan's stomach turned, he knew one of them would be Holly, already dead. He soon realized his mistake. It was not Holly. His brief feeling of relief was shattered by the devastating realization of the victim's identity. Katherine lay atop the rock, her eyes closed, her arms folded across her chest.

MacBridan ran up to her, placing his hand on her neck. Her skin was clammy to the touch, and it took a few seconds before he could detect a faint pulse. "Thank God," he muttered. It had been his second prayer in less than ten minutes. Maybe when all this was over he'd join Obermann back at the monastery.

"She's alive," he said as he gently picked the old woman up, getting her off of the cold stone.

"So is this guy," said Obermann. "But from the amount of blood on him, I'm not sure what kind of shape he's in."

MacBridan moved over next to Obermann. He did not want to look at the second body, for he was reasonably certain that it would be either Harry or Smithers. Instead, he found himself staring down at the young deputy. "It's Deputy Goodman," said MacBridan. The deputy's thick hair was matted with blood. It had run down to cover much of his face and neck. He lay on his stomach, nearly spread eagle, his right arm folded under him. MacBridan noticed that his holster was empty.

Father Collin paid little attention to any of this. He placed the bag on the ground next to Altar Rock and proceeded to pull out the items he needed to begin his work. "Keep your eyes open," he said. "We are not alone."

As if on cue, light sprang from the ruins of the old church steeple. Dozens of candles blazed to life, all of which had been placed across the crumbling walls that lined the top of the bell tower. In the midst of the candles stood three figures, motionless, wearing monk's robes. To MacBridan they looked like something out of *Canterbury Tales*, their faces obscured, hidden deep within the hoods of their garments.

Obermann left the deputy where he lay, moving in beside the priest. MacBridan also edged closer to Father Collin, unsure of his next move. He looked around, trying to find a safe place to put Katherine. It was then he spotted another of the hooded figures.

"Over to your left, where the path leaves the woods. We've got one more of them," warned MacBridan.

"Saw him," answered Obermann. "There's also one at the base of the tower." MacBridan looked, finally catching sight of him in the dim light. Like the others, he stood perfectly still, blending in with the rock wall behind him.

Father Collin carried on, not allowing any of this to distract him. A small gold box rested in front of him. He had begun to chant, while at the same time trying to light the incense he'd placed in a large, beautifully etched burner, a long brass chain attached to its top.

"You're too late, priest!" The voice was loud and full with a harsh grating quality to it. It had come from one of the figures upon the tower. "Behold your fallen church."

The figure to the left of the dark priest on the tower stepped forward, and from beneath its robe, brought out the Cross of St. Patrick. He held the cross in front of him, upside-down, inverted. MacBridan recognized the artifact that had eluded him for so long.

MacBridan quickly laid Katherine down next to him in the grass. "You want the two on the ground or the three in the tower?"

"The two on the ground," answered Obermann.

Father Collin stood at the base of Altar Rock. The small gold box contained the host. He held it in his right hand. "I'm ready to begin," he told them, "but this is going to take a little time. No matter what happens, you cannot allow them their final sacrifice." Father Collin's Irish accent much more pronounced.

Obermann had drifted a couple of paces away from Altar Rock. MacBridan stood to his right. The hooded figure holding the Cross of St. Patrick remained completely motionless. The one standing behind him raised his arms and shouted something in a language MacBridan did not recognize. Once finished, he kept his arms raised to sky, quiet now, perfectly still.

MacBridan was poised to attack, ready to take out the two coven members in the tower. These people had already killed many times without mercy. They had tried to kill him. They had attacked Katherine, and he knew they would soon kill her as well. A numbing feeling of despair ran through him as he thought about Harry and Smithers. He could only imagine what had happened to them. With all this filling his mind, he had no qualms as he stood ready to help Obermann cut them down. The sad truth was that he was looking forward to it.

"You ready?" asked Obermann. His voice was as calm as if he were preparing to order lunch.

The extreme silence amplified the cocking of a gun. "Nobody moves," the voice from behind them commanded. The dull, smacking sound of someone being hit was closely followed by a gasp of pain. Father Collin fell hard, hitting the ground between them. MacBridan could see that a small cut above his eye had started to bleed.

"Drop the guns, now, or I'll put a bullet in the priest's head."

There was little they could do and they let their weapons fall to the grass.

"Good. Now step forward. That's it. All right stop. Kneel down and place your hands behind your head."

MacBridan ignored this, turned around and looked at the man. "Officer Goodman, glad to see you're feeling better." MacBridan realized that the deputy had been lying on his gun and silently cursed himself for not having checked him more closely.

"Much," said Goodman. His smiling face a hideous mask, grinning out from under the dried blood. "Now do as you're told or I'll break the old girl's neck while you watch."

"You brought her here?" asked MacBridan.

"That's right," said Goodman. "Your two men went down almost as easily as you did that night during the storm when I knocked you into the bushes. I'd have finished you then if she hadn't come out with that shotgun."

"So that's why Beninger never found out who was watching the house. He had you doing the looking."

"Beninger was a lazy fool," sneered Goodman. "He came to depend on me for almost everything."

"Sheriff's going to wonder where everybody is when he shows up at Mrs. Chamberlin's with Holly and nobody's home."

Goodman laughed, "Sheriff Beninger won't be showing up anywhere ever again. He's dead, MacBridan. Just like your men."

It was all MacBridan could do to keep from charging at Goodman. "Before this night ends, you're going to die," said MacBridan. "You have my word on it."

Obermann had not turned to look at Goodman. He'd watched the hooded figure by the trees rush in to join the deputy. He too held a gun.

The man pulled the hood of his robe back. "Shut up, MacBridan, and do as he says," said Scar Face. "We were told to take you alive, but I'm more than willing to ignore that in your case. Now on your knees. Do it."

MacBridan and Obermann briefly looked at each other and then knelt down. They faced Altar Rock and the ruins. They could see that the coven members up on the tower hadn't moved, but the one at the base of the tower had disappeared.

"Bring forth our offering to the eternal lord, marking the beginning of his earthly reign." The grating voice filled the area. After saying this, the figure on the tower lowered its arms.

MacBridan, helpless to do anything, watched as two more hooded figures emerged from the ruins. They supported someone between them as they slowly made their way down to Altar Rock. MacBridan's heart fell as he recognized the person they were nearly dragging. As he had feared, it was Holly Carpenter.

***

The slow climb up the hill on his hands and knees had been excruciating, the pain in his head relentless, grinding him down. Both knees, as well as the palms of his hands, had suffered cuts and punctures as he crawled up the hill, but Beninger hadn't noticed. Something inside was driving him forward with single purpose.

He finally reached the crest of the hill and slowly lowered himself to the ground, resting his head on his hands. He'd made it. He couldn't believe it, but he'd made it.

Beninger heard voices but couldn't distinguish what was being said, much less who was saying it. He lifted his head and looked around. The scene that greeted him was unreal, frightening. His head injury had to be affecting his vision for everything glowed with a greenish light. About twenty yards in front of him was Altar Rock. It took some effort, but he finally recognized MacBridan. Beninger watched as MacBridan and another man knelt to the ground.

The ruins of the old church were further up the hill to his left. From where he was lying, he couldn't see them all that well, but he did see the hooded figures moving down the hill toward MacBridan. Although he wasn't certain, he was pretty sure that it was Holly Carpenter being held up between the two of them.

A strong wave of nausea surged through him. Beninger lowered his head back down on his hands. He tried breathing deeply, doing all he could to keep from throwing up again. He didn't know what to do. Physically he knew he couldn't move from where he was. The realization then hit him that he'd failed, had failed them all. MacBridan had tried to warn him, but now there didn't seem to be anything he could do.

***

Scar Face and Deputy Goodman stood guard behind MacBridan and Obermann. Father Collin and Katherine still lay on the ground, both unconscious. The two men holding Holly struggled with her as they had trouble picking her up and laying her on Altar Rock. The smaller of the two figures then placed candles on each corner, lighting them as he went. They appeared to be just like the black candles MacBridan had previously found traces of.

While the candles were being lit, MacBridan watched the other man bring out a scalpel, carefully cutting open Holly's blouse and exposing her swollen belly to the hellish scene around it. The man then laid the scalpel next to her. All of them turned to face the tower and waited.

The Dark Priest, as MacBridan dubbed him, began to talk in the same, strange language he'd used before. When he stopped, the remaining coven members pulled back their hoods. MacBridan couldn't believe that it was Dr. Appleton standing next to Holly. The man who had lit the candles was young, and quite thin, but MacBridan didn't know who he was. This, however, wasn't the case with one of the figures on the tower. The bright light from all the candles made it easy for MacBridan to recognize Benny, Macy's friend from the Box Car Bar. MacBridan couldn't help but wonder if Benny might have ratted Macy out to the coven. Only the Dark Priest and the figure holding the cross remained hooded.

The hooded figure turned and handed the Cross of St. Patrick to the Dark Priest, keeping it inverted. The Dark Priest looked to the sky and began to chant, the harsh words echoing across the clearing. The other members of the coven joined in, mimicking the chant.

It didn't take long before MacBridan could feel the ground begin to tremble. Across from them, at the far side of the clearing between the ruins and Altar Rock, the earth broke, cracking open with a loud, tearing noise. Continuing to widen, the ground split like a festering wound, small flames licking along its jagged edges, but nothing else could be seen. A dark shape suddenly sprang from the pit, taking its position at the edge, snarling in defiance. The sudden movement startled MacBridan, and he found himself staring into the glowing green eyes of a massive hound. Like the pit it came from, the creature was black as pitch.

The coven's chant droned on, steady, constant. MacBridan's eyes remained fixed on the hound. Then, slowly, the dark creature he'd encountered twice before slowly began to rise up from the terrible gash rent in the earth. It was more human in its form and the terrible cold that accompanied it rushed over them, affecting everything in the clearing.

The too familiar, nearly debilitating fear gripped MacBridan, choking the breath from his body. This time there was no escape, no one to help, nothing he could do. The cross that had saved him before was being used against them. MacBridan watched the creature as it hovered over the pit, he knew his death was imminent. A death he couldn't begin to imagine.

* * *

The cold rushed over Beninger. His eyes opened, and he realized that he had nearly drifted off. Calling on what little remaining strength he had left, he lifted himself up with his arms to see what was happening. He didn't see the dog, or the demon hovering behind it. All he saw was Holly, lying on Altar Rock, men all around her.

Beninger leaned over on his left side, and with his right hand, reached for his gun. He fumbled with the strap that held the gun in place. In his entire career as Sheriff, he'd only needed his weapon maybe three times. He definitely needed it now. He pulled the large caliber revolver out of its holster and brought it up before him. Carefully, he cocked the hammer, extended his arm and tried to take aim.

But the pounding in his head caused his hand to shake, throwing his aim off. A small, smooth stone, the size of a brick, lay just to his left. Using his elbows for leverage, he dragged himself over to it. This time, lying completely prone, he held the gun with both hands, resting them on the stone to help steady his aim.

***

Dr. Appleton picked up the scalpel, quickly wiping Holly's stomach with a swab. It appeared to MacBridan that he was preparing to open Holly's womb. This was it. He tried to think of something, but there was nothing he could do. The chanting pounded on. The Dark Priest turned to face the demon and started to slowly raise the inverted Cross of St. Patrick in tribute to the demon's arrival.

A shot rang out from the woods, taking all of them by surprise. Scar Face cried out as the bullet ripped through his shoulder blade, spinning him around. Scar Face's gun flew from his hand, and Obermann dove for it.

Acting on instinct MacBridan flung himself backward, heavily colliding with Goodman, catching him right at the knees. The deputy had spun around to face this unexpected threat from the trees and didn't see MacBridan coming. The force of MacBridan's lunge caught him off guard, sending him to the ground. MacBridan rolled over and launched himself on to Goodman. Goodman's gun lay a foot away from him, the impact with the ground having jarred it from his hand. Before he could get to it, MacBridan landed heavily on the deputy's back, driving him into the ground. The two men rolled over and over, struggling for position. The deputy's strength surprised MacBridan, and he found himself being slowly pushed down on his back. Goodman put all his weight into it and with both hands began to strangle MacBridan.

The Dark Priest and his two followers also turned their focus toward the woods, looking down from the tower, trying to figure out who had fired the shot. The Dark Priest uttered a command, pointing to the trees and the hound sprang from its position at the edge of the pit, leaping forward to charge its prey. With the chanting having stopped, the ceremony disrupted, the demon started to squirm, a silent struggle to keep from being pulled back into the pit began.

Obermann grabbed Scar Face's gun, came up on one knee and fired. The bullet caught Dr. Appleton high in chest, just below his neck, lifting him off the ground and sending him away from Holly and Altar Rock. At the same time, the smaller man rushed at Obermann, swinging his fist at his head. Obermann turned into the punch, deflecting most of it with his shoulder, leaving the other man's midsection exposed. He rammed the pistol's handle into the thin man's stomach then immediately brought his hand straight up, slamming it into his chin. The thin man's head snapped back. Obermann's fist smashed into the man's throat, crushing the larynx, and he fell to the ground, choking to death on his own blood.

MacBridan struggled but couldn't break the iron grip that Goodman had on his neck. His vision started to blur. In a last desperate act, he let go of Goodman's wrists and rammed his thumbs deep into the deputy's eyes. Goodman screamed, releasing the hold he'd had on MacBridan. MacBridan threw the deputy off of him, got to his feet and kicked at Goodman's head before the other man could recover. The blow nearly flipped the deputy over. The struggle with Goodman had brought MacBridan close to his own gun. He bent over, picked it up, and turned back to Goodman. Only scant seconds had passed, and MacBridan was astonished to find the deputy already up on one knee, struggling with something on his ankle. Without hesitation, MacBridan fired two rounds as Goodman brought his hand up, pointing something at him. MacBridan's first shot hit Goodman in the head, the second burrowed into his chest. Goodman fell on his back, the small pistol he'd had strapped to his ankle gripped in his hand.

The hound tore across the clearing. Beninger never really saw what it was, but managed to get off one more shot at the blur of motion that rocketed towards him, moving with impossible speed. The hound, nearly as large as Beninger, crashed into him, striking the sheriff with tremendous force. Beninger's gun flew from his hand, the breath knocked from his body. The hound looked down on the helpless man, both of his massive paws resting on Beninger's chest. In one swift motion, it clamped its jaws down on Beninger's neck, its teeth sinking into the cartilage, and shook the life out of him.

"The tower," shouted Father Collin, "fire at the tower. We have to keep them distracted. MacBridan, help me." MacBridan was surprised to find the priest standing up. Although a little unsteady on his feet, he was trying to get Holly down off Altar Rock. MacBridan helped the priest and they lowered her to the ground, next to Katherine, who remained unconscious. Obermann fired twice at the remaining coven members, but they had already taken cover inside the tower.

"We have to get the Cross of St. Patrick away from them. It's too powerful to leave in their possession. I need Obermann with me; he knows how to assist me with what I have to do. MacBridan, you have to get it away from them. You cannot let anything happen to it. That would be disastrous for all of us."

Without hesitation, MacBridan took off for the tower. He'd sprinted halfway up the hill when heard the Dark Priest shout another command. MacBridan glanced at the demon. It remained fixed over the pit and seemed to be struggling, unseen forces tearing at it. The coven hadn't been able to get full control over the demon before Beninger's timely intrusion, but it did have control over the hellhound.

The black beast emerged from the trees and took off down the hill. MacBridan dove to the ground, rolling to his right, trying to escape its deathly charge. But the hound passed by MacBridan, and he realized that it wasn't after him at all. It was after Father Collin.

"Father Collin!" shouted MacBridan. "The hound. Look out!"

Father Collin had already swept the black candles off the surface of the Altar Rock, replacing them with pieces of the host on each corner. He turned and faced the charging beast, holding before him the large sword he'd used earlier in the cemetery. Father Collin continued to chant as the hound bore down on him. Still yards from the priest, the demonic hound leaped into the air. The priest moved slightly to his left, squatted and brought the sword around in an upward, arching motion. The blade glowed with the blue white light and deeply slashed into the hound's belly. The creature burst into a ball of bright blue flame. It fell to the ground and began thrashing about. Screams from the demon echoed the screams from the hound's throat.

"Get up," shouted Father Collin. "The hound is gone, but if we don't get that cross away from them they may yet pull that horror from the pit. Hurry!" With that, he turned his back and continued the ceremony to sanctify Altar Rock and ground around it.

MacBridan pulled out his sword and entered the ruins, turning towards the tower. Just as he was about to step into the tower he caught sight of something moving off to his left, but not in time to get out of the way. The chain struck him hard across his left shoulder, reaching to the center of his back. The force of the blow sent him staggering into the doorframe, his sword clattering to the ground. He sensed more than saw the next blow coming. Ducking down, he rolled away. The chain barely missed his head, sparks shooting off of the stone wall of the tower.

MacBridan made it to his feet, his left arm almost useless, numb from the hit he'd taken. Benny stood in front of him, blocking the door. He held the chain with both hands, swinging it back and forth. "I've been dreaming about this, MacBridan. Ever since that cheap shot in the bar, ever since you got Macy killed," said Benny.

Benny didn't have a gun or he would have used it by now. The Dark Priest probably knew that. Therefore, MacBridan figured, the only chance he had of making it up those narrow stairs with any element of surprise, was to take care of Benny without using his gun.

"Macy died because he understood more than you about what's going on here," said MacBridan. "He tried bringing me the cross as a bargaining chip, something that he knew I wanted bad enough that I'd agree to help save his life, as well as yours."

"What? Save our lives?" chuckled Benny. "MacBridan, you're the one who needs saving."

"Macy knew that he was being used, all of you are, grand promises of all that you'll be paid for helping them, all the privileges you'll have. Benny, once tonight is over, they won't need you anymore. They'll kill all of us. Macy understood that and was asking me for help when that creature killed him. When they killed Vickers, Macy realized that they would end up killing the rest of you. Benny, if they succeed, they'll feed us all to that thing," said MacBridan, constantly looking behind Benny, adding to the ploy he was running.

The chain hung limp from Benny's hands. He stared at MacBridan, suddenly unsure of his position. He mulled over what MacBridan had said, thinking, trying to decide what to do. MacBridan didn't have that long.

"Benny!" MacBridan punched the name out. "Behind you, look out!"

Benny whirled around. "Where? What?"

It was all MacBridan needed. He rushed in before Benny realized he'd been taken, coming in low and slamming into him with his shoulder. The impact lifted Benny off his feet and MacBridan drove him backwards. They crashed into a statue of an angel holding a spear and the head of the spear burst through Benny's chest, narrowly missing MacBridan's head. Benny's body spasmed twice before going limp. MacBridan stared at the impaled body, trying to determine how badly his own arm had been hurt.

He then turned away and entered the stairwell. The absolute darkness made the tight, winding passageway seem even more constricted. He wondered what else was waiting for him on the steps in the darkness. What other hideous creatures did the coven control? No! He couldn't allow his thoughts to go there and tried to shake them off as he continued his slow climb up the stairs. As he neared the top, he could hear the Dark Priest chanting, the words unintelligible. MacBridan carefully looked out and spotted the priest and his remaining disciple on their knees, in a corner of the tower out of view from Altar Rock and effectively out of Obermann's line of fire.

"I should kill you without hesitation," said MacBridan.

The Dark Priest stiffened and they both stopped the chanting. The demon screamed out its rage at this new interruption. MacBridan looked down. The demon had grown in size, becoming more defined, but still suspended above the pit. Father Collin and Obermann had stayed at Altar Rock. A ring of white candles now surrounded them. Holly and Katherine were both lying on the ground, inside the ring. Father Collin knelt outside the ring, the cross held before him, speaking as loudly as he could. The Latin words called on the Almighty to smite the creature, condemning it back to the pit from which it had come. Obermann walked in a circular motion, inside the ring of candles, waving the incense burner as he walked.

"You've proven yourself to be far more resourceful than any of us ever imagined you would be," said the Dark Priest. "Unfortunately, you and your pitiful friends are too late to stop us. I'd ask you to join us, but I know you're too stupid to appreciate the power that I'd be offering you. No, MacBridan, it is your time to die."

"Who are you?" asked MacBridan. The man was a total stranger to him.

His smile was unnerving, the light of insanity burning in his eyes.

"I'm Dr. Emerick Wilson. It's so unfortunate that we couldn't meet before now, but I did enjoy spending time with your associate. It was so nice of her share with me all that you were doing, keeping me updated. All of us laughed at how little you actually knew."

"So the information on New Haven was a distraction. I thought so, it didn't sound right."

"You should have taken my advice. You might have survived the night."

"Yeah, well Emerick, as it turns out, I'm the one with the gun," said MacBridan, fingering the hammer back. "Now gently set the cross down, and I do mean gently. It is the only thing keeping you alive."

Although MacBridan could clearly see the Dark Priest's face, but his follower's face was hidden by a hood. He could feel the hatred lancing out from beneath the cowl. The demon screamed out, its cry lancing through his body, causing him to shudder.

"Now, last chance," MacBridan shouted. "I said put it down!"

Emerick stooped over, slowly lowering the cross to the floor of the tower. As he started to straighten up, his disciple's right hand shot out. MacBridan had no chance as a small dagger flew through the air, piercing his left shoulder. He cried out, falling backwards, just missing the opening in the platform leading to the staircase. Despite the pain, he managed to get off a shot, catching the disciple in the chest. The disciple's head flew back and the hood came off. Lucy looked backed at him in disbelief, clutching her chest as she staggered a couple of steps then fell over the edge. MacBridan's gun slid from his hand as he dropped onto the hard stone flooring. The dagger was firmly planted into the same shoulder that Benny had already injured with his chain. The pain from the dagger burned like fire, almost more than he could take.

With a triumphant yell, Emerick charged at MacBridan, diving on to the helpless man. MacBridan kicked out just as the he descended on him, his foot connecting with Emerick's stomach, sending him rolling into one of the low stone walls. Emerick's head hit hard enough to momentarily knock him senseless.

MacBridan could hear his name being called, but it seemed to be coming from miles away. A weakness began to spread from his shoulder to the rest of his body. He struggled to sit up, the small blade imbedded in his shoulder.

"MacBridan, are you alright? MacBridan!" It sounded like Father Collin, but MacBridan wasn't sure. The pain in his shoulder was getting worse.

Somehow, he managed to get to his feet and looked down.

"MacBridan, do you have the cross?"

"Yes," he answered, but that one word took far more effort than it should have.

"Pick it up and hold it towards the creature," shouted Father Collin.

MacBridan staggered over to the cross, nearly losing his balance as he reached down for it. The pain from his shoulder continued to spread, joining forces with the weakness coursing through him. Poison, he realized, the blade had been coated in poison. With his right hand, he held the cross up, but nearly dropped it as he saw that the creature had risen well above the pit, almost eye to eye with him. The demon glared at MacBridan and began to drift toward him.

"Pray, MacBridan. Pray to God now," shouted Father Collin. The priest began to walk toward the pit, holding his cross up, chanting his prayers. Obermann followed with the incense burner swinging from side to side.

MacBridan didn't really know any prayers. It was not something he'd recently had a lot of experience with. He stood there, not knowing what to do, and simply began to ask for help. "Help us, God. Please help us, God," he mumbled over and over, his eyes locked on the creature. He felt the Cross of St. Patrick as it began to grow warmer, the bluish white light beginning to dance around its edges.

Emerick recovered from his fall and managed to stand up. He looked at MacBridan and the light that was building around the cross. Glancing down, he could see Father Collin approaching the pit, the same blue white light glowing brightly from his cross. The combined power of the crosses forced a scream from the demon more terrible, more wretched, than any that it had uttered before. MacBridan actually felt the tower shudder in response to the demon's cry. It writhed in mid-air as the light from the crosses grew. MacBridan continued to pray, unable to take his eyes away from the horror that slowly kept inching toward him. All his remaining strength was focused on the thing before him.

Again, the earth trembled, but now the pit was starting to close. The light from the two crosses had become so bright that it was nearly blinding. The creature, totally consumed in agony, struck out in desperation, lunging at the tower and MacBridan.

Light suddenly blazed from the Cross of St. Patrick, shielding MacBridan from the creature's attack. Forced away from its tormentor, the demon reached out and grabbed Emerick. He screamed, struggling to free himself as he was lifted from the tower. His struggle became even more frantic as he realized that he was being pulled into the pit with the creature. MacBridan's last glimpse of Emerick's face burned into his memory. It was a face consumed with complete and total terror.

"No!" he screamed. "Help me!"

The demon fell from the sky, back into the flames from the pit, dragging Emerick in with it. The earth shook violently and slammed shut with such a force that rocked the tower, pieces of it falling away. The force of the tremor sent MacBridan to his knees. He laid the cross down as gently as he could, no longer able to hold it up. He crawled over to the wall and looked down. Father Collin stood where the pit had been. Unbelievably the creature was gone. They had won.

MacBridan tried to get up, but this time his legs would not cooperate. He'd recovered the cross, but knew that it would be up to someone else to give it back to the church. His vision blurred, and he was having trouble keeping his eyes open. He tried to call out to Father Collin but couldn't. Together they had defeated a terrible evil, a horror that lived beyond MacBridan's darkest imaginings. Perhaps providence—a true God he'd never known—had brought MacBridan to New Westminster for that very purpose. It was MacBridan's last thought as he descended into the void.

EPILOGUE

(SIX WEEKS LATER)

The unusually warm December evening brought many people out and, even as the sun prepared to set, still they swarmed around the south entrance to the Central Park Zoo in New York City. An assortment of bright holiday sweaters and light jackets took care of the multitude enjoying the rare warm weather with Christmas only ten days away. Numerous decorations added to the festive spirit, further enhancing the special magic unique to this park. Tens of thousands of small Christmas lights coated the tree branches and, with the oncoming evening, they would soon be visible.

Father Collin rested on a bench across from the zoo entrance, slowly sipping his coffee. Like so many of the people he watched, this time of year held many special memories for him. It was a time in which he could find peace, a time that even he could escape the harsher realities that so often filled his days.

"Quite a different scene from the last time you and I went for a walk through the woods, isn't it, Father?"

Father Collin turned and looked up at the man standing next to him. "Ah, Mr. MacBridan, so good to see you up and around. How's the arm?"

"Better," said MacBridan as he sat down next to the priest. A sling held his left arm nearly immobile, protecting his shoulder from any exaggerated movements. "Fortunately for me the poison she had on that blade was too weak to do any permanent damage. Doctor says that given the time, and if I continue to do exactly as he says, I should heal up good as new."

"Excellent! That is so good to hear," said Father Collin. "I was sorry, though, when I learned what happened to your colleagues."

"Yeah, that was pretty hard," said MacBridan. He'd not really talked to anyone about this; at least not about how he felt. An abundance of self-imposed guilt lay heavily across his shoulders. "Smithers died almost instantly. Harry, on the other hand, even though he still has a long road in front of him, should eventually recover. The blow to his head resulted in a pretty serious concussion, and he badly fractured his arm when he hit the floor. For a while there, they weren't sure whether or not he'd pull out of it, or even if he did what kind of shape he'd be in. As it turns out, Harry's either the luckiest guy alive or has one of the hardest heads around. Personally I think it's all of the above."

Father Collin stood up, lightly placing his hand on MacBridan's shoulder. "Let's go for a walk, shall we?" he said, moving away from the crowd.

MacBridan walked beside the priest and for a while, neither man spoke, reluctant to revisit the horror of their last meeting. "I understand," said Father Collin, "that Mrs. Chamberlin is doing quite well."

"It's been a few weeks since I last spoke to her, but Dolinski has told me that she is doing just fine. For a woman her age, she is amazingly strong, especially when you consider all that happened to her."

"She and I talked many times in the weeks following the assault on her home," said Father Collin. "Her faith is quite strong and I must agree with you, she is a very impressive individual."

"I spotted Obermann off to your right when I came up to the bench. Will he be joining us?"

Father Collin chuckled at this. "You remain very observant, but then you demonstrated that skill to me early on. No, he knows that I want to spend some time with you, get some things cleared up. He'll just follow along to make sure that we are not disturbed," said Father Collin.

"Are you expecting some kind of trouble?" asked MacBridan. "It's been some time, and I'll admit that the night did end a little abruptly for me, but if memory serves, we didn't leave any bad guys standing."

Father Collin gave a grim smile and said, "No, we were most efficient. But you need to understand that the threat is never really gone. Our enemy may suffer setbacks but make no mistake, we haven't defeated him. Satan will continue to provide temptation, challenging men with God's gift of free will."

"That night on the tower I found Satan to be represented by a very sick man and a remarkably evil woman. Assuming I even cared about political correctness I'd have to accuse you of disparaging men by referring to the devil as 'him,'" said MacBridan.

Father Collin laughed again. "Yes, guess I should be more sensitive to those kinds of comments, but some things will never change, especially with an old dog like me."

"Father, I was glad to get your call. There are several questions that I haven't been able to answer."

"Too much time has passed and I must apologize for that, but then there was so much that had to be done. Your messages did get through to me, I'm only sorry that it took so long to get back with you."

"What became of Holly? Even Dolinski is vague on that. Other than she is recovering, he really doesn't have any other information."

With the sun disappearing behind the horizon, the air quickly began to cool, coming more in line with the season. Father Collin continued his steady pace down the path. He folded his hands behind his back and lowered his head, collecting his thoughts. The heavy scent from the surrounding pine trees drifted over them as they passed through a densely wooded area, with several large boulders strewn amongst the tall pines. "It might be better to first let you know how we got everyone out of there."

"That'd be nice. To be honest, I thought I was a goner. There wasn't anyone more surprised than me when I woke up in that emergency room," said MacBridan.

"It was even closer for Holly, but then, despite her condition, we couldn't leave until I had finished sanctifying the ground where the creature disappeared, just as I did around Altar Rock. We came too close that night, too close, and I couldn't leave anything to chance. Anyway, as soon as that was completed I went back to look after Holly and Mrs. Chamberlin. Obermann went to the tower to see about you."

"Obermann?" said MacBridan. "I didn't know he cared."

"Try not to be too disappointed in what I'm about to say, but I don't believe that he was actually motivated by any hidden feelings for you," said Father Collin with a small smile. "As you said earlier, we didn't leave any bad guys standing, but we had to be certain. Ubel checked on the bodies by the tower and then climbed up to look for you. We feared that you were beyond our help," explained Father Collin.

"How did he get me down off that tower, that couldn't have been easy? I'm not a little guy to begin with and my time with Mrs. Chamberlin added a few pounds that I didn't need."

"You weren't completely out of it, and even though you did need a great deal of assistance, the two of you managed to make it down. Obermann left you sitting on the ground outside the old church and then went to check on Beninger."

"Beninger was a good man, a brave man. Dolinski told me that the blow to the head he got at Holly's house should have finished him, and yet he somehow managed to drive through those woods to Altar Rock. We owe him our lives," said MacBridan.

"And so much more. Had the coven been successful our whole world might have changed, but we'll talk more about that later. We have learned so much."

The path they had been following intersected with another, broader path and they turned to follow it, running parallel to the street that was just outside the park. MacBridan didn't see Obermann, but that didn't mean anything. He knew he was near.

"Obermann moved Beninger out of the way, and then found the two cars parked in the woods. The station wagon belonged to the antique shop. Obermann got it started and drove it right down to Altar Rock. We were able to lay Holly down in the back of it. By that time Mrs. Chamberlin had started to come around."

"I understand that she'd been drugged." MacBridan said.

"Yes, they brought her along as an insurance policy against you. Here too we were blessed that they hadn't yet harmed her. They were too cocky, too certain that they'd already reached a level of invincibility," said Father Collin.

"Not hard to understand why. To tell you the truth, Father, I didn't think that thing could be stopped."

"Once we got everyone in the car, I drove the three of you to the hospital. Ubel followed us in Beninger's cruiser. I parked right outside the doors to the emergency room and then called the hospital to let them know you were outside."

MacBridan stared at the priest. "You left us there?"

"Yes," answered Father Collin, "and under the same circumstances, I'd do it again. We had to be certain that we had gotten all of them and there simply wasn't any time to waste. Had I stayed, I would have been trapped at the hospital for hours, if not more, talking with the police. No, the risk of other coven members escaping while I was stuck there answering a bunch of questions simply couldn't be taken."

MacBridan nodded, "Makes sense. I'm guessing you went to the antique shop."

"Good guess," said Father Collin.

"Not really. You know, Father, you compliment me on how observant I am, and yet, in retrospect, I can't quit thinking about a really obvious clue that we all missed. Course, at the time I didn't know that I was looking for one of the devil's minions. Still I find her audacity amazing."

"What are you referring to?"

"Her name. The antique shop was called *Furr's Antiques.* Her first name was Lucy. Get it? Lucy-Furr. She and her leader, Dr. Wilson, must have been laughing at us the whole time."

"Now I know I'm getting old," said Father Collin. "Age is a cruel master."

"Were any other coven members waiting for you?" asked MacBridan.

"No, the shop was empty, which was good. It gave us the opportunity to thoroughly search it," said Father Collin. "All we found were copies of two very ancient manuscripts in Lucy's desk, one of which my order didn't even know existed. Each dates back to the mid-thirteenth century and provides intimate details of all that needs to be done in order to fulfill several different grimoires. Our concern is that we never did find the originals. It scares me when I think that they're still out there and who might be in possession of them."

"I was told that the antique shop burnt to the ground that night. Not being one who believes in coincidence, do I even have to ask how that happened?"

"That too was our doing. Here again we couldn't risk the originals being found by someone else, or, for that matter, anything else that we might have missed falling into the wrong hands. Fire is the great purifier."

"Do you even bother going to confession, or have they just given up on you?" asked MacBridan. "You'd have to spend night and day saying Hail Marys."

"We've already been down this road, Mr. MacBridan. My order is tasked with fighting Satan wherever he appears, and we can't afford to be timid in our approach."

MacBridan laughed at this. "Timid is not a word I would ever use to describe you or Obermann."

"From there we went back to the church and parked the cruiser near the footbridge. I called the Sheriff's office and expressed my concern, stating that the cruiser had been there for some time, but that I couldn't find anyone around it. This hit them pretty hard. They were already looking for Beninger, who had been missing for several hours, and in addition to that, they'd also lost contact with Goodman. Needless to say, they responded rather quickly. As soon as the deputies arrived, I told them of my earlier conversations with Sheriff Beninger regarding the nightly goings on out at Altar Rock and they immediately took off to see if he was there. You, of course, are well aware of what was waiting for them."

"Yeah, that was quite a massacre."

"Yes. So many violent deaths in such a small community are rather daunting. It is believed that Sheriff Beninger and Deputy Goodman confronted a group of devil worshipers who had kidnapped you, Holly and Mrs. Chamberlin and took you out there to be used as human sacrifice. Sadly, they died in the fight. Fortunately, thanks entirely to their efforts, you were able to escape, and Mrs. Chamberlin drove you and Holly to the hospital. The church has been most cooperative, and fortunately, I've not been asked to provide any additional details."

"Nice and neat," said MacBridan. "In case you don't know, the state police are having trouble with that story, but so far they haven't been able to knock any significant holes in it. They've questioned me several times and probably wouldn't have believed me if it hadn't been for Katherine backing up my story, which I'm assuming I owe to you."

"On the ride to the hospital I told her to keep it simple, that both of you had been kidnapped by the coven, that she was drugged by them almost immediately and that's all she knew until she came to at Altar Rock."

"That pretty well sums it up," said MacBridan. "I confirmed with the police that the coven kidnapped us at gunpoint and took us there to be sacrificed. Finding Harry and Smithers further corroborated our story. That reminds me, who sent the police out to Mrs. Chamberlin's?"

"You have to thank Ubel for that," said Father Collin. "He brought it to my attention that for Mrs. Chamberlin to have been at Altar Rock, something must have happened to your men. He phoned in an anonymous tip about hearing shots at her house. We prayed that they had merely been incapacitated, but unfortunately it turned out to be far worse than that."

"It was a busy night in New Westminster," said MacBridan, his thoughts once again returning to Harry and Smithers.

"The community is still very much in shock, terribly shaken, and will be for some time to come I'm afraid. The fear was that one, or more, of the killers might have gotten away. The day after the event, my order sent three more priests to help me. On the surface we were there to minister to the towns people, but in reality it allowed us to make sure that we had someone with Holly at all times."

"Which I guess brings us back to my earlier question of what became of Holly?"

"There we have some good news. Both she and her husband Ian are with us now. They are continuing to recover and the baby is doing quite well."

"It doesn't make sense to me why they spent so much time isolating her, getting her drugged to the gills just to use her as a final sacrifice. Wouldn't it have been much easier to just show up that evening, kill Ian and take her to Altar Rock?"

"Had that been their goal, yes, that would have been much easier. However, if you'll remember, it was my assumption that all they wanted was to use her and the baby as a final sacrifice. I was mistaken. As I said a few moments ago, we have learned much, which, for the most part, came from studying the manuscripts we found at the antique shop. Someone, and we believe it was Lucy, jotted down notes regarding the coven's activities on the back of the manuscripts. Most revealing. The notes detailed how the coven was gradually drugging Holly. This was done over the course of several days so that they could control her, but at the same time not endanger the baby."

"So it was the child that they were actually after?" asked MacBridan.

"Yes, and here's a very interesting detail. In order for the grimoire to work, Holly had to agree, had to willingly give her consent for the coven to use her child."

"I don't believe she'd ever do that," said MacBridan. "That would make her one of them."

"Yes, it would. Once we'd read the grimoire and understood all that was needed, that particular point raised grave concerns with us. However, we have spent a great deal of time with Holly and our talks with her have given us the details of exactly how they tricked her into doing this. If nothing else, they were quite clever," explained Father Collin.

"So they didn't do it by threatening her?"

"They couldn't. The grimoire clearly states that the mother, of her own free will, has to agree that she will give up the child. Any method of intimidation would have spoiled their plan. Holly told us that during one of her first visits with Lucy, Lucy gave her a very modest house-warming gift, an antique pumpkin carving kit. Lucy got her to agree to not only carve a specific pattern in her first pumpkin, but to recite a verse that came with the kit. Holly thought it was innocent, quaint in fact, and was drawn to the idea of starting a Halloween tradition in her new home. She'd carved many pumpkins as a child growing up and had no idea that what she was doing carried dark implications."

"Didn't the words to the verse give her some clue to what she was doing?" asked MacBridan.

"The verse wasn't written in English. Although we can make some reasonably good guesses as to what language the verse was written in, Holly told us that she didn't recognize it. Therefore, she had to sound it out, and, as she had given her word to Lucy, did the best she could. The events that took place the second after she completed this little ritual are fantastic. She told us that the pumpkin seemed to come alive, that flames roared from inside it, then rose up off the table and nearly attacked her."

"Father, at this point there is very little that I wouldn't believe. So what did they need the child for?"

"The coven's goal was not to just raise a powerful demon out of the pit to use for random killings. They planned for the demon to live in this world and needed the baby to use as its corporal home. Over time it would have grown into a beast in human form with enormous power, but I assure you, there wouldn't have been anything human about it."

"That brings several unsettling possibilities to mind," said MacBridan.

"Worse than you can imagine," explained Father Collin. "With its power and their knowledge they could have summoned forth many more demons and creatures out of the pit, virtually opening the portal to Hell, signaling an end to life as we know it. Over time they truly would have become unstoppable."

"Dr. Wilson surprised Cori more than me. She had no idea that she was feeding the enemy inside information."

"Yes, we believe he was the brains behind the outfit and was the one who gave the grimoire to Lucy. He directed their affairs from a distance, but was there each time they summoned the creature. His method of controlling the gang was by not sharing all that he knew. Without him, they would never have gotten as far as they did. When Vickers strayed, as Macy did later, he used the demon to show the others what would happen if they tried anything."

"I trust that his office and home fell under the same level of scrutiny."

"And then some, said Father Collin. "We didn't find anything at this office, but we did find some remarkable documents at this home. If nothing else, he'd knew what he was doing."

"Any insight as to what his motive might have been?"

"At the end of the day it was power," answered Father Collin. "Perhaps a little revenge too, but mostly power. Growing up he'd been one of those nerdy kids who got pushed around. Wreaking havoc in New Westminster was probably his way of getting even for all he'd suffered. He nearly succeeded in turning New Westminster into Hell on earth."

"That's a concept I don't want to think about," said MacBridan. "Even today, though I know all that happened in New Westminster, that I witnessed so many things that are beyond belief, to me it still seems more like a terrible, terrible dream than anything to do with reality. Problem is, with this dream there's no waking up, and I know it'll never go away."

"You've had much to deal with, and, I presume, no one to talk to regarding all that happened," said Father Collin. "How are you handling things?"

"I've talked with Cori some, but I can't tell her half of what I saw. She already believes I'm partially crazy, and I'm not ready to confirm for her that I've lost what little I have left. The first couple weeks, when I was at home recovering, my nights were pure misery. I'd jump at almost anything, and if I did manage to fall asleep, the nightmares would start right up. It's going to take me some time, Father, but eventually I'll come to grips with it. I have to."

"You don't have to do this alone. Although I'm sorry to say I won't be here, there are others in my order that are ready to work with you," offered Father Collin.

"If the need arises, I'll let you know. The dreams have stopped, but I'd be lying if I didn't tell you that at times I question my own sanity. Hell actually exists. I pray Heaven does also."

"It does, Mr. MacBridan, it most certainly does," said Father Collin. The priest stopped, faced MacBridan and placed his hands on MacBridan's shoulders. "Despite all that you experienced and all that you have had to deal with since then, you must also understand that you have been extremely blessed. Yes, you witnessed evil—true evil in its purest form—but you also witnessed the hand of God. You were witness to His power and His ability to overcome any and all evil. There are millions of Christians worldwide who pray every day for the very privilege that has been granted to you. Take heart, my son, you are greatly loved."

MacBridan stared at the priest. Strangely, he found himself close to tears. He nodded and moved away from the priest, continuing their walk.

"Thank you," said MacBridan, his voice just above a whisper. "I never really looked at it that way. Time, Father, it's just going to take me a little more time."

They passed by a small shelter that protected two benches from the elements, and continued to follow the path as it started to work its way up hill. Eventually MacBridan asked, "How did they drug, Holly?"

"It is interesting to see how they manipulated Holly and Ian from day one. The coven member at Altar Rock, the smaller man helping Dr. Appleton with Holly that night, was Paul Lovett. He used to be one of the few local real-estate people in New Westminster. Like the rest of the coven, he too was looking for the right person to come along to supply them with the child they needed. About a year earlier, Lucy, under another name, had quietly purchased the farm that Holly and Ian ended up buying. Their original intent was to find a homeless woman who was pregnant, befriend her and put her up at the farm. No one would miss someone like that, and once the baby came, the coven's plan would have been complete."

"Enter Holly and Ian, stage right," said MacBridan.

"Exactly. When Ian and Holly walked in looking for a home, it played right into their hands. Here was a young couple, looking for just the right house to start their new family. It was made to order for them. Not too long after the moved in, Holly became pregnant, a little piece of news she shared with anyone who would listen. Holly and Ian certainly weren't homeless, but they had very little family, and what few relations they had were several hundred miles away. The coven controlled the price on the farm and made sure the young couple got a deal that they couldn't walk away from. Over time, Lucy made contact with them and became friends with Holly. We found a tea with some very special ingredients at the antique shop and at Holly's home. We're certain that Lucy gave it to Holly and that is how they administered the drug. Although it would have given Holly a mild boost as she drank it, it also contained a drug that gradually built up in her system, weakening her."

"Wouldn't that have endangered the child they were after?"

"It could have, certainly, but then there was Dr. Appleton. Another active member of the coven, he knew what she was being given and carefully monitored the levels in her system. Lucy made the tea for Holly, and Dr. Appleton let her know the right amounts to put in each batch as time progressed. Had all gone their way, Dr. Appleton would have taken the baby that evening and the creature would be with us now."

"Do we know who ran Ian down?" asked MacBridan.

"No, we don't, and we probably never will, but I'm positive it was one of the coven who simply followed him to Boston and then hit him with their car."

"Where are they now?"

"Holly and Ian are with us," answered Father Collin, "and will be for some time. They both need the time to recover and frankly to adjust to being new parents. They have a very healthy little girl who will run them ragged."

"You still haven't answered my question. Why the secrecy? They're not still in danger, are they?" asked MacBridan.

"They could be. We don't know who has the original manuscripts. We don't know if Dr. Wilson was working with anyone else outside New Westminster. Did we get all the coven members that evening, or did we just deal with the members that lived in New Westminster? Try to think of what my order is doing as the church's version of a witness protection program. We will resettle them, and we will always watch over them, especially the child."

"What will become of the Cross of St. Patrick?" asked MacBridan.

"The church is very grateful for its return. Eventually it'll be sent back to the church from which it was stolen, but for the time being it will reside at the Vatican, also to be studied. You did remarkably well, Mr. MacBridan. You stood your ground against a terror when most people would have crumbled under. We are very impressed with you, with your abilities, and may have need of your services in the future."

"No thank you, Father. Once is enough. As it is, Halloween will never be the same for me again. Going forward, the scariest thing I want to face is Dolinski's coffee."

They had stopped walking. Father Collin turned to MacBridan and took his hand. "Thank you for all your help. It has been a pleasure knowing you, but I can't promise that we won't meet up again. Fate has an interesting way of bringing people together."

"You believe in fate, Father? Doesn't that go against the rules somewhere?" asked MacBridan, a smile on his face.

"Ah but you see, I'm Irish also, and that makes me a special Catholic," said Father Collin. "Remember James, our enemy is relentless. We've won a battle, but not the war. And for all that you did, you are now a marked man. You have a target on your forehead and the enemy has you in their sights."

"You're not helping my insomnia," said MacBridan.

"Good. That was not my intent. Always be watchful. Go with God, James MacBridan, you will be in my prayers."

"Goodbye, Father, it has been interesting. You'll not be forgotten."

Father Collin smiled at him and started down a path that led back into the park. Twenty yards down, MacBridan saw Obermann waiting for the priest. Obermann nodded at MacBridan and then turned and walked away with Father Collin beside him.

Now there goes the odd couple if there ever was one, MacBridan thought. He exited the park and began to look for a cab that would take him back to the office. As he waited, his hand reached up and felt for the crucifix he continued to wear under his shirt. He hadn't taken it off since his night at Altar Rock and knew he never would. He'd also gone to mass, something he hadn't done on his own in years. Although it was still too early for him to completely comprehend all that had happened, all that had changed in him, he found himself praying that he'd never be tested this way again.

MacBridan turned to follow the path out of the park and collided with a young woman, nearly knocking her to the ground. They grabbed on to each other to keep her from falling. "I am so sorry, are you alright?" asked MacBridan.

"I'm fine, I think," she said as she straightened her jacket, taking a step back from MacBridan. "I sincerely hope this isn't how you pick up women?"

MacBridan couldn't believe his luck, this girl was absolutely stunning. In her early thirties, she had dark brown hair with bright, amber colored eyes and a figure her jacket couldn't begin to conceal.

"At this point I'm really not sure what I can say that's going to make me come off looking good. My name's James MacBridan. I'd just finished talking to a friend of mine and I'm afraid my mind was elsewhere."

She smiled at MacBridan and her laugh was almost magical. "Okay, James MacBridan, I can believe that. You look like the kind of guy who deserves a second chance."

"That'd be nice. It's been a rough few weeks."

"I can see that," she said, lightly touching his arm. "My name's Samantha, I'm in real-estate. Here's my card. Give me a call sometime and if you promise not to run me over again we can meet for coffee." With that, she smiled and walked off into the park. MacBridan watched her as she walked away. Yes, Samantha, you will most certainly be getting a call. With the evening ending on a high note, he smiled to himself and headed out of the park.

***

Samantha continued on a little bit further, then stepped off the path into the trees. Waiting for her were two large, rough looking men wearing jeans, heavy work shoes and leather jackets. Her expression instantly changed from kind and pleasant to dark and angry, a hidden fury burned in her eyes. She led them back out onto the path and nodded in the direction MacBridan had gone. "That's him."

Without a word, the two men started up the path after MacBridan. Father Collin's warning had been timely. The war had only just begun.